THE RETURN OF
CAPTAIN
JOHN
EMMETT

Also by Elizabeth Speller

Biography
Following Hadrian:
A Second Century Journey Through
the Roman Empire

Memoir
The Sunlight on the Garden:
A Family in Love, War and Madness

THE RETURN OF
CAPTAIN
JOHN
EMMETT

Elizabeth Speller

virago

VIRAGO

First published in Great Britain in 2010 by Virago Press

Copyright © Elizabeth Speller 2010

Frances Cornford's poem 'Youth' is reproduced from her *Selected Poems*
by kind permission of Enitharmon Press.

A CIP catalogue record for this book
is available from the British Library.

Hardback ISBN 978-1-84408-607-8
C-format ISBN 978-1-84408-608-5

Typeset in Centaur by M Rules
Printed and bound in Great Britain by
Clays Ltd, St Ives plc

Papers used by Virago are natural, renewable and
recyclable products sourced from well-managed forests and certified
in accordance with the rules of the Forest Stewardship Council.

Mixed Sources
Product group from well-managed
forests and other controlled sources
www.fsc.org Cert no. SGS-COC-004081
© 1996 Forest Stewardship Council

FSC

Virago Press
An imprint of
Little, Brown Book Group
100 Victoria Embankment
London EC4Y 0DY

An Hachette UK Company
www.hachette.co.uk

www.virago.co.uk

For my brother, Richard, and for my nephews Dominic, Tristan, William, Barnaby and Charlie, who, had they been born exactly one hundred years earlier, might all have found themselves on the Western Front.

You were only David's father,
But I had fifty sons
When we went up in the evening
Under the arch of the guns.

Lieutenant Ewart Alan Mackintosh
(died Cambrai 1917)

PROLOGUE

*T*hey gathered in the dark long before the train arrived at the small station. It was mostly women: young mothers holding tightly wrapped infants, elderly women in shawls, black-coated middle-aged matrons alongside grown children. There were men too, of course, some already holding their hats self-consciously at their sides, and a cluster of soldiers stood to one end of the platform near the bearded stationmaster. Even so, the men were outnumbered by the women as they always were these days.

Occasionally the station buffet sign creaked or a baby wailed and the isolated murmur of one woman to another was almost indistinguishable from the faint sigh of wind, but mostly there was quiet as they waited. Still others stood a little further away. In the houses on either side of the line, behind lighted windows, silhouetted occupants held back curtains. Below them, at rail-side garden fences or on the banks, stood a handful more. On the far platform, almost out of reach of the lights, it was just possible to pick out one individual, swathed in a dark coat and hat, who stood at a distance from the rest. The stationmaster looked across the rails with some apprehension. In a long career he had never had a suicide, but tonight was different; this train's freight was despair and sorrow. However, the watcher seemed calm, standing at a reasonable distance from the platform's edge, with the width of the down track separating his stiffly upright figure from the expected train.

They felt it before they heard it. A faint vibration in the rails seemed to transmit itself to the people waiting, and a shiver trembled through them, followed by a more audible hum and finally a crescendo of noise as the train, pulled by its great dark engine, appeared around the bend. Tiny points of fire danced red in its smoke and singed the grass. The last hats were removed hurriedly and one young woman buried her face in her companion's chest. The soldiers stood to attention and, as the train thundered by without stopping, its compartments brilliantly illuminated, they saluted. A wave ran through the crowd as several of the spectators craned forward, desperate to catch a momentary glimpse of the red, blue and white flag, draped over the coffin of English oak, before its passing left them to the dark loneliness of their changed world.

As the crowd slowly dispersed, almost as silently as they had assembled, the stationmaster looked along his platform once more. Now quite alone on the far side of the track, one figure stayed immobile. Hours after the stationmaster had gone to his bed, reassured in the knowledge that it was six hours until the milk train, the last watcher remained solitary and now invisible in the darkness, waiting for dawn and the last battle to begin.

CHAPTER ONE

*I*n years to come, Laurence Bartram would look back and think that the event that really changed everything was not the war, nor the attack at Rosières, nor even the loss of his wife, but the return of John Emmett into his life. Before then, Laurence had been trying to develop a routine around the writing of a book on London churches. Astonishingly, a mere six or so years earlier when he came down from Oxford, he had taught, briefly and happily, but on marrying he had been persuaded that teaching was not a means of supporting Louise and the large family she had planned. After only token resistance he had joined her family's long-established coffee importing business. It all seemed so long ago, now. There was no coffee, no business – or not for him – and Louise and his only child were dead.

When his wife and son lay dying in Bristol, Laurence was crouched in the colourless light of dawn, waiting to move towards the German guns and praying fervently to a God he no longer believed in. He had long been indifferent to which side won; he wished only that one or the other would do so decisively while he was still alive. It would be days before the news of Louise and their baby's death reached him. It was not until he was home, with his grief-stricken mother-in-law endlessly supplying unwanted details, that he realised that Louise had died at precisely the moment he was giving the order to advance. When he finally got leave, he had stood by the grave with its thin, new grass while his father-in-law hovered near by, embarrassed. When the older man had withdrawn, Laurence crouched down. He could smell the damp earth but there was nothing of her here. Later, he chose the granite and spelled out both names and the dates to the stonemason. He wanted to mourn, yet his emotions seemed unreachable. Indeed, after a few days shut up with his parents-in-law, desolate and aged by loss, he was soon searching for an excuse to return to London and escape the intensity of their misery.

As he sat on the train, returning to close up his London house, he had felt a brief but shocking wave of elation. Louise was gone, so many were gone, but he had made it through – he was still quite young and with a life ahead of him. The mood passed as quickly as it always did, to be replaced by emptiness. The house felt airless and stale. He started packing everything himself but after opening a small chest to find a soft whiteness of matinée jackets, bootees, embroidered baby gowns and tiny bonnets, all carefully folded in tissue paper, he had recoiled from the task and paid someone to make sure he never saw any of it again.

Louise had left him money and so he was free to follow a new career. It did not make him a man of substantial means, but it was enough for him to tell Louise's father that he wouldn't be returning to the business. Even if Louise had survived and he were now the father of a lively son, he doubted he would have continued buying and selling coffee beans. The war had changed things; for him life before 1914 was a closed world he could never reach back and touch. He could recall banal fragments of people but not the whole. His mother's long fingers stabbing embroidery silks into her petit point. His father snipping and smoothing his moustache as he grimaced in the looking-glass. He could even remember the smell of his father's pomade, yet the rest of the face never quite came into focus. His memories were just a series of tableaux, disconnected from the present. Louise, and the small hopes and plans that went with her, were simply part of these everyday losses.

He'd rented a small flat, a quarter the size of the town house he and Louise had lived in for their eighteen months of marriage before he was sent to France. It was in Great Ormond Street and on the top floor, with windows facing in three directions so that the small rooms were filled with light. There he could lie in bed listening to the wind and the pigeons cooing on the roof. He rarely went out socially these days but when he did it was usually to see his friend Charles Carfax who had been at the same school and had served in France. Charles was someone to whom nothing need be explained.

Sometimes as he gazed out across the rooftops Laurence tried to picture where he might be in a year's time – five years, ten – but he couldn't imagine a life other than this. At Oxford he had been teased about his enthusiasms: for long walks, architecture, even dancing. That excitement was a curiosity now and he had stopped worrying that he had drifted away from friends. He no longer had any imagined future different from the present.

Where he felt most alive was sitting in the chapel of Thomas More inside Chelsea Old Church, wondering at the man's courage, or in All Hallows by the Tower where bodies, including More's, had been brought after beheading at the Tower. Somehow horror was blunted by thirteen centuries. Churches, he thought, weren't buildings but stories; even their names fascinated him. However, when he tried to re-create that excitement for his own book, he was reduced to stone and floor plans and architectural terms. For St Bartholomew the Great, his notes read: billet moulding, cloister, twelfth-century transept. Yet when he was sitting, resting his eyes, he had sometimes sensed the monks brushing by him on their way to Compline, or stumbling bewildered through the teeming streets after Henry VIII had evicted them, while the building survived as best it could: as stable, forge, factory or inn, before it returned to what it was meant to be.

He had had a happy childhood, adored by parents who had produced him quite late in life, but both had died unexpectedly before he was sixteen. His much older married sister, Millicent, had been like a second mother, but she had moved to India before their parents died, remaining there with her large family and a husband who was part of the colonial administration. She had tried her hardest to persuade her young brother to join them and, when Laurence turned out to be surprisingly stubborn in refusal, sent him stories by Rudyard Kipling, which revealed India as a magical and dangerous place. He still kept one book near his bed, unable to imagine his sensible sister amid the gold elephants, turbaned elephant boys and rearing rattlesnakes on the cover. A distant aunt agreed to be his guardian and this satisfied Millicent, if not his need for love and comfort. In due course he went up to Oxford where his tutor had been something of a father to him from the day he arrived at Merton College as an undergraduate. Shortly before his death a year or so ago, this kind, unworldly man had introduced him to a publisher who had shown surprising interest in Laurence's diffidently proposed work.

Meanwhile his sister wrote regularly with an innocent assumption of his love for Wilfred, Sally, Bumble, James and Ted, his unknown, unimagined nephews and nieces. Given her determination never to speak of anything unpleasant, her letters only increased his feeling that Louise and the war were something he'd dreamed up.

For a while young widows, or girls who had once been engaged to officers in his regiment who hadn't made it through, made it fairly clear that his attentions would be welcome. He was nice-looking rather than conventionally handsome, with thick dark hair, pale skin, brown eyes and strong nose, a combination that sometimes led people to assume a non-existent Scottish ancestry. Unable to cope with the possibilities on offer, he invariably withdrew with the excuse that he needed to focus on his research. His married friends had been kind after Louise's death but he felt uncomfortable in their houses, watching their family life unfold. He had tried it once. He had journeyed down to Hampshire for a perfectly undemanding weekend of tennis and cocktails, country walks and chatter, then found himself in the grip of overwhelming anxiety. As they trudged through waist-high bracken and followed earth tracks through thickets of dense flowering gorse, he found himself jumping at every rustle or crack of a branch. He made his excuses straight after Sunday lunch.

Sometimes now he could go a week or more without revisiting the smells and tremors of the war, and a whole month without dreaming of Louise: that unknown Louise, ever pliant, ever accommodating. It was an irony that he thought about the dead Louise a great deal more intensely than he ever had the living woman, and with real physical longing.

Just once he had weakened. He was walking alone late when a woman stepped from a doorway.

'On your own?' she said.

He thought she had a slight west country accent.

'I say, you're a quiet one. You on your own?'

Inadequately dressed even for a mild winter's evening, she smiled hopefully.

'Do you want to get warm?'

His first thought had been that he didn't feel cold. His second, that she looked nothing like Louise.

Her back curved away from him as she took off her clothes, folding them carefully on a chair. Then she turned to him. Standing there, in just her stockings, her body thin and white and her bush of hair shocking and black, he was simultaneously aroused and appalled. She watched him incuriously as he took off his shirt and trousers. Then she lay back and opened her legs. Yet when he tried to enter her she was quite dry and he had to spit on his hand to wet her before he pushed hard against her resistance. He couldn't bear to look at her. As he took her he wished he had removed his socks. When he had finished she got up, went over to a bowl on a stool in the corner, half hidden behind a papier-mâché screen, and wiped herself with a bit of cloth. He paid, noticing she wore a wedding ring, and went briskly downstairs into the dark where he drew mouthfuls of night air, with its smell of cinders and drains, deep into his lungs. He was lost. Too much had gone.

CHAPTER TWO

*N*early three years after the war, John Emmett came
back into his life. There had been six weeks without
rain. Night and day had become jumbled and Laurence often
sat in the dark with the sash windows wide open and let the
breeze cool him as he worked, knowing that when he finally
went to bed on these humid August nights he would find it
hard to sleep. Only the bells of St George's chiming the quar-
ter-hours linked him to the outside world.

Then, one Tuesday teatime, he was surprised to find a letter,
addressed in unfamiliar handwriting, lying on the hall table.
Later he came to think of it as *the* letter. It had been forwarded
twice: first from his old Oxford college, then from his former
marital home; it was a miracle it had got to him at all.

He sat down by the largest window, slipped a finger under
the flap and tore it open. Late-afternoon sunlight fell across
the page. Neat, cursive writing ran over two pages, covering
both sides, the lines quite close together and sloping to the
right. He turned it over and looked for a signature. Instantly,
foolishly, he felt a jolt of possibility.

Dear Laurence,

Writing to you after so long feels like a bit of an intrusion especially as you once wrote to me and I never answered. My life was difficult then. I hope you still remember me.

I heard that you lost your wife and I am dreadfully sorry. I met Louise only that one time at Henley but she was a lovely girl, you must miss her a lot.

I wanted to tell you that John died six months ago and, horribly, he shot himself. He seemed to have been luckier than many in the war, but when he came back from France he wouldn't talk and just sat in his room or went for long walks at night. He said he couldn't sleep. I don't think he was writing or reading or any of the things he used to enjoy. Sometimes he would get in furious rages, even with our mother. Finally he got in a fight with strangers and was arrested.

Our doctor said that he needed more help than he could provide. He found him a place in a nursing home. John went along with it but then the following winter he ran away. A month later a keeper found his body in a wood over thirty miles away. He didn't leave a letter. Nothing to explain it. We had thought he was getting better.

I know you saw much less of each other after school, but all John's other friends that I ever met are gone and you are the only one, ever, who John brought home.

I am sure you are a busy man, but I would be so very

grateful, as would my mother, if you could talk to me a little about John. We loved him but we didn't always understand him. We can't begin to know what changed him so much in the war. You might. I've written three letters to you before and not posted them; instead I just go over and over his last months. I know it is a lot to ask and I'm presuming on a feeling that maybe you don't share – that we had a bond – but could we meet? I will understand if you feel you have nothing to say, of course; we knew each other such a long time ago and you have had your own troubles.

Yours sincerely,
Mary Emmett

Laurence leaned back in the chair, feeling the heat of the sun. Mary Emmett. She was right, he would have liked to have known her better. He remembered a lively, brown-haired girl with none of her brother's reserve. He had first come across her while he was at school, then been surprised by how she had changed when he bumped into her again in Oxford at a dance three or four years later. Yet he had recognised her almost immediately.

Although she was not a beauty, she had an attractive, open face with – and he smiled as he remembered it – a schoolgirl's grin at anything that was at all absurd. They were seated at the same large table and kept catching one another's glance, but by the time he could detach himself from his neighbours, to ask her to dance, her friends were wanting to leave. They talked for perhaps ten minutes, which he wished had been longer.

Then, not long before the war, he'd seen her again at the Henley regatta. It was soon after he'd met Louise, and Mary Emmett seemed to have an attentive male friend, but he recalled meeting eyes that were full of laughter when they sat opposite each other at some particularly pompous dinner party. Candlelight shone on her pearl necklace and he thought he remembered the shimmering eau-de-nil satin of her dress. He had thought, if water nymphs existed, they would look much like her. He had a sense of connection which was far stronger than any actual contact between them and afterwards, impulsively, he had written to her. He had never received a reply and soon his life was overtaken by marriage and war.

He read the letter again and slowly the impact of her news sank in. What on earth had led the self-contained but confident boy he had known at school to kill himself, having survived four years of war?

CHAPTER THREE

*J*ohn and Laurence had arrived at Marlborough on the same day in 1903. Laurence's first impression of school was of warm reds and rusts: one handsome, square brick building after another and the early autumn colours of huge horse-chestnut trees. He was small for his age and after a sheltered childhood the changes came as a shock.

Amid the clamour and occasional brutality of a large public school, the two thirteen-year-olds had banded together with Charles, who had been there a term already, Rupert — who later died in Africa — and Lionel, who was destined for the Church. But it was John Emmett who was the unacknowledged leader. He appeared fearless and was dogged in the pursuit of justice. When he was younger, things simply went wrong for those who crossed him; as he got older, he would quietly confront anyone who made a weaker boy's life a misery.

John Emmett had very little interest in the sort of success that schoolboys usually hungered for. Although good at most games, especially rowing, he was unimpressed by being selected for teams; he drilled with the cadets but made no effort to be promoted; he sang in the chapel choir but by sixteen was privately expressing doubts about God. He argued with masters with such skill that contradiction seemed like enthusiasm. He was a natural linguist. He even wrote poetry, yet avoided being seen as effete by the school's dominating clique of hearty sportsmen. Yet although many respected him, nobody would have called John their best friend. For the young Laurence he represented everything that was mysterious and brave.

John was notorious for his night-time adventures. One summer Laurence went out onto the leads of the roof, swallowing hard to try to conquer his nausea at being four storeys above the stone-flagged courtyard. There was nobody else he would have gone with. It was a perfect, absolutely clear night and the sky was filled with stars. Laurence looked up, feeling giddy as John named the galaxies and planets above them.

'Don't like heights, do you?' John said, matter-of-factly. 'Me, I can go as high as you like, it's being shut in that gives me the heebie-jeebies. But look,' he pointed, 'tonight you can just see the rings of Saturn with the naked eye.' He stepped dangerously near the edge, silhouetted against the bright night sky.

It was from his father that John had learned all about the stars. He would use his father's opinion to settle arguments decisively; Laurence could still hear his solemn tone of voice: 'My father says . . .' When Laurence finally went to stay with John, the year before they were to take university entrance, he found that Mr Emmett was in fact a bluff gentleman farmer, whose main topic of conversation was shooting, whose hobby was stargazing through his old telescope and whose closest confidant was a small terrier called Sirius.

'Dog star, d'ye see?'

John and his father seemed to understand each other without speaking and on several mornings Laurence woke to find the two of them already up and walking the fields.

He had liked the warm informality of the Emmett household. There was a freedom there he had never known. When Laurence's parents died, the Marlborough code meant that no one actually mentioned his new status as an orphan. When John came into Laurence's study a day or so after his mother's funeral to find him red-eyed, he had asked him to stay during the holidays. The Emmetts lived in a large, rather isolated house in Suffolk. Rooms were dusty, furniture faded. The grass on the tennis court was two inches high and choked with dandelions and the worn balls were as likely to go through the holes in the net as over it. There was a croquet lawn of sorts on a slope so steep that all but the most skilful players eventually relinquished their balls to the small stream that ran below it. Mary, very much the little sister then, went in barefoot to retrieve them and tried to sell them back. She was always paddling in the stream, her legs were invariably muddy, he recalled, and she had a ferret she took for walks on a lead. Was it called Kitchener? The following Christmas the Emmetts had sent him a present of an ivory-handled penknife with his initials on it. He had it with him in France.

He looked again at her letter. Why had they lost touch? He supposed they had rapidly become different men on leaving school but the truth was that John had probably grown up more quickly than he had. Laurence remembered being surprised to hear that Emmett had joined as a volunteer at the beginning of the war. John was the last person to be swayed by popular excitement and at Oxford he liked to speak of himself as a European. The only jingoist in the Emmett family had been John's father, who toasted the King every evening and mistrusted the French, Germans and Londoners. Laurence thought, uncomfortably, of his own, discreditable motives for volunteering and hoped his friends would be equally surprised if they knew that truth.

For a moment he felt a surprisingly intense sadness, the sort of emotion he could remember once feeling quite often. Now that odd, passionate schoolboy was gone, and, judging by the address on Mary's letter, so was the lovingly neglected house. John had been different when so many of them were so ordinary. Laurence counted himself among the ordinary sort. If the war hadn't come, they would all have become stout solicitors and brewers, doctors and cattle-breeders, with tolerant wives and children, most of them living in the same villages, towns and counties they came from.

For much of the war Laurence had hung on to the idea that he would go back to the small world he had been so eager to leave. Only when the end of the war seemed a possibility did life suddenly become precious and death a terrifying reality. Both he and John *had* returned, but now he knew that death had caught up with John and, moreover, by his own choice.

Laurence's second reaction as he read Mary Emmett's letter was a sinking feeling. He couldn't bring John back, nor could he tell her anything she wanted to hear, and he hadn't – as far as he knew – served near him in France. The truth was that he had heard nothing directly from his old school friend since they'd left Oxford. At university they had effectively parted ways. John had gone into a different college; his circle were clever men: writers, debaters, thinkers. Laurence had fallen in with an easier set, who held parties and played games, thinking of little outside their own lives. Laurence had migrated to London, surrendered to the coffee trade and married Louise. John had apparently gone abroad to Switzerland, then Germany. Laurence had read his occasional reports in the London newspapers. They were usually cameo pieces: Bavarian farmers struggling to make ends meet, the chocolate-smelling girls in a Berne factory or a veteran who had been Bismarck's footman. As tensions rose in Europe, he supposed John's small contributions had slipped out of favour. During the war one of his poems had been published in a newspaper but apart from that his work had disappeared from view.

Laurence had nothing new to give Mary. He told himself that a visit to Cambridge would simply raise her hopes, and probably her mother's too. If she came to London he couldn't think where he could take her. But he couldn't forget the kindnesses shown by all the Emmetts when he was a lonely boy without any real family of his own.

Dressing for dinner with Charles, he took out his cufflinks and there nestling beside them was the little ivory-handled penknife. That decided him. He was deluding himself that any kind of book was taking shape and a few days away from stifling London could do no harm. But as he walked through the London streets to dinner, it was Mary's conspiratorial and almost forgotten smile which occupied his mind.

'But why the hell didn't you tell me?' he asked Charles later, as they sat back in deep armchairs, nursing their port.

Charles coughed, loud enough to make two men sitting across the room look up. His still-boyish face flushed with embarrassment. 'Unforgivable. I was in Scotland when I heard. My cousin Jack's place. Damn cold. Then I forgot.'

'Why did he do it?' Laurence asked himself as much as Charles.

'Usual thing, I suppose. France? Seems to have taken some men like that. Mind you,' Charles reflected, 'he was home when the West Kents really took a pounding. Back in England – smashed leg, something like that. Must have avoided the whole scrap. Perhaps he felt he didn't deserve the luck.'

Charles seemed to have regarded his military service as a bit of a lark. He'd embraced war as an escape from destiny in the form of the successful family leather factories and he flourished in the infantry. He had escaped death, serious injury or illness for three gruelling years and had been mentioned in despatches twice by the time the war ended.

They both fell quiet. Laurence gazed at the flare of copper chrysanthemums in the fireplace. Eventually Charles broke the silence.

'Look, I'm sorry I didn't fill you in about Emmett. I know he was a jolly close friend at school but then the Harcourts didn't make it either, nor did Sorely and that odd chap Greaves you liked so much, and that Scot – what was he called – with the terrible temper. The one who joined the RFC? It's not as if we'd all been in touch and I rather thought you'd had enough of talking about that kind of thing. You know, with Louise and everything. No-go area and all that.' He reddened again.

'Lachlan. It was Lachlan Ramsay who had the temper,' said Laurence quickly. 'But yes, I did admire John. His odd courage; his independence. What may have happened after the war doesn't alter that. It's a shame.' He paused. 'Quite honestly, I wish I *could* say he was my friend, but he wasn't, not really. *Friendly*, while we were at school, but not a friend. Hardly even that at Oxford. A few words if we'd met in the street, no more.'

As he spoke, one of the two older men who had sat across the room from them got up to leave. His companion rose to follow him. Charles, who had been glancing in their direction for the last half-hour, jumped up from his chair and went over to shake the first man's hand, and was then introduced to the other. The slightly younger man had a distinguished and intelligent face, the older one a slightly stiff military bearing.

As Charles sat down again he looked pleased. 'You know who they were, of course?'

Laurence never knew who anybody was, however eagerly Charles assumed that figures who loomed large in his own life were as significant in anyone else's.

'Gerald Somers,' Charles said triumphantly, and then when Laurence failed to respond quickly enough: 'Major general. Zulu wars. Boer scrap. Mafeking. Enough medals for a jubilee. A real hero, not just medals for other men's courage. Of *course* you know who he is, Laurence. Mind you, he's not so popular with the powers that be now. Got some very unfashionable views on military discipline.'

Simply to be left in peace Laurence nodded. 'Of course.' These ageing generals loved their hanging and flogging, he thought wearily.

'Well, they can't say much. Not to his face. Career like that and gave both his sons to his country. The other man was Philip Morrell. Used to be an MP. I'm surprised you didn't recognise him, Laurence. Though he's a Liberal, of course. His wife is Lady Ottoline, sister of the Duke of Portland. *You* know. Bohemians. Absolutely terrifying.'

Laurence had at least heard of the Morrells and their circle, so felt able to nod. 'Absolutely. But why would Mary write to me?' he added.

Although even as he said it, he realised Charles was right – attrition had been high among their school friends. In the aftermath of the last few years, her choice was limited.

✳

When he got in, Laurence sat down to write to Mary Emmett. He kept it brief, just his condolences and a gentle warning that he doubted he could throw any light on anything, but would visit as soon as she wanted. Then, with a sense of urgency – her letter had taken eight weeks to find him – he went out into the dark to post it. When he returned he lay on his bed, unsettled by the heat, and by thoughts of John.

CHAPTER FOUR

*I*t was a perfect early September day, the sky a cloudless deep blue, as Laurence's train crossed the flatlands of eastern England. It was not an area he knew well or found particularly attractive but on such a fine morning it was hard not to feel a sense of well-being. As the train gathered speed leaving London behind, he had felt a wonderful sense of liberation despite the probable awkwardness of the day ahead. The fields spread away to the horizon, all bleached stubble and hayricks, and occasionally a line of elms marking a road going from one small village to another. Nothing seemed to move, although as they rattled across a level crossing a horse and cart laden with hay and two bicyclists waited to cross.

His mood stayed calm even as they drew into Cambridge and he left the train. The country summer had straggled into the city; Michaelmas daisies and roses grew in tired beds by the station, and a few ripe blackberries hung on sooty brambles in the no-man's land between the platform and the picket fence. On the platform a group of young women laughed in the pastel shade of Chinese parasols.

Rather to his relief, he recognised Mary Emmett almost immediately, standing outside the ticket office in a pale-green dress and a soft straw hat, her wavy brown hair caught in a bun at the nape of her neck. Her once laughing greenish eyes were solemn. But when he approached she smiled and he saw the girl he remembered in the older, thinner face.

She put out her hand. 'Laurence,' she said, 'welcome to Cambridge. Thank you so, so much for coming.'

She had a wide, pretty mouth and when she talked a dimple appeared to one side. She looked genuinely delighted to see him, and only dark smudges under her eyes hinted at sadness.

They took a bus, which drove slowly past the Botanic Gardens – a dark-green jungle behind tidy railings. The warm stone buildings of the ancient colleges lay on either side of them.

'Now,' Mary said as they got off by Magdalene Bridge, 'here we are at the crossroads of duty and pleasure: we could go home but if we do we'll get caught up with Mother and Aunt Virginia. She lives with us now, as a companion for my mother.' She made a face.

Laurence waited to see where the other road led.

'Or,' she continued, 'seeing as it's such a perfect day, we could go out to Granchester for early tea. We could take the bus or even punt. Do you punt?'

'Well, I could punt more than a decade ago. I suppose I could test my surviving punting skills if you feel brave?'

'I can actually punt myself.' She smiled. 'It's just much more fun to be a puntee.'

However he had thought the day might turn out, Laurence had never expected to be drinking lemon squash under trees so heavy with fruit that under their weight the branches had curved to the ground to form green-latticed caves. They made good time up the river. After tying up next to a couple of other boats, and swatting away midges at the water's edge, they walked through meadows to the tearooms. Apart from their footsteps in the dry grass, the only sound was a distant corncrake.

Mary asked whether he'd read Brooke's poem about the village and Laurence felt absurdly glad to be able to recite at least some of it.

'I met him, you know,' Mary said. 'I don't think he was very impressed – I was far too young and not nearly clever or beautiful enough for his set, but John liked him. They'd come over here and talk and read. That's how I first knew of the tearoom. But I love the river. Cambridge can be so dusty and yellow but the river is always so cool and green. It reminds me of our old house out here. I'd live on an island or a houseboat if I could.'

'You'll be horrified to know that when I was at Oxford I used to think you were like a water nymph,' he said. For a second he couldn't believe he had blurted out something so ridiculously inappropriate but she looked so delighted and happy at his absurd revelation that he laughed with her.

Laurence began to wonder whether the whole day would pass without either of them mentioning the reason for his visit. It was only the almost untouched seed cake on her plate that suggested Mary Emmett was more anxious than she appeared. He was fighting off sleepiness from the punting and the sun as he sat in his shirtsleeves, eyes slightly screwed up against the light. He had become adept at sensing the turn of a conversation so that he could head off any direction that led to Louise and sympathy. Now he found himself on the other side, trying to reach a place where John could be there quite naturally.

'Is your mother all right?' It was a lame question.

'No,' said Mary. 'No, she's not, actually. She was never very strong and she's just retreated from the world. All the anxiety about John during the war, and then a brief happiness when he came back. Then it was soon obvious things were badly wrong, and she was scared and embarrassed by his violent out-bursts. He got involved in a fight, miles away, and was arrested. He wouldn't talk about it but he would have been charged if he hadn't been admitted into a nursing home. All the same, she wasn't sure whether she should have let him be put away — because we *were* putting him away; we both felt it. He would-n't speak and something was wrong with his arm; it made his life even harder that he couldn't use it. He needed us. Needed somebody who loved him.'

'I'm sure he understood,' Laurence said. 'I'm sorry, that sounds such a cliché.' However, he was wondering whether John might also have needed distance from his over-protective mother.

'Yes, but the place was too far away and he was among strangers and I'm not even sure they — the people in charge — were all very *nice* people. Not very kind. And the worst thing of all was that truthfully it was quite a relief to have him out of the house.'

Her voice wobbled. Laurence automatically put out his hand to comfort her and cursed himself for being a fool as it neither reached her nor was noticed. After a second he with-drew it. There was silence for a minute or two, except for wasps buzzing round the jug of cordial.

'Do you really think he was mistreated?'

'Well, not actively mistreated, but not always understood. He was complicated.'

She described what she knew of John's last days, though the story she told was not greatly amplified from her long letter.

John had settled into Holmwood, an institution in the market town of Fairford in the Cotswolds. It had long been a hospital specialising in neurasthenia. Before the war it had taken men and women in more or less equal numbers but soon it began to fill with troubled officers.

'Shell-shock: that's what they call it now. To give them their due, they got John speaking and he'd put on a bit of weight by the last time I saw him.'

'Who was actually in charge?' asked Laurence.

'A Doctor Chilvers was in charge medically but his son had a share in ownership, I think; he seemed to have a lot of influence in how things were done. Although Dr Chilvers was quite old, he seemed to be doing his best. His son, George, was thirty-five or so but I didn't get the feeling he'd served in the war. He's a solicitor. I didn't like him. The staff were nervous of him, I thought. And either there's family money or they're doing quite nicely out of Holmwood. Is that unfair? I suppose it is.' She rushed on, 'Why shouldn't they do well? Somebody has to care for these poor men.'

'Did anyone expect things to turn out so badly?'

'I would have said suicide was the last thing he'd do. Earlier, maybe. Not then. I saw him about six weeks before he — escaped — and he was a bit restless. But in a way I thought that was good. He hated being cooped up; said he had things he needed to do, which must mean he intended to have time to do them in, surely? He talked a bit. About Suffolk. Lots about our father. He said he had regrets — he didn't say about what but I assumed the war. Yet that last time I thought he was more himself, if anything. In fact, I went back more hopeful than I had for ages. I even suggested Mother went over to see him.'

She stopped and breathed in deeply. They were both so still

that a sparrow hopped on to the table and pecked at crumbs. As she began to speak again, it flew a few feet away to perch on a chairback.

'She never did, of course. She never saw him again. That Christmas Day he was taken ill in church or pretended he was. A Holmwood attendant followed him out but John either knocked him out or just pushed him out of his way – it depends which version you believe. And John ran off and ended up dead in a wood. Heaven knows how long he'd been there. He could have lived rough for a while, I suppose. It was an awful, awful shock.

'Anyway, apparently Dr Chilvers told the inquest – we didn't go; my mother would have been terribly distressed and I couldn't face it on my own – there was a blot on John's copybook at Holmwood: he'd "absconded" only weeks earlier. Absconded! When he'd gone to Holmwood voluntarily.'

She was sitting forward now, her elbows on the table. Sun filtered through the brim of her hat on to her skin. She was beautiful, he thought.

'After that they'd been keeping him under closer confinement for a bit,' she went on. 'That alone would have driven him mad. No wonder he broke out. But Chilvers' slimy son backed up the doctor and one of the attendants said John was volatile.' She looked upset and paused as if waiting for him to see the injustice of it all. 'As if the rest of their patients were models of composure. They kept referring to what they called a violent attack on their warder outside the church. Not pointing out it was the only way John could get away.'

Laurence must have looked puzzled because Mary added, 'Of course, men like John do kill themselves sometimes. I know that. In fact there'd been another death there – right in the house itself – only a few months before John arrived. But

26

on the day John disappeared, they didn't call the police out for twelve hours while young Mr Chilvers drove around, trying to retrieve their lost patient with minimum fuss. If they'd got others involved they might have found John before he did it.'

Although her hand was trembling slightly her voice remained very calm. She ran her finger down the side of her glass.

'But it was a stranger who died, you see. He'd left us years ago.'

Laurence wished he could tell her he had heard from him, wished he could have explained that stranger to her. He wanted to believe he would have made contact if he'd known John was in trouble, but he feared that he wouldn't. He should never have lost his friend in the first place.

'Look,' he began, unsure what he was about to commit himself to and whether he was complicating a simple, if sad, event. 'I could see if I could find out anything. I mean, I don't know if I would be able to do any more than you have, but I could at least ask around people he and I both knew. At school, mostly, possibly at Oxford. See whether any of them had heard anything from him since the war. I have the time.'

Even as he said it, he knew he was only setting himself up to disappoint her. So many in their year were gone now and John had had no intimates, anyway. 'People at school' would simply mean Charles Carfax. But her face brightened irresistibly, so he continued, 'At a pinch I suppose I could talk to the people at Holmwood, see if they come up with anything.' As he said it, he thought how unlikely it was that he would be any match for the professionally discreet.

'When John died — afterwards — they sent a trunk with his things,' she said. 'There's not much in it, just clothes and books. Little things.'

A look of such extreme sadness came over her that he was embarrassed to be faced with her emotion and uneasy remembering his own reactions to Louise's possessions.

'But there might be something you'd make sense of. There are sketches and writings, a few photographs. You might see something, knowing a different side of John to us.'

He didn't know how to tell her that he felt he had never really known her brother at all.

It was getting cooler. Laurence paid for tea and they walked back to the punt, now alone on its moorings. Light breezes made the return journey faster but chilly. Mary sat, eventually accepting Laurence's offer of his coat, while he made what seemed like interminable progress downstream. After a bit she took over and he surrendered the pole with gratitude. His shoulder muscles were burning with exertion but he was damp with sweat and soon felt cold. They were both weary by the time they were back on land again.

They walked the short distance to the Emmetts' new house in silence. Laurence, remembering their Suffolk home from years back, was surprised by the dull meagreness of the tall, narrow house they lived in now. The brick was greyish-yellow, the proportions of the windows cramped. Below the railings, ferns and mosses had encroached on the damp basement. What had happened to their leisured existence before the war?

CHAPTER FIVE

*A*n elderly woman opened the door. Was it the same maid he remembered from long ago, Laurence wondered; she wasn't in uniform but few domestics were now. He smiled encouragingly but she just motioned to them to come in.

'My aunt, Miss Virginia Peel,' said Mary. He hoped his smile hadn't been patronising.

Mary took him into a small drawing room where, despite the warmth outside, Mrs Emmett sat by a fire. To cross the room and shake her hand, he had to squeeze between occasional tables and around a large chiffonier. Every bit of furniture that had looked at home in an affably neglected manor house appeared to have accompanied them to Cambridge. The effect was oppressive, the pieces heavy and grandiose. Weak light filtered in through thick lace curtains under a velvet pelmet. Even Mary seemed to wilt. Her mother sat on a button-back chair like a relic of another age.

'Laurence,' she said and held out a soft hand, 'how good to see you again.'

He would not have recognised Mrs Emmett. She was much smaller than he recalled and a certain excitability, which had amused him when he was a boy, was entirely gone.

'How good of you to come all this way and see Mary. She doesn't get out nearly enough.' She looked towards her daughter. 'She doesn't see much of her old friends. I don't know why. Everybody used to love Mary.'

They talked politely, touching on her son for only a second, and then only to locate them all in time.

'That was before John died, of course,' Mrs Emmett had replied to Laurence's asking when they had moved to Cambridge.

Mary jumped in at this opportunity. 'I thought it might be nice to let Laurence have one of John's books. You remember we discussed it. As a keepsake.' He could tell that Mrs Emmett actually remembered nothing of the sort and it crossed his mind that there had never even been a conversation on the subject, but Mrs Emmett smiled again vaguely.

'Oh yes, lovely. What a good idea. Certainly he should have something. Do you like poetry? John was very keen on poetry, you know.'

Laurence had worried that they would have to sit and have a second, awkward, tea, but Mary's mother seemed unconcerned with such social niceties and after a few minutes they were able to back out of the room.

John's things had been put in one of two small rooms under the eaves. As they climbed the three flights of stairs, Mary said over her shoulder, 'You don't have to take anything. I simply wanted an excuse to show you John's things without having to explain.'

Their feet clattered up a last uncarpeted flight into a small, peaceful room with a casement window. It held an iron bed, a wooden chair and a washstand. On the bed lay a trunk and a box. It reminded him a bit of school.

'We never used to come up here,' Mary said, as if the room still surprised her. 'But my aunt needed John's old room, and now this is all that's left of him . . . It's hard.'

She opened the wooden box first. A battered hip flask lay on top of a yellow and black striped scarf. Mary picked it up and held to her face, smelling it.

'A school house scarf,' she said. 'Not a Marlborough scarf and not his, though I like to think that a friend gave it to him to keep out the cold. He had it with him until the end.'

Laurence took the scarf from her. He didn't say that it had probably belonged to a dead man. He picked up the corner and saw what he expected: embroidered initials and a school number next to it. He wondered what the schoolboy MS142C had been like and what had happened to him. What sporting boys in what house in what school had worn these colours? School with its numbered individuals was just like the army, he thought.

Mary was rifling through the box. 'Holmwood sent it back to us. Most of what was with him, on his body, was burned,' she said hurriedly, turning her face away. 'But there should have been a watch. It had been my grandfather's and my father bought a new chain for it when John went up to Oxford. Though I suppose it could have been damaged.'

The corner of her mouth twitched so minutely that if he hadn't been watching her closely, he might have missed it.

'These were returned to us.' She turned round, holding out an oilskin tobacco pouch, a crumpled handkerchief and a worn woman's hair ornament. She then lifted up a lined sheet of paper with writing on it and a photograph. 'The contents of his pockets. Pathetic, really. The note and photograph were in the empty pouch.'

He took the photograph from her. A deep crease ran across it and the corners were dog-eared. It was a picture of soldiers, taken from a short distance away. The image was poor quality and overexposed along one edge. Nor had they posed for it; in fact, the group seemed unaware of the photographer. They were mostly young and unsmiling. Some were smoking in a huddle. The closest was more of a boy than a man, noticeably slighter and shorter than the rest. Standing alone, leaning back against a pile of logs, his eyes half shut but looking more relaxed than the others, was a sergeant. Close by were two officers; one was considerably older, in his late forties, Laurence guessed. The younger had turned half away from the camera. Could it be John? Mary didn't comment. In the background was a cobbled farmyard. A single bare branch overhung open stalls with a covering of what looked like light snow.

He turned the picture over. In the corner was a fairly formal monogram in purple ink – the developer perhaps? He looked briefly at the sheet of paper; across the top was the word 'Coburg' underlined, and below it 'Byers' and then 'Darling' in older, pencilled writing. Next to it in different ink was written 'B. Combe Bisset and then Tucker/Florence St?'

Who had taken the photograph, and why had John got it with him at his death? Impossible to know. Were Byers and Darling men in the picture? Was Tucker a street or a person? Combe Bisset was presumably a British location and Coburg a German one. But then he thought of all the nicknames they gave to trenches in France, a stagnant pit called Piccadilly and a sand-bagged Dover Way. As he thought, he was fiddling with the metal comb, a small, cheap, gilt trinket. A unicorn's head surmounted its bent spikes, with what might be letters or simply decoration.

Mary set aside a battered tin of geometry instruments and

lifted out a book on birds. He opened it at the bookmark. John had written down the margin: 'Wonderful golden orioles singing at La Comte. April '17.' The page showed a plump, bright-yellow bird with the caption '*Oriolus oriolus*'.

'He and my father loved birds,' Mary said, as she handed him three more volumes. 'Heads in the air – birds and stars – both of them.'

On top was a well-worn copy of *The Iliad*. Laurence remembered struggling through it at school. He put the other books on the bed and opened the Homer. Sure enough, it was inscribed: *John Christopher Rawlston Emmett, College House*. He reached for a small anthology with a cover in pristine khaki. He thought every soldier had been given a copy on embarkation to France. It was titled *Spirit of War*, a collection of stirring works for impressionable young men. He exchanged it briefly for Browning's *The Ring and the Book*. Mary handed him a book in a brown slipcover. Taking it from her, he read the cover: Karl Marx, *Das Kapital*. He prised apart the curled-up page corners and stared at the mystery of dense Gothic script.

Mary had pulled some notebooks from under the remaining contents. The first was a mixture of sketches, poems and bits of prose. Here and there a cutting had been stuck in. She tipped a page towards him: it was a charcoal drawing of the old Suffolk house. The second book was smaller and the writing in it more cramped; following round the bottom margins of pages and up the sides.

Mary stood close to him and turned the pages slowly. There were sketches of infantrymen in a camp lying propped up with mugs of tea, and then one of a young soldier enveloped in a waterproof cape and huddled behind sandbags. They were awfully good, Laurence thought; the sense of relentless rain was invoked with a few pencil strokes. The whole of the next page was a half-finished portrait of a nurse sitting by an oil lamp, its light accentuating her bone structure. Mary handed the open book to him. He turned the page again. On the left was a studio photograph: French undoubtedly – he had seen hundreds like it – of a solid young woman, posed naked but for her hat and boots. Her hands were clasped behind her neck, the hair under her arms and between her legs was as dark and thick as that under her hat. Laurence looked up sharply but Mary was absorbed in the earlier notebook.

There were two poems on the following page. They both had the same title, 'A Lament'. The first, a sonnet, had the initials JCRE underneath. He remembered John's poem he'd read in the newspaper. This one was better, he thought. The second poem, although also handwritten, had been pasted in; the writing was quite different. It was signed 'Sisyphus'. It was long, with no real structure and incomplete sentences, yet its words painted a picture that brought the combined sensations and sounds of warfare back to Laurence so strongly that he found himself gripping the book tightly. The strange fragments summoned up the inescapable proximity to others and the simultaneous loneliness of life near the front line, of profound bonds between men dependent on each other, yet having perhaps to pass by the same men lying dead in some muddy defile.

Laurence wondered why John had stuck the poems in together. John's poem was highly competent, moving even, but diminished by the extraordinary quality of the unknown Sisyphus's work.

As Mary unlatched the trunk it emanated a faint and disconcerting stale male scent: sweat, tobacco, hair oil and mothballs. The contents were somehow depressing: towels, a worn tartan blanket, some cheap blank writing paper and envelopes. A pair of indoor shoes in need of a polish and lovat bedroom slippers lay over a couple of folded newspapers, presumably there to protect the clothes from the shoes. He picked up the top paper; it was dated the previous November. The front page had a grainy picture of the train bearing the Unknown Warrior arriving at Victoria Station. Under the slightly damp newspapers was a layer of clothing: much-washed vests, long johns and a box of collars. An army greatcoat lay under a thick navy comforter of the sort Laurence remembered well, knitted by mothers, aunts and wives who had always believed that a chill on the chest was the most formidable enemy of all.

There were four unframed photographs tucked between layers of clothes. The first was of John's father standing outside Colston House with his dog and a shotgun. The next was a studio portrait of a very young John, and Mary younger still, posed in a big chair. Some glue and a torn bit of dark paper remained on the reverse, so it had presumably been taken from an album. The third surprised him; he recognised himself, Lionel, Rupert and Charles in stiff collars and dark jackets, posing for the shot. The fourth was small: a little boy in a sailor suit with dark hair and eyes who he guessed was John. He was disconcerted to find John had held such attachments to the past and felt a momentary discomfort at revealing the inner life of such a private man.

'But this is what I wanted to show you.'

Mary pulled out a lined schoolbook. Again she opened it and handed it to Laurence. There were fewer words than in the earlier books, large, single ones or short phrases scrawled across the page. One read *Göttes Mühle mahle langsam, mahle aber trefflich klein*, but he had no idea what it meant.

The pictures were no longer portraits and small landscapes.

Ghoul-like faces – eyeless, formless – rose, dripping, out of some viscous glue. He turned a few more pages: bodies, German soldiers by the look of the uniform, thrown outwards by a central explosion. A rat was crouched on the corner of the next page, a subaltern's pips hanging from its claws and a human grin on its mouth. He turned over the page. A man slumped away from a post, almost on his knees but restrained by a rope with his hands behind him, a blindfold over his eyes. Dark, shiny pencilling over his shirt indicated mortal injury. The lead had pierced the page at one point. Six soldiers were standing with their guns half raised. Along the bottom on both sides of the next double-page spread men walked, single file, with bandaged eyes, one hand on the shoulder of the man in front. They'd been gassed, Laurence assumed, or were prisoners. It was hard to tell from the uniforms. The quality of drawing was still very fine, which made their impact acute.

Laurence turned the page again; he hated seeing all these nightmarish images here in front of Mary. Until now he had been unable to reconcile the boy he had known at school, as well as the man revealed by his possessions and whose sister loved him, with the kind of person who would blow his brains out in a winter wood. Now he had become privy to the preoccupations of a different sort of man.

There were a few blank pages, then one last drawing, in pencil. In it a girl lay apparently dead across some sacks, one arm thrown behind her, the other across her chest. Her head was turned to one side, her hair was tangled. What was most shocking was that her skirts were raised, showing her nakedness underneath. One stocking was torn, the other leg was bare, her foot turned outwards.

He suddenly realised that he had been silent for some time. When he glanced up, Mary had moved to the window and was half turned away from him, looking out. She still clutched the striped scarf. There were tears on her cheeks but her crying was silent. She pressed one end of the scarf to her eyes. He left the book on the bed and went over to her, putting his arm clumsily round her shoulders. She stayed immobile for a second before turning towards him. He held her for a minute, conscious of the scent of her, and of the scarf, and of her hair against his face, the slightness of her body against his chest. It was the first time he had touched another human being, apart from trying to comfort injured men, he thought, since he had last held Louise in the darkness of their bed. But then he remembered the whore in Soho just as Mary broke away, covering her embarrassment by pulling a handkerchief out of her sleeve.

'I'm sorry,' she said. 'I can't bear thinking what must have happened to him out there. After I found it I was going to burn it so that Mother never saw it, but it turned out she didn't want to look at John's things. She has his photo by the bed and that's enough for her. A tidy relationship.' She raised her eyes to his. 'She always did like everything to be nice and everybody to be happy. She can't cope with complicated things. I'm quite sure she wishes John had simply died in action like half the other officers in his regiment.'

It occurred to Laurence that Mary must feel suffocated in this claustrophobic house with two prematurely old women.

'Look,' he said, 'I'm happy to do anything I can to help but you're wrong in thinking I knew your brother well. I knew him. I liked him. I liked him a lot. But that was a long time ago.'

Mary looked at him. 'You probably knew him as well as any of us, then.'

She rummaged through the trunk, under the heavy layers of clothing, then sat back on her heels.

'No, wait a minute,' she said, hurriedly, 'I've got something in my room I want you to see. You stay here.'

Laurence sat on the chair, hearing her clatter down the second flight of stairs. It was stuffy under the roof, and moving John's things about had raised dust, which shimmered in the light. He walked to the window, lifted the latch and pushed. The window seemed stuck fast. Dead flies lay on the sill. He banged on the frame with the side of his clenched fist and then harder with his hand protected in the sleeve of his jacket. It burst free, explosively, and swung wide to allow in a rush of fresh air. Old moss and flakes of paint fell on to the floor; God knows when it had last been opened. The light beyond the slate roofs showed that evening was not far away. He looked at his watch. It was getting late. He was standing at the window when Mary returned with a manila envelope.

'Look, I'm going to have to be off soon if I'm to catch my train,' he said. Her face fell instantly. 'We can meet again,' he went on hurriedly, 'but I'm supposed to be at dinner in London tonight.' It was only with Charles but he had left it too late to change the arrangements. 'I've got half an hour.'

'John was engaged once, you know.'

Laurence found himself surprised, not because he couldn't imagine John liking women, but simply because he couldn't imagine him being that intimate with anyone.

'She was German, her name was Minna. She lived near Munich. A lawyer's daughter, I think. He met her before the war, presumably when he was travelling. Well, *obviously* before the war.' She shrugged. 'We'd never got to meet her. Her family had been going to come over in 1913 but then everything caught up with us and they never came. My father died late that year. John came home for the funeral and he never went back to

38

Germany. Then, when war seemed inevitable, Minna's father forced her to call off the engagement. A good thing probably. She was very young. It was made worse because she died not long afterwards. Appendicitis, John said.'

'There's no picture of her?'

'No. He did have one once although I never saw it after they separated. He took her death quite hard. But there may have been other people in his life that we knew nothing of. He left a will before he went to France; they all did. When he came back from the war he made another will. We didn't know anything about it and it wasn't with the family solicitors. He used a small London firm. They sent us a copy. It wasn't very different — he provided for my mother and me — but there were three individual bequests as well. One was to a Captain William Bolitho whose address was a convalescent home. One was to a Frenchman, a Monsieur Meurice of . . . somewhere that sounded like Rouen. Doulon — no, Doullens, I think — and the other was to a married woman. I've got her name downstairs. Sadly the Frenchman and all his family were untraceable. Even the village was gone. The solicitors are holding money in case he is found. There were no reasons given for any of the bequests.

'Captain Bolitho was in John's regiment. He survived although apparently he lost his legs. But nobody knew anything about the Frenchman or the woman. I wondered whether they had been . . .' She paused. 'Well, whether they had been close, I suppose, and whether he would have written to her if they were. In the end I never tried to speak to her and she never contacted us, though the solicitors could have passed on any letter to us.'

She looked at him with an expression he found hard to read. Her eyes were steady and almost on a level with his.

'Look,' he said, quickly, aware of the clumsiness of his timing, 'I'm really sorry but I do have to go very soon.' He glanced at his watch again. He was going to be lucky to catch the half past six train. 'But if you want me to try to contact Bolitho or this woman, I'll gladly make enquiries. Nothing that would embarrass you, enough to put your mind at rest.'

Although Mary was silent, she looked much happier.

'Might I take the note he had with him?' he asked. 'It might be useful.' Though he couldn't think how. She nodded and reached for it.

'Why don't you come up and see me in London?' he said. 'Next week, say? We could go to a concert, if you'd like that. Have you been to the Wigmore Hall? I could try to get tickets. We could talk more then. In the meantime I'll think whether there's anything else I can do.'

Mary visibly brightened. 'I'd love that. I went there with John just before he joined up and before it was closed down. It must have been before 1914, because it was still a German business. The Bechstein Hall, it was then. They were still playing Schubert and Brahms: dangerous German music.' She smiled again. 'John's favourites. It was the only time we'd ever gone anywhere like that together. It was only because somebody else had let him down at the last minute.'

He went downstairs ahead of her, said a rather perfunctory goodbye to Mrs Emmett and her sister and shook hands on the doorstep with Mary who was clearly trying not to cry. He wanted to say something to help her, but then she thrust a sheet of paper at him. He was puzzled for a second until he realised it was a copy of John's will.

Speaking fast, she said, 'You probably think I'm just not accepting it, John's death. But I do accept it. We'd lived with that possibility for four years. It's really his life I'm trying to understand. There's this hole where I should know things. And then there are things I *do* know — such as the people in his will whom we'd never even heard of, and my impression that he was definitely getting better — that I simply can't make sense of.'

He took her hands in his. She bit her lip, looking at him without speaking. 'I'll do everything I can,' he promised.

He caught a bus to the station and only made the train by running down the platform. Once in a seat, he rested his head against the window and his breathing calmed. The train gathered speed. He had to close his eyes against the setting sun and, drifting on the edge of sleep, he reflected on the afternoon.

He was disoriented by his encounter. It wouldn't be hard to be attracted to Mary Emmett — he had been in a way, all those years ago — yet he knew he was now responding to emotions and a vulnerability that had nothing to do with him.

He took out the will. Mrs Gwen Lovell was the first beneficiary — or was it Lowell? The legal hand was clear but the letter 'v' less so. Her address was 11 Lynmouth Road, Kentish Town, London. Bolitho's address was a convalescent home at Brighton. Those bits would be easy, he thought.

CHAPTER SIX

*L*aurence managed to get home, change and still be only a quarter of an hour late, but he was so tired he feared being poor company. He and Charles sat down to eat in an almost empty dining room.

'Everybody's on the moors,' Charles grunted. 'Lucky devils. But you look as if you've come hot saddle from Aix to Ghent.'

'Actually I went and saw John Emmett's people today.'

'Did you, by God?' For once Charles looked surprised. 'What are they like? I heard they were cooped up in some ghastly place in Cambridge.'

'Mary's a really nice girl. I hardly recognised her, though.' It wasn't true but he wanted to resist acknowledging the impact she'd made on him.

'Bad business,' said Charles, picking up his glass and half closing his eyes in appreciation of the wine. 'Have they taken it hard?'

'Well, it doesn't help that he didn't leave a letter.'

'They've really been through it,' Charles reflected. 'Pa died suddenly before the war, I heard from Jack – that's the Ayrshire cousin — and the Emmetts can hardly have come out with anything, once they'd paid off his debts. The mother was always pretty batty, he'd heard tell — must be where Emmett got it from — and more so when they had to sell the house. And before then, John gets engaged to some Fräulein and it takes a war to get him out of it. And the sister, Mary, my aunt said had been involved in some scandal with a married man. Takes a war to get her out of that too. Blown to smithereens at Vimy Ridge.' He added as an afterthought, 'Jack said he had been at school at Ampleforth with the fellow. RC. Can't remember the name. Nice chap, though notoriously flighty wife.'

Laurence was shocked by the lurch of his heart. He was unable to distinguish whether his annoyance was with Charles, Mary or himself. To his astonishment and discomfiture he felt jealous. Mary wasn't what he'd taken her for. Immediately he knew he was being ridiculous. Not only did he hardly know her but she had not volunteered anything about herself to him and why should he have expected her to? He was being a fool. She must be in her mid- to late-twenties by now. Why shouldn't she have had another life, a life away from her family? Why shouldn't she have been happy for a while?

'John's father can't have been too profligate as John was able to make generous bequests in his own will. One to a chap called Bolitho.' Laurence knew he sounded gruff. 'Served with him, apparently. Do you know him?'

Charles's social antennae meant that, even unasked, he could provide chapter and verse on just about any officer or outfit he had come across.

'Bolitho? Bill Bolitho, I expect that'll be; he was with John's lot,' he answered, almost like a music-hall memory man. 'Good man. Legs shot off in 1917. Well, not shot off but gangrene or something. One, anyway. Not sure about the other.' He paused, thinking. 'So Emmett left him some money? Not entirely surprising that he felt grateful, I suppose.' His expression belied his words. 'More surprising to find Emmett had any to leave. Jack's usually spot on about stuff. Emmett and Bolitho served together in France. Emmett was inspecting a redoubt when it collapsed. Nothing to do with Jerry, just one of those things. Two other chaps with him died but Emmett wasn't far in and I heard that old Bolitho dug like fury and got him out. Banged him about, got him breathing. Heroic measures. Emmett must have remembered when Bolitho was invalided out.'

'And a Frenchman who's disappeared and a woman called Lovell, or Lowell? Does she mean anything to you? She lives in London now, Kentish Town way.'

Charles thought for a moment. 'No,' he said. 'No. Can't say it does. No, don't personally know any Lowells, Lovells or whoever. Or anybody at all in Kentish Town.' He looked amazed at his own fallibility. 'The Cat, the Rat, and Lovell the Dog, rule all England under the Hog.'

Laurence stared at his friend, speechless.

'Richard III's nasty chums,' said Charles, happily. 'Only bit of history I remember from school. So, this Miss Lovell, an heiress too now, is she? Some floozy of Emmett's? Well, at least she sounds English this time. Always a dark horse, that man.'

'*Mrs* Lovell, I think.'

Charles raised his eyebrows. 'Just so,' he said.

After the strangely disquieting day in Cambridge and the dinner with Charles, Laurence half expected Louise to come; she so often did when he had drunk a bit. Trying to avoid her, he delayed getting undressed. Eventually he fell into bed around two, thinking briefly about the sun and the river. He must have fallen asleep as the next thing he knew it was morning; he had been woken by a bee buzzing angrily between curtain and windowpane. He flicked it out into the day and lay back. Despite his aching shoulders and back, he felt content, relaxing in the early light, recalling his meeting with Mary, and he pushed away thoughts of her now-dead lover.

He considered the feasibility of actually contacting people who had known John. What questions could he reasonably ask on her behalf? Nothing too wild; there was a limit to how far anybody wanted to look back these days. He simply hoped to give Mary some sense of her brother's war and of what others made of him. He thought of his own sister, as he almost never did, and reflected how very little she would know about him if he should die suddenly. He pulled out his bedside drawer and found the picture he had of them, side by side, just before she left to go on honeymoon and out of his life. He was already taller than her. All these photographs looked so real, yet were as much illusions and ghosts as oil paintings in a gallery. He had left all those he had of Louise in their London house. He thought back to the family portrait of the Emmett children. Who was the baby, he wondered? Had they once had a younger sibling? He felt sorry for Mary, now the lone survivor.

He felt happy in a way he hadn't for years at the thought of simply walking over to the concert hall to check the pro-gramme. To satisfy his conscience, he wrote solidly all day. The pages at the end of it suddenly looked remarkably like a proper chapter.

He decided to start following up John Emmett's trail the next morning, although when he woke heavy skies threatened rain, putting him in two minds whether to postpone his day's plans or not. There was, after all, no hurry: John Emmett had been dead for nine months or so.

The postman delivered a letter from Charles. He took out the single, crisp page with a smile. Having inherited and swiftly sold the substantial business built up by four generations of Carfaxes, Charles had time to involve himself in other men's lives. Sometimes Laurence wondered whether, in the absence of war, Charles was bored.

Albany

10 September 1921

Dear Bartram,

Before you turn detective, because any fool can see that's what you've got in mind, and probably a lady behind your transformation into Mr. Holmes, I thought I might help you by tracking down Bolitho. Turns out he's not in a convalescent home and not far away. Lives in a mansion flat in Kensington with his wife. Not doing too badly, I'm told, and quite happy to have visitors. Anyway, he's at 2 Moscow Mansions, South Kensington. I had an aunt who lived in the same block before the war, full of faded gentlefolk. I think the Bolithos must be on the ground floor. You're on your own with the mysterious Mrs Lovell, though.

Charles

The following week, Laurence met Mary off the train at Liverpool Street. He stood right under the clock, excitement turning to nervousness and then to embarrassment as he realised two other men and a single anxious-faced woman were sharing his chosen rendezvous. It was a cliché. He was a cliché. He moved further away. There were a surprising number of people on the platform: a gaggle of girls in plaits with identical navy coats and felt hats pulled down hard on their heads, while they, their trunks and their lacrosse sticks were overseen by two stern-looking ladies; it was obviously the beginning of term.

All these journeys momentarily intersecting here, he thought. All the farewells. A stout older man huffed by, preceded by a porter with a large case. From childhood, Laurence had always been drawn to inventing lives for unknown people. This man was a Harley Street physician, he decided, whom the war had saved from retirement. Now he was off to a difficult but profitable case in the shires. Laurence looked up at the clock; the Cambridge train was already ten minutes late.

Perhaps he and Mary would forever be meeting like this. He still felt uneasy in stations. Memories of three journeys to or from France still haunted him. The first time, nervous but confident, he was ridiculously over-equipped: a Swaine Adeney Brigg catalogue model, his uniform stiff, his badges bright and untested, chatting eagerly to new faces, wanting to make a good impression on the two subalterns travelling out with him. They were all so junior that they had no choice but to sit on wooden benches in the crowded compartments, back-to-back with ordinary soldiers. It was winter and the fug of cheap cigarettes, the range of accents and the stink of stale uniform was overwhelming. He observed the contrast between excitement in some men and grim disengagement in others.

The second time – when a period of leave in May, spent with Louise and some friends in Oxfordshire, had cruelly reminded him of all he had to leave behind and that the gap between normality and hell was only a day's travel – had been hideous. He had sat on the train taking him back to the front almost unable to speak. That time he had recognised the silences he had met on his first embarkation.

Much later, he had returned to England on a hospital train. Although he had travelled in reasonable comfort on this

47

journey, when he got off it was to a sea of stretchers bearing casualties, some in blood-stained bandages, others apparently blind or minus limbs. The sight of them was more shocking, lying on a familiar London platform, than amid the chaos of injury and mutilation he'd encountered in the trenches. He remembered an orderly and a nurse leaning over one man. She pulled his grey blanket over his head as she signalled to two soldiers to carry him away. Contemplating the horror of the man's long journey, the pain and disruption of coming home, just to die next to the buffers, Laurence had turned his head away.

He jerked back to the present. The landscape of khaki and grey faded away. The Cambridge train was pulling in with a last exhalation of steam. He watched various individuals pass but he could not see Mary.

She had almost reached his end of the platform before he recognised her. With her hair covered by a deep-crimson hat and wearing a coat, she looked different: more sophisticated and more in control. Everything about her declared her a modern woman, he thought as she drew closer, yet her eyes were less confident as she searched the crowd and she clutched her bag tightly to her. He was grinning like an idiot; he could feel his cheek muscles aching. He waved, although it was quite redundant; she was near enough to have seen him already and then she was in front of him. Quite on the spur of the moment he kissed her on the cheek. She smelled of Lily of the Valley.

'Laurence,' she said, with her amused, crooked smile, 'it's so good to be here.' She looked round almost excitedly and took a deep breath of anticipation.

'We need to get a cab,' he said, gently ushering her through the crowds, his hand in the small of her back. 'We've got plenty of time so we could have tea before the concert. If you'd like that, that is? Talk a bit and so on?'

'Talk a bit,' she said teasingly but then laughed. 'Oh Laurence, I love just being here. Getting away.' Her voice became more serious. 'We'll have a bit of time afterwards though, I hope?' He was very conscious of her body even through the small area under his palm and through a wool coat. She broke away only as a cab drew up.

Within a quarter of an hour they were sitting over tea in Durrants Hotel.

'I struck lucky with Captain Bolitho,' he told her happily. 'Nice wife too. It all seems quite straightforward.'

His confidence that evening, the uncomplicated nature of the story he had to tell, was something Laurence would remember long afterwards.

CHAPTER SEVEN

*L*aurence had been surprised to get a letter by return of post from William Bolitho, suggesting he come to lunch the following day. He had taken a bus and then, following Charles's very precise directions, walked through the streets to Moscow Mansions.

Mrs Bolitho had opened the door. She was slim and of middling height with curly auburn hair and an intelligent face. Bolitho sat by a window in the sitting room with a blanket over his lap. The shutters were folded back and light poured into a slightly shabby but pleasing room. Some draughtsman's drawings, mostly of big but unfamiliar houses, hung on the largest wall, and on the wooden floor lay a rose and indigo Persian rug faded by the sun. One wall was lined with books; the other was dominated by an abstract picture of strong ochre and black squares and curves, with odd glued and painted newspaper scraps. Laurence had no idea what it meant, but he liked it.

Laurence turned as Bolitho reached out to shake him by the hand. It was a strong grip that matched the strength of character in the man's face. Bolitho had caught the direction of Laurence's gaze.

'It's Braque,' he said. 'Well, not *a* Braque, obviously, but a copy.' Then he went on, 'It's very good to meet you.'

Laurence sat down in a deep chair opposite William. They talked for a while about nothing particularly significant, although Laurence was trying to gauge the man and suspected William was doing much the same with him, until Eleanor suggested they move through for luncheon. He tried not to look shocked when she removed a blanket, revealing one of William's legs apparently ending at the knee, the trouser neatly pinned up, and no sign of the other limb at all. She helped William into a wheelchair, bracing it with her foot, while he swung himself over.

'Can I help?' Laurence asked, although it was obviously a practised routine.

'No, no it's fine,' said William. 'Most chaps in my situation sit in the wheelchair most of the day but I get damn bored. I prefer to move about.'

Eleanor pushed the chair through double doors to the small dining room where a table was laid near the window.

Any fear he'd had that the meeting would be gloomy and difficult was dispersed over a simple meal of cold meats, boiled potatoes, sweet pickled beetroot and a blackcurrant fool. The Bolithos were excellent hosts and the affection between them was tangible. William had been an architect before the war, he told Laurence, and still hoped that he might find a job that would allow him to work again. Laurence glanced at his wife whose face was one of determined good cheer as her husband spoke.

'I was trained in Glasgow and studied in Vienna. There's so much I'd like to be part of — so much happening in architecture that's exciting, innovative . . .'. His face lit up with enthusiasm. 'It's difficult, of course, but with all the new building in London I'm keeping my ears open. I write letters, I keep up with my reading and so on.' He indicated a pile of journals on a table. 'Eleanor says it can be only a matter of time.'

'Sadly,' she said, 'they're as short of young architects now as they are of so many other professional men.'

Apparently ignoring her earnestness, William looked over his shoulder, his waving fork indicating the room and the painting behind them.

'Alternatively, I do feel I might have a good future in forging Braques,' he said. 'Cubism seems to invite it, really.'

An hour or more went by without Laurence really noticing time pass but it was long enough for him to realise, as he had with Mary, that he was quite useless in controlling the direction of a conversation. He let it find its own level. Eleanor held forth on the prospect of the Independent Labour Party ever winning an election. Her enthusiasm and intelligence were infectious and William, who must have heard it all before, looked on with evident pleasure. Laurence found himself telling them about his teaching and his reservations about the book he was writing.

'But obviously you want to talk about John Emmett's will?' William said eventually, with no embarrassment. 'Well, one of the things we were able to do with his bequest was to buy a gramophone.' He looked towards the corner. 'Tidy, isn't it?' As Laurence followed his glance, William added, 'I expect you're wondering where the horn is. You see, it's got a pleated diaphragm instead, it's the latest thing. I first saw it out in France, as we had one in the mess at HQ. A friend has just sent me Beethoven's complete works. They've just been recorded.' He picked up a couple of crimson-centred records and carefully slipped them out of their brown-paper covers. 'Beautiful. And Bach as well. There's much more interest in him these days. About time too.' He looked completely happy, Laurence thought. 'Frankly, Emmett's bequest changed our lives. The sum he left us surprised us both.'

'It was being able to move here, you see,' said Eleanor. Just fleetingly she sounded defensive. 'It wasn't all about luxuries, however welcome.' She smiled at her husband and then turned to Laurence. 'We really wanted more room; with the wheelchair you need more space to manoeuvre — you can imagine. We were in Bayswater, but it was small and William was a prisoner if he was on his own, and then there was Nicholas.' Laurence must have looked puzzled because she went on, 'Our son. He's nearly three now.'

Laurence tried not to let his surprise show on his face. Eleanor laughed.

'The flat seems a lot smaller with him around; he's never still for a minute. Today he's at my sister-in-law's near by with his little cousins.'

She got up to carry the plates through to the kitchen and called back, 'Moving here, living near her, has made a huge difference to us all. She's a widow — my brother Max was killed at Cambrai. Now we can all start again.'

Laurence looked at William and saw a handsome man with thick, light-brown hair, which was just beginning to turn grey around his ears; the first lines of middle age only gave his face more expression. Any pity Laurence had felt for him on arrival had long subsided.

After they'd finished lunch, and Eleanor had left to fetch their son, the two men settled back in the drawing room. William took out his pipe and held it in his hand without lighting it.

'You were a close friend of John Emmett's, then?'

'Well, the thing is, I *wasn't* a particular friend of his,' Laurence began. 'I was while we were at school, I suppose, but I'd hardly heard from him since; in fact I didn't even know he'd died until his sister – Mary – contacted me. It's just that his family were very kind to me when I was young and so I thought I might help them a bit by trying to find out more about his state of mind.'

'No letter, I gather? Or so the solicitor told us.'

Laurence shook his head.

'Hard. I'm unlikely to add to what you probably know already but I can tell you it was damned odd hearing about the bequest and, of course, hearing it with the news of his suicide.'

'But you saved his life, didn't you?' said Laurence. He wondered how William felt now that the life he saved had been thrown away.

'Not really. In fact, not at all. I just happened to be there. Anyone would have done the same. They did, in fact.'

Laurence recognised English diffidence. No doubt he would have explained it like that too.

'It was in the run-up to the Somme. He was in a covered trench just outside Albert. It was an old one that had been blown in a while back and was being redug. They knew their stuff, those sappers. Though the chap in charge of the sector had come across from HQ at the time because there was some question of whether the earthworks were viable at all. Rightly, as it turned out.

'Emmett had gone down there with a corporal and two other men who were stringing up some cables. It was probably rotten wood that did it. We'd run out of decent material for revetment by then and we were reusing timbers that had been waterlogged. It had been hot and dry for weeks and I suspect the wood had simply dried out too quickly, even underground. You know what it was like.'

Laurence nodded.

'Anyway,' William went on, 'I was just standing there in the sunshine, glad it was all quiet. I can remember it exactly because one of the men had just brought me a flint arrowhead. The whole river valley was full of Iron Age remains. Every time we dug, these things were turning up — stone axes some-times. Everyone knew I collected them so if they found any odd-looking bits they brought them over. I've still got some.' He waved at a cabinet against the far wall. 'This one was tiny but a beauty; you could see where it had been chipped around the edge as if it had been done yesterday. Perfect. When, bang, there's this God-awful crack and a few seconds of dull rum-bling under the feet, and the tunnel's gone. A great puff of dirt comes back out of it, smelling of damp and worse things, to be honest. That damn awful smell.

'My immediate response was that we were under fire and we all ducked down instinctively, but within seconds we realised the tunnel had gone. I started trying to tear at the debris and the earth with my hands, but it was hopeless, the entrance was almost completely blocked. The sergeant called for proper tools and someone went for an orderly. I went in with the ser-geant — Tucker, as I recall — and we took turns clearing it. Another lad helped. I think he was the servant of the visiting sapper officer.'

The name Tucker registered almost immediately with Laurence. Although a common enough name, it was also on the list John Emmett had with him when he died.

'It was Tucker who ran the risks, no question; we still weren't entirely sure whether they'd found a shell. Tucker had had his run-ins with Emmett but on that day he was digging like a man possessed to get him out. He reached one of the soldiers in a few minutes or at least got hold of his feet. We pulled him clear but he was in a bad way. Tucker cleared his nose and mouth but apparently he was gone within seconds – the man was his friend, someone said – and then the orderly arrived and had him taken off.

'One of the soldiers dug with anything he could find and while Tucker was still dealing with his friend, I changed places, without much hope really, and I found John there about twenty feet in. Cleared the filth away to help him breathe. The tunnel hadn't fallen in all along its length. The nearest section had come right down and did for the man we'd got to first. Further in the timbers had held on one side and collapsed on the other, so they were at an angle across the trench. John lay under this; the top half of his body was towards us. He was conscious and had air, but his right arm was caught under him, his back and legs were buried by the earth and he couldn't turn his head. Even the timber above him was bowing and there was a steady trickle of soil. I don't mind telling you I was on a hair-trigger to run out of there. I always hated those tunnels, especially re-digs. But slowly I calmed down and realised I couldn't smell explosive or burning.'

William turned in his chair, opened a carved box on the side table, took out a silver lighter and a tobacco pouch and proceeded to fill and light his pipe. He drew the smoke in, slowly and deeply.

'I started excavating round him, hoping to hell the whole thing wouldn't fall in.'

'And you got him out?'

'Well, he was a lucky man in the event; scarcely a scratch on him, but he wasn't doing too well down there. Covered in sweat, ashen in the light of my torch and gasping. Eventually Tucker had to finish the job. I was too big, you see. Tall man, back then . . . couldn't squeeze through properly. Every time I moved, I scraped against the sides and brought more stuff down, but Tucker was wiry, almost skinny, he could wriggle about down there. Until we had John out, I thought he must be bleeding somewhere, even wondered if he'd die before we'd got him clear. Ghastly look on his face. But nothing; well, a broken finger and ankle, but nothing major that you could see. It turned out he'd also injured a kidney, which eventually saw him sent back to Blighty, but what he was suffering from right then was fear, I suppose. Simple, unalloyed fear. We weren't supposed to be frightened, not so that it showed. Now when you look back, you can see that fear was the rational response to much of it, but there was another set of rules then, wasn't there?'

Laurence nodded silently. He had never been able to say outright, 'I was frightened.' The band of iron round his chest might have been so tight that pain shot down his arms and his fingers tingled as he laboured to draw in a breath, but he'd always hidden it, or at least he hoped he had.

Bolitho went on matter-of-factly, 'The men could scream for hours out in no-man's land, especially the young ones. Disturb your rest for a bit, rather like a neighbour's barking dog, but eventually you'd learn to sleep through. Officers, though, were supposed to be above all that. You might have been a Sunday school teacher or a corn merchant back home, but get a commission and all your emotions had to be left at the door.' He inhaled on his pipe.

'And there was Tucker,' Bolitho continued after a while, 'who was close to losing his stripes for this and that, working like a dervish to get John out. Absolutely fearless; on his stomach practically keeping the ceiling up with his own body and the whole thing creaking in a way that made you remember how many hundredweight of earth was above it, lying with his body pressed against John, so close that he could have kissed him just by dropping his head a few inches. Yet when we finally pulled John clear, only minutes before the whole damn thing fell in with one last, long rumble, and Smith left in what was now his tomb – pray God he was dead already, not a squeak from him – I saw Tucker was looking at John with a sort of amused contempt and something nastier: triumph, I'd say. And he didn't seem that bothered by the corporal – Perkins was his name, I think – getting it, either, given the man was what passed for a friend.'

'And no bequest from John for him?'

Bolitho tapped at his pipe. 'Unlikely. There was definitely business between John and Tucker. Something going on.'

'Business?'

'Haven't a clue what it was,' William said breezily. 'Just an impression. Antagonism of some sort. Tucker had his finger in various pies. Buying and selling, doing favours, even dead men's effects, some said. He nearly went down over some rabbit-skin fiddle.'

'Rabbit skin?' Laurence wondered whether there was a whole lexicon of army jargon that had passed him by.

'You remember rabbit stew? Sometimes more stew than rabbit, sometimes the men claimed it was rat? Procurement people made a fortune on selling rabbit skins. Hundreds of thousand of pounds from clothes manufacturers to warm the slender necks of shop girls and kindergarten teachers, with fur collars straight from the mess kitchens. Only Tucker had seen the opportunity first and he'd been selling them locally. Argued he thought it was all just rubbish. Got away with it, but only just. His mate, Perkins, who'd enlisted with him and who was definitely part of the scheme, called him Bunny from then on, but nobody else would have dared.'

'How on earth had he got to sergeant?' Laurence asked.

'Well, they were very short of NCOs at the start and he'd been a factory foreman, somewhere in the Black Country, so actually he was quite good with the men – the ones he hadn't taken against – and he was fearless, albeit vicious, or he would have been in trouble before. But there were always rumours. The men said he was a devil with the ladies and we'd nearly had him up on a charge for selling coloured water as a cure for the clap. The lads didn't like getting the lecture from the MO, and Tucker's stuff worked a treat because most of them never had the clap in the first place. First-timers, boys, with nothing worse than a guilty conscience. But we were a long way forward at that time, so there weren't a whole lot of mesdemoiselless in petticoats waiting for Tucker's blandishments. I seldom dealt with him directly but the man was a clever opportunist and, I can quite believe, a brute at heart. And he'd disappear from time to time. I suppose we thought he might have been out poaching.'

Again Laurence must have looked puzzled because William's expression changed to one of weary distaste.

'You must have come across them. Loners? Men made for killing? Couldn't have enough of it, so went out to find the odd extra German for sport or mementoes?' He ran a finger across his throat.

Laurence nodded. Angels in the sky; bullets deflected by prayer books or cigarette cases; football armistices; berserkers. Battlefields acquired their own myths; he'd rarely found much truth in them.

William went on, 'Still, John had him down for something else. He wouldn't say, or not to me – I was new to the unit then – but he clearly loathed the man. I went to see Emmett once he was strapped up and waiting to go. He was still very pale but quite composed, and he asked me about Perkins, and where Tucker had been when the tunnel collapsed. He was more suspicious than grateful. I told him I hadn't seen Tucker at all until everyone came running and that he owed his life to him. But I got the feeling that John thought Tucker might have had something to do with the accident itself. Perhaps that's a bit strong. He didn't say anything specific and he'd had a bad shock.'

'He didn't like small spaces,' Laurence said. 'He had claustrophobia, I suppose. Even at school.'

'God.' William puffed at the pipe. 'Must have been hell, then. He was two hours down there, at least. Must have seemed like a lifetime. Anyway, a few weeks later everything goes up. John's in hospital, locally until the casualties start pouring in, then shipped home. Never gets a chance to call it with Tucker. Not then.'

'And when he died he left you the money?' Laurence said. 'Do you mind me asking?'

'Of course not. It was as much a surprise to us as I fear it must have been to his family. In fact, when John's solicitors wrote, we asked them what the family's circumstances were. Didn't want to leave them in dire straits. Can't say but that the money was helpful – you can see how it is – but no reason for them to do without. Chap said that he didn't know the family personally but that John had left his people the house they were already living in, which he owned, and most of the rest of his estate. The solicitor seemed to think their needs were covered quite well. Eleanor wrote to the family, too – partly with condolences, partly to try to find out what John had meant by it. No answer.'

Laurence stayed silent, trying to remember if Mary had mentioned a letter.

'They're not in trouble are they — the Emmetts?' William looked concerned.

'No. There's no question of that. His mother and sister would be grateful you saved him, even though the end came as it did. They just — well, his sister mostly, to be honest — wanted to understand.'

William nodded. 'It's a funny thing,' he said slowly. 'I was angry when I heard John had shot himself. There were so many men who didn't come back, and then John makes it, and makes it in one piece, and then . . . puts his family through all that. But Eleanor understands it. She saw plenty of men with their nerves gone. She was a nurse; that's how I met her. Shell-shock, that's what they call it now, and it didn't seem to matter how strong a man was before the war; it could hit anyone, any time.' The faintest of smiles flickered. 'Well, not Sergeant Tucker, obviously. War had its own rewards for his sort.'

Laurence thought of Charles, another man whom war suited very nicely. Charles was an ideal officer: not over-imaginative, unflappable and robust. But what happened to those men who had found some pleasure in the fighting and the routines, once it was all over?

'As to what pushed him over the edge,' William went on, 'who can tell? I've no idea. He came back from convalescence in England once he was patched up but I never saw him again. I'd been injured by then. We were wiped out, or damn nearly, at Lateau Wood. One leg virtually blown off.' He pointed to the limb, which ended at the knee. 'Other leg went septic. I hovered between life and death — I don't remember a thing — and was nursed by Eleanor, who viewed their having to take off the other leg as a personal insult and wasn't prepared to put up with me dying after all her labours. I don't know exactly what John did when he got back. Seconded to another outfit's my guess.'

'And Tucker?' Laurence asked, not quite knowing why.

'No idea. I expect he survived. His sort tended to. Probably came home with his clap tonic and the Military Medal in his bag.'

William was starting to look tired. Laurence fired off one last question. 'I don't know if you were told but there were another two bequests besides yours. A Mrs Lovell. That doesn't mean anything to you, does it?'

Bolitho shook his head. 'The solicitor implied there were other beneficiaries, mostly to put my mind at rest about taking the money, but he was far too circumspect to volunteer names and I didn't ask.'

'Not Tucker, anyway,' said Laurence, feeling guilty that he'd been so much less discreet than the legal advisors. 'So there were limits to John's gratitude. And there wasn't any Lovell involved in the rescue?'

'No, I'm pretty sure not. Perkins died. I think it was Smith who was probably buried alive. There was Tucker, and the major's batman and a couple of other Welsh lads whose names escape me, if I ever knew them. But I don't think I remember a Lovell at all. Not there, anyway. Certainly never came across a Mrs Lovell. What are you thinking: somebody's wife? Mother?'

'I haven't a clue. It's the wildest of wild cards. I hope to speak to her, if she still lives at the address I have.'

'And could she even have been somebody's sister? A Miss Tucker or Perkins or whatever at one time, I suppose?' William said. 'Or maybe she was a young widow with hopes of being a Mrs Emmett?'

'Possibly. And a Frenchman – called Meurice? No bells ringing?'

William shook his head.

✻

It took Laurence nearly an hour to tell Mary about the afternoon and his impressions. She had not interrupted once although at one point she picked up a biscuit, broke off a piece, dipped it in her tea and carried it to her mouth, all without dropping her eyes from his face. He liked her for it.

'Bolitho was a good man. Perhaps you'll meet him one day. His wife too. If it helps, John's money must have made a big difference to a decent couple. There's a child too: a little boy.'

Mary looked thoughtful. Finally she spoke. 'Thank you. It means a lot, even these little bits: John's war in mosaic. He never told us how he got injured. We didn't think much of it; we saw it more as a good way of keeping him from the fighting for a while. We didn't know Captain Bolitho had saved his life, only that he'd been in the same regiment. John simply wrote and told us that he'd been in an accident. He didn't mention the sergeant at all, but being trapped would have been hellish for him: John hated being in small spaces or, really, being constrained in any way. Even rules irked him.'

Laurence nodded. It had been obvious at Marlborough. He wondered again why on earth John had rushed to volunteer, to become part of such a regulation-bound environment. 'But didn't Eleanor Bolitho tell you some of this in her letter?'

She frowned. 'They never bothered to write. None of the beneficiaries wrote,' she said, with a trace of bitterness.

'How odd,' Laurence said.

It didn't sit with what he'd seen of the Bolithos and contradicted what William had told him.

'Look, we need to push on to catch the concert, but I did wonder whether I should go and see Mrs Lovell soon. Unlike Bolitho, we really haven't a clue how John knew her but she must know why she was a beneficiary. Although Bolitho was certainly surprised, he wasn't completely at a loss as to why the bequest came to him. One thing I did mean to ask you was where John was when he got in the fight you mentioned? Presumably he was wherever it was for a reason?'

She shrugged.

'Never mind. It's probably nothing but then there's Coburg,' he went on. 'It was written on that list John had.' He could see he had lost her. 'It's just that Coburg's in Germany, in Bavaria. And you said John had been engaged to a girl there, in Munich I think you said, which is also in Bavaria.'

Mary didn't respond.

'I know it's all a bit far-fetched. I just wondered whether he'd had any correspondence with someone there.'

Mary still didn't answer. She looked down at her lap, turning the clasp on her handbag and finally raising a solemn face to him. 'He didn't tell me much. Ever.' She seemed keen to change the subject. 'Look, I ought to give you some money. I do have some. From John. It's not fair that you do all this charging about at your own expense.'

She gazed at him intently. He couldn't help smiling. She was so beautiful and so alive. A long lock of hair had fallen forward and curled towards her lips. She blew it away, then tucked it back behind her ear.

He almost let slip that he was enjoying all the 'charging about', but it seemed tactless. 'It's good to be busy, funnily enough,' he said. 'I haven't really done anything, not since the war.' He paused. 'Not since Louise — died. Not really. I've only been writing because I had to do something.'

Suddenly, her hand was on his, and stayed there, calm and warm. She said nothing.

They had to hurry to the concert hall. The concert began with Elgar's *Salut d'Amour*, and then there was some Debussy, which he liked less, though he thought how Louise would have enjoyed it. Next was a Brahms quintet, which drew enthusiastic applause. Mary was rapt. He was aware, all the way through, of her closeness. From time to time her knee touched his. A couple of times he stole a glance at her in profile. The second time she caught him and returned a small smile.

As they left the auditorium he left her for a moment while he went to fetch her coat. She was standing behind him as he queued. Reflected in the wall of mirrors above the attendant he saw that a man had stopped to greet her and had even taken her hand in his. Their bodies were very close as they talked, Mary's head bent towards his to catch his words. Then she looked towards Laurence's back and obviously said goodbye. The man was quickly gone. The attendant handed Laurence their belongings and he returned to Mary, expecting her to explain, but as he helped her into her coat she simply said, 'Wasn't that fun!' Her face, however, was serious and pale.

All the way to the station he wanted to ask her who the man was but could think of no way to raise it that didn't seem clumsy. He told himself that if the meeting had been insignificant, surely she would have explained. As the wish to know loomed larger, the opportunity to do so receded. He could think of nothing else to say. Mary kept looking at her watch in the dark of the cab. From time to time she gave him a nervous and, he thought, slightly distant smile. She was no longer eager to talk but anyway they made it with just minutes to spare. As she stepped up into the carriage, she placed a hand on his shoulder and kissed him on the cheek. He waited until her train had gone, waving with a jolliness that he didn't feel.

He decided to clear his head by walking back. The city was quiet. The monumental architecture of the great financial institutions rose up either side of him, dark and oppressive. He supposed they had fought to protect these as much as they had the idea of village greens or royal palaces, had fought to keep things as they were. The dome of St Paul's came into view against the night sky, its silhouette softened by a veil of cloud. The night was cool and slightly damp; autumn was well on its way now with leaves beginning to fall from the plane trees. He felt indescribably sad.

That night was the first bad one for a while. The banshee scream of shells. The distant crump of other men's catastrophes. The stink of burning and sweat, and all the time his heart pounding. He placed his hand on his chest to steady himself but his heart pulsed loudly through the dream. He put the whistle in his mouth. He was supposed to blow but couldn't get enough breath. Then somehow he was alone in the remains of a traverse, digging as fast and as desperately as he could. It was raining and Louise was there, under the earth. The wet soil made his hands ache with cold. His fingers found first her face and then her nose, entered her open mouth, felt the edges of her teeth. As fast as he dug, earth fell on her from above. Rain pooled in the crater he had dug to let her breathe and slowly, though he held her muddy hair, it filled up and she slipped away from him.

CHAPTER EIGHT

*F*inding a man in France was obviously far beyond his resources, so Laurence mentally set Monsieur Meurice on one side. Kentish Town was another matter entirely. He had decided not to write to Mrs Lovell but simply to go to her house on the chance he would find her in.

At four o'clock he arrived at the address given in John's will. It was a small, slightly shabby, dark-brick house, one of thousands like it in London. He noticed grass sprouting in the gutter and that a single spindly rose needed deadheading. Rain was pattering on a faded canvas screen hanging over the door and when he knocked, several tiny spiders were dislodged. No one came. He looked up at the grimy windows and thought how Mrs Lovell must have welcomed John's bequest. He knocked again and called out self-consciously. 'Mrs Lovell.' He waited for a while and then turned away. A woman in a print pinafore was watching him from over a bowing fence.

'They're long gone,' she said. 'Those Lovells. Four – five years? She kept it nice but there's been another lot since and they've gone too. Bad drains.'

'Do you have an address?'

'No, but my daughter might. Used to help with the children. She liked her.'

She turned and went into her own house, leaving the door open. He heard no voices but a few minutes later a skinny younger woman came out with a baby in her arms. She handed him a grubby bit of paper with an address written in capital letters.

'That's where they were, last I heard.'

It was a fifteen-minute walk, through increasingly heavy rain, to a modest street, but one much less drab than the first address. The semi-detached house sat back behind a low hedge where large cobwebs held drops like jewels. The smell of privet after rain was one he always associated with London.

A tiled path led up to a dull black front door. He walked up and pulled the bell, hearing it jangle in the rear of the house, and almost immediately he heard swift footsteps inside. The door swung open and a young woman stood there, her fair hair loose on her shoulders. She had a sleeping cat draped over one arm and looked surprised, as if she had expected someone else.

'Can I help you?' She was much younger than he'd imagined, just a girl really, but her face was quite composed.

'Mrs Lovell?' Laurence began.

'*Miss* Lovell,' she replied. 'Catherine Maude Lovell.'

Laurence was suddenly and embarrassingly aware of how impulsive his decision to visit had been. In his haste to help Mary he hadn't thought of the effect of his enquiries on those at the receiving end. How the hell could he explain himself to the slender girl in front of him?

'I'm looking for someone called Lovell who knew one of my friends.'

'Who?' she said.

'A man called Emmett. Captain John Emmett.'

There was no sign of recognition on her face.

'He died a few months ago.' He was beginning to feel it was hopeless. Rain was starting to fall again.

'My brother was killed in the war,' the girl said, matter-of-factly. 'But I don't know a John Emmett. Perhaps it's my mother you want? She's out but she should be back soon. I thought you were her, forgetting her key again. You could wait if you want?'

How could he have been so stupid? Of course this girl was too young to have known John. She was what — fifteen? Younger? But he had at least established that the family had a son who had fought. That was the likely connection to John.

He followed her indoors with some relief; water was now trickling down the back of his neck. A daily woman, by the look of her, emerged from the back of the house. She took his hat and coat, shaking them out as she did so. Catherine Lovell showed him into a small sitting room. It was neat, respectable, perhaps a little old-fashioned, and decidedly cold, but there were some good books in a glass-fronted case. He looked sideways and read those with larger lettering on their spines: Trollope, Dickens' *The Old Curiosity Shop*, Sir Walter Scott, Tennyson, Wordsworth; it was more or less the sort of collection he had at home. There were even some bound operetta scores. The girl sat opposite him talking to the cat.

Eventually he heard the door open, and the gasps and protestations of someone retreating from a downpour.

'Martha. Martha, oh thank you — no, I'm not soaked. I had my umbrella. Just take my hat and coat and put them in the scullery, not too near the stove, mind.'

A handsome woman, in her early forties perhaps, came

through the door. She was dressed entirely in dark blue and, like the room, her dress was sedate and unremarkable. But she had an alert face, pale, fine skin and hair almost as fair as her daughter's, though fading with middle age.

Catherine jumped up and spoke before either she or Laurence had a chance to do so. 'He's looking for a man called Captain Emmett.'

'Catherine —' Mrs Lovell looked anxious for a second but then her expression lightened. 'Not now, my love, I don't even know who our visitor is. Mr — ?' She had a slight provincial accent.

'Bartram,' he said, 'Laurence Bartram. I'm very sorry to intrude, Mrs Lovell, but your daughter suggested I came in and the rain . . .'

Although Mrs Lovell had every right to be put out by his uninvited presence, she shook his hand and smiled. 'Quite right too, Mr Bartram,' she said. 'Catherine,' she nodded in the direction of the door. 'Can you go and ask Martha to make tea? Stay and help her, I think.'

The girl made a face. She was younger than he had guessed. She left the room and the door banged slightly behind her.

'Look, I'm awfully sorry to barge in like this,' Laurence said. 'It's obviously not convenient.'

'Not at all, Mr Bartram.' She sat down. 'It's perfectly convenient but I'm not sure how I can help you.'

'This is going to sound frightfully rude, I'm afraid,' he began, 'but I represent the family of John Emmett. We, that is, they — his sister — gathered that John had left you a small amount of money . . .'

A flush swept up her neck and face, and he regretted leaping in.

'But I never wanted the money. So much money. I never

expected it. I never even knew about it until a letter came from a solicitor at the beginning of the summer.'

'No one has any problem at all with the bequest. Not at all.' Laurence spoke in what he hoped was a soothing voice. 'They were glad it had come to you,' he improvised.

Heaven knew what they actually felt. He was embarrassed to see that she thought he was in some way attacking the propriety of it.

'It's just that John Emmett killed himself. His family has very little idea why he did so. His mother's a widow. He has a sister. Forgive me; they just thought that you might have been a friend or the wife of a friend of his.' He didn't want to say outright that he'd just been told she too had lost a son. 'They never wanted to bother you.'

'Still, I understand it no more than you, Mr Bartram,' she said. 'Until a year or so ago I had never heard of Captain Emmett. And then I received a letter from him. Just a few months later I hear that he has died in that dreadful way, leaving me all this money. Discovering that we had received this from a complete stranger, and a stranger who had then killed himself, was very disturbing.'

'A letter?' Laurence hoped he hadn't sounded too excited.

'Yes. It was an odd letter in its way, but then it turned out to have been written only weeks before he took his life. It came in November last year. Captain Emmett said he wanted to meet me, that he had something to tell me about Harry, my son. I can't remember his phrasing but he was quite pressing. However, sadly, he never made an appointment.'

'Do you still have the letter?' Laurence asked.

'Not any more. I'm sorry. But I knew men sometimes wrote to parents of friends who'd been killed and I was grateful to hear from him.'

When she went to fetch the tea-tray he paced around the room. To one side of the door were two silhouettes: a boy and a younger girl. He presumed they were Catherine and her brother. There was a lithograph of a Gothic-looking castle and an old theatre poster in a frame. A young woman in an elaborate feather headdress stood singing, hands clasped. He looked closely. It looked like Catherine, but could be a much younger Mrs Lovell.

She returned, set a teapot, china and a plate of cake on a small table, then sat in a chair with her back to the window.

'Did you reply?' he said. 'To the letter?'

'Of course. But he never wrote again.'

There was an awkward silence, which she filled abruptly.

'You knew Captain Emmett well? It must be very terrible for his family.'

Laurence hastily swallowed his mouthful of Dundee cake. Crumbs fell on his tie. 'I was at school with him, but he wasn't a close friend. Not really. Not as adults.'

'But Miss Emmett, his sister, she is a friend?'

'Well, I suppose so. I don't really know her either. I mean, not well.'

She looked at him quizzically. 'My husband died when Captain Emmett must have been scarcely more than a child,' she said, effectively pre-empting his next question. 'He was older than me and had been an invalid for many years. He died in Nice when Catherine was three. Then my son was killed in the war.' Her eyes dropped to her linked hands. She wore no jewellery. 'He was twenty-one. Now we are just the two of us.'

This time the silence seemed infinite. To say he was sorry seemed an absurd irrelevance.

'Harry volunteered as soon as he was eighteen. He was buried near Le Crotoy. But I am told his grave is lost.' She looked at Laurence. 'Captain Emmett must have been a friend of Harry's. Don't you think so? I met only one or two of his friends, and one died out in Flanders, but I don't remember an Emmett. Wouldn't he have told me?'

'I simply have no idea. But certainly one of the other bequests, apart from his family, was to an officer who served with him, so it's possible. Was Harry in the West Kents?'

This time it was she who had a mouthful of cake, so she shook her head. He put down his plate and when he looked up she had turned to gaze out of the side pane of the bay window.

'You know all these stories people tell about how they were lying in bed one night and their loved one walked in, or they were out walking and heard a voice calling them from far away, and soon after the news came of their death? How they just *knew*? Well, nothing like that happened to me,' she said quietly. 'If it *were* possible, then it would have. We were very close, you see. He was quite a solitary boy and he would share things with me: stories, pictures, shells, birds' eggs.

'One afternoon Catherine and I went walking on Parliament Hill Fields. It was March and we were trying to fly a kite. We weren't very good: it was Harry's kite really and he was so clever with it. Finally it went soaring off and caught round a chimney. It looked like a flag: white, red and black, and I said to Catherine that we had better escape or we might be arrested as foreign agents.' She smiled, more to herself than him. 'We came back laughing to the house, just clutching the string, and when I turned a corner I saw him. The telegraph boy. Standing at the bottom of our steps, just out there.'

She turned her head a little towards the window.

'I held Catherine's hand so tightly that she cried out, and I turned round and I walked with her across the road and back to the green, and then I ran and ran, pulling her along, and she kept stumbling and she started to cry, and I looked up and saw the kite, bright on the rooftops, and I knew it was no good. I couldn't turn the clock back an hour earlier, or a day, or a year, or three years. We sat on the grass for hours until it got dark and rather cold, and finally a woman came out from the houses, and she spoke to us and was kind, and she and her husband walked us home and there it was — the telegram. My neighbour had it. She had told the boy "no reply". She knew, of course.'

The rush of words stopped. She swallowed hard.

'We hadn't been here that long. It had gone to our old address first. It was weeks since he'd actually died. So, you see, I wasn't even thinking about him when I thought I still *had* him, before I knew he was gone. Who knows what I was doing at the moment he died. Peeling an apple? Riding on a tram? Shopping at Swan and Edgar? Who knows what *he* was doing? I didn't. Was he killed immediately? Did he linger in pain? I dreamed of it, of course. Not every night but often. As one does.'

Laurence thought how natural she seemed to think dreams of the dead were. He never admitted to anyone that he dreamed of Louise.

'I dreamed of him dying in every imaginable way, but it was worse when I dreamed he was alive. I could smell him, touch him, and then I'd wake up and it was new agony all over again. But you've lost someone yourself?' she ventured, obviously noticing his unease. 'Someone close to you? Not just Captain Emmett?'

Laurence said nothing for a few seconds. Finally he said, 'A long time ago,' and knew she didn't believe him.

The room was starting to darken but she made no attempt

to turn on the light, not even when she went out to the kitchen to send the maid home. When she returned, she seemed to have come to a decision.

'You know, I would very much have liked to know what Captain Emmett had to tell me. He probably knew Harry, possibly had some details about his death. But I don't think I ever shall know now what he wanted and I don't want to try to find out. For a long time I did but I owe it to Catherine to make a proper life for her, not one overshadowed with grief.' She paused. 'It's different for me, of course. For me life is over.'

Laurence sat forward.

'I'm so very sorry,' he said, and he meant it. 'I wish I could help, I wish I could tell you more about John Emmett; there must be a connection but I've found nothing, yet.'

'No,' she said, 'I'm not asking for that.'

She looked down at her hands. It was obviously time for him to leave and in saying goodbye he was not surprised that she didn't ask him to keep in touch with her.

On the way home, Laurence was cross with himself for not asking her a bit more. However, he had been unnerved by the depths of sorrow behind her dignified exterior and it had seemed to him that she didn't want her daughter to overhear their conversation.

As he left he'd said, 'I don't have a card, but . . .' He plunged his hand into his coat pocket to find only the Wigmore concert programme. 'I'll give you my name and address in case you want to talk to me.'

He tore off a bit of the back cover and started to write. She didn't offer him anything better to write on and he felt a bit of a fool, but it seemed a courtesy after he'd invaded her afternoon without warning.

'Thank you,' she had said and then added, 'So you like music, Mr Bartram?' She picked up the programme as it lay on the console table.

'Yes, I do,' he replied.

'I was a singer once,' she said almost off-handedly. 'Classical repertoire mostly. I trained for over four years. I sang on the continent but gave it all up when my son was born.'

'The Elgar was wonderful at this concert,' he said after a few seconds. 'It made me feel that things were getting back to normal.'

He cursed himself for not thinking. He was talking to a woman whose life could never be normal again, yet she actually brightened and nodded in agreement as she skimmed the programme before handing it back. He hovered on the doorstep for a second, made his farewell and walked towards the main road deep in thought.

People didn't just inherit money from strangers. There had to be a link and he would find it. He felt that he had at least established that John had a reason, even one known only to John, for the bequest. One he'd meant to explain, perhaps. But what had made him change his mind?

CHAPTER NINE

When Laurence got home there were, unusually, three letters waiting. A plump one was from India and he set it aside for later. The second was from his publishers. The third was in unfamiliar handwriting.

Dear Mr Bartram,

There was something I wanted to ask you but I didn't want to speak in front of William because he needs to look forward, not back to the war. We all must.

However, you may not have realised, and it didn't seem the time to raise it, but I knew John Emmett for a while. I doubt William will have thought to tell you.

I nursed him out in France and of course that's how I met William, too. I just wondered, for my own peace of mind, whether you were quite certain that John's death was deliberate. You see, although John may have been troubled, he was strong in his way. He had inner resources – talents. He wrote, he could draw marvellously. He had things to live for, however difficult his circumstances.

You do hear of people being careless while cleaning a gun, say (though I'd like to know how he had hidden a gun if he was being treated for melancholia). But I just hope somebody who didn't know him properly hadn't jumped to any conclusion just because he was ill after the war. Someone told me that tens of thousands of men are trying to claim pensions for nervous conditions and they are probably the saner ones. Anyway, they are not all killing themselves. I'm sorry to bother you and to ask you to keep my letter to yourself but hope, in time, you might be able to reassure me that things were properly investigated. John Emmett was an exceptional man.

Yours sincerely,
Eleanor Bolitho

Laurence read it twice and sat back in his chair. Her words on the need to face forward carried echoes of Mrs Lovell's determination but, knowing Eleanor Bolitho had been a nurse in France, he should have thought to ask her whether she knew John. Nevertheless, he had never considered for a minute that John's death could have been an accident. Was that naive of him, being so ready to believe the man he once known and admired had loaded his gun and shot himself in the — what? temple? mouth? He'd had a corporal once who'd shot himself, though no one was sure whether it was because he was careless or had had enough. The shot had gone through his chin and taken off the back of his head.

Eleanor was right. He had accepted the story at face value because John was already unstable. It dawned on him that he knew very little about how John had died. Where *had* he got the gun? Plenty of officers had held on to their pistols, although it was officially frowned upon, yet he imagined any nursing home would have searched their patients' belongings. John could have got one from someone else but that would mean that there was someone out there who knew more about the suicide and yet hadn't come forward. Given John was dead, it had never seemed to matter where the gun had come from.

Once Laurence started to consider what he did not know, or even what Mary might know but had not volunteered, he realised how little substance there was to the account of John Emmett's death. Where was the wood where the body was found, for instance? Mary had said it was on the edge of the county.

He pulled out an elderly atlas of England from his shelves. Fairford was in south-east Gloucestershire, almost on the border where three counties met: Gloucestershire, Oxfordshire and Wiltshire. But Somerset, Monmouthshire, Herefordshire, Worcestershire and Warwickshire also shared boundaries, though much further away. How far had John travelled before dying? Where was the inquest held?

He wasn't sure whether acting as Mary's private detective was quixotic or ridiculous, but there were surprisingly positive aspects to it and not just the emotions he was trying to suppress regarding Mary herself. He'd enjoyed meeting William and Eleanor Bolitho and he was intrigued by Mrs Lovell. He had wondered briefly whether either she or her daughter had been John's lover, but the girl was far too young and he just couldn't see Mrs Lovell's charms appealing to a man in his twenties.

He was still puzzled by John having that much money to leave. It didn't fit in with the gossip relayed by Charles. He could ask Mary, if he phrased it subtly. But at least John's will had established a scale of things. Bolitho had received a good-ish sum for helping John survive an accident, although Bolitho had represented himself as little more than an observer. Whatever Mrs Lovell had done, it was evidently of slightly less importance than that, judging by the size of the bequest. The lost or dead Frenchman, M. Meurice, had been left half the sum Bolitho had received. Doullens was near the battlefields of the Somme. Had Meurice helped John out there in some way?

Realistically, Lovell and Meurice had to be connected through John's military service. Bolitho certainly was and, anyway, war had been John's occupation for most of the years leading up to his incarceration and death, leaving little time for anything else. Was it possible that Mrs Lovell, like Eleanor Bolitho, had been a nurse in France? It seemed highly unlikely as she had a young daughter. Yet whatever the connection was, it had not existed, or had not been pressing enough, for John to recognise it in his previous will, made in 1914. Yet perhaps that first will had been made with very little thought of death as a real possibility. It was just a routine for all departing officers and they were all such gung-ho optimists then.

He mulled over a few other vague ideas. Could Mr Emmett Senior have been married before, and Mrs Lovell been a half-sister of John's? Unlikely, he thought; she and her daughter were unusually fair-haired and fair-skinned, while John, like his father, was dark-haired and brown-eyed. Anyway, in that case Mrs Lovell would surely have recognised the name Emmett instantly when she received the letter and he doubted John's father was old enough to have squeezed in an earlier marriage. It was equally unlikely that Catherine Lovell was actually an illegitimate child of Mr Emmett and Mrs Lovell, making her a half-sister to John and Mary.

So, the uncomplicated and old-fashioned Cecil Emmett –

a man whose main relationship seemed to be with his animals and the kitchen garden, and who refused to spend a night away from home — hardly seemed the type to maintain a handsome widow in a North London villa. His favourite phrase had been, 'Always set things right,' which he applied to everything from not leaving tennis balls in the rain to having cottages repaired for aged tenants while his own roof leaked. However, there were also Charles's allegations about his carelessness with money.

Could there really be some connection with Germany? If so, Laurence couldn't begin to think how it could be unravelled now. By the time it began to get dark, he had decided to ask Charles to check the name Lovell with some of his army cronies. Charles would find the mystery irresistible. He should have asked Mrs Lovell for her son's regiment but Charles would enjoy finding it.

The one idea he'd been mulling over since his first meeting with Mary was seeing Holmwood for himself. He had rejected his initial vague notion as reckless once he got home, but in the absence of other answers he was starting to think that it wouldn't be so difficult to carry off; he could simply present himself as looking for a place for a troubled relative. It would be a gesture to prove his commitment to finding out more about John Emmett.

The next morning he wrote to Mary to propose it again. She wrote back by return of post and with such enthusiasm that his heart sank slightly as he realised he was now committed to a deceit. However, his spirits rose at the rest of her letter, which described the easterly wind, leaves falling, Michaelmas undergraduates wandering about like lost schoolboys in their gowns, and how she had been to a recital in Trinity chapel which she thought he might have enjoyed. She added, almost as an afterthought, that she had found a few more of John's things although there was nothing remarkable among them. Next time they met, she'd bring them. She hoped this would be soon – she underlined the word soon. It was a very different Mary, more informal and light-hearted than in her earlier letter.

Buoyed up by her tone, he wrote to Holmwood immediately. Mary had said they had installed a telephone system although he was in no great hurry. Wanting it to seem like an ordinary enquiry, he created an older brother, Robert, who owed quite a lot to a character in a book by John Buchan, but was, additionally and essentially, given to melancholy and seizures, having being injured at Loos. He went out to the postbox straight away, before he could deliberate any further, but after he'd posted his letter he wondered whether the fits were too much. On the way back, he picked up a newspaper from the news boy in the square; since he had started involving himself with John Emmett, he had found his broader curiosity for the world returning intermittently.

When he got in, not being in the mood to look at his work, he opened his sister's letter. It was full of the usual cheerful inconsequentialities and devoid of any sense of what she was thinking, only of what she – or, more often, other people – were doing. He felt saddened by the distance that had come between them; even the vocabulary of her life seemed old-fashioned, as if time as well as oceans separated them.

He thought back to school and the days when his parents were both alive. His father had been a handsome man who, his mother feared, had an eye for other women. Laurence remembered how funny this had seemed at the time, when he was fourteen or so, with his father in his late forties, and his mother sensitive to any straying glance or conversation.

'Oh Laurie,' she would say anxiously, 'your teacher, Miss Beames, do you think she might be generally considered pretty? Did you see your father talking to her?' Or, whispered on a bus, 'Did you see the way your father looked at that young lady he gave his seat up to? Did you get the feeling he knew her already?' His sister would roll her eyes.

Who would be interested in that old man? Laurence had thought to himself then.

He wondered who young Wilfred, his eldest nephew, took after. At the end of the year he would find out. When he had eventually read his sister's latest news, he was alarmed to find that his oldest nephew was being sent to school in England after Christmas. He could tell that his sister wanted him to be Wilfred's guardian. He rather hoped the boy had not inherited too many characteristics of his sister's stout, red-faced husband but he was nonetheless glad his dead parents had living grand-children.

Now he scanned an account of a vast industrial explosion in Germany and briefly felt compassion for the families of the dead, whatever their nationality. Pity was like blood returning, painfully, to a leg with cramp. The other lead story concerned the hunt for the killer of a senior police officer who had been shot dead as he left his office. The policeman had been involved in two high-profile cases with violent foreign gangs. A police spokesman said there were still no clues but there was an increasing problem with the number of side arms in cir-culation after the war. Laurence thought, briefly, of John. Would he have killed himself anyway, even if he hadn't had a gun?

In an opinion piece he discovered that Brinsmead Pianos had opened under new ownership. He read this article in more detail. Louise's piano – his piano – had been a Brinsmead. He thought the firm had been broken by the piano workers' strike of the previous year. Guns. Strikers. Discontent. He found himself wondering how Eleanor Bolitho would see it all. An editorial in his paper viewed Brinsmead's re-emergence as a triumph of capitalism over the Bolshevist threat. From what Eleanor had said of her political beliefs, he thought she might rejoice in the workers asserting themselves, even if it did lead to a dearth of music in middle-class parlours.

Next to the pianos was a poor picture of a politician and an illustrious army commander, speaking together at a public meeting in Birmingham. They were arguing that war, any war but especially the Great War, was not a matter of heroism but endurance. They had been heckled at first, the article said, but the hecklers had themselves been shouted down. Laurence recognised the men; it was the pair Charles had been so excited to meet at his club: Morrell, the former MP, and the retired general, Somers. He had been wrong in his assumption that the retired officer would be a stickler for the harshest dis-cipline. Perhaps speaking out now was another form of courage.

It was interesting, Laurence mused, reading on, how some people were beginning to feel they could say these things now without their patriotism being called into question. Charles had told him that another MP – Lambert Ward – whose own recent service with the Royal Naval Reserve had provided him with a shield of valour, had demanded executed deserters be buried in military graves with all the other fallen soldiers. Charles himself was surprisingly indifferent.

'Who cares?' he said. 'One way or another, they're all gone.'
Until John Emmett rose from the dead into his life,

84

Laurence had almost convinced himself the war was history but now he saw that its aftershocks rumbled on and on, and that peace had nothing to do with signatures and seals on a paper.

He started to read about the paper poppies they were making for Armistice Day this year. It was a new idea — started in America. He couldn't imagine wearing one; he even disliked fresh poppies — but perhaps some families wanted a visible sign of all they had lost.

The wind had got up and the windows rattled. He tore a strip off the page and wedged the frame fast. He returned to the mutilated newspaper and started on an obituary of a centenarian who had fought under Elphinstone in the First Afghan War and survived the massacre at the Gandamak Pass. His last thought as the paper slipped to the floor was how small wars used to be.

Over the next week his own eagerness to get going was matched by a lack of any action elsewhere and yet he couldn't settle to writing. Charles had bought a car and had been trying it out by motoring from one friend's house to another across the southern counties. He wouldn't be back for a day or so. There was no further word from Mary. What was she doing, he wondered. How did she pass the weeks in Cambridge?

After a couple of days' reluctant progress on his book, a letter finally brought good and bad news. Dr Bertram Chilvers, Holmwood Nursing Home, Fairford, Gloucestershire (proprietors Dr B.G.S. Chilvers MD, and G.H. Chilvers) would be delighted to show him round his establishment and discuss possible treatment for Captain Robert Bartram. Trains ran from Paddington to Fairford, changing at Oxford. The station was on the outskirts of town but it was only a ten- to fifteen-minute walk. If Mr Bartram let them know what train he would be catching, a car could be sent to fetch him. If he required accommodation overnight, it could be arranged at the local hotel. It would be helpful, it concluded, if he could obtain a letter from Captain Robert Bartram's doctor to assist in an assessment of his condition.

'Damn,' said Laurence aloud. 'Damn, damn, damn.'

He considered forging a letter of referral but realised almost as soon as he'd hit on the idea that it was hopeless. Doctors all knew each one another and anyway he was sure to get the vocabulary wrong and they'd smell a rat. At the very least he would have to account for the absence of such a letter.

Suddenly he thought of Eleanor Bolitho. Could she help him construct a plausible document? While she had as good as asked him not to disturb William again, he could, under the guise of answering her letter to him, ask for help. He dashed off a note to her before dining at Charles's club.

When he arrived in Pall Mall, he could tell Charles was eager to talk, but they got dragged into a small group digging in on their positions on the gold standard. Finally, as brandy was brought into the smoking room, Charles, who had been fidgeting with impatience throughout the latter part of their dinner, could describe his attempted pursuit of Mrs Lovell's son.

'Truth is, old chap, he doesn't exist. Bought this new book, fresh off the press – bound to come in handy: *Officers Died in the Great War*. Five dead Lovells in there. Not a lucky name. But not our man. The first . . .' He counted off on his fingers: 'Colonel Frederick Lovell: career soldier and far too old from what you've told me. Number two: Captain M. St J. Lovell RFC – a possibility, but then we have number three: his brother Lieutenant H.B.E. Lovell. He died in 1917, but I think you said our boy's an only son. Four, Captain Bruce Lovell, went down with Kitchener on the *Hampshire* en route to Archangel in 1916. Best hope,' his finger hovered, 'was five: another subaltern, Royal Fusiliers, enlisted in London, nineteen years old: Richard Ranelagh Lovell. Promising but he's too early: missing in action, Mons, 1914.'

'Missing?' Laurence said.

'Yes, missing, but it's pretty certain what happened to him. I checked. Was seen badly wounded but pressing on. Seen to be shot again and falling, and by his adjutant. Know that man myself, as it happens. Married to a cousin. Third cousin, really. I'm off to see him for the weekend. Two soldiers in his platoon saw this Lovell's body but they had no chance to bury him. Body gone by the time anyone got back there. Whole place was unrecognisable by then. Him too, no doubt. So it's simple,' he concluded dramatically. 'Your Master Lovell didn't die in the Great War.'

Laurence responded slowly, without pointing out that it wasn't *his* Lovell. 'Perhaps, though I can't think how, he isn't dead, then? Perhaps he survived?'

Charles was beaming before he had finished the sentence. Laurence had gone exactly where he intended.

'No suitable Lovell dead *or* alive, old chap. All checked. Friends plus Army List. Of eight surviving Lovells, four left the army: one's a barrister; one lives on an annuity; two returned home north of the border; one went to South Africa; one, a Lovell-Brace, is a Hampshire landowner. One Lovell is still serving and currently head of the Staff College. No dead commissioned Lowells in the right place either. I remembered you weren't sure of the spelling the first time you mentioned him, or rather her, the heiress of Parliament Hill. Perhaps the lady's a fraud?'

Laurence thought that Charles was much cleverer than he let on and that he also had a great deal too much time on his hands.

'No,' he said, 'I'm quite certain that she had a son and that he was killed. She thought John might be a friend of his.' To manufacture grief like hers, he thought, would have required the skills of a consummate actress.

He left late, declining Charles's invitation to bring Mary Emmett to the Savoy next week. He knew Charles would try to pick up the bill, which Laurence would indeed have trouble meeting, but he also wanted to keep Mary to himself for the time being. As he walked home briskly in the cold he realised that his one certainty – that the deaths of Emmett and Lovell were connected – had been obliterated by Charles's energetic enquiries.

That night he wrote to Mary and remembered to ask whether he could have the photograph of the soldiers in the farmyard. He wanted to see if William Bolitho could identify any of those in it. He told her that he had not really advanced his search and he hoped she wouldn't be disappointed. Even so, there were some things he kept to himself.

CHAPTER TEN

*I*n the morning a letter came from Eleanor Bolitho. She agreed to meet him the next day in a teashop he'd suggested near the British Museum. She would have to leave spot on four to fetch her son, she said.

When he arrived she was already waiting, her elbows on the table, reading a book. He read the spine of it as he struggled for a moment to pull his arm from his coat before sitting down. It was John Galsworthy's *The Man of Property*.

'Hello,' she said evenly, putting the book to one side.

Eleanor didn't seem a person for light chatter or any degree of deception, so he simply expanded on the explanation in his letter and the need to fabricate a medical history for a mythical brother. But first he told her what he knew of John's deterioration once he got home. It seemed only fair. He explained Mary Emmett's fear that her brother had been mistreated at Holmwood and added some of the ideas he'd had about John's death.

For a few seconds her face showed no discernible emotion. Then she said, simply, 'I don't doubt she's right. There are far too many greedy, amoral people taking advantage of sick men and of their families, who are bankrupting themselves to have their loved ones looked after. Or,' she added darkly, 'so they believe. I've heard about a couple of such places. Something should be done about them. This government should do right by ordinary people. We should have a different sort of politics now that everything's changed so much. We shouldn't be trying to do things the same way, which ended up killing and mutilating half the men in Europe.'

She paused just long enough for Laurence to signal a waitress. Her pale, creamy skin was flushed.

'Did you ever read any of John Emmett's poetry?' she asked abruptly.

Laurence's heart sank. He didn't want any diversion at this point. 'Not really. Only the one that was published in the paper.'

'Do you like poetry?'

'Yes. Some of it, anyway,' Laurence said, hoping she wouldn't ask him to explain which bits.

'Well, John's poems, his early ones, were very much a young man's work: pretty pastoral scenes usually with a pretty Dresden shepherdess: his little Minna, sitting in them.'

'Minna?'

'His fiancée. He was engaged to be married in about 1912, I think. She was a German girl. She died. When he talked about her I always felt it was Goethe and Schiller and Schubert he'd really fallen in love with.' She was silent for a second. 'Didn't you know about Minna?'

'Mary Emmett told me but I'd forgotten her name.' He was trying to calibrate the extent of Eleanor Bolitho's knowledge of John Emmett. He'd previously assumed a very slight relationship.

'And now you're also wondering how I knew so much about John?' she asked, in a slightly teasing tone and looking him straight in the eye.

'Yes.'

'And about poetry?'

He smiled.

'Well, the answer to the second question is that before the war broke out I was reading English at Cambridge – at Girton College. We couldn't graduate but we could study. I wanted to be a teacher. But circumstances changed,' she paused, 'and I became a nurse. Which has been a more useful skill, as it turned out.'

She breathed in deeply.

'The answer to the first question is that when John came into my field hospital, it was all very quiet; lovely, very early summer weather, I remember. Beds made, bandages rolled, shrouds waiting, quarts of iodine and carbolic acid and chloroform, but no patients. Not yet. We had half a dozen soldiers plus two young officers who were ill rather than injured. One had jaundice, I think. And a Canadian major who'd been kicked by a horse. We were waiting for the big push. It was uncannily quiet, in fact. Quite eerie in its way. Not far from the hospital Irish soldiers were digging pits, great long graves, for all the dead they were expecting. The other nurses and I kept taking water out to the men; they were in surprisingly good spirits, standing there cracking jokes while up to their knees in earth amid a sweep of grass and wild oats. Anyway, John was brought in from his regimental aid post one afternoon; he'd been injured in an accident. He had various middling injuries. But he seemed quite shocked and had bad flank pain. By the next day he started bleeding quite heavily from a kidney, so we kept him in.'

'And your husband was brought in then too?' Laurence added.

'Good heavens, no, this was much earlier than that. I met William when he was fighting for his life. No, there was just John and the three others. They were the only officers.'

'Can you remember what the major's name was?' asked Laurence.

'No,' she said. 'I haven't a clue. I'm sure they didn't know each other beforehand, if that's what you're thinking, and the major was moved out in a day or so. The boys were just boys. They ate together and played draughts. Only John was there for any length of time.'

She stopped.

'The MO wondered, though only to me, whether John might be adding blood to his own urine. But we never confronted him.'

Laurence must have looked puzzled, because she added, 'He appeared to be bleeding from his kidneys, but the blood could have come from anywhere.'

'You mean he was faking it?' Despite himself, he was shocked.

'Faking the degree of visible damage? Possibly. But not faking the fact he was hurt or needed care.

'After a couple of weeks things heated up and he was sent back home, lucky man. The injury had saved him. The mass graves were filled and overfilled, but he wasn't there. But when he was there and when nobody else was,' her voice dropped a little, 'I was on night duty and he couldn't sleep. The trench collapse had really rattled him.'

'Being trapped,' said Laurence.

She nodded. 'In those circumstances you get to know a man quite well.' She looked sad.

'You were saying about his poetry?' Laurence said, remembering the limits on her time and that he *had* once seen another poem of John's – when he was in Cambridge with Mary.

'All I was going to say was that after John was injured, he stopped,' she said briskly. 'Writing poems. He said it had gone. He said he had been a minor poet at best and now not even minor. It wasn't true but it's what he felt.' She hesitated. 'They were all in touch with each other,' she went on after a while, 'the would-be poets – and there was a sort of magazine he put together, even after he stopped writing himself. It had all kinds of stuff in it. Some was pretty awful, to be honest, but John said it didn't matter if it helped people to stay sane. One or two were marvellous. I remember him reading some to me. It was very late at night and warm. We had the windows wide open and you could smell the countryside. In all that misery, it was a single perfect hour.'

Laurence watched her face. She had been in love with John Emmett, he thought.

'Can you remember any of their names?' he asked.

'Most of the ones I read had pen-names. Some of their subjects were pretty strong, not likely to go down well with the general staff. And he wasn't supposed to circulate poetry, not poetry like that. You weren't really even supposed to keep diaries were you? Though I imagine that was honoured more in the breach than the observance, as they say. John said he knew who most of the poets were but nobody else did.'

Laurence suddenly remembered the other poem he'd read from John Emmett's trunk in Cambridge.

'The name Sisyphus doesn't ring any bells, does it?'

'The man in the myth doomed to push a boulder up a hill for ever?'

Laurence nodded.

She paused. 'Yes, there *was* a Sisyphus. I'd have forgotten except that, much later, John showed me a couple of his and asked what I thought of them. They were really, really good. But I've no idea who Sisyphus was in real life.'

'So, how did you come to know that John had other troubles? Neurasthenia?'

'Well, I saw him a second time. The last winter of the war. He was admitted in a state of collapse: congested lungs, a fever, but more than that. He was a broken man, much worse than before. He scarcely spoke. He couldn't sleep. He had nightmares if he did. He had black moods. Just right at the end he started to improve a little. He came out for walks despite the cold.' A ghost of a smile flickered and was gone. 'But it didn't last. I suppose, looking back on it, the strange business of his paralysed arm was part of it.'

'Paralysed arm?' Laurence was puzzled.

'Yes. Towards the end of this second stay, he began to lose the power of his right arm. He said he'd had pins and needles and weakness since the earlier trench accident and then, suddenly, he couldn't use it at all. He couldn't write properly, do up buttons, cut with a knife: all those kinds of things. Major Fortune tried the usual tests: skin pricks, offering him a glass of water and so on, seeing which hand he used if he was caught by surprise, but he was consistent; his hand hung useless at his side. They decided it didn't matter as he was going home anyway. It was going to be someone else's problem.'

She stopped quite suddenly and then looked at her watch.

'So,' she went on, 'we could use some of that for your fictitious patient. You could say to the Holmwood people that your brother is presenting with hysterical conversion – that's the proper name for John's arm problem – plus insomnia, sudden alteration in mood and feelings of guilt after this head injury; they're classic symptoms.'

Laurence stopped her. 'Would you mind if I wrote this down?' he said. As he scrawled on another piece of paper, he looked up at her; she looked much more cheerful and seemed almost to be enjoying the fiction.

'Say it seems obvious that he'll always be an invalid. They'll like that if they're dishonest: the thought that they might keep him and his pension for ever.' She attempted a scowl. 'You could say he has mostly refused medical help until now. That might help explain the lack of a medical report, and emphasise that he generally had a bad war. You men like those sort of euphemisms. And you can say that poor Dr Fortune – the MO at our field hospital – died last year.'

Laurence raised his eyebrows.

'Heart attack at work,' she said. 'Unjust after all he'd been through. Though you could make up a few horror stories from your own experience, no doubt.'

'I was quite lucky actually,' said Laurence, quickly. 'Nothing really terrible ever happened to me. Nothing especially bad. Not to me personally.'

Eleanor looked at him for a long time. He felt uneasy under her gaze.

'Didn't it?' she said finally.

They sat over the table for another half an hour or so while he scribbled notes. She even suggested that he give her name to Dr Chilvers. She had at least been John's nurse and she was prepared to blur the time and place where she had looked after her patient.

'Anything to make life a bit more difficult for these charlatans,' she said. 'They should be struck off. If they're real doctors to start with,' she added portentously. Laurence thought that Eleanor made an impressive enemy but he didn't want her to see that he was amused.

At four, just as she had warned she must, Eleanor rose to leave. As she was pushing her chair back, he suddenly thought of something else.

'Do you know whereabouts in Bavaria Minna came from?' he asked. 'Does Coburg ring a bell?'

'Sorry,' she said, shaking her head. 'I don't think I ever knew.'

'Did you know her full name?'

'No. He didn't talk much about her. Not to me. Though I think her first name was really Wilhelmina. She had an older brother; I do remember that.'

'Did you see John again?' Laurence asked as he helped her on with her coat. 'After the war?'

'No,' she said. 'No. I married not so long after the war ended. But we kept in touch by letter from time to time. I liked him. He was special. And very alone.'

'I suppose John had a pen-name too?' he said, just as they reached the door. Why the hell hadn't he got his ideas together until she was on the point of leaving?

She thought for a while. 'It was Charon,' she said rather sadly. 'The bearer of the dead.'

CHAPTER ELEVEN

*T*here were two letters waiting for him when he returned home. He tore open the one from Mary as he walked upstairs. Out fell two photographs. One was a cheerful portrait of John in a rowing vest, taken at Oxford, he guessed. The other was of the group of soldiers; the picture he'd seen that day in Cambridge. Even allowing for the fact it was of poor quality, there was something grim and defeated about the men. He picked up the letter.

Dear Laurence,

It goes without saying that the happy photograph is precious to me. John never looked so carefree after he returned from France.

I am sorry I've been slow to write — I've been quite busy and my mother has been unwell. It occurred to me that I know so little about you, although talking to you helped me. You have a skill for understanding — maybe because you are a writer.

Perhaps we could meet once you have been to

Holmwood? The set-up there is not quite what it seems,
I think. But I don't want to influence you.

    Yours,
    Mary

Laurence was still sufficiently objective to recognise that she
was being disingenuous in the last sentence. Nor was research
into Norman architecture likely to fit anyone for insights into
the human condition. Still, he wondered whether he might
bring Mary back to his rooms one day. What would she think
of it? The rooms were well proportioned, and she would like
the views over London. He opened the piano lid and pressed
a key; it reverberated endlessly. God knows when it had last
been tuned. It had been Louise's pride and joy; in the end it
was the only thing of hers he could not face putting in a sale.
The piano stool was covered with a worn tapestry of a horn
of plenty, embroidered by his mother.

    The bedroom, on the north-east corner of the building,
was always colder than the other rooms and tonight the wind
was wailing round the corner of the building. He felt suddenly despondent; his reactions were those of a boy, not of a
man, a former soldier and a widower. Underneath his romantic fantasies he recognised a much darker physical desire for
her. It had first swept over him when Charles had implied that
she was not the innocent girl he had taken her to be. Surprised
by the knowledge of her passionate affair, he had also been
aroused by it, as well as the fact that, unknown to her, he possessed this piece of her secret self. He lay there in his chilly
bed, remembering what it felt like to have a woman beside
him, her naked legs against his where her nightgown had
ridden up, her back curved into him and his arms around her
warmth.

He woke feeling sick and shivery. His eiderdown had slipped off and the sheets had bunched down the bed, leaving the rough blankets irritating his skin. His ears were hot and ringing. The usual formless horrors slipped away from him once he switched on the light and straightened his sheets. He lay back. How could he ever explain all this to Mary or to any woman, he wondered, and despaired.

He knew it was useless to stay in bed; sleep would not return. As he walked into the other room he remembered that he had forgotten to open the second letter. There was the large, even handwriting: perfectly straight across the page as if Charles had internalised the ruled lines of the nursery. It took him three sides to communicate that he had been away for the weekend, that the Alvis was a marvel, that a group of friends Laurence had never heard of were on particularly good form, and that he had something quite rum to tell Laurence. It ended firmly: 'We need dinner, old man. Not the Club. Fancy a bit of a change. How about the Café Royal? At seven on Thursday?'

Although he woke up tired, the following day was clear. He decided to go over to the Bolithos and show William the photograph. It crossed his mind that the implicit bargain in exchange for Eleanor's help with Holmwood, was that he didn't bother her husband, but he promised himself that he would not linger.

Eleanor was out when he arrived. Their charwoman opened the door. He felt a degree of relief. William seemed genuinely pleased to see him. Despite the chill from half-opened windows and a strong smell of paint, the main room had taken on a feel of spring since his last visit.

'Chinese yellow,' William said, 'Eleanor's work.' He looked

down ruefully at the floor where a couple of yellow drips had hardened. 'She's a rather impulsive handywoman. But sit down. Ethel will make some tea.'

'Look, I can't stay,' Laurence said, 'and I am awfully sorry to pester you again but I wondered if I might show you a picture? I'm simply trying to identify the men in it.'

William seemed perfectly calm when he took the photograph. Though Eleanor had said he needed to move forward, he showed no sign of distress. If he hadn't known otherwise, Laurence would have thought he was a man glad of company and eager for something to do.

William turned slightly so that natural light fell on the picture. 'Well, that's John, you may have realised that?'

Laurence nodded; it confirmed his guess.

'And the others, well, that's odd — it's the MO, Major Fortune. Good man. A volunteer who never even had to be there. Must have been fifty if he was a day: a perfectly good career as a surgeon at St Thomas' Hospital. And, oh, there's Sergeant Tucker — the man I told you about, looking pleased with himself.'

He held the photograph out to Laurence and pointed at the figure leaning back against a log pile. Tucker was a sinewy, almost feral man. The others looked pretty miserable as they pulled on cigarettes or gazed down at their feet, but Tucker just looked calm.

'I don't know any of the others; at least — no, the one on the end there, I don't know what he's doing here, but he's the man who helped pull John out of the tunnel collapse. The sapper major's servant. I was thinking about him after we spoke last time and I remembered that he could do the most astonishing tricks with numbers. Give him fifty numbers and he could add them, subtract them, whatever you liked, in seconds, or work out sequences: you know, one – three – five and so on, only much harder ones. The lads used to try to catch him out. He was there while Major Whoever-it-was was billeted with us. He was a prodigy, though he and his officer reminded me a bit of a circus ringmaster and a performing elephant. Wonder what happened to him?'

From the hall, they heard someone come in. The front door closed. Laurence could hear Eleanor talking and the voice of a small child. The door to the room opened. A small boy with dark-auburn curls rushed in and climbed on to William's lap. When he saw Laurence, he buried his face in his father's chest. Eleanor followed her son, her expression drawn and irritated.

'Mr Bartram,' she said, tightly, as if she'd caught him out in some peccadillo.

'I'm sorry,' he began.

'*What* a surprise,' she said. 'I'm sorry I wasn't here, although perhaps you'd anticipated that, but as you can see we're quite busy this afternoon. Perhaps you could come back another time? If you let us know beforehand we might arrange an easier day?'

'Eleanor . . .' William began, while the boy turned to look shyly at Laurence, but his wife ignored his attempt to head her off.

'I'd like to give Nicky his tea now and William is tired.'

She looked fixedly at Laurence and under the intensity of her gaze he finally said 'I'm really very sorry. I shouldn't have come without warning.'

'But he needed me to identify a photograph,' William interrupted firmly. 'I wasn't much help, but I got a couple of the men, though I've no idea where it was taken.'

Eleanor put her hand out and he gave it to her. She looked at it briefly. 'John Emmett,' she said. 'Of course. He must be getting more attention dead than he ever did alive.' She handed the picture back.

'Eleanor . . .' William began.

'Well, it's true,' she said, 'when he was alive he was an embarrassment. His moods, his obsessions, his unpredictability: all too difficult. Not a modest hero adding lustre to a county drawing room, but a man who couldn't cope, shut away in some rotten asylum. Now he's dead we can all think about how we wish we could have helped him, or, if we couldn't, how it would have been better if he'd been blown to smithereens with his reputation intact.'

William said less mildly, 'I don't think that's entirely fair.'

Laurence thought again how well she knew John Emmett and wondered whether William noticed or minded her evident loyalty to the dead man. He decided now was not the time to defend Mary.

'No, I'm sorry,' she said. 'Whatever my feelings, I'm being rude. But I really must go and get Nicholas's tea now.'

She hung back and Laurence realised she was expecting him to go first. He tucked the picture in his wallet, said a hasty goodbye to William, who seemed diplomatically unaware of the degree of tension in the room, and he smiled at Nicholas, still on his father's knee. The little boy smiled back. Eleanor led him out and closed the door behind him.

By the front door she stopped, looked up at him and spoke quietly but fiercely. 'Just because William's stuck here and can't get out doesn't mean you can just come and go as if he had no life except to assist you. I helped you as much as I could. William did too but we want to move on. John's dead. We're not. We're very grateful for the money but it doesn't buy you or Miss Emmett a right to our lives.'

*

He got to the Café Royal first that evening. Charles arrived, slightly late, full of apologies and long technical explanations about the Alvis. He seemed quite good-humoured as if having it break down was all part of the fun. When finally they were settled, Laurence regaled Charles with his brief and difficult visit to the Bolithos.

Charles seemed hugely amused.

'Oh Mrs Bolitho, that Bolshevik firebrand. She's famous for it. Not a girl to cross. Jolly clever. Good person to have on your side, though.' He picked up his glass and held it up to a candle so that its garnet-like depths glowed. 'Ask Mr Lenin.'

'Is she really?' Laurence asked. 'A Bolshevik, I mean?'

'Well, she's certainly a fighter. Damn good nurse, I hear, but my mama wouldn't have had her in the house before the war. Suffragette, Fabian, bluestocking: that kind of thing. Not that my mama knew her not to have her, of course. Didn't have her sort in Warwickshire, but Mama read about them in her paper and always said she wouldn't receive anybody who thought females should have the vote.' He sighed. 'Poor Mama. She must be turning in her grave. Still bending Father's ear in paradise and all that. Not paradise for him really. Still, I should think Mrs Bolitho's politics would make even Ramsay MacDonald's hair stand on end.'

'Good Lord.' Laurence found he was full of admiration rather than shocked. 'And William?'

'Heaven knows. Never met him. Not likely to now, really. Suppose he must go along with it if only for a quiet life. But he's probably counting his blessings: Mrs Bolitho was always a bit sought after. Healing hands, that kind of thing. Pretty too. General surprise when she married old Bolitho but then nurses do that: marry their patients and so on, even without legs. There's a child, isn't there? So his wounds haven't stopped him enjoying the benefits.'

He beamed at Laurence. In anyone else such a statement of the obvious would seem prurient but Charles simply seemed happy for his fellow officer.

'Lucky man,' he added.

Laurence was just about to ask him more about the circumstances of the Bolithos' marriage when Charles dropped his own thunderbolt.

'Motored down to Lewes last week and guess who I met there?'

He left a pause for Laurence to go through the motions of guessing.

'Surprise me,' Laurence said, slicing into his turbot.

'Well, I was staying at Frant, you know, Tolly Pitt's house. Third cousin. He married a lovely girl – not really a girl, she must be twenty-eight if she's a day. She was engaged to some cavalry man who got it right at the start, but then she meets Tolly, love at second sight, a year or so back and then she inherits Frant off one of those useful aunts these girls have, and it turns out Tolly loves her too. We had a spot of dinner and a jolly good walk along the coast. You know how these weekends go.'

Charles was momentarily diverted by his pheasant, but after another mouthful he went on.

'Anyway, this Octavia is a lot of fun but keen on church, that kind of thing. So we were off for luncheon in Tunbridge Wells with someone Tolly knew from the regiment when Octavia decided we should all go to church there rather than in the village. To cut a long story short, halfway through the service Octavia obviously sees someone she knows across the way: lots of looks, little smiles, fingertip wiggling – delight, surprise:

that thing they do — and she whispers to me during the inter-minable sermon that it was a girl she'd known from driving some sort of canteen lorry for returning soldiers at Victoria Station in the war. Steaming tea, fragrant English girls — wel-come back warrior — you know. When we're all peeling out, rather relieved to be swapping the chilly sea of faith for a good roast, she's chatting away to her, obviously trying to persuade her to join us or come over the next day.

"'I'm afraid I can't,' says our new chum, just as we come within earshot, "I'm staying with a friend. He's not well enough to travel." Then Octavia sees me and Tolly's sister coming over together and introduces us: "This is Mary Emmett. Charles, I think you must have been at Marlborough with her brother, John?"'

Laurence had been following his own train of thought while Charles's story slowly circled its way to a conclusion, but Charles's words jerked him back into the conversation.

'Aha,' said Charles triumphantly, spearing a parsnip, 'thought that'd make you sit up. So I said, of course I did and I was sorry to hear the news, terrible thing, etcetera etcetera, and I can see why you're so keen to scout about for her — nice-look-ing girl, though a bit of fresh air needed to put a blush in those cheeks — and I said all the things you'd expect. So then I said, "And I think you know my great friend Laurence Bartram," and she was completely thrown. The look that crossed her face was not of fondness and grateful admiration at your very name, but nearer to horror, to be honest. Anyway, after that, I regret to say, old chap, she couldn't get away fast enough. Though Octavia had extracted a promise from her to come round — hard person to refuse, Octavia — the next time she was in the area, and got her address in Cambridge, she didn't even stay to meet Tolly and nobody could be intimidated by old Tolly. But then later I thought Miss Emmett didn't want my friend Laurence to know she was in Tunbridge. But why on earth shouldn't she be? And why should he care?'

'Where did she go?'

'Heaven knows. I wasn't going to *follow* her. She was quite on her own and she just trotted off down the Pantiles. Almost as if she were scared we'd follow her. Octavia thought she was embarrassed about her brother: suicide, scandal and so on. In fact, I got the distinct impression that Octavia rather thought I was de trop for mentioning it, though it was she who brought up the subject of John in the first place, but I think Miss Emmett was fine with all that. It was me knowing you, I'm certain, that caused all the consternation.'

Finally he stopped, looking expectantly across the table. As Laurence tried to appear indifferent to what he'd just heard, the silence lengthened until Charles couldn't resist adding, 'What do you think?'

Laurence longed to check whether Charles was certain that Mary had said she was staying with a man, but to do so would be to make himself look a fool. He hadn't been concentrating at the crucial point in the rambling story. Wasn't it her mother who was supposed to be needing her care? He felt irritated by Charles's speculations and, above all, he felt angry with himself.

Eventually, and it must have been obvious to both men that it was an effort, he said lamely, 'Yes, I seem to remember she had friends down there.' Then to move away from a gratuitous lie to one of his oldest friends, he added, 'Did she look well?'

Charles looked at him closely for a second. 'Well, as I said, I thought she looked a bit tired.' Of course he'd said that, Laurence thought, and stopped himself from asking any more questions.

'Are you all right?' Charles raised an eyebrow. 'Your fish is getting cold.'

Charles's plate was empty but for a couple of game chips, which he transferred so quickly from plate to mouth with his fingers that the action was almost imperceptible. He wiped his hands and moustache with his napkin.

'Do you know, I think you're a bit keen on the mysterious Miss Emmett, Laurence. Who could blame you? She's a handsome girl and since Louise died you've turned yourself into some kind of recluse, so personally I'm delighted to see an old friend back in play, but, for what it's worth, whatever she was doing last Sunday, it didn't look as if it was making her particularly happy.'

'I don't know,' said Laurence and stopped.

He realised as he spoke that behind the vague reply was a profound truth. The chasm of what he didn't know was huge. Mary was the least of it. Everything he thought he knew when he was eighteen had been meaningless. Everything he had thought his at twenty-one was gone. That was undoubtedly why he was devising hare-brained schemes to chase dead men and why he was so fond of Charles who had seemed old at thirteen and would seem young at eighty.

For want of anything else to say he blurted out, 'I'm actually going down to the home, asylum, call it what you will, where John Emmett was a patient. Next week. Just to see whether there's anything I can find out for . . . Mary.'

'Wasn't that somewhere in the Cotswolds? Oxfordshire? Gloucestershire?' Charles asked.

'Fairford. The nursing home is called Holmwood, it's in Gloucestershire. It's an hour or so west of Oxford by train.'

'Well,' Charles said, brightening up, 'no need to go by train. We can both go in the car. Good to try her out after her temperamental fit the other day and I haven't got much on during the next week as it so happens. We could leave early, stay a couple of nights somewhere and come back after you've spied out the land.' Reading the expression in Laurence's face, he added quickly, 'Unless you're taking your Miss Emmett and want to go *à deux*, of course?'

When Laurence shook his head, Charles continued, 'Wouldn't get in your way. Have a walk. Take the air. Lovely countryside. Who knows, even pick up a bit of gossip?'

To his surprise Laurence found the thought of going with Charles, even travelling in his car, was a pleasant one. All the same, he needed to explain more about his enquiry.

'I'm afraid I'm not exactly going as myself,' he started. 'I mean, I am going as myself but I'm not going to represent Mary Emmett. We didn't want the Holmwood people to be aware of my specific interest in John's death. I've sort of invented a brother – Robert – whom we might need to place in the care of a nursing home. Bad experiences in Flanders . . .' He tailed off.

'Well, you are a dark horse,' said Charles happily. 'Reminds me of Bulldog Drummond. Marvellous read.'

CHAPTER TWELVE

*T*he journey started off more like a voyage. It had been raining all night and it continued to pour as they drove out of London at dawn. There were very few other vehicles on the road. Charles swerved vigorously to avoid standing water on some streets, yet water seeped in round the passenger door. The interior of the car smelled of leather and oil, and the windscreen and side windows were soon misty with condensation. But by the time they reached the country roads beyond Slough the clouds broke up, and when they stopped briefly at an old inn at Hurley at midday it was beginning to get slightly warmer as the sun emerged.

Laurence's back ached as he pulled himself upright. It had done so since the war. 'You've got an old man's back,' Charles said as he swung himself nimbly out of his seat.

After a pint of beer, they crunched back through rusty drifts of leaves and bright-green spiked conker cases split open on the steaming path. When they returned to the car, Charles pulled back the roof and strapped it down, then took out two woollen scarves, goggles and a map, giving Laurence the less disreputable scarf. Charles set his goggles in place and looked every bit the fearless aviator his driving suggested. Once Laurence got used to the noise and the air rushing past, he relaxed. When they stopped the car a couple of times for Charles to look at the map, he could hear birds and smell the earthiness of the damp countryside. They made little attempt at conversation; Charles occasionally shouted a brief commentary on the car's performance, which was mostly lost to the wind and the engine, and Laurence made vaguely appreciative gestures with which Charles seemed satisfied.

At one point, where the road was straight and wide, he slowed to ask whether Laurence wanted a go, apparently indifferent to the fact that his friend had never driven a car in his life. Having received a firm refusal, Charles lit his pipe and drove on, occasionally beating off the sparks which dropped on his coat.

They passed through Maidenhead, Henley, Wallingford and Wantage: towns of Georgian brick houses and pale stone bridges with broad and tranquil views of the Thames.

Henley was the only place Laurence had visited before, for the 1911 Regatta. It had been one of the hottest weeks of a blazing summer. He'd stayed with an aristocratic Oxford companion: Richard Standish. The house stood a little way from the town, its park slightly raised above the river. The first morning he had got up early. The air was warm even before the sun rose and as it came up a veil of mist lingered over the water. It was silent at the river's edge, the surface dark and unbroken between the reeds. Standish's people had a large house party. He and Richard and a cousin of Richard's, all unexpected guests, had to share a long attic room in the servants' quarters, under the eaves where they could hear doves cooing while they lay on top of the bedclothes in the stifling heat. It was the week Laurence had met Louise.

Louise, then seventeen, was also staying with friends: a large, noisy family with five daughters. He had sometimes wondered whether their meeting and subsequent attraction had all been based on the fantasy that was that regatta week. Louise was being pushed by her mother to set her sights beyond her mercantile roots. He was lonely and without any family. That week he was ensconced with his titled friend while Louise was nestled at the heart of her ebullient hosts. In those contexts they both seemed to offer what the other most wanted. In fact, when he tried to remember when he first saw Louise — surely this was a crucial moment in any tale of love — he was hard put to separate the pale blur of cream and blue dresses, spinning parasols and straw hats, the chattering and the giggles, into separate young women.

John Emmett was there too, he suddenly recalled, though where he was staying he was not sure. He had forgotten that fact completely but now it occurred to him that was actually the last time he'd seen him. Into his mind came a picture of John standing barefoot on a slip in a rowing vest and shorts, slender but well muscled. It had slipped his mind that John was such a good oarsman. He was not a dedicated one; although he could have been first class, he always maintained a position of ultimate disengagement. Was that just the pose of a very young man, he wondered? But John had rowed for his college, which must have required some commitment. Was there a girl beside him? He rather thought there was, smiling and laughing with an easy familiarity under a ridiculous hat. Was that his fiancée, the Bavarian girl? Had she ever come to England?

Just as Laurence was basking, content and almost hypnotised by the vibrations of the car, lulled by memories of summer and cool water, a bump in the road and a mutter from Charles startled him and instantly his mood plummeted. Of all of them, excited and noisy, it seemed that only he was left. That June, eating strawberries in the shade of pavilions or watching the dripping boats lifted from the river, such a thing would have seemed impossible. They were all so much *there*, so permanent in their world. He had occasionally wondered if it was actually he who was dead and excluded, while the others continued together, missing him from time to time, but busy somewhere else. Suddenly, surprisingly, his eyes stung and a desperate fear swept over him that he would weep, sitting in the front seat of Charles's car, travelling along autumn roads in England, and that if he did so he would be crying not for the dead but in terrible self-pity that things he'd enjoyed had been taken away. He lifted his head to the oncoming wind, glad that his smarting eyes were hidden.

They passed a flock of children coming out of a village school. Several girls in pinafores waved, while small boys in short trousers and boots shouted at the sight of the car. Charles hooted twice. Smoke rose from cottage chimneys. A dog ran out at them yapping and in danger of hurling itself under the wheels in its fury.

They came through Wolvescot, right on the border between Oxfordshire and Gloucestershire according to their map, and gathered speed going downhill between an avenue of trees. Charles jabbed his finger vigorously out of the side window and, leaning forward, Laurence could see some sort of tall, dark tower emerging from a dense copse on a nearby hill. There was something Gothic about it, isolated in the English countryside.

'The Folly,' Charles shouted. Laurence remembered it from

an outing at school; they must be nearer than he thought to the Wiltshire border.

The countryside became more undulating; the sun was almost directly in their faces, yet it was getting colder. Laurence pulled up his greatcoat collar around the scarf and sank lower in his seat. Charles had come up with the name of both an inn and a small hotel, suggested to him by friends.

They finally rolled into Fairford along a narrow street of honey-coloured, terraced houses. They passed the hotel, a tidy Georgian house, just as they came into a large market place and stopped. An inn, the Bull, occupied almost one full side of the square. Its low, mossy roof and small windows gave it an appearance of great age.

Charles stood by the car, looking from one establishment to the other. He pulled off his goggles; each eye was surrounded by a disc of white in his grimy face.

'Shall we try the inn first?' he asked, to Laurence's surprise. 'Village hostelry by the look of it; sort of place one might find oneself buying a drink for a local and picking up a bit of gossip. Hotels only have guests, strangers like us, nothing to be gained there.'

Not for the first time, Laurence looked at him in admiration.

As they walked into the dark, low interior of the inn, the landlord appeared, looking surprised, wiping his hands on his apron. Charles took a large, plain room with double windows overlooking the market square, while Laurence chose a much smaller bedroom with a beamed ceiling and a tiny fireplace, but a view towards the spire of Fairford church. A boy brought in their bags and they agreed to meet in half an hour.

After a while there was a knock on Laurence's door and a plump girl stood with a large jug of steaming water. 'D'you want the fire lighted?' she asked.

Laurence shook his head and took the jug from her. He heard the squeak of floorboards as she went downstairs. He hung his coat in a wardrobe that smelled strongly of camphor, then, stripping off his jacket, shirt and vest, poured the contents of the jug into the bowl on the washstand and leaned forward, steeping his arms halfway to his elbows. His skin tingled with the sudden heat.

Peering into the speckled glass over the basin, he realised that his face was as creased and filthy as Charles's – no wonder the landlord had looked surprised. He was quite stiff and weary, as if he'd had a day's exercise rather than a ride in a motor car. When he'd washed he lay down on the bed and pulled the eiderdown up over him for warmth. The bed sank deeply beneath him, softened by age; it reminded him of school where generations of boys had shaped the mattresses into hammocks. Under the feather pillow was a horsehair bolster.

He lay on his back, looking at a ceiling yellowed with age. With his ankles crossed and his hands on his chest, he was as still as an alabaster knight. All he needed was a small dog under his heels, he thought. He was drifting. The eiderdown became an ancient flag over the catafalque. He remembered a cathedral where his father had taken him as a child. Military colours and standards hung high in a side chapel, flag after flag, generation after generation: stained, torn, repaired and decayed. The lower ones were still dyed deep red and blue, and retained threads of tarnished gold; the highest had faded into soft, bone-coloured gauze, the distant regiments and battle honours that they represented as invisible as their mottoes had become. He must have been very small because his father had been holding his hand.

*

An insistent rapping at the door woke him.

'Laurence. Are you coming down?'

Laurence looked at his watch but had to strike a match to read it. He'd been asleep for nearly two hours. He swung his feet out of bed and pulled on his discarded jacket.

'God, Charles, I'm sorry. I must have just dropped off,' he said as he opened the door.

'Not a problem. I've been having a little look around, spoken to our landlord: font of wisdom, and he's happy to serve a simple dinner in the parlour. You dress and I'll see you downstairs in a quarter of an hour, say?'

'Yes. Of course. Sorry, just went out like a light,' Laurence said.

When the door closed he lit the lamp then scrabbled to find a clean shirt and socks. He peered in the glass again, damped down his hair and combed it through with his fingers. He hardly recognised the man with the deep lines round his eyes and a few first grey hairs. When had he got so old?

CHAPTER THIRTEEN

*D*ownstairs a coal fire burned in a back room which smelled of smoke and tar. Plates of cold tongue, chunks of fresh bread and some cheese had been set out on a table next to a stoneware jar of pickles.

'I hope the beer suits you,' Charles said. 'Local brew but the landlord assures me it's good.'

Laurence was ravenous and the food was much better than he'd expected. There was occasional laughter from elsewhere in the building but muffled by thick walls, and from time to time a heavy door slammed shut. Otherwise the only sound was of their knives scraping on the plates. The beer was as good as Charles promised and when the girl he'd seen earlier came in to take their plates and refill their tankards, he sat back, content.

'Nervous about tomorrow?' Charles asked.

'I expect I should be but in truth I'm quite curious.'

'See what you can extract for Miss Emmett?' Charles looked amused as he pulled out his tobacco pouch.

'Actually, it feels more as if I'm doing it for John himself and, less creditably, my own curiosity. But it's certainly because of Mary's suspicions about how the place was run. Eleanor Bolitho, too — she was pretty damning about these set-ups. Not that I can do a thing about it anyway.'

Charles was concentrating on tamping his pipe.

Laurence went on, 'It sounds terribly worthy, doesn't it? I really just want to get a look at these people.'

'You need to keep an open mind, that's all,' Charles said, slowly. 'Not because I personally doubt for a minute that things go on that would make your hair stand on end. In fact, from what I've heard, quite literally there's electric stuff and so on. Wouldn't be allowed on a chap in Wormwood Scrubs, yet their families empty their coffers for it.' He reached for the pickle jar. 'But what really bothers me is that you're not a very good actor. Never were. Seriously, old chap. Think you're so British, sang-froid and so on, when really your face is an open book. When you go in and meet Dr Caligari, you've got to be believing they might help Reginald.'

'Robert.'

'Just testing you.' Charles continued, unperturbed, 'Take the embarrassment of the unhinged Bertie Bartram off your hands. Possibly even make him better. Return him to the bosom of his relieved family. Or keep him safely out of it. You've got to look as if you hope they can work miracles, not as if you suspect them of negligence at best and atrocities at worst. You've got to forget everything those girls told you. I mean you're dealing with mind doctors. They'll be on to you in a minute. Well, half an hour, certainly. Probably charge you two guineas to boot.'

'Thank you,' Laurence said simply.

'Still,' Charles said after a moment's pause while he sawed an inch-thick slice of bread off the loaf, 'they're not entirely popular in Fairford by all accounts.'

'The landlord?' Laurence guessed.

'Well, I only had a brief chat. Explained we were down here to find a place for your brother, stricken war hero and all that. Turns out he — our landlord — was at Mons same time as my lot, and lost a nephew in the Glosters. Main gripe seems to be that Master Caligari — what is the man's name?'

'If you mean the son, it's George Chilvers.'

'Yes, well, young Chilvers didn't fight. He had been a keen cricketer, so was apparently healthy, and he's not a medic himself, so no reserved status. Bad feeling all round especially as most of the lads in these parts fought together and took a drubbing in '17.'

'But that doesn't mean that Holmwood itself is suspect,' Laurence said.

'No,' Charles conceded. 'Apparently one of the older attendants who made it back lost an arm. Worked at Holmwood before the war, when it was a place for mad gentlefolk — men and women. Came home, hero's welcome, medal, expected to get his place back as Dr C had promised, but young Chilvers laid him off three months later while Pa was away. Said he couldn't pull his weight. He — the ex-employee — believes he was got rid of because he didn't approve of young Chilvers' marriage.'

'But why on earth should a warder have an opinion, or anyone care if he did, about his employer's marriage plans?'

'Because, old chap, it seems that Chilvers married a wealthy heiress.'

'And so?' There was obviously more to come.

'And she had been a patient at Holmwood. That's how Chilvers Junior met her. She'd tried to kill herself.' Charles couldn't keep a triumphant note out of his voice. Laurence was astonished that he'd managed to keep this juicy morsel of gossip to himself for so long.

'Well, you were obviously a lot more alert after our drive than I was.'

'I'm hoping to find out more tomorrow. Our man, the disgruntled warder, usually comes in for a drink on Wednesday lunchtime. He's bringing a friend who still works there. So I plan to be in the bar with a generous wallet while you are interrogating the Chilverses.'

Despite sleeping so deeply before dinner, Laurence was pleasantly tired when he got back to his room. A small fire was burning and the thin curtains had been drawn, the water bowl emptied and his bed straightened. He opened the window a little, slipped between the cold sheets and slept until morning when he woke with an aching bladder and, loath to use the chamber pot, went briskly downstairs, the linoleum cold under his feet. On the way back up he crossed with Charles going downstairs with equal urgency.

Half an hour later after a agreeably silent meal of thick bacon, dark-yolked eggs and blood-pudding, they planned Laurence's day.

'Got the wind up yet?' asked Charles hopefully.

'Not really. Either I get some information or at least a general feel for the place or I make a complete fool of myself, get away quickly and never have to see them again.'

'Or they could take you for a maniac and strap you into a straitjacket,' Charles said benignly. 'But although the locals may grumble, the place is quite well thought of by the nobs. Landlord, the wonderfully named Cyril Trusty, by the way, tells me that they've had various scions of the great and good tucked up in there. Lord Verey's heir for a start, and the son of a bishop, though Trusty can't remember which one. Not much of a man for matters theological, our landlord.'

'And where do all these pillars of the establishment stand on shell-shock, then?'

'Well, I don't think Verey's been giving speeches in the Lords,' Charles said. 'Probably not too keen for the world to know the heir's of unsound mind.'

Laurence decided to walk up to Holmwood. It lay on the edge of the small town, the landlord had told them, sketching out a pencil map.

'You'll know it when you see it,' said Cyril Trusty. 'High walls and spikes on top. To stop them scarpering. Impale 'em instead. Doesn't look as old as it is. Bits added on. Solid. Paid a fortune to install proper asylum locks just before the war. Had to get a man from London. Ordinary locks won't do for lunatics. Ingenious type, your madman, they say.'

Chapter Fourteen

*L*aurence's appointment was at eleven and he set off along the riverbank with a quarter of an hour to spare. Where the path reached some water meadows he looked back to see the fine church standing on higher ground. It reminded him that the churchyard at Fairford was the last place anyone had admitted to seeing John Emmett. Which way had he gone then, Laurence wondered? Not across the meadows, obviously, as that would have led him straight back towards Holmwood, the direction he was taking now. Not due east, as he could see a wide river and no sign of a bridge. And if he'd turned down into the market place, along the main road and towards the station, surely he would have been identified, if not as himself, certainly as an outsider: a patient. Beyond the church lay farmland as far as Laurence could see, with a few stands of beech and a Dutch barn right on the horizon. John must have headed that way.

Presumably the main service on Christmas Day was Matins. John's disappearance could have been discovered no later than midday, once the church party got back to Holmwood at the latest, though the youth he'd stunned in order to escape must surely have raised the alert before then. That left three to four hours or so of decent daylight to look for him. But it also meant that John would soon have needed shelter.

Could he have known anyone in the area? Could someone have come to fetch him? It would have needed a car. Branch-line trains ran a reduced service on Christmas Day and, anyway, he was sure the police and Holmwood people would have checked at the station. But in concentrating on how, he was no nearer knowing why. Where was John going so determinedly and who could he have persuaded to help him if that was what he'd done? And why hadn't that person come forward?

He had a sense that he was almost on to something when the sight of what he guessed were the closed gates of Holmwood distracted him. A large iron bell pull was set in the wall beside a small nameplate. He couldn't see Cyril Trusty's promised spikes but he noticed that the small upper windows, at least, were barred like a prison. The rooms up there must be dark, he thought. The building he was approaching was tall and square, its roof shallow and, unusually for the area, he noted, of slate rather than Cotswold stone. That added to its slightly sombre appearance but the man who opened one gate a minute or so later had a perfectly pleasant expression on his face.

'Mr Bartram?'

He stood back to let Laurence through. Inside, an oval of grass was studded with a few fallen crab apples. A cream Bentley was pulled up by steps to the front door. It was one of the few cars Laurence could recognise. He thought of Charles, who was able to identify anything on wheels at any distance and by any visible part. Charles would love this car. Perhaps one of the eminent parents was visiting a son?

'Could you come this way, sir?'

A gravelled drive wound away behind a shrubbery but they were heading to a pillared porch on the left.

'Sorry.' Laurence caught up. 'Just admiring the motor car.'

'Mr George's car,' said his guide. 'He's a great man for cars. Dr Chilvers now, he still takes the trap if it's fine, but Mr George loves a beautiful bit of machinery.'

They came into a half-panelled hall. Stained glass in the door filtered a wash of colour on to the stone floor but the space was mostly lit by a skylight three storeys above. The building was absolutely quiet, smelling of beeswax and, faintly, of cooking. It took Laurence back instantly to his prep school. Wide stairs curved up to a landing while several doors led off the hall. The man knocked at the nearest one and opened it without waiting for a response. The room he entered was a large, book-lined study, a room to receive guests rather than treat patients.

Dr Chilvers looked more the rural doctor than hospital physician. Dressed in a shapeless country suit, he was a spare man in his sixties, his hair sandy grey and wavy above a pale, almost waxy face. As he stepped forward his eyes held Laurence's. His handshake was firm. The doctor's demeanour was presumably intended to put Laurence at ease but, perhaps because he was here under false pretences, Laurence felt decidedly on edge.

'Come in, come in.'

Chilvers indicated an upright leather chair, then sat down himself behind a wide and tidy desk.

'You came up last night? Stayed at the Regent? It's comfortable enough and the owner is a good man. Used to work for us, in fact, but took on the hotel when his late father became ill.'

'Actually, I'm at the Bull.'

Chilvers looked surprised. 'The Bull?' he said, as if, although he recalled it, it was an effort to remember where it was. 'Well, there's not much alternative, when the Regent is full, I suppose. We do have a couple of guest rooms here but we tend to keep them for family. Of patients, that is. Especially ladies travelling alone or where a visit seems likely to be distressing.'

Laurence nodded.

'Did you come by train?' Chilvers asked.

'No. I motored down with a friend.'

'Quite so. Quite so.'

Again Laurence had the feeling that it would have been better to have conformed to expectations.

'You're here about your brother,' Dr Chilvers said in a slightly brisker tone of voice. He put on his spectacles and pulled over a sheaf of paper from the right-hand side of his desk. The first page was blank.

'I should tell you at the outset that at present we have no room at all. We take a maximum of eight patients. This permits us to give highly specialised care, adapted – I think I may say with confidence, very finely adapted – to individual patients' needs. However, I would anticipate a vacancy, possibly two, in the very near future. One patient returning home. Very much improved. The other into longer-term convalescent care. We could be looking at –' He reached for a large morocco leather diary, opened it, leafed through a few pages. 'Certainly before New Year. Late December, I would imagine. Would that be suitable?'

Chilvers evidently mistook for something else Laurence's look of alarm at the conversation's swift and specific direction, because he continued, 'Of course we haven't discussed your brother or what we could do to assist his condition, but I feel it is important not to hold out any false hopes for an immediate solution.' His eyes met Laurence's. 'Families come to me, some accustomed through rank or wealth to resolving a problem with some immediacy. But in these cases a swift and satisfactory outcome is not always possible. Despair is not susceptible to the usual processes of society. It is not just those who enter here but their families who may find their circumstances have very much changed. We help them all adapt.'

Chilvers had made this speech before, Laurence was sure. He nodded again, then he found himself saying aloud what he was thinking. 'It sometimes feels as if the fixed points have moved. It's as if we can't be sure how things might fit together any more.'

He spoke quite urgently and stopped, suddenly embarrassed, but Chilvers did not seem to find it odd.

'I think the essential aspects of human nature remain unchanged,' the doctor responded. 'Love, fear, jealousy, indolence, opportunism, hope — even nobility of spirit — but the relationship of one to another may have altered; some aspects may have moved to the fore, others have receded. Of course for every man whose response is to tread carefully, recalculating those fixed points,' he paused and looked at Laurence, 'others abandon it all and live lives of remarkable recklessness.

'It seems to me,' he continued, 'that one might argue that man has evolved to be a warrior; indeed, few generations have escaped that role. Of course, I was not there,' he gave a respectful nod to Laurence, 'but I judge, from speaking at length to many of the recent war's more invisibly injured, that what was hard for them was a lack of clarity — in orders, aims, even as to whether engagements had been won or lost, and the constant anticipation of random catastrophe. The realisation that the traditional skills of the top-class fighting man — strength, courage, dexterity with his weapon and so on – might not be rewarded, not even by a heroic death, but rather, that a man's fate depended almost entirely on the inequities of fortune. It exploded profound understandings of what it meant to be a soldier.'

Laurence stared out of the window where crimson Virginia creeper blocked a full view of what was obviously a lawn beyond. After a matter of probably a few seconds but which felt like several minutes, Chilvers seemed to throw him a lifeline:

'Have you read your Homer?'

'At school.' However, he'd known men who had their Homer with them on the battlefield. He'd heard less talk of Homer's inspirational qualities as the war ground on.

'*The Iliad* gives us an impeccable account of battlefield injuries. No machine-guns, no tanks, no aeroplanes, but the injuries themselves – those ancient and terrible descriptions – and their prognoses, are absolutely accurate. Injuries to the brain, piercing wounds to the liver, known even then to doom the afflicted. But what does Homer not show us?' Laurence knew no answer was expected and Chilvers moved on without pausing for one: 'The casualties die swiftly, if dramatically, and at the end of each day the living usually retrieve their dead, then get back to a campfire and their comrades. No mention of mutilation or lifelong physical disability there. No shellshock.'

Laurence finally found his voice. 'There wasn't much mention of all that in *The Times*, either.'

Chilvers gave a dry laugh, dispersing the intensity. 'True, but then *The Times* was for fathers and commanders of earlier wars: the mouthpiece and the vindication of the establishment. *The Times* was information, *The Iliad* a celebration. *The Iliad* was a romance stiffened by historical fact. *The Times* was fact with fiction as emollient.

'You'd be surprised at how many men I see, men who thought war would be something like Troy. Not the regulars, of course; they were emotionally better suited to the stresses of conflict, and not so much the conscripted, who were either resigned or resentful. But in the volunteer there is shock, bewilderment, even a sense of betrayal. They couldn't compare their war to the Zulu wars, not that half-naked men with spears didn't have a trick or two to teach them. The Boer War was fought against God-fearing farmers, not a proper army, and, anyway, we won. Their grandfathers could have told them a thing or two about conditions in the Crimea, but many of those old combatants were never able to speak of it at all. So these young men go off with a few weeks of basic training, and three thousand years of Homer in their pockets and, more dangerously, in their heads and, in every sense of the phrase, they come to grief. When they get home, reeling with Homer's deceptions, the *Times* readers at the breakfast table tell them they've got it all wrong.'

All those barely contained arguments he'd had with Louise and her parents, Laurence thought, with him trying to control a degree of anger and exhaustion which they didn't deserve. They had no idea. Any of them.

'In this war,' Chilvers said, 'men weren't fighting for the King or for Britain and certainly not for "little Belgium", but for apple blossom in a Kentish orchard or the smell of caulking ships on the Tyne, or the comradeship of a Rhondda pithead. Men find it easier to risk their lives for provincial loyalties.'

'Or because they have no option,' Laurence said. It was odd, though not unpleasant, to find himself on the receiving end of a well-honed lecture, but he could hear a note of bitterness in his own voice. 'And they returned to find that the things they thought they were fighting for suddenly seemed hopelessly sentimental and irrelevant.'

Chilvers made no reply and Laurence continued, brusquely, 'I didn't join myself until late 1915, when I could see conscription was imminent.' He felt ashamed for lying unnecessarily.

He failed to say that the circumstances which led him to do so began when when, after a single, clumsy sexual encounter — his first — which he thought Louise had found distasteful and which she certainly tried her hardest to avoid ever afterwards, she had become pregnant. Perhaps it had damaged their relationship more than it had their prospects. They were engaged at the time and he was working for her father. He could not tell Louise, much less her furious mother, how much he had wanted her: the curve of her lip, the fine bones of her ankles in white stockings, the womanly smell of the back of her neck, under the weight of her pinned-up hair, so different from the flowery perfume she wore or the hot linen scent of her dress. Feeling her under him, as he pressed deep inside her, he had felt complete. Neither Louise's obvious discomfort, nor even his own dawning shame could diminish the deep joy of it. As a result, they simply brought forward their marriage, but she miscarried soon afterwards. Having married her, he swiftly felt an appalling need to escape.

For the first months he was amused, watching her set up the small but handsome house bought with her family funds. As the countries of Europe issued ultimatums and mobilised their armies, he looked on as she chose curtains and furniture with her mother, selected a housemaid or a lapdog, played the piano and invited her friends round. All the while he had a sense of his life becoming immeasurably smaller. He knew his own horizons were not vast when he met Louise and he disliked himself for being unable to enjoy her complete happiness in making them both a home. She was not even particularly demanding; there was simply an implicit invitation for him to admire her domestic skills. He had acquiesced in everything.

His first positive, independent action in marriage had been to lie to her and tell her he had received his papers. They had been married just eighteen months. She never knew that he had volunteered.

So he had gone and, despite the news coming in from the front, he sat on the train to Dover almost exhilarated at the opportunity of war. All that followed had seemed entirely merited by this first act of treachery.

'You were working until then?' Chilvers asked, breaking into his daydream.

'In my father-in-law's business. My wife is dead,' Laurence added quickly to cut off any possible question.

'I am sorry,' Chilvers said, and paused.

After some seconds he spoke again.

'But we must speak of your brother.' He took out his pen and wrote down the details of the fictional Robert's name, date of birth. 'You said in your recent letter that he had been in a sanatorium in Switzerland and that his own doctor has died, so I assume you have no access to his records? Never mind, sometimes it is easier to come to these cases without preconceptions. I am sure we can track them down if we need them, but military medical records are, I have found, lamentably inadequate.'

Laurence felt a lessening of tension. One major hurdle had been cleared easily.

'Regiment?'

It had taken Charles and Laurence some time over the previous week to place Robert in a suitable regiment. 'Instant pitfall, this,' Charles had said. 'You can count on someone's cousin having been in the same outfit, however obscure it might be, and that same cousin being clapped up in Holmwood. You know how it is with cousins?'

Laurence had no cousins but through Charles had observed their mysterious degree of social penetration.

'And for God's sake keep him out of the Artists' Rifles; being mad is practically a prerequisite for joining.'

In the end Charles had suggested an empire regiment. 'That's where a lot of oddballs ended up.' They had debated the merits of the Canadian and South African Expeditionary Forces.

'Anyway, Chilvers was far too old for service, even as a medic,' Laurence had said, 'and his son was never a soldier, and Holmwood's a tiny place, and it's not as if the existing patients have a committee of acceptance. It's not White's, Charles.'

He was finding that dissembling was moving from a necessity to something approaching a game with someone to share it with. Charles had given him a long, appraising look.

'Queen Victoria's Own Madras Sappers and Miners,' Laurence now said confidently to Chilvers.

'Do you have a connection with India?'

'Yes,' said Laurence. 'At least my sister — *our* sister — lives out there with her family.' It was strange to be telling the truth, briefly.

'And you have other siblings?'

'No.'

'Parents?'

'Both dead.'

Chilvers wrote carefully, his expression attentive. Laurence tried to ignore a pang of guilt.

'Your brother is unmarried?'

'Yes.'

'This must be quite a burden for you,' Chilvers observed matter-of-factly. 'The sole responsibility for an invalid is never easy.'

'I have an aunt,' Laurence said. He needed the aunt to provide a place where Robert was currently domiciled.

'Any illnesses before the war?' he asked.

'We both survived diphtheria as children,' Laurence said, letting the imaginary brother share his infections. 'Otherwise just childhood diseases.' He was becoming more relaxed, soothed by the anodyne questions.

'Any sign of previous mental instability? In your brother's case or with any other family member?'

Laurence was briefly surprised; it was not as if shell-shock was hereditary.

'No.'

They went on to discuss Robert's general background and then his present condition and treatment, all mapped out for Laurence by Eleanor Bolitho. Laurence had learned it by heart and hoped it didn't sound too pat.

'I should warn you,' said the doctor, 'not to expect miracles and not to be disappointed if there are setbacks. What we sometimes see is that when a patient is taken out of his usual environment to this place where there are few expectations of him, least of all to be the man he once was, and with our regime, good food, plenty of rest and encouragement to move beyond his war experiences, he visibly improves, sometimes quite fast. Splendid for his loved ones, of course. But sometimes the cost of dismantling the habits he may have assembled to help him bear the unbearable – abandoning him unarmed, as it were, to confront his memories – may leave him vulnerable. We've had men who arrive here refusing to sleep, or who never speak. We have men who compulsively follow exact and occasionally quite outlandish routines: who won't remove soiled clothes or bathe. One, I recall, kept his ears plugged with wool and Vaseline jelly. All of these protections are barriers; all serve to keep them as solitaries. We try to equip a man with better ways to confront the terrors he suffers but there is nevertheless a dangerous period of raw, unprotected insight.

'There was a mother once whom I particularly recall; her son came in as a living body inhabited by a dead man. He lay in the dark, mute, apparently unhearing, curled up, facing the wall. He responded to neither heat nor cold, pinprick, bright light nor sudden noise. To be honest, I thought it was a hopeless case. He was very frail: his temperature was always abnormally low, his pulse slow; we wrapped him in blankets and hot-water bottles, and we chafed his hands. We fed him by tube.

'We did everything for this patient. My son urged me to have him removed to a larger, probably more permanent institution, but his mother begged me to keep him. She didn't want him moved again. She sat there, stroking him, talking to him. About his dog, about fishing. She brought the seasons into the room: leaves fell, snow drifted, corn ripened in the fields, the pond at home dried up, the barley was gathered in, the wind brought down an old barn. She continually changed the photographs by his bed. She put books there for him, which she selected carefully and replaced every so often. Sometimes they were children's picture books, some were boys' adventure stories. One was about Captain Scott's expedition, I recollect.

'And slowly, over months and months, he improved. Astonishingly, he improved. His senses came back. His wits came back. He began to eat, to talk, to read and to smile when he saw his mother. To remember. Eventually she suggested he should be allowed home for a weekend and we agreed. He cut his throat in his mother's bed on his first evening back. He wrote one line to say he simply couldn't live with his memories. His mother told me she sometimes wished he'd been killed outright in Flanders or that she'd accepted him as he was before we treated him.'

Chilvers was obviously still moved by the case. He looked drawn and tired. Laurence felt uncomfortable, hearing this tragic account in response to his own lies.

Chilvers took off his spectacles and started to polish them. 'In a little while, I shall get my son to escort you round the premises and explain a little of how we treat such cases as you go along. I find that is usually the most effective way of covering all the possibilities.' He rang a small bell. 'But in the meantime, no doubt you have questions of your own?'

Laurence struggled to articulate the apparently innocent but potentially fruitful enquiries he'd planned with first Eleanor and then Charles's help, and the questions that he felt Chilvers would expect him to ask if he really had a brother in need of care. For reasons he could not put his finger on, their discussion had unsettled him. He also knew that he had come prepared for a charlatan, even a sadist, and Chilvers, although perhaps a little certain in his ideas, was neither. Confronted with Chilvers' insights, and given that the man had naturally enough heard plenty of stories of war from his patients, Laurence was acutely aware that it was he who was in fact the impostor.

'By the way,' the doctor said, 'I wondered how you heard of us. I assume it was a personal recommendation?'

Laurence flailed. 'Yes.' Could he name the Emmetts? Would the family of a runaway suicide have suggested he put his brother in the same institution? Suddenly a conversation he'd had yesterday came to him.

'It might have been Lord Verey, I think. I met him at a dinner. For charity,' he improvised. 'And I mentioned Robert only towards the end.'

The room was silent. Laurence thought that he probably cut an implausible figure as a dining companion for the great and good.

Then the doctor said slowly, 'As I believe I mentioned earlier, we are always discreet, but I think Lieutenant Verey's case — a very sad situation — could be considered one of our successes. His physical injuries were so severe that I thought at first his state of mind was entirely contingent on those limitations. It was also obvious that he would need virtually full-time nursing care and I had some doubts as to whether he would be suitable for Holmwood at all. We pursue quite . . . *vigorous* treatment here and to have cases that are not susceptible to any kind of improvement is bad for the morale of the others, quite apart from taking up a bed that might be better used by another. But his lordship was very insistent — perhaps at that stage he felt a confidence only a father could — and he was happy to support the hiring of extra nursing staff. Young Verey improved more than I could ever have hoped.'

Before Laurence could respond, and while he was still trying to disguise his relief that his improvisation had succeeded, there was a knock on the door and a man, probably in his middle thirties, came in. Though the newcomer was slimmer and lighter-haired than Dr Chilvers, the similarity was such that Laurence realised it must be his son. There was a certain formality in their response to each other but presumably that was because Laurence was there.

'George,' the doctor said. 'This is Captain Bartram.'

Laurence shook hands with George Chilvers. Even-featured

and of average build, he was as handsome as had been reported and in a way Laurence suspected would be attractive to women. His reddish-gold hair was slicked to a sheen and his trim figure was enhanced by expensive tailoring.

'Perhaps you could show Captain Bartram around?' the older man suggested. 'After that, we might meet to discuss any further questions he might have.'

They moved into the hall. A slight man in his twenties was crossing it from one room to another. His trousers were so loose, Laurence noticed instantly, that they had been gathered in deep folds and were held up by an old tie used as a belt. The man stopped when he saw them and started to go back into the room he had just left. Doctor Chilvers moved towards him and placed a reassuring hand on his arm, nodding towards his son and Laurence. Laurence observed Chilvers' firm but comforting demeanour: while he talked, he kept his hand gently where it had lain and looked the man in the eye. Eventually the younger man smiled slightly and glanced at Laurence.

'How do you do?' he said softly and then hurried into the next doorway.

CHAPTER FIFTEEN

*L*aurence was surprised how exhausted he felt when he got back to the Bull. If he had been able to admit his real interest to Chilvers, he felt the doctor could undoubtedly have helped him. Except that if he had mentioned John, Chilvers would probably have disappeared behind a screen of professional reticence. Seeing the place had been helpful and fairly reassuring, but Chilvers' own perceptions had both disturbed and moved him.

A couple of hours later, he and Charles were exchanging information: his incomplete impressions for Charles's more substantial progress.

'Well, apart from the fact that our disgruntled one-armed friend and his chum could drink both of us under the table, it's been a useful exchange, ale for ill-will. I was glad when the landlord called time, though,' Charles said. 'But to start with: there's something his sister either didn't know or didn't tell you. Emmett was front man on a firing squad. Dr Chilvers told the coroner that his patient had been very troubled by the execution.'

'Neither Mary nor her mother attended the inquest,' Laurence said. He was certain Mary had no idea. 'But, God, poor man.' He'd known one young officer who was ashamed that he'd faked illness to get out of presiding over a firing squad but, as the subaltern said, he would have felt ashamed either way.

'And another odd thing,' Charles remembered. 'This was probably just a straightforward bit of trouble-making but the sacked employee commented in passing that given that one of Emmett's main symptoms was paralysis of the right arm, it was strange that he'd managed to shoot himself with it.'

Laurence sat forward. 'Are you sure?' Although the symptom tied in with what he already knew.

'Sure he said it, sure Emmett had it or sure that he was naturally right-handed? All three. I can remember him on the cricket pitch. Good bowler. Chilvers' evidence stated that Emmett's right arm was useless. Police surgeon was equally certain that he couldn't have done it with his left. Perhaps because it would have been the wrong angle? Anyway, my man had been involved in the treatment, which at the subtler end was a matter of trying to trick John into forgetting his arm didn't work: handing him a book, or whatever came to mind. They tried tying his other hand behind his back for days at a time, and, at the more dramatic end, giving him electric shocks to stimulate the muscles.'

Laurence grimaced.

Charles said ghoulishly, 'Regular Dr Frankenstein. Are you sure you didn't see wires?' But he didn't wait for an answer. 'Strangely, he'd shot himself through the heart, not the head.'

'Less messy. Definitely no letter?'

'Nothing much at all, I think. I did ask. A few bits and pieces and our jolly old school scarf near by. Faithful till death and all that. Neatly folded. Coroner saw the deliberation as evidence of intent. Removed it to be sure of his shot. Much what you'd expect except for no note. Damn hard on the family, not having a letter. I suppose they got the scarf. Not much consolation.'

'It wasn't Marlborough colours actually – Mary showed it to me – and hardly his sort of thing anyway, I'd have said. But where was he between-times?'

Charles shrugged. 'There were any number of barns and outhouses he could have holed up in until the hue and cry had died down, they say. They reckoned if John could have got hold of some food, he could have survived a week or two before he emerged and sauntered off to get a train. Perhaps not from Fairford, where they'd probably circulated his picture, but from a neighbouring village perhaps.'

'Do you know exactly where they found him?'

'The Folly. On the hill. We passed it yesterday. I pointed it out – at Faringdon. Well, obviously we all knew it from school.'

The location came as a shock. Folly Wood had been such a strange place, always in shadow. But it made it much more likely that John had gone there of his own volition. Why was it more painful to think of him seeking out somewhere familiar to end it all, Laurence wondered? He thought of the young Holmwood patient who had died in his mother's bed. Was that a last frenzied act of rage or a final refuge in the safest place he knew?

'Frankly, when I realised both the degree of disaffection even in the man currently employed there, and the fact that we are never likely to be coming back, since I for one would certainly choose an alternative therapeutic establishment if I were to suddenly believe that I was Napoleon Bonaparte,' Charles said, 'I came clean, or cleanish. That's when I learned some interesting facts about Emmett's time there. Most interesting of all, he had visitors. An army friend and two members of the family.'

'"Army friend" could be anybody,' Laurence said, although he recalled that Mary had given the impression he had few left. 'And Mary visited, but I thought that his mother stayed away.'

Charles lowered his voice, although the room was empty. 'Yes, Mary did visit. In fact, *two* sisters did. More than once.' He paused. 'One was dark-haired and cross, though a bit of a looker, as the man who still works there tells it: presumably your Miss Emmett; and the other was red-haired and crosser.'

'Eleanor Bolitho?' said Laurence, astonished, simultaneously realising that there could be any number of redheads in John's life.

'That's my guess,' said Charles. 'Do you think it's true that redheads always have tempers?'

'Charles,' Laurence butted in, 'when did these so-called sisters come, did you ask him that?'

'It *was* Eleanor,' said Charles, 'because one time she brought her boy with her. Moreover, in addition to my deductive guesswork, and though both girls gave their name as Emmett, our man overheard John saying his fond farewells and he called her Elly. He remembered thinking it was a rather sweet, feminine name quite at odds with her personality.'

Laurence laughed. 'What had she done?'

'Well, the only thing she approved of was the food, I gather. Demanded that arrangements should be made for John to be accompanied on daily walks, if they weren't prepared to let him out on his own. She took him out once but they wouldn't allow it the other time she visited. Dr Chilvers was away and they needed his permission, they said. She was impressively furious and all else followed. She inspected the library and declared it inadequate. Was incensed that all the patients well enough were made to go on church parade. Harangued Chilvers Junior about John's room; he had been moved to one of the barred ones. She said he was hardly likely to jump out, although my man pointed out, with a certain degree of satisfaction, that jumping out, in a manner of speaking, was exactly what he did when he got the chance. But she was angriest of all to hear that John had been put in close confinement simply for leaving the building without permission. Close to tears in her fury, apparently.'

'They were right too about not letting him out alone,' said Laurence. 'Though, in fact it was churchgoing that was to give him the chance to escape. So perhaps the Holmwood people knew him better than she did.' He kept to himself Eleanor's assurance that she had not met John after the war. 'And actually, I found Dr Chilvers quite impressive. 'It was the son I took a dislike to.'

'Even my complainant says the old man's a decent chap, dedicated to his patients, if a bit on the zealous side. But he's not well, goes up to London for treatment. Probably a hopeless case, he reckons. Says the doctor's lost stones in the last year. It's when he goes away that young Chilvers gets to impose his stamp on the place: changes treatment, sacks people at will. The old man rarely stands up to him. And of course the staff know it will all be his when his father shuffles off his mortal, so they mostly toe the line. Not many jobs in these parts.'

Laurence thought that if he'd been less focused on his own deceptions, he would have guessed Chilvers was ill from his pallor and thinness.

Charles was gaining momentum. 'And he was shot with a Luger.'

Laurence looked up, sharply. 'Well, that should have made

it easier,' he said. 'To track down, I mean. Not many of those in circulation. No recuperating German officers in Holmwood. Plenty of our lot got hold of them but it was a side arm for the flashy type.'

'I had a Luger,' said Charles, after a momentary pause. 'Still have, in fact.'

'How?' said Laurence and immediately wished he hadn't.

'I captured it.' His eyes caught Laurence's momentarily. 'Off a dragoon Hauptman to be precise. I was a good shot, it was the best side arm around and I was keen to live.'

'But did John have a Luger – or any gun at all?'

'All the witnesses thought not. But they would, wouldn't they?'

There was a long silence.

'You're still thinking he wasn't the Luger type,' said Charles.

Laurence didn't answer. He was thinking that George Chilvers was precisely the sort of man who would have a Luger, had he not been the sort of man who avoided military service completely, but he felt irritated with himself for both pointless thoughts.

'Well, lots of us weren't the type for lots of things, but we changed,' said Charles.

There was another, longer silence.

'In fact the records showed he'd turned in a perfectly regulation Webley at the end of the war. It came up at the inquest, of course. Which was in Oxford, by the way. Doesn't mean he hadn't acquired anything else, though. But what did you make of the place? How do they fix them up?' Charles looked hopeful.

'Straightforward, really,' Laurence said, thinking back. 'Dr Chilvers believes routine splints the broken mind in the same way that a splint holds a broken leg.' He realised he was quoting him almost verbatim. 'They have to get up at the same time each day, they have to take meals. They're allowed a short rest after lunch, otherwise they're not allowed to return to their rooms and sleep during the day. Chilvers said this is partly to counteract the insomnia that's a major problem. Church on Sundays.'

Thinking of church brought him back to Eleanor's complaints.

'Chilvers said he didn't care whether they believed in God or not.' He remembered this clearly, because it seemed quite a worldly view from an otherwise old-fashioned man. 'He said it was good for them to have the pattern established. They have to confront the outside world – some of them have huge problems with people, apparently – and church services give an opportunity for this within a familiar context. And he said they didn't really have enough to do on Sundays. 'A bit of a walk and some singing is good for them; it's all exercise, in its way, Chilvers had said.'

'Not surprisingly one or two are quite angry with God, but, as a general principle, we like to have these things out at Holmwood,' the doctor had added. He had been close to a smile, Laurence had thought.

Charles was uncharacteristically silent.

'There's a ward, I suppose you call it, holding two men at present, for those whose physical condition is poor,' Laurence continued. 'Some patients are injured, but young Chilvers explained that some melancholics simply cease to eat. Here they are fed and treated for physical illnesses before they get the mind stuff. These two both looked pretty sick to me. One had a tube taped to his cheek. I couldn't wait to get out of there, to be honest.

'Apart from that, it was like any officers' convalescent home.

Piano, comfortable drawing room, newspapers, though Dr Chilvers told me earlier that occasionally they withheld these if current events were likely to distress occupants. A small library; actually I didn't think it looked too bad, though I didn't do an inventory of the titles.' He smiled at the thought of Eleanor's inspection. 'Tennis court. A couple of inmates helped with the garden from time to time, young Chilvers said. Found it calming. Both Chilverses referred to treatment rooms, but I was shown only one. It has a bath, water nozzles, sitz baths, hydrotherapy, all rather old-fashioned, it seemed to me.'

'My man says they have all the latest electrical stuff,' Charles interrupted, 'though I suppose they don't want to frighten a potential paying customer.'

Laurence remembered that Eleanor had talked of electric shocks being given to those with false paralysis of limbs. She talked as if it were fairly standard.

'I really didn't see anything like that. Sorry, Charles. But what was interesting is that young Chilvers told me that all comforts were withheld for what he called "misbehaviour". They have to earn them. And there's a secure floor: the top floor, where patients in a state of agitation are confined. The windows were barred, I noticed, from the outside. Presumably that's where John was incarcerated. I was shown only an empty room on the second floor, made up ready for a new arrival. Nice enough.'

'Why not keep them downstairs if they think they're going to leap out?'

'I suppose downstairs they could escape more easily?'

'Did they say anything about suicide to you?' Charles asked.

'Well, only in a general way. I mean, for God's sake, Charles, I could hardly interrogate them on their failures. Young Chilvers said that it had happened, though very rarely, in the twenty years that Dr Chilvers had been running the place. It seemed rude to ask what "very rarely" meant in numbers.'

He had been quite pleased with how he'd raised the question of his fictional brother's threats of suicide. George Chilvers hadn't looked particularly surprised.

'Six,' said Charles.

'Six?'

'Suicides. Four since the war. One other was actually just discharged, and one was before the war, but, listen to this: that one was a girl of twenty. She got out somehow, lay down on the tracks just outside Fairford Station and waited for some hapless train driver to chop her in three. Her family asked for a post-mortem, which the coroner granted, and, as it turned out, she was five months pregnant.'

'Was that why she was depressed?'

'It might be why she killed herself but it wasn't why she was melancholic in the first place. She'd been admitted eight months earlier. Nearly a scandal, certainly there were nasty rumours. Staff reckoned she was sweet on young Chilvers; a single man then, of course. One female nurse – now dismissed – had said Chilvers had been found with the naked patient in a bathroom. He was using a high-pressure hose on her: she was soaked and squealing. Chilvers insisted it was treatment for hysteria. A different attendant, who went up to check her room when the alarm was first raised, says he saw a letter addressed to Chilvers in an envelope on her desk. At that point, naturally, nobody knew she was dead, but when he went back to check later, no letter.'

As there had been no letter after John's death, Laurence thought, though the incidents must have been years apart.

'My man said that "these sort of letters" seldom helped

anybody anyway,' Charles went on. 'They were just self-pity. "The same old stuff they were on about every day," he said.'

'Did people really think George Chilvers was the father of the dead woman's child?' said Laurence. 'Or is that just a sacked man's bitterness?'

'I think they did. Though apparently some said Chilvers Senior could have drugged her to have his way with her. But probably that was black humour. He's a widower, has been for years. Married to the job. All the same, it had to be someone from inside; she never left the place, and George Chilvers already had a bit of reputation as a lady's man. Mad ladies. Sad ladies. I got the impression that his eventual marriage to another patient was not so much for the money but forced upon him by his old man to prevent a further scandal.' He paused. 'Well-made chap, from all accounts – well, the account I got.'

'I suppose he's handsome enough in his way,' said Laurence. 'But patients? Surely he could find someone who wouldn't put his reputation at so much risk?'

'Well, he's not a doctor like Papa, so I suppose he could get away with it. Perhaps he's attracted to highly strung girls. Young ones. Lonely. Rich. Can't have been difficult.'

'Yet he is a solicitor, and you said Cyril Trusty seemed to think they'd done well out of a couple of bequests, but then I suppose doctors do, don't they? Quite often?'

'Except the clientele must be rather younger than the run-of-the-mill spinsters of a practice in Bognor Regis. The Holmwood patients wouldn't be expected to die in the normal run of things,' Charles said, 'though one of my Bognor great-aunts was quite mad. Great-Aunt Caroline. She should have been locked away, without any question. Would have saved a mass of trouble.'

He absent-mindedly tore off a piece of bread and soaked it in his beer.

'All this talk of George Chilvers' love life diverted me,' Charles went on. 'We were on suicides: John, most recently. Before him, there was some flying ace who hanged himself, apparently at the prospect of going home, though he had pretty hideous burns so it's a bit more understandable. A major in the Glosters who seemed better but turned out not to be, and after him a chap who certainly made his mark on the establishment. Apparently they've got some kind of atrium, with a glass roof, several storeys up?'

Laurence nodded. It was a slightly grandiose description of the entrance hall.

'He got out on the roof through the attics and threw himself head-first, not off the roof into the garden as you might expect, but in through the skylight, and dashed his brains out on the flagstones in the middle of the house.'

'Good God,' Laurence said. 'How appalling. The poor people who found him.'

'Poor chap himself, I'd say,' Charles observed. 'Not poor George Chilvers, as he'd recently made up a will for him. Mind you, no personal bequests, so scandal kept at bay with this one, but a tidy little chunk to Holmwood itself. In gratitude. So my man says.'

CHAPTER SIXTEEN

*L*aurence was looking forward to regaining the peace of his own territory, though it was only when they stopped for a light lunch that he and Charles had any further discussion.

'So. What's your next step, old chap?'

'Hard to know. I didn't like young Chilvers, although Dr Chilvers seemed professional yet sympathetic. The place itself gave me the willies, but then the condition of the men who end up in places like that doesn't exactly bring peace of mind. I didn't feel as strongly as Mary, or Eleanor apparently, that something was rotten.'

He wondered, but didn't say, whether this was simply because, unlike them, he knew about war and what it could do to men's minds as well as bodies. Though Eleanor must have seen much of it too. He also had the first solid information that directly contradicted an account given to him by anyone involved in John's life. However, Eleanor Bolitho was already so cross with him that it was hard to contemplate querying her story or any approach to her that might bear fruit. What if, by some coincidence, John had known two red-haired spitfires? He was grasping at straws, he knew.

'Well, will you be settling your poor lunatic brother there?' said Charles. 'I imagine it will come as the greatest relief to the family to see him locked up.'

Laurence didn't answer. He was considering what it would be like to have a brother, even a mad one. Would he put him in Holmwood? Despite Mary, despite Charles, he thought he might. His reservations lay with the son – too glib, too willing to generalise about the imagined experience of battle.

At one point they had been peering into the small ward. The nearest man lay in bed with his eyes closed. There was a zinc bowl on the nightstand and a sour smell of vomit about him; a bottle of what looked like milk hanging above the bed was passing down the tube into his nose.

'FE again,' said George loudly. 'Flanders Effect.'

The man in bed was startled. His head on the pillow shook and his fingers clutched at the blanket. George made no attempt to soothe him. Laurence thought he detected a flicker of disdain in Chilvers' face but it was quickly replaced by a perfectly businesslike demeanour.

'Some of these people should never have been expected to fight in the first place,' he said.

Laurence agreed with the sentiment but found himself unable to answer. He suspected his reasons for believing it were quite different from Chilvers'. It was on the tip of his tongue to ask the man about his own service but he kept silent, thinking that however delightful it might be to prick Chilvers' confidence, it was hardly worth provoking him.

'Do you know,' Laurence said now, 'I realise that I more or less forgot about Robert once I'd left Dr Chilvers' study. I don't think I mentioned him to George more than once or twice.

Must have looked damned odd. He didn't ask me either, too busy selling the place. Still, I suppose it doesn't matter now. Not likely to see him – any of them – again.'

Charles gave a slow smile. If it hadn't been Charles, reliable, straightforward Charles, Laurence might have thought there was something devious in it.

'My man,' said Charles. 'I saw him again, last thing, as the lad was putting our bags in the car. He said Mrs Chilvers, Mrs *George* Chilvers, late resident of Holmwood, was a bit sweet on John Emmett. Or vice versa. Or mutually. Can't have pleased George too much.' He attempted to look inscrutable but couldn't resist sounding pleased with himself. 'Now there's somebody it might be worth talking to, if we could ever get near her.'

He paused, but when Laurence didn't respond, added, 'Apparently everybody there thought that Emmett had been moved up to the top floor as a punishment for talking to George's wife. Not for some falling-out with a warder or trip out without a pass.'

Laurence felt faintly exasperated that Charles had come out with this only now.

'Did you find out where she – where *they* – live?'

'Used to live in a flat above the old stables near Holmwood but Dr Chilvers thought it better for her to live away from somewhere that had mixed memories for her. That was recently, though. After Emmett's death possibly? Now they live out of the village – in a biggish house; she was a wealthy woman, of course – in a rather isolated position. That was courtesy of our good host Cyril Trusty. He says George Chilvers has just about got her locked up. Some of the servants at Holmwood – maid, cleaner, cook – do turns there. Not a great improvement on her original circumstances.'

'What a bloody odious man,' Laurence said, louder than he intended.

'Ah, Sir Laurence, knight-errant. Dragons skewered, enchanters foiled, moustache-twirling seducers thwarted, dungeons breached. Damsels in distress a speciality.' Charles's smile took the sting out of his words.

'I'm being ludicrous, aren't I?' Laurence said.

'Not at all, frankly. Though I'm not sure where it all goes from here.'

'I just can't think what to tell Mary. I had mixed impressions of Holmwood so I'm hardly likely to produce a coherent line for her. The firing squad link would horrify her and I can't tell her about Eleanor. She might go round there and God knows what scenes there'd be.'

'Laurence,' said Charles patiently, 'you're not a hero in one of Mr Drummond's books and she's no swooning maiden. She survived her brother's death — whatever the cause. She asked you to look into it a bit. What did you think? That they were all going to be palpable villains, keeping the deranged wretches chained up in the dripping cellars? Then how on earth would they have taken in so many wealthy and often well-connected families for so long? Or did you hope they were going to come clean and provide a tidy solution at your command? Yes, he did have a gun hidden away. Sorry, slipped the mind. Yes, we found a letter behind the wainscot only last week. Turns out he had some incurable wasting disease and wanted to save his loved ones the pain of watching his prolonged expiry.'

'But what if he didn't exactly kill himself?'

Charles looked incredulous.

'No, hear me out. Maybe someone didn't put a gun to his head but deliberately drove him to it. What then?' Laurence was astonished at his own recklessness.

'Well, I'd ask who?' Charles said, surprisingly calmly. 'Who could have done? Who would have done? Why?'

Laurence thought for a few seconds before saying without great conviction, 'George Chilvers. He'd be top of my list.' He stopped, faced with Charles's look of astonishment. 'No, of course you're right. Is it more likely a depressed man killed himself or that he was murdered by persons unknown? It never entered Mary's head and even Eleanor doesn't think that. Forget I said it.'

Reflecting on Charles's assessment the next day, back in London, Laurence was still surprised at the perspicacity behind his comments. He started to write to Mary about the trip but gave up after two muddled paragraphs. In the end he simply agreed they meet as she'd suggested. But by the time he'd stuck down the envelope, he'd also decided on one further journey. After that, he thought he would stop living someone else's life and get back to his own. His slender manuscript lay on the edge of the desk, very tidy, but, to his shame, a fine layer of dust covered it. He drew an M on it with his finger.

He went out to post the letters. The sky was palest blue with fast-moving clouds. He walked as far as Coram's Fields, where he sat down on an empty bench. There was a folded newspaper abandoned on the damp wood and he read the headlines. Opposite him an old man was tossing crumbs to a dozen squabbling pigeons. A nursemaid holding a well-wrapped small girl by the hand walked past, pushing a perambulator. Laurence smiled at the child and she looked back at him curiously as she passed by.

As he walked home he read a piece about the next month's Varsity match. Having finished with the paper, he put it in the

dustbin beneath his own steps. He looked up to see his neighbour, a man who rarely left his rooms, appear in the doorway.
There was invariably a faint smell of cats about him. He thrust
out a letter to Laurence.

'It's for you,' he said, almost reproachfully. 'Picked it up with
my own post.'

'Thank you.'

Laurence examined it, failing to recognise the handwriting.
His neighbour nodded and retreated back to his flat.
Laurence's eyes followed him briefly. It was possible the man
was no older than he was but life had aged him.

He hung up his coat and opened the envelope, expecting it
to be from a woman: the writing was what he vaguely thought
of as artistic. His eye went to the bottom of the page. This
time the letter was from William Bolitho.

Dear Bartram,

   It was very good to see you the other day. I realise
Eleanor may have given you a different impression but I
have enjoyed our brief talks. I rather envy you having a
meaty task to get your teeth into, though I continue to
regret Emmett's death. He was a decent man. You must
not take Eleanor's rebuffs to heart. Eleanor is very
defensive of those she loves. It is a sterling quality – I
doubt I would be here were it not for her – and I count
my blessings even though she sometimes overrates threats
to my welfare.

   What I wanted to tell you, though I fear it may be of
slight use in your enquiries, is that I remembered the name
of the major who was billeted on us in 1917 and whose
batman helped rescue John Emmett in the tunnel collapse.
The man who was in your photograph. Calogreedy was

his name. Name like that, can't think how I ever forgot it.
Ex Indian Army man. God knows what his servant was
called; all I can remember of him is his accent – broad
west country – Somerset, perhaps, if that helps at all. It's
quite a coincidence but yesterday I was checking some
small investments I have and I noticed a firm called
Calogreedy and Weatherall were quoted on the stock
exchange. As far as I can tell, their business is locks, safes,
strong-rooms and so on. It was such an unusual name that
I remembered the major instantly and I thought there
might, just, be a connection.

I hope this is helpful and that when things are calmer
we shall meet again. In the meantime I shall take the
slightly clandestine step of handing this to Ethel to post.
Yours,
William Bolitho

Laurence ran back downstairs to where his scavenged newspaper lay on top of the rubbish in the bin. Self-consciously he
looked around to check he wasn't observed and smoothed it
out on the wall, brushing tea leaves off its back page. He suddenly had an image of Louise's father scrutinising the financial
pages, making gruff noises of approval or concern and occasionally putting a mark against certain figures. He remembered
Louise's mother objecting to her husband tucking his silver
propelling pencil behind his ear while he read. For a brief
moment, his father-in-law felt more real to him than any
memory of Louise.

Laurence's fingers travelled down the columns. Calogreedy
and Weatherall were there; their shares seemed to be healthy.
He put the paper back in the bin. The next day he would try
to find out where they did business.

He was relieved that William Bolitho had been in touch; Eleanor had been so adamant that he was causing her husband distress that he had been almost persuaded of it, although, if anything, Bolitho seemed bored by the constraints on his actions. John's death must have eased the Bolithos' circumstances, but it could never have given Bolitho any kind of life. Fleetingly, he wondered whether Eleanor could have been petitioning John for financial help but Eleanor was only a collateral beneficiary anyway. Had she simply become over-involved with John while she nursed him? Or was it a passionate love affair, independent of war, and was it reciprocated? The period when she would have visited John at Holmwood would have been well after she got married so an enduring love affair seemed unlikely.

He wondered whether Eleanor knew about John's role in the firing squad. Whether she was friend or nurse, it was not unlikely she shared his secrets. Not that this one was his alone; there would have been plenty of others at an execution, of course.

He stared at the photograph he'd received from Mary and remembered Chilvers' evidence to the inquest, stating that John was preoccupied by the event. This photograph was one that John had carried with him to his death. Bolitho had identified John, Tucker and the sapper's servant. They were all men involved in the trench accident, yet this was clearly winter and Bolitho had said the collapse took place in the heat of summer. Could they also have been part of a firing squad? Although the presence of the medical officer meant it could have been an execution detail, there were also plenty of times when soldiers clustered together, looking glum and waiting for action. Yet who could have photographed the men and why? Whose was the monogram on the back?

He'd never seen an execution but tales of them circulated from time to time. Sometimes he thought that their circulation was deliberate; it made it clear to nervous soldiers that whilst the Germans might be aiming to kill them on one side, the forces of their own military discipline were equally lethal on the other. Like every other aspect of the war, horror stories abounded. Everyone knew someone who knew someone who'd been involved. The officer who was supposed to deliver the *coup de grâce* fiddling with a jammed revolver; executioners calling out to a friend or brother tied to a stake; right down to the straightforward humiliations: the condemned soldier losing control of his bowels or bladder, the young ones crying for their mothers. Better to go towards the guns or through the wire.

Trench tales were always about removing choice, he reflected; the good soldier was a resigned soldier. The good soldier never wasted time thinking about alternatives.

CHAPTER SEVENTEEN

Finding Major Calogreedy turned out to be Charles's easiest task so far. There were only two Calogreedys who'd seen service in the war. Calogreedy and Weatherall had offices at Lambeth. A telephone call established that Calogreedy was in the office, running the business, and had indeed seen action in France. Laurence made an appointment to go over and see him the following Friday at midday, ignoring Charles's efforts to lure him to a party in Suffolk.

'But we're celebrating,' Charles had said and added, 'Funny choice of day to track down this Calogreedy.'

It was not cold so he decided to walk. He passed down a peaceful Kingsway towards Aldwych but as he got nearer to the Strand he seemed to be crossing the tail-end of a crowd, the bulk of which he could see pushing westwards towards Whitehall. The mass of people were hardly moving. Just out of sight, but still just audible, was a brass band. He listened and recognised it as a hymn. He knew the words to it. 'Victor, he rose; victorious too shall rise, They who have drunk His cup of sacrifice.' Hearing it so unexpectedly made a great impact on him. Although he was far from sharing its sentiments now, the music was as powerfully evocative as ever; to his horror, the conflicting emotions made him shiver.

As the hymn died away he realised with a shock the significance of Charles's apparently throwaway remark. Almost simultaneously the bells of Big Ben rang out over a nearly silent London. Eleven o'clock. It was Armistice Day. This year there was a ceremony at the new Cenotaph and a few of those around him were wearing the paper poppies. They looked oddly frivolous but the expressions on the faces in the crowd belied that. Whether the crowds wanted to see the King or wanted to honour their dead, everybody was looking back, either in sorrow, as here, or in jubilation – going to the races or, like Charles, preparing for a party. The country was divided: between those who wept and those who danced.

Except he was doing neither. Only three years had passed, yet he had forgotten it was the eleventh. Peace descended more abruptly around him now than it had in 1918; he could hear the flutter of squabbling pigeons on a window ledge. The sky above him was uniformly grey.

He remembered when the news had come through in France. He'd been in a makeshift stable, examining a sick horse. They were trying to decide whether to shoot it. The horse was coughing and rolling its eyes as a young farrier tried to restrain it. Its jaw was dark with saliva and it looked completely mad. The new adjutant had rushed in but was stopped in his tracks by the sight of the deranged horse. Then he said, 'It's over.' And for a second Laurence had thought he meant they should hurry up and shoot the horse. Once he understood what the officer really meant, his first thought was that it would be marvellous to have a clean collar every day. His second had been a feeling of such profound pointlessness that even remembering it now made him want to weep.

When the silence came to an end, he crossed over Waterloo Bridge, which was bitingly cold in the wind, and then moved into the shelter of buildings on the south bank of the river. He walked briskly along York Road towards Lambeth. The business was easy to find: a middle-sized factory abutted the road. Above a wide archway the words 'Calogreedy and Weatherall' were spelled out in ironwork. The buildings were quite old but the sign looked new. When Laurence entered the gateway a young man in a dark suit came towards him.

'Mr Bartram,' he said, holding out his hand. 'Would you please follow me, sir?'

Calogreedy's office was just across a small yard. Laurence stepped forward and greeted the tall man who had stood up behind his desk. As the door closed behind them, a distant background of banging and grinding became fainter.

'The men all wanted to come in, business as usual, but we stopped for the commemoration,' said Calogreedy, shaking Laurence's hand and nodding back towards the yard. 'I said a prayer. It was appreciated, I think, but one never quite knows.'

Calogreedy was obviously a military man, upright and with decisive movements. He had dark hair, a neat moustache, blue eyes and weathered skin. He was about forty-five, Laurence guessed. The entire wall behind him was covered in photographs. Some looked recent and were of what Laurence presumed was the factory floor: with workbenches, presses and tool racks as a background to ten or so men in overalls. One picture was of Calogreedy shaking hands with a government minister. The more faded ones were either regimental or apparently taken in India: a tiger shoot, a magnificent picnic overlooking a fort in the foothills of some mountains, and one of what looked like the 1912 Durbar. The King and Queen stood pale and stiff under a silken canopy, dwarfed by ostrich-plumed officers, jewelled maharajahs and ornately decked elephants. It might as well have been another century.

'Well, to start with, you've certainly found the right man. Funnily enough, the only other serving Calogreedy – I believe – was my brother Godfrey. He's a director of the company, too, and might as easily have been here today, but I'm clearly the man you are after. Basil Calogreedy. A regular. Indian Army.' He nodded to the photographs. 'Sappers.'

Laurence wondered, briefly, whether Calogreedy had been in the same outfit as his fictitious brother, Robert.

'Came out in 1919 and bought this business. We've been expanding ever since. Weatherall was a sleeping partner. Very much asleep, in fact, as he passed on before the war, but the name means something in the locks and safes world so we kept it. Doing well. Factories in Birmingham and Bristol. Unfortunately, we live in hard times: men come out of uniform and there's no job for them.' He sat back, placing the palms of his hands flat on his desk. 'Outcome: desperation. Burglary. Petty theft. Solution: good locks. All the men I take on have been in uniform. We owe it to them. Find they can't get skilled positions because they've been out of their trade for four years and some fifteen-year-old is being trained up for a pittance.'

He shook his head in apparent disbelief at his own words before his attention returned to Laurence.

'I can't think I've much to contribute but perhaps if you fire off some questions, something I say will be of use. Strange business, your friend's death. Sadly not unique, though.'

'It was very hard for his sister and widowed mother,' said

Laurence. Then, hesitantly, 'Do you remember an incident in 1916? I believe you were passing through a village near Albert where there was a collapse of a major trench system. Two men killed, one injured? My friend was one of those men.'

Calogreedy wrinkled his brow. 'It happened all too often,' he said, but it was obvious that he knew what Laurence was talking about. 'I wasn't actually there on that occasion – I was surveying another stretch. It was my servant who helped get the men out. They were lucky. Lucky not more men were down there, I mean. I'd been sent forward because the diggers were anxious about the stability of the trenches; they were pushing ahead at terrific speed. HQ wanted them back in commission, but they didn't have the materials to prop the new tunnels adequately and the ground was chalky; tree roots a problem, as I recall, and they kept running into abandoned German trenches. Anyway the collapse simply bore out my judgment. Three or four men, including your fellow presumably, were underneath when it caved in. Byers, an officer and an NCO got the survivor out.'

'Byers?' said Laurence, remembering the name on John's list.

'Yes. Leonard Byers. He was my servant – a good man; tremendous aptitude for figures. Farm boy. Bit of a phenomenon. If commissions were awarded on intellect alone, he'd have been an officer of engineers. As it was, he just proved that if you had a good batman the war could be a very much more congenial experience. Started off as a bit of a joke, getting him to do mental arithmetic. Lads used to throw questions at him and lay bets on how long it would take him to tot up forty numbers, that kind of thing. He was always quicker in his head than anyone doing the same sum on paper. Heaven knows where he got his abilities from; left school at twelve and, from what he tells me, they never got the farm to pay. But I've kept him with me. Man who showed you in.' He nodded at the door. 'He married one of our lady typewriters the same year we set up and I've half a mind to bring him on to the management side eventually. One day. Just need to persuade Godfrey who is a conventional chap. Can't see the brain behind the rough edges.'

'Byers was your mess servant in 1916?' Laurence asked. He had temporarily forgotten that Calogreedy was rumoured to have kept his batman with him when the war finished. It was not so odd for a regular officer but usually the relationship became one of master and valet. The making of such an easy connection, after so much information that had seemed to go nowhere, caught him by surprise. He was looking for a Byers, and for the batman, and now they had turned out to be one and the same.

'Was there a Darling or a Coburg there?' It was a very long shot and he wasn't surprised when Calogreedy shook his head. His mind was evidently still on his employee.

'He's had a tough time recently because of all the palaver over the death of his cousin a few months back. Poor chap was murdered. In cold blood. Can you believe it? Policeman came here to tell him as the nearest surviving relative. He took it badly. Can understand why: his cousin makes it unscathed through three and a half bloody years in France and someone does for him while he's milking cows. As I said: desperate times — desperate men. But have a word with him in a while; he'll be in his office until late.'

'I do have one other question.' Laurence hesitated. 'It's a slightly strange one. Perhaps this should be for Mr Byers himself and you may not know the answer anyway, but was he ever part of a firing squad?'

It was obvious he had hit on something. Calogreedy's face answered for him.

'A bad business. He really shouldn't have had to do it. I was on leave or I would have stopped it. He was forced into making up numbers because so many had dysentery at the time and even then there was a bit of malice in his selection, I think. The condemned man was an officer, you see.'

Laurence stiffened. The execution of an officer was virtually unheard of. He struggled for a second to take it in.

'His own men were loath to do it,' Calogreedy said, 'but once the sentence had been handed down and confirmed, I expect the powers that be wanted to get it over with as quickly as possible. At least Byers didn't know the man, but neither did he really know anybody else on the squad except for the sergeant and a couple of the officers. And although he was a country lad he wasn't even very good with a gun. Needed spectacles.'

'An officer executed?'

'Yes. Poor fellow. Cowardice, I imagine. Of course you can't make exceptions but still, he was very young, I gather. There were chaps out there who couldn't have commanded a tea party, much less an assault on a machine-gun post.'

'You don't—?'

'Remember his name? No. Absolutely not, if I ever knew it. Not very good on names. I dare say you could find out. Careful how you go with Byers — touchy subject. All this stuff in the papers now: accusations of summary justice and so on. Though it beats me how you can expect much subtlety in military law, not in the field, not when there are men out there who couldn't find their way into battle with a map. So deciding theoretical degrees of guilt when the German guns were rumbling in the background . . . Well, a lot seemed to depend on local morale and setting examples, nothing consistent about it. But, d'you know, I only ever read of one other officer being

executed. They were tougher on the whole: good schools, independence, team sports, values. Byers won't welcome talking
about it, I can tell you. I'll have a word. Smooth things over.
You'll need to be persistent.'

It was obvious that Calogreedy had little else to share with him
and Laurence stayed only long enough not to seem impolite.
He was eager to speak to Leonard Byers and Calogreedy made
it easy for him by taking him across to a smaller office on the
far side.

'Look, it's almost their lunch hour. He might feel more
relaxed off the premises. Take a walk, that kind of thing.'

Calogreedy strode ahead, pushing open a door. Laurence
looked up at the spitting rain without enthusiasm. Inside the
office, surrounded by graphs and diagrams, Leonard Byers sat
hunched over a desk between hefty files, writing notes against
columns of figures in front of him. He didn't hear the door
open or see them standing there at first. When he did he
looked embarrassed, jumping up while straightening his tie.

'Sorry to disturb you,' Calogreedy said, 'but curiously it
turns out that although it was me that he had come to see, you
were, in a manner of speaking, really the man Mr Bartram was
after all the time. He was hoping you might be able to help
him look into the death of his friend. Anyway, take your time.
Nothing urgent to do here.'

It might have been Laurence's imagination but he thought
he detected a look of wariness cross the younger man's face.
Although it was gone almost immediately, he looked uncomfortable even as he belatedly reached out his hand.

Calogreedy paused in the doorway. 'Difficult times. But try
to help him, old chap. I'd be grateful, you know.'

CHAPTER EIGHTEEN

*L*eonard Byers had a pale, serious face, a faint shadow of stubble on his chin and purple hollows under his eyes. One lens of his wire spectacles was cracked. Laurence remembered that he had only recently, and violently, lost a close relative. Most people still assumed that talk of death meant talk of the war, but here they both were with enough distance from it to have experienced death in peacetime.

Byers, who was slight in build with intelligent eyes, looked younger than his years. He must be in his mid-twenties at least but could have been five years younger. He faced Laurence unsmilingly. A farm boy, Calogreedy had said. Yet here he was, translated by the war into an urban clerk on the banks of the Thames.

Byers motioned him to a spare chair and sat down behind the desk.

'I'm sorry,' Laurence said. 'I gather this is a difficult time for you. Death in the family. Not a time to answer questions, perhaps?'

'My cousin, Jim,' said Byers, 'back in the summer. But it's all right, ask what you like. If the major thinks it'll help.' He looked unconvinced. 'Nothing'll bring Jim back.' He took off his spectacles and held them in front of him.

Laurence could hear a slight west country burr in his voice. 'You must have been close?'

'Well, close as lads. We were the same age to the month. Almost like twins when we were young 'uns. Up to all sorts. I was the clever one but he was the sportsman. Strong. Ran like the wind. Star of the village cricket team before the war. When they still had a team. But when he went back to the farm in 1918 and I followed the major here, he wasn't so happy. Didn't say as much, mind, but I could tell he thought he'd got a raw deal. It was just him and the old man. I should've gone to see them more, but it's a long way and I was helping the major get things going. Then I met Enid — she's my wife now — and we were saving. But I should have gone down. It wasn't fair on Jim.

'The farm hadn't been properly run in the war. Couldn't get the labour, it was all girls and old men. Didn't buy in new animals, let a few bills go unpaid. Couple of bad harvests, didn't keep the repairs up to scratch and it's an old place, needs work on it all the time. After the war, for all the talk, nobody gave a . . .'

He seemed to struggle to find a respectable word.

'Nobody cared if a tatty little farm went to the dogs. Stupid thing is, neither of us had to fight. We were needed at home. Essential work, they called it. But to tell the truth, I was bored and wanted to see the world.' He frowned. 'Which I did. And we both thought that girls would be all over a man in uniform. Which they weren't. And once I'd joined up, then Jim wasn't going to be left behind in the mud at Combe Bisset. Went to find some nice foreign mud of his own. Come Christmas, he just signed on the line. Went in as a private, came out with his stripes. Uncle looked like he could carry on with the lads we'd got, but then he fell off a roof he was fixing and his leg was never right, and of course eventually the younger lads were itching to get into uniform too.'

'Your uncle?' The conversation had moved a long way from where Laurence intended it to go but he wanted to gain the young man's trust and Byers seemed willing to talk about his family catastrophe.

'Yes. That's what made it worse. The old man had been pretty well bedridden since Jim'd got back. But he liked to sit in a chair by the window upstairs. He saw it all.'

'The death?'

'The murder.'

'He saw the person who did it?'

'He did that. Though a fat lot of help it's been. Man in a hat and a coat. That's only half the population, then. Arrived by car probably, though left it out of sight. My uncle said he heard it but never saw it. He'll have been right about that: his eyesight's not great but his hearing was always spot on. So it was a man with the nerve to drive within earshot of the house and to see off our dog, and she's a nasty bit of work. A man who carried a gun and didn't hesitate in using it at close range. Twice.'

'Twice?'

'Once in the chest and then a second, head shot, once he was on the ground. The police said the first shot would have done for him. He can't have known anything. The second was just to make sure.'

'How extraordinary,' said Laurence. 'Did the police have any ideas at all who it might have been?'

'No. I mean, Jim'd never been anywhere, excepting after he

joined up. We were brought up on the farm. Both his parents died when he was very young. My father died of lockjaw when we were boys. My uncle looked after my mother and both us cousins in return for her keeping house. She passed on just before the war. Anyone Jim knew, I knew. I'd have known if he'd got into any kind of trouble. We had the same friends, got into the same trouble – but only the schoolboy kind: scrumping, girls, playground knuckle fights. Nothing out of the ordinary ever happened to Jim until the day somebody came all the way out to the farm and shot him. Nothing to nick, either. No reason to it.'

'What kind of gun was it?'

'Not a shotgun. A pistol. Kills him, then blows his face off,' Byers said bitterly.

Laurence was surprised. When Byers had spoken of a final shot to the head, he'd been thinking of a single bullet, a military *coup de grâce*.

'They might of got his tyre tracks,' Byers was saying, 'and had some hope of tracing the car, the major says, but the police and the local doctor had driven backwards and forwards down the same track by the time those clods thought of it. Mashed into nothingness, it was. But what did they care? Single man, mucky farm. Probably thought he'd been after some other yokel's wife.'

'How dreadful for your uncle.'

'Yes. It was. He comes down the stairs on his . . . on his behind, must have taken him for ever. Got himself out in the yard. Found Jim, but there was nothing he could do for him and no way he could get help. Lucky he didn't die of cold, poor old man. Didn't have an obliging bone in him but he didn't deserve that. The girl found him – the one who did the milking. Him and the dog sitting in the muck, and then Jim's blood splattered all over the yard. But it did for him really, the old man. The farm was sold. The money that was left after the creditors had their take went to pay a widow in town to look after him in her home. Me and Enid didn't see a penny of it,' he added defensively.

His face softened. 'Funny thing is, when the police first came, I thought, just for a minute, that Jim'd done it himself. Topped himself. He was that fed up. So, just for a minute there was a queer kind of relief that he hadn't. Mind you, I wasn't the one who had to find him. The old man wasn't beyond covering up a suicide: that generation, you know, and a bit on the religious side. He could of made up cars and strangers, but not the gun. Jim had a shotgun — crows and rabbits — but it was still back in the house. Didn't have it with him so obviously wasn't expecting any trouble. Hadn't been fired for a while, the police said.'

Laurence's head was buzzing. 'Do the police think the assailant knew your uncle was there as well?' he asked.

'God knows. Local man would of known, but anyone else — probably not. Bastard was taking a risk but then he was carrying a loaded gun. Not so much of a risk if you've got a strong stomach and more of us around now have seen some sights would've turned us before the war.

'A few days earlier a man came into the pub in the village. It's a mile or so's walk from our farm. It was early and nobody much was in there but he had a half of cider. Kept himself to himself but was pleasant enough. Might have been useful information if the landlord didn't help himself to his own spirits all day. All he could remember was the man spoke like a gentleman and asked where the farm was. And he didn't even remember that for a week. The stranger took himself off. Where he went, if it was him, for the next day or so, who knows? If he had a car, he could of gone anywhere. But I'm certain Jim had no more idea than I do why anyone would want to kill him in the first place.

'You'll be thinking he might of got involved with something in France I don't know of,' Leonard Byers rushed on. The circumstances were obviously still bothering him. 'The major got me to see a senior policeman friend of his. But he was really just doing it as a favour for the major. Small fry, me and Jim, but people will do all sorts for the major.' He looked almost proud. 'A London policeman. Mullins. Turned out I'd sort of met this Mullins when we were both in France. He thought Jim had got mixed up with some bad lads there. But Jim didn't get into any funny business. We weren't close like we once were, but he would still've told me if anything was really wrong. He just said his time out there was mostly uncomfortable or frightening. He said it was his duty and, like all duty, boring but unavoidable.'

Laurence nodded. Byers' assessment was well observed. He was also relieved that he was talking so freely, although most of the time he avoided eye contact.

'I would of known if he'd been caught up in anything so odd that someone would've come hunting for him over two years after the war ended. After all, he was hardly in hiding, was he? He wasn't scared. He was right back where he started. He didn't expect *anything* to happen, not ever again. That was his gripe. I don't suppose we'll ever know. Too careful, too planned, Mullins said, for a homicidal maniac. Everyone knows us down here. Whoever it was, he wouldn't have got that far without being clear precisely who he was about to shoot. And he did get right up to him. Looked him in the face. Perhaps Jim knows the answer but he's past telling.'

Awkwardly Laurence asked, 'Would you like to go for a beer

or something? The major's quite happy for you to take time away . . .'

'I'm temperance.'

'Oh. Right. A walk?'

Byers looked to the window. 'It's raining,' he said flatly.

There was a long-drawn-out silence. The door of the small iron stove rattled as wind came down the pipe. Laurence was absorbing the fact that Combe Bisset was one of the names written on the list John had carried at his death, but now was not the time to bring this up and he knew he was avoiding a more difficult topic.

'Look, I'm sorry to have to ask you this,' Laurence began in a rush, 'but were you ever part of a firing squad?'

Byers shoulders tensed. He looked down, turned his spectacles over in his hands. His lips tightened. For a minute Laurence thought he was going to refuse to speak.

'So that's why you're really here. The major told you, is that it? And he wants me to tell you?' he said, stiffly. 'Why do you want to know? For the papers? It's all over now.'

'I asked him — your name had come up — and he said you'd help me,' Laurence said, not quite truthfully. 'It's just the friend that he mentioned, the friend whose death I'm looking into, may have been connected with it.'

'You think he was involved in that dismal bloody mess?' Byers looked suspicious.

Laurence felt for his wallet and took out the photograph. 'Is this you?' he said.

Byers took the picture. He stared at it impassively. 'Jesus,' he said. 'Mr Brabourne and his ruddy camera. Could never leave it alone. I'm surprised he didn't take one of the actual shooting as well.'

'Brabourne?'

'First Lieutenant Tresham Brabourne. They called him "Fiery". He wasn't so much fiery, though, as some kind of fizzing grenade that you're not sure if it's a dud or it's about to turn you to mincemeat. I'd been under him early on in the war. We were bantams. Short-arses. Never thought I'd see him again. He was so green, so lacking any normal sense of self-preservation, the lads there said just following him was the most dangerous thing you were ever likely to be asked to do.' Byers' face relaxed momentarily. 'Nineteen, twenty perhaps? Not that I was any older. Apparently his mama had given him the camera as a goodbye present. Perhaps she thought it was going to be like a touring holiday. Going to visit family friends in this or that chateau, chomp on snails and frogs' legs for dinner? When he went on leave, he hopped off to Paris. Brought back some champagne one time. Wanted to be a writer or some such, though what he really loved was his camera. No, I remember now, he was going to be a newspaperman when he got out of the war. Which was about as likely as the Kaiser being invited back for tea at Buckingham Palace. If ever there was a man with a short lifespan it was Mr Brabourne.

'He'd been told about the camera. You couldn't have people taking any old pictures. He thought he could sell them to the papers, I suppose. Make his reputation. But he was heading for trouble if he was caught again. He could probably even have been charged with spying, though I expect his family knew people in the War Office. His sort did. But this,' he tapped on the picture with his forefinger. 'It has to be Brabourne's work. He was there. We were there. He was the only one who could've taken this.' He paused. 'Was Mr Brabourne your friend?'

Laurence shook his head. 'No. Can you tell me what's going on in the picture?'

'Apart from the fact that we're about to see off some poor bastard, which you obviously guessed already. Look, I decided way back never to talk about it. Never even to think about it, if I could. You just come in here . . .' He was struggling to contain his anger. 'I don't know who you are. I've only said this much because the major.' He put the picture on his desk, laying it face down as he pushed it sharply towards Laurence.

'I'm sorry,' said Laurence, trying to disguise the excitement he felt at the confirmation that the image was of the firing squad. 'I really wouldn't be bringing it up if it wasn't important. It's just my friend has a sister and she doesn't understand why he died. He shot himself, you see. And he was part of all this and felt much as you did, I think.'

He waited to see whether Byers would give him an answer. He sensed it was no good pushing him further.

'Then, assuming he was an officer, your friend must be either the MO, the padre, the APM – the assistant provost marshal – or the captain,' Byers said, after several minutes. His tone was resigned. 'Empson, I think his name was.'

'Emmett,' said Laurence.

Byers nodded and picked up the photograph again.

'Emmett,' he said. 'Right.' He fell silent again. 'You know, this wasn't the first time I'd met your friend the captain. I came across him before this business. He was a lieutenant then. I was passing near Albert but didn't know anyone. He asked where I came from in Devon. He could place anyone by their voice. I told him Combe Bisset. He said his mother's maiden name was Bisset. Next day the trench collapsed on him. Looked nasty, but he was lucky. Lucky then, anyways.'

Laurence was about to ask him about the collapse but then the young man pointed to himself in the picture. A slightly plumper self, but even more tense than he looked now.

'Watkins,' he said, moving his finger to the man next to him. 'Welsh nutter.' His finger moved again: 'Vince somebody, a cabinet maker in real life, a Londoner, on light duties with his rupture. Not the sort of light duty he had in mind, I'd imagine. Next to him — a man whose nerves were all over the place. Wound us all up.' His finger moved on. 'This one — nickname was Dusty. I suppose that means he was called Miller — Dustys usually are, aren't they? Can't remember this one at all, he was on the end. One of Dusty's lot probably. Just a lad. Two were from the poor bugger's own company. They were sick about it. Said their officer was no worse than any other. Old man's the doc,' he pointed, 'and very unhappy. Your friend, Emmett there. And that evil bastard — sorry,' he looked up at Laurence, 'but he was — is — Sergeant Tucker. He's the one that had it in for me.'

'In what way?'

'Well, they were making up a squad. Nobody wants the job. General feeling was that it was a rotten business. By all accounts, the poor useless bastard they'd got it in for was round the bend. And because he was an officer. You'd think some of them might have gone for that on general principles, but most felt it would bring bad luck. Not Sergeant Tucker, though. He was in his element. It wasn't personal or anything; he was just a nasty bit of work. I'd met him before, too, funnily enough, same accident you just asked me about. One of Tucker's so-called mates had been suffocated. Tucker was supposedly trying to help him until a medic came. The others were all trying to get the rest out, but I'd turned round and watched Tucker, and I can tell you he wasn't lifting a finger to help his friend. He was leaning over him but it looked more like he was putting his hand over his mouth rather than clearing it of earth. He saw me looking and moved to block my view. When I met him again, I hoped he'd forgotten me.'

Laurence made a non-committal grunt.

'But he never forgot anything.' Byers was obviously thinking. 'Frankly, he made a bit of a mess of it, your friend. As for me, half the regulars were ill. The others were all bellyaching. I was there waiting for the major to get back from Blighty. I shouldn't have been there at all. It's difficult when you don't belong, when it's not your outfit. At night I had to kip with the others and Tucker had it in for me from the start. The other lads were taking the rip but most of it was pretty good-humoured. One pretended to put on an apron and dust the place down. When I went out for a piss, they made out I was picking flowers for the major's billet. But Tucker, he was all for me being a nancy-boy. Called me the major's girl. Called me Leonora and soon they were all at it.' His cheeks flared red. Then he said, almost aggressively, 'Look, you really want to know all this stuff? It's not pretty, any of it. Not the bit with your friend in either. Not stuff his sister and mother would want to know.'

Laurence had no idea where it was going: but he was simultaneously apprehensive and eager to hear the rest of what Byers had to tell. 'Please,' he said, 'you've no idea how useful this is. I won't pass on all the details.'

He hoped Byers' evident loyalty to Calogreedy would keep him talking, rather than asking himself why Laurence needed the details if he was not intending to use them.

Byers took out a crumpled handkerchief. For a second Laurence thought he was going to cry and felt a flash of embarrassment, but the young man simply rubbed the lenses of his glasses. 'What started it was that, the first evening, I was there when Tucker was selling some German stuff. Most of it was the usual: belt buckles, badges. He had a ring and a watch with its glass smashed, a beautiful thing, an officer's probably, but it still went, and a pen, and a couple of photographs of some Fräuleins, that he'd nicked from dead men's pockets, and some letters nobody could read in that funny writing of theirs. Oh and some fancy drawers and a hair ribbon he'd taken off a French lass. But some of it was plain disgusting and that's what everybody wanted to buy. He had some collar flashes stiff with blood and then he'd got something in a little jar of inky liquid. He handed it over to me, saying, "You'll like this, Byers, it's right up your street." I thought at first it was some sort of small animal he'd pickled, but then from the grin on his face I knew it was something much worse. I shook it a little and then I saw what it was.' He stopped, looking uncomfortable. 'It was a part of a German. His thing. Organ. It was stinking. I almost dropped it there and then. Of course it could have been anybody's if we'd stopped to think. After all, there were enough dead bodies about, but he'd got them all falling over each other to have it. Even Watkins who was forever talking about sinners and hellfire.

'Anyway, he's asking for bids, and some of them are offering money and some are trying to trade for tobacco or sweets or saucy pictures. The young lad – his eyes are on stalks. You can see Watkins wants the drawers but there's the Holy Book holding him back, and Dusty is offering for different combinations of stuff, but Tucker keeps adding or subtracting according to what he chooses. Finally they agree, but I can see Tucker's added up the total wrong. So I correct him. I mean, that's what I'm good at. The look he gives me. Well, of course he was trying to cheat them. Not for the money but as a game. But I didn't know him then, did I? I hadn't taken to him on account of his being too chummy with the young soldiers, but I didn't know what a sick bastard – sorry, again, sir, but it's the truth – he was. And then some of the men start to laugh and I know I've had it.

'Two days later the rumour that's been going round – that

some young officer, who they've had locked up in the guard-house, and who'd been done for being a coward, has been sentenced to death – turns out to be true. Tucker comes in late, happy as Larry, tells us he's looking for volunteers for a squad. Of course he doesn't mean "volunteer" and he doesn't get any. Well, only Dusty, who's half-witted and would put his hand up to go over the top in a tutu armed with a stick of Brighton rock if an NCO asked him. The others don't like it. The one with nerves is shaking. Two of them know the officer. I don't, of course.

'He wants ten but he'll settle for seven and a burial party. There were a lot of men on sick, granted, but I knew it would only be a matter of time until he picked on me. And it was. He played about, pretending he wanted X or Y, who turned out to be puking up somewhere or on leave, and then he said, "Oh Byers, just the man. You like doing officers favours. Well, you can do this one a favour by shooting straight." Bastard,' Byers muttered, almost to himself.

'That night they billeted us in the farm, the one you can see in the photograph. Nobody slept much, bar Dusty who snored the whole night through. What with that and Watkins reading aloud from his bible, and the cold, and the prospect of what was to come, it was a horrible night. Too long and too short at the same time, if you know what I mean. For once Tucker was in with us. Just lay on his back, no trouble to anyone for once, not sleeping: you could see the glow of his cigarette in the half-dark. Captain Emmett came in about six. He looked pretty sick too.'

'And this Brabourne, was he part of the squad, then?' asked Laurence.

'No. He didn't pitch up until we were about to do it. Just in time to take our photograph, I suppose.'

Laurence was puzzled. 'But what was he doing there?'

'I was told that he was part of the trial. The one who's put in to defend someone but never gets them off. But I mean, Mr Brabourne, they might as well of shot the man right there.'

Laurence saw they'd arrived at the point which he should have clarified to start with.

'And the prisoner was?'

'Mr Hart. Another lieutenant.'

Laurence realised that he'd increasingly expected to recognise the name, whatever it turned out to be, but Hart meant nothing to him. 'Hart?' he repeated, blankly.

Byers looked unhappy. 'Whatever he'd done, and Vince said he'd left them all in a ditch, being shot at, and done a runner and been found stark bollock naked spouting balderdash, he was brave enough in the end. We were hanging around for a while beforehand; that's probably when Brabourne got his picture. It was a dark morning, a bit of snow, not light enough at first. Then Emmett gives us a little speech, though you can tell his heart's not in it: about how sometimes duty asks strange and difficult things of us just as necessary as fighting the Germans. Chin up. Soon be over. That kind of thing. Probably read it in his officer handbook.

'Tucker marches us off. It's still sleeting and my boots have a hole in them. I remember thinking I shouldn't be noticing this now. The captain comes over, says, "All right, lads?" I hear myself saying, "My boots are leaking." It just come out. Captain Emmett gives me a hard look. There's a post, and some rope. Well, you must know how it goes. Tucker puts me on the end next to him. So as he can have fun watching me, no doubt. Then he mixes the rifles.'

'Mixes the rifles?'

'You must know. Being an officer.' He looked incredulous.

'Shift your rifles about. Of course it means you're not firing with the weapon you're used to. Not that I'd fired more than twice anyway.'

'I'm sorry – I misunderstood.'

But truthfully Laurence had never given it any thought; it had seemed at first like an uncharacteristically humane idea but of course it would be a shambles in its effect. And by the time a man was shooting a fellow soldier, his sensibilities were probably past protecting. By the time he'd been six months in France, he would be pretty well inured to most of war's surprises.

'Then Tucker loads them; supposedly one's a blank, that's what they tell you, but if it was, I knew I wasn't getting it; Tucker was way too chipper with me. Dusty lights a ciggie behind a hand and Captain Emmett shouts at him to put it out. Then we're all silent. It's just breathing and sloshing as we stomp our feet up and down to keep warm. Watkins starts muttering, "I know that my redeemer liveth." Tucker says, "No he don't, Watkins. Not here." Then Tucker must have heard something because we all have to stand to attention. And then we see them, and I thought I was going to pass out, my heart was racing so fast in my chest. Tucker's looking like it's the best thing he's seen in ages.'

Byers faltered. His shoulders rose and fell a couple of times.

'The lieutenant's stumbling along with his hands tied behind his back. The padre – one of the young ones, gripping his book and not lifting his eyes from the page, though you'd have thought he'd have known the words by heart – walks a little in front of him, reading prayers. The two men who'd been guarding him are either side and the APM – I suppose to execute an officer they needed to do it right – following on.'

Byers was speaking at an increasing speed, his initial

reticence having transformed almost into eagerness to get to the end.

'They're bringing him along at quite a lick and the ground's rough and he nearly falls when he sees the place, but the corporal steadies him. They have him tied to the post in a jiffy. He doesn't struggle though he says the ropes are too tight. The corporal has a scarf but Hart won't have a blindfold. He looks at us and he seems a bit puzzled. The lad beside me, he looks down. It's worse for him because he's served under him. Part of me's thinking, at least if his boots is leaking, they won't be troubling him long.'

The look he gave Laurence was almost an appeal for understanding.

'Nerves; it was just my nerves. The MO steps forward, pins a white card or something over his heart. He's shaking his head just a bit, as he backs away. Could of been the sleet melting off his hat. The padre goes on with his "I am the resurrection and the life" stuff and then steps to the side, looking at the ground all the while. Funny, the things you notice. The APM reads out the sentence and leaves us to it, walking back the way he come. Never looks back. He'd got a car waiting, they said.'

Byers looked momentarily uncomfortable but after a brief hesitation he went on.

'Then Captain Emmett calls out, not loud enough really, "Ready", and there's the first click and then Mr Hart shouts out, "Goodbye, lads. Shoot straight and for God's sake make it quick." And the captain, he seems startled. Instead of going on, he stops. Then starts again: "Ready, aim, fire." Which we do.

'But the thing is, we *don't* shoot straight. First off, we're not using our own weapons. Dusty had been tippling out of his flask all night; God knows where he got it but he'd had plenty.

Watkins is so busy with his mutterings about Jesus that his aim's all over the place, and the lad next to me whose name I can't remember shoots even before the captain has given the order to fire, he's that jumpy, and he hits the bloke all right, but not in the heart. We can all hear him moaning. Vince fires when he's told to, I think, and so do I, but I'd never even had to shoot a real person, not close up. Hart slumps against the ropes. As for Tucker, he shoots, but after me and he gets him in the leg or the belly or somewhere, and he was a good shot. Famous for it. Wasn't nervous either. It's Tucker's shot that makes him fall forward and the weight of him pulls the post with him at an angle and the ropes give way and he's on the ground and we can see he's bleeding. It doesn't take the MO to make it official. He's alive. We all look at Captain Emmett. Not just us but the padre and the MO and Mr Brabourne. It's the captain's mess to sort out now.'

Laurence felt cold with disgust. The inhumanity of it all.

'Captain Emmett takes his pistol out of its holster. He steps up to Hart, who's moving slightly. He hesitates and it looks like Hart's trying to speak. God knows how. Captain Emmett should have just ended it there and then. But he stoops down and tries to hear what Hart says. Puts his hand on his arm. Then he stands up again, whiter even than he was before. His arm with the gun is just hanging at his side. He looks up towards the MO and Mr Brabourne and for a minute nobody moves. Mr Brabourne looks back. The MO moves forward but stops. Hart's sort of coughing. His leg's twitching.'

Byers swallowed hard.

'Then suddenly Tucker walks across to the captain. He pushes Hart half over with his boot, reaches out and takes the captain's pistol out of his hand. No resistance at all. He shoots Hart, straight in the face. Then he takes Captain Emmett's hand, puts the gun in it, salutes sharpish, and walks back to the rest of us.'

Byers fell silent and when he spoke again his voice was husky.

'It was all wrong, all of it. It's why I took it so bad with Jim, it brought it all back.'

He put his spectacles back on and looked defiantly at Laurence.

'Tucker marches us off back to the farmyard. But not before we could all hear someone throwing up, Mr Brabourne, I think it was, but then whatever you say about Mr Brabourne, he'd had guts to be there; he didn't have to be. Could have been the padre, mind you. He was green too. God knows what happened between the officers. We don't see the MO and the padre again; they went off someplace else, and Captain Emmett and Mr Brabourne get back a while later. No mention of any irregularities. Nothing. No comeback I ever heard of against Tucker. Nor against your friend, Captain Emmett. Our secret. But Tucker, when the officers come in, he's standing next to the captain and the captain won't even look at him, when Tucker calls out, "Byers, there's an officer here needs his boots cleaning," and I look down and Captain Emmett looks down and there's blood and brains and stuff all over his foot.'

The room was suddenly silent. Then, slowly, sound crept back in. Laurence was aware of a clock ticking and a squeak each time Byers moved in his chair. His own grated as he pushed it back. Incongruously he could hear a blackbird somewhere outside. Byers was looking down and absent-mindedly tapping his pencil on his desk. Slowly Laurence picked up the more remote noise of metalworking and someone shouting.

'Thank you for telling me,' he said. 'You're a brave man. It can't be easy to go back over it.'

'None of us were brave, ever,' said Byers. 'Bravery's when you've got a choice.' He blinked as if finding himself somewhere he didn't quite expect. 'I'm not a man for fancies but sometimes I think we were cursed after. Dusty was gassed, I heard. Not in an attack but by some stupid lamp in a dugout. Probably too drunk to notice. Vince's body was never even found after the last push at Ypres. I heard Watkins went raving mad after his twin brother was killed, and he was locked up. The padre was done for when they took a big German dugout. Some well-meaning lad tells him there's a little shrine in the corner still with a cross. Padre rushes in, marvelling. Booby-trapped. Blew him to kingdom come. And the APM, a hard man, they say, survived the war, went back to the police here in London – he was the copper the major knew. Just the other week he was shot by some villain with a grudge. I saw it in the paper. Now you tell me Captain Emmett's done himself in. I'm not even surprised; it was a stinking business from start to finish.'

'Yet you're still here.'

But even as he spoke, Laurence was considering the reach of coincidence. Most of the casualties Byers had spoken of were straightforward, but if the assistant provost marshal had been murdered the balance seemed to shift.

'Right,' said Byers. 'Well then, that leaves me and Tucker and the MO. Who knows about the young one whose name I've forgotten and the one with the shakes. Tucker's alive and kicking, of course. Alive, at any rate.'

'Our secret,' Byers had said. But not many shared it now. He didn't tell the younger man that the MO had died.

'Enid's brother-in-law, Ted, who'd served with him, said Tucker came out and took himself back up to the Black Country. Hasn't managed to hold down a job, though, I hear.

So perhaps the war did get him in the end? Ted's a Birmingham man and he saw him a year or so back, though not to speak to. Had a wife all along, did Tucker, and some kiddies. The devil looks after his own's all I can say.'

'And Mr Brabourne?'

'Never heard of him again. Doubt he made it through. Like I said, he was a schoolboy on a spree. Right out of his depth.'

Laurence wondered about Tresham Brabourne. In ideal circumstances, advocates at courts martial were chosen from those who'd had legal experience before the war but circumstances were seldom ideal. With a military manual, a so-called Prisoner's Friend might try to construct a defence. It was surprising, though, that an officer hadn't been represented by someone who'd been a barrister in civilian life. However, if they'd been in a hurry, and his family either hadn't been notified or hadn't been well connected, then someone like Brabourne might be the best the accused could hope for. All the same, he had accompanied a man he'd defended, presumably to the best of his ability, to a horrible death. He didn't have to be there. That made him a bit more than the careless boy that Byers took him for.

Could Brabourne still be alive? Rumour had it that if a man defended the accused too energetically, he found himself on all the worst sorties afterwards. Simply defending Hart might have shortened the odds on young Brabourne's survival.

When he looked at his watch, Laurence was embarrassed to see that over an hour had passed. He jumped to his feet, apologising.

'No matter,' said Byers, although he looked relieved. 'I'd said I'd never talk about it again but now I have. It doesn't change anything. The major knew, of course, and I'd spoken of it to Jim, but I've never even told Enid. I don't want her to know the man I was then. I'm only talking of it now because the major brought you in. All my anger's gone Tucker's way but the war just gave Tucker his head. Yet who else is there? The system? The generals on both sides? The Kaiser? The hothead who chucked a bomb at that duke in Serbia? Truth is, I don't even know *who* to blame. It's the same with Jim's death. A great unknown enemy out there that I can't even hate properly.'

Laurence had a sense that there was something Byers had withheld from his account. 'And there's nothing else you want to tell me?' he asked.

Byers was rotating a pencil in his fingers; it twirled like a propeller. Suddenly he lost control of it and it spun across the room. Momentarily Laurence followed its trajectory with his eyes. It hit the wall. When he looked back, Byers seemed not to have noticed; his fingers were still moving.

'Isn't that enough?' he said.

Laurence put his hand out and after a moment's hesitation Byers shook it. The rain had stopped and men were struggling to get a large safe on to a pallet as Laurence walked across the yard. There was no sign of Major Calogreedy.

He strode out through the open gates and turned left. The Thames was brown, with foam from one of the industrial works forming a pale scum along the pilings. It was chilly down by the river. Laurence could smell the dankness of the water and the smoke of a thousand afternoon coal fires.

As he walked back along the Thames, he found himself hoping that Leonard Byers' marriage was a comfort to him. On the point of leaving he'd asked him whether he would ask Mrs Byers' brother-in-law where Tucker could be found. Byers doubted he knew — but he gave him the name of the pub he'd been told Tucker drank in: The Woodman.

'I've never been there, never been north of London, but he said that's where to go if I was ever up in our Birmingham works and wanted to look Tucker up. That was his idea of a joke.'

CHAPTER NINETEEN

*H*e was impatient to see what Charles could unearth so rather than wait until their usual rendezvous, Laurence scrawled a note to him with the few details he had about Hart and Brabourne in the hope Charles might find out something by Thursday, when they were due to meet. He didn't even know Hart's first name. He kept the thrust of the story to himself; he was interested to see its effect on Charles when he retold it in person.

Seeing Calogreedy and Byers caught up in their working lives, Laurence had felt guilty. Recently he'd hardly picked up his own work. That was the trouble with his research: too solitary, too quickly set aside. His publishers were easy on him and, in a sense, the small income Louise's money had provided was a trap. It was time he did something more demanding. Not in business like Calogreedy and Weatherall, and certainly not a return to coffee trading. What did begin to attract him was going back to a classroom, not the tutoring he'd done after leaving Oxford, but something more structured. He wondered whether he could get a beak's job at a good school.

On Thursday night Charles's club was almost empty. They both chose lamb chops with Cumberland sauce. The lamb was beautifully tender and sweet but Laurence scarcely noticed as he struggled to recall every detail of what Byers had told him. When he had finished, his friend whistled through his teeth.

'We had a private who faced the death penalty for sleeping at his post but the colonel was never going to let it be carried out. It was enough the lads thought it could be. Kept the rest awake. But bad for morale, these things. Shooting an officer. Rotten luck that old Emmett drew the short straw. They usually made a subaltern do the dirty work. As always. Byers give you anything else?'

'That was it,' Laurence said. 'Resentful but frank.'

Charles said, 'I heard there was a point when the powers that be wanted to quash the rumours that there was one rule for officers and another for the men. From what you say, this Hart seems to have been the best they could do for an example. Don't imagine it would have happened if his people had known the right people.' He stopped and gave it some thought, then said, 'Damn odd about the batman's cousin, don't you think?'

'There's something odd all round. I keep thinking there's something I'm missing,' said Laurence. 'John seems to have been making amends for things that happened in the war. Leaving money to Bolitho after his terrible injury, unburdening himself to Dr Chilvers. Various people seem to have noticed an improvement in his mental state towards the end of his life. It seems unlikely Mrs Lovell's son was part of either the trench collapse or the execution of Lieutenant Hart, although he might have been involved in the court martial, I suppose. But he was apparently close to his mother, and never told her about it. So what is John's connection with Lovell — or even Mrs Lovell herself? It's quite possible there was something else there that he was trying to put right. John served for over three years. God knows what else happened. And what about the unknown Frenchman?'

Eventually Charles spoke again. 'Well, there's another possible line of enquiry re Hart. Young Tresham Brabourne's alive, you'll be surprised to hear. Or he was when he came out of the army in December 1918.'

Laurence found his spirits lifting. He'd instinctively taken to the unknown Brabourne and was glad he was still around. His survival disproved Byers' gloomy predictions. If they could find him, Brabourne's account of John's state could be invaluable. He might even know of a connection with a Lovell.

'But no idea where he is, I'm afraid. There's his mother's name as next of kin.' He pulled out a bit of paper from an inner pocket. 'Fulvia — they go in for funny names, these Brabournes. Mind you, she's not Brabourne, either. She's Green. Mrs Fulvia Elizabeth Green. Must have remarried. But the only address is Beverley, Yorkshire. Brabourne joined up in 1915. Profession, pupil in chambers. All of which is a fat lot of good to us. Leave it with me and I'll see what other sleuthing I can do. Or we can go north to find him?'

'So he was training at the Bar? That's why he defended Hart.'

'Possibly. Poor disgraced Hart. My cousin in the War Office clammed up about Hart, or any execution. Papers not public and they're currently sensitive to parliamentary concerns. Whatever that means. But the records are in chaos anyway. He just gave me the enlistment details. His name was Edmund. A Londoner when he joined up, if this Hart is our boy. Which he probably is, though it's quite a common name, but the date's right. Born in Winson . . .'

'What kind of place is that?' Laurence asked.

'A small place,' Charles replied. 'In Gloucestershire, I think. A coincidence? No profession given, which is not so surprising as he was only eighteen. Parents, Mr and Mrs P. Hart. Very informative,' he said dryly. 'At least there's a street this time, but no name or number and you can hardly go from door to door saying, excuse me, was your son shot as a coward? Families try to cover these things up. In fact, they often don't find out until they begin to smell a rat when the pension doesn't come through. Still, more officers were sentenced to death than you'd think. Just not shot on the whole. Recommendations to pardon or commute hurtling across the Channel like whizz-bangs. Hart was unlucky.'

'What a bugger.'

'Yes. I expect he thought so,' said Charles. 'Beastly business. God knows what it did to Emmett. Mind you, what was he thinking? Once Hart was wounded he should have just finished him off. It makes it all much worse for the men who misfired. Everyone has the jitters in these sorts of situations but he was the officer. And as for Tucker, he should have been sorted out way back, it seems to me. Insolence, abuse of power, bullying, contravention of King's Regs. Weak leadership there, letting a rogue NCO call the tune.'

'And now I'm going to have to go and confront the man himself,' said Laurence.

'What?'

'Well, something set John and Tucker against each other and that something apparently culminated in the fiasco at the execution. They obviously loathed each other. And Byers hinted that Tucker's ministrations to his own friend after the trench

189

accident were murderous rather than medical. Though his actions were vague and Byers hated the man, so it may be wishful thinking.'

'So you think you can track down Tucker, wherever he might have got to?' Charles spoke slowly. 'And might I add that Tucker is hardly in the same league as Tresham Brabourne when it comes to distinctive names? Then you're going to tell him that the man he persecuted, by the sound of it, was your chum, whom he drove to his death, and then he's obligingly going to tell you exactly what it was all about, man to man, and you can bear the news to the fair Mary Emmett and set her mind at rest and ensure her everlasting gratitude. Is that how you see it?'

'Well, no, obviously not. But I don't have to show Tucker how partisan I am. I can think of some legitimate reason for seeing him. If he's fallen on hard times he might even talk in exchange for money. And actually I do know how to find him. He's in Birmingham.'

'Ah, that rural hamlet. Should be easy, then. And I expect he has war heroes, brimming with derring-do, travelling up from London to ask his opinion on this and that every day of the week?'

'I know exactly where he is. At least I know how to find him. In a public house.'

Charles gave him a long look. 'Of course. Simple. Apart from anything else, Tucker could be dangerous. He doesn't sound like a man to cross. My cousin says the final wartime death toll is going to be a loss of about one in four or five officers and rather less than that for other ranks, one in eight, say. Mind you, that doesn't include poor buggers with half-lives like John and Bolitho. Maybe a third of us were casualties of some sort. Some outfits were hit badly, obviously some got off lightly, but what we're talking about here is a complete reversal of that ratio: almost everybody connected with Tucker is dead. Some died well after the hostilities.'

'Well, the soldiers died in action. Byers' cousin can hardly be counted and policemen do, occasionally, die on duty. John made his own decision. Probably.'

Charles looked thoughtful. 'What do we know about the death of the police officer, late APM, then? Mullins, was it? When was it for a start? Have the police got anybody for it?'

'I don't know. No idea,' said Laurence. 'I vaguely remember seeing a headline. I suppose I can find out but it must have been weeks, maybe even months ago.'

'My point exactly. If it's a question of killing their own, the police won't rest until he's caught and hanged. Not a casual crook, I'd say, if he's managed to elude them. Anyway, when did you last hear of the death of any senior policeman?'

Laurence shook his head.

'I'm not being overly dramatic,' said Charles, 'but think about it. Even Byers' cousin's death could have been someone wanting to get back at Leonard Byers, someone with a nasty line in vindictiveness, and from everything you've told me about Tucker, he seems to fit the bill.'

'Charles . . .' Laurence began.

'You think it's improbable? *I* think it's improbable but it still makes me cautious about you tootling off to track Tucker down. Think, man, what was really shocking about Tucker's behaviour over Hart's death? He shot him in the face. Unnecessary. Maximum damage. Maximum impact for onlookers plus public contempt for John.'

'I know what you're getting at,' Laurence interrupted, 'that whoever it was deliberately shot Byers' cousin in the face. Whom do we know who has a taste for that kind of thing?

Who might want to send a message to Leonard Byers? Tucker. That's why I'm going. All roads lead to Tucker.'

'But I don't think yours should. He strikes me as one of those men who hated all officers on principle.'

'John wasn't shot in the face,' Laurence said. 'He didn't even shoot himself in the head like most suicides.'

'No,' said Charles, 'but you've already started to wonder whether it really was suicide. Could you still put your hand on your heart and tell Miss Emmett her brother killed himself?'

Laurence's optimism was flagging, yet it had all seemed to be coming together less than a week ago. Not perfect, but approaching coherence.

'It simply makes it more important that I try to see Tucker,' he said. 'Why would anyone disguise John's death to look like suicide? If there is a single killer he certainly didn't bother to do so with Byers and Mullins.' He felt foolish even articulating it. 'And I keep asking myself, why would anyone be doing this?'

'Any chance you've still got your gun?' Charles asked, and then, seeing the look on Laurence's face, went on, 'No, of course you haven't.'

'I'm not getting on a train at St Pancras armed to the teeth anyway, if that's what you've got in mind. I'm not a gangster. This isn't America,' Laurence retorted. After a moment's hesitation he added, 'But I'll tell you what. I won't go rushing up there just yet. Before I do, I'll check the archives for the story of that policeman's death. No danger there and it's easily done.'

'And I'll try to track down Brabourne,' said Charles. 'Then if, and only if, we feel it's necessary to head north, we'll both go. No, don't protest,' he interrupted as Laurence started to speak. 'Safety in numbers. Tucker's a maniac. Don't want to find myself buying back your tenderest parts pickled in a bottle, do I?'

'You think Tucker's more likely to talk to two strangers than one?' said Laurence. 'I don't.'

'No. But I think he's less likely to attack two than one. His sort go for the safe bet. Anyway, I'd like to look the man in the eye.'

They finished their dinner, Laurence turning down the offer of brandy and cigars. Charles walked with him to get his coat. Impulsively, Laurence shook his hand, holding it with both his own.

'Thank you,' he said. 'You've been more of a help than you know.'

Charles looked simultaneously pleased and embarrassed.

'I was getting bored, you know. Before. At least with the war you knew where you were.'

CHAPTER TWENTY

When he arrived home his rooms felt cold and unwelcoming even when he'd lit the fire. He made some thick, bitter cocoa and warmed his hands on the cup. There were things he thought he'd never know for sure but the biggest remaining question mark, apart from Tucker's role in all this, was why Gwen Lovell had been left money by a stranger and why they couldn't find Harry Lovell's records.

But then another thought struck him. They'd all made the assumption that Lovell was an officer. He had done it from the start himself. Mrs Lovell had never said so but he'd taken it for granted because, although in visibly reduced circumstances, she was a lady and also because of her assumption that John, a captain, might plausibly have been her son's friend. Friendships were rare across the ranks. But whether or not you went into the ranks wasn't always a matter of class. Sometimes it was one of preference.

He'd read of a famous headmaster's son who'd set out to be a conscientious objector, but when half the young men in his village had died he had finally joined up, refusing the commission his education entitled him to. Eventually he had won the Victoria Cross. There were plenty of others. One school friend, he'd heard, had gone into the Royal Flying Corps as a mechanic, simply because he was fascinated by the engines.

It was much rarer the other way. A costermonger or a miner didn't get a commission, however good a soldier or however bravely he fought. Although an exceptionally able bank clerk or a seed merchant might work his way up to major if casualties were sufficiently high, he doubted they'd find an unstinting welcome in the mess. Even in the face of imminent death and conditions of massive discomfort, the nuances were always there. Snobbery, prejudice, bullying: all of it transported straight from the playing fields and drawing rooms of English society. He had been guilty of it himself, assuming the son of the well-spoken Mrs Lovell would automatically have held a commission.

If young Lovell was the link between John Emmett and the bequest to Mrs Lovell, and Lovell was a private soldier, not an officer, the puzzle became more complex still, simply in terms of numbers. It was just possible that the man his mother had described as sensitive and music-loving might have refused a commission despite his background. He cast back to the events that people had described to him over the last few weeks and thought how often he'd heard the phrase 'some corporal' or been told of 'a young soldier' or 'a private – I don't think I ever knew his name'. He felt momentarily dispirited but then recalled that Lovell, though an interesting loose end, didn't seem to be at the centre of his enquiry. Why was he making everything so complicated?

As he got ready for bed, he thought about seeing Mary again. Tomorrow, no, he tipped his watch to the light, today, she'd be here, in London. Yet since her unexplained encounter with Charles in Tunbridge Wells and that fleeting exchange with a stranger at the Wigmore Hall, he was wary. He could hardly ask her to explain herself.

Several hours later, when she appeared waving vigorously from the far end of the platform, so that the pompons on the ends of her scarf danced on her coat, the minutiae of his concerns about her fled away. She tucked her arm in his as if they were the oldest friends in the world. Her other arm clutched a bag to her body.

'Gosh, it's cold,' she said. 'Do you think it's going to snow early this year? It'll make the winter seem awfully long.'

She had put on a little weight, he thought, and it suited her. Today the cold had also flushed her cheeks and her eyes sparkled.

'How've you been?' he asked once they were settled on the bus, knowing that he really wanted to ask what she had been doing.

'Oh, all right. You know. Up and down but I think, on the whole, more up than down. It's not so easy for my mother.'

'But she's still got you,' said Laurence.

'Maybe you always count the cost of what you've lost more than what you still have,' she said. 'Anyway, she was always trying to get rid of me — marry me off. Ghastly men. Whiskery bachelor academics, mournful widowers.' She looked mortified. 'Oh Laurence, how frightful of me. I'm dreadfully sorry.' She put her warm, gloveless hand over his. 'I didn't mean you or anyone like you. It was just a joke. I talk too much, always have, especially when I'm trying to impress someone. Say things I shouldn't even think.'

He was more amused than anything else, though glad she might want to impress him.

As he helped her down from the bus he said, 'Perhaps she's

eager for grandchildren. Another generation to live for.' He added swiftly, 'There, that sounds awfully clumsy too. I don't mean to suggest your only purpose is to produce babies as her consolation.'

'You're probably right, though,' said Mary. 'Ideally they'd be boys and the oldest one could be called John. The youngest too, possibly. That should do it. A girl called Johanna in the middle. But I need to find the right man first.' He knew she was teasing him as she squeezed his arm a little more tightly.

'Let's get out of the cold and have tea,' he said, already turning up a street in the direction of the British Museum. They were walking too fast to talk easily.

It was the same small place that he had used to meet Eleanor. The waitress who took their order seemed completely indifferent to them. Her cap was pinned far back on her crimped yellow hair and with her lips coloured into a surprised-looking bow, she looked like a large, rather peevish doll. In any case she was too busy watching the door, waiting for somebody she evidently expected. But nobody else ever arrived; the room was theirs. Laurence curved his cold fingers round his cup.

Before he could start to tell Mary of what he still thought of as his detective work, she took out a brown envelope from her bag.

'Look,' she said, 'these were things I found in the bedside cupboard in John's room. They were just odds and ends that came back with his things from Holmwood, so we shoved them in there and forgot about them. Nothing very exciting. A couple of laundry lists, notes of some birds he'd seen in the garden. You see,' she said, pulling out a lined sheet, 'he did have some interest in what was going on.'

Laurence took the bit of paper. The writing was uncontrolled but the content was clear:

Blackbird.
Mistle thrush, M. and F.
Great tit.
Blue tit (nesting in garage wall?)

Beside it John had sketched a blue tit, a coal tit and a great tit, and labelled them.

Chaffinches.
Woodpecker (heard, but never seen).
Hedge sparrow — lots.
Pipit? Chiffchaff.
Wren (in honeysuckle outside music-room window)
Red kite. A pair. Just once, walking out. Mewling over the river valley. Wonderful. N. was a little frightened at first. Larks. 'All the birds of Oxfordshire and Gloucestershire.' Went as far as river watching them through Dr C's glasses. As agreed did not throw myself in!

Another, much neater hand, had added:

Greater puff-chested yellow fiddler. Fine plumage; watchful demeanour. Mates prolifically with weaker females. Harsh and irritating repetitive cry. Minemineminemine. Moneemoneemonee. Rarely leaves his natural habitat, where he is king of his tattered little flock, for the open countryside where the woodland animals might tear him apart.

They looked at each other.

'It's nice, isn't it?' said Mary, hopefully.

Laurence, lost in the last sentence, was startled for a second but realised she meant the birdwatching. It was true, he could feel John's old enthusiasm. The quote was Edward Thomas, he thought. This was the first he'd seen of a John he recognised in anything he'd heard about him since the war. It went a small way to dispelling the image of him as just an angry and unstable officer. Nor had he been alone, from the sound of it. Could his timid companion, frightened by birds of prey, have been the fragile Mrs George Chilvers, he wondered?

'But who do you think wrote this?' he asked, pointing to the foot of the page.

'Well, I assumed it was *about* the younger Chilvers. Not an actual bird, obviously. I suppose it could be anybody. Briefly I thought it might be John writing about himself; it has his sort of wit, and even calling himself a coward . . . but nothing else fits. He was never puffed up and couldn't give an earthly for money. He worried about my father when Daddy kept putting too much on the horses – Daddy was a bit of an optimist where racing was concerned and our mother used to rage at him – but I don't think he was happy when he discovered that my maternal grandparents' wealth had always been entailed to him.'

Laurence mentally ticked off one question: which was how John had had any money to leave Bolitho and Mrs Lovell, and how the Emmetts came by their current house. Had John got everything simply because he was the male heir, he wondered?

'And the bottom bit's not John's writing,' she said. 'He had to use his left hand because his right was paralysed. And all those tails like umbrella handles on the Ys, not him. If not Mrs Chilvers, another inmate, perhaps?'

Even as she spoke, Laurence felt certain the unknown companion must have been Eleanor but he didn't want to raise this with Mary yet.

'A disaffected member of staff?' she suggested. 'And it could be *about* anybody. But my money's on Chilvers. Did you see the man's driving gloves?'

'What were they?' John asked, trying to sound light-hearted and disguise his discomfort at withholding information. 'Mink, studded with emeralds, or spiked metal gauntlets to incapacitate any motorist who impedes his way?'

'Well, nearer the mink. Bright-yellow kid, fine and soft. Must have cost a fortune. I know because when we met, he had just got out of that car of his and rather creepily he shook hands — well, he squeezed hands — without taking them off. It was like warm loose skin against my own flesh. Disgusting. Had his poor wife with him. Like a mannequin. All the latest fashions — French probably. Perfect hair. Perfect marcasite earrings. Enviable hat. Well, I was envious. Fox stole. Just the thing for a madhouse in some rural back of beyond.'

She stopped and seemed to consider what she'd said.

'Poor woman. She didn't say a word and he didn't introduce us. A life sentence, however many hats.'

'Rumour has it, she was the one with hats in the first place. It's he who wasn't in gloves until she came along.'

Mary summoned a half-hearted expression of scorn, but she was focused on pulling a pamphlet out of the manila envelope. It was poor-quality paper that had obviously been rolled up at some time. She tried to smooth it out on the table, weighing down one end with the sugar bowl. The front cover had an ink drawing of a cluster of stars and across it, in what might almost have been potato print, the word *Constellations*.

Inside the front cover was a short typed paragraph, signed only: Charon. He read it.

'Read, stranger, passing by. Here disobedient to their laws, we cry. 1916.'

The epigraph echoed something he knew from school. Ancient Greek, he thought, but the words were not quite right. He read on. The following pages were all typed poems. After a few pages he came to the one he'd seen scrawled in one of John's notebooks back in Cambridge. He turned it to show Mary. She nodded. 'That one again,' she said. '"Sisyphus".'

He read it for a second time. Its brilliance struck him, just as it had in the stuffy attic at the end of the summer. Once he had been an enthusiastic reader of poetry but since the war he had read very little. He found the best modern poets so disturbing that he was invariably left melancholic; the worst were excruciating lists of rhyming clichés. This poem, however, was beyond categorisation; there was a strangely mystical feel about it. He remembered reading Gerard Manley Hopkins at Oxford. This Sisyphus had the same mad beauty in his writing. Reality had all but disappeared and what was left was like the unease of a dream.

'I can't understand it,' said Mary. 'In fact the more I try, the less I succeed — but when I relax, I seem to absorb it. Or something . . .' She trailed off embarrassed and then said as if to defuse her emotional response, 'But it's bit affected, this pseudonym stuff. I mean, they're not boys in the classical sixth. Why can't they just use their initials if they're feeling coy? Anyway, if they'd put their names to them, they might be famous by now.'

'They wouldn't risk it,' said Laurence. 'It had to be private unless it was frightfully gung-ho, our glorious dead, noble sacrifice sort of stuff. The one John had published earlier was just on the right side of the divide. But most were never intended for publication. Although this is obviously a bit more than the work of a few friends.'

He remembered what Eleanor Bolitho had told him about John publishing poetry, his own and others', and was certain this was the project she'd spoken of. Again, he felt forced to keep information back until he'd tried to speak to Eleanor but he felt fraudulent presenting knowledge as a conclusion.

'Someone's typed it, for a start; it's in semi-circulation, I think, and well before the war ended, judging by the date on the introduction.' He turned back a page. 'I mean, look at this one, it's not satire, it's simply contempt: "The pink brigadier lifts his snout from the swill." I don't think it would have advanced anybody's career.'

Opposite the farmyard ditty was a neat traditional poem. Unlike much of the poetry, this was oddly cheerful and complete. So many of the poems were raw and rough-edged. Yet here was a tidy pastoral sonnet. The work of an optimist or a blind man. Blue speedwell, bluer sky, skylarks, hawthorn after rain. Distant guns like summer thunder. Laurence rather liked it. The pen name was 'Hermes'.

'Hermes,' said Mary, 'the messenger.'

'The winged messenger,' said Laurence. 'And Sisyphus had a vast rock to roll uphill for ever, and Charon rowed the dead, of course.' He looked again at the page. 'Would you mind if I borrowed this?' he asked. 'I can see it's fragile but I'll be really careful.'

He gave her no reason. There was none beyond a wish to read it, at his leisure and unobserved.

'Have it all – everything – if it helps.'

He refilled Mary's cup with lukewarm tea. The waitress was outside, peering up the street. He could no longer put off recounting his interview with Byers. What he told Mary was pretty faithful to what he'd heard, though omitting the severed penis and the brains that had splattered on John's boot.

Nonetheless, when he had finished, her head was bowed. She was absolutely silent and then two tears dropped from the end of her nose on to the willow pattern of her plate. She rubbed her nose with her hand, rustling around in her bag and her pockets, apologising and sniffing, until Laurence found his own handkerchief, clean, even ironed. She dabbed rather ineffectually, then held it across her eyes, almost hiding behind it. Then she sat for a minute with the handkerchief screwed up in her hand and her hand bunched against her forehead. Eventually she took a deep, slightly uneven breath.

'I'm sure we could have helped if he'd spoken to us.' Her eyes filled with tears again.

'I think,' said Laurence very cautiously, 'that many men – just couldn't talk about things. It was as if once they put words to it, it would overwhelm them completely. And they didn't want to place that burden on people they loved. Couldn't.'

Mary sniffed but he thought it was an encouraging sniff.

'Even now, if I meet another man my sort of age, we know we probably share the same sort of memories; we don't discuss it but it's there between us. But with families there's a sort of innocence. It can be exasperating' – he thought back to Louise's patriotic certainties – 'but sometimes it's easier to be with people who haven't been,' he searched for a word, 'corrupted,' he said finally. He knew that he had moved from the general to the particular, revealing himself more than he'd intended.

'But the price is that you'll always be alone,' Mary said heatedly. 'And a whole generation of women are excluded. Redundant. Irrelevant.'

Laurence nodded. He thought of Eleanor Bolitho and wondered how different it must be to be with a woman who had shared some of the horror.

'It's not fair. You don't give us a chance.' Mary's voice rose slightly.

'The man I was telling you about — Byers. He's not been married long. Yet he's never ever told his wife all this.'

'And perhaps Mrs Byers has lots of things she'd like to tell him. Of fear and loneliness and never knowing who was coming back or in what shape. Sitting. Waiting. Perhaps you should ask us whether we'd like to know? We're women, not children.'

'He means well . . . he's trying to protect her.'

Mary snorted, or something like it. 'So from now on we conduct our relationships in a dense fog with areas marked *do not enter*. Brilliant, Laurence.'

He didn't know how to respond. He didn't want to tell her she had no idea. That he, at least, *couldn't* put the past into words, not that he wouldn't. His heart was beating erratically.

'So do you have secrets tucked away? Do *all* you men have secrets?' she asked almost angrily.

He wanted to say, 'Do you?' but instead he said, 'Yes, of course I do.' Then he found himself blurring his truth. 'Everybody has secret bits of their life, I suppose.' He tried to stop it sounding too much like an accusation.

She nodded almost imperceptibly, suddenly calmer. 'Was it all really, really awful? Out there?'

'No. Some of it was boring. Some of it was funny. Living in a cottage with two other subalterns and a French family: the mother giving birth noisily upstairs while we ate sausages and lentils. Some of it was plain ludicrous. There were two men in my platoon, and every time we seemed settled for more than a week, they'd start growing vegetables. And rhubarb. A year or so later we passed through the village again and the rhubarb was thriving – the only thing that was, amid the ruins. Nearly all of it was uncomfortable. Some people enjoyed bits of it, especially at first. My friend Charles; he was a natural. He was good at it. His men respected him. He liked his men. I liked mine. Most of them. But we both had an easy war compared with some.'

He had a sudden image of a soldier beaming at him. It was Pollock, the fat man, khaki uniform straining. There never was such a man for belching. He could do it to 'God Save the King'. The men counted on his last lucky belch each time they went over the top.

She sat quietly for a while, gazing at the closed pamphlet. Eventually she said, 'I'm glad in a way we have that list of bird-watching. That's a long time after the worst of it. So at least I know that he didn't always feel as wretched and raging as he was when he came back. This,' she picked up the list, 'is a John I recognise. Look, he can even joke about not throwing himself in the river. He's simply glad to be alive. I think he is, at last, I really do.'

'Yes.' Strangely, his own reaction to glimpsing this hour of pleasure was sadness.

'But come the winter, it all goes wrong.'

He couldn't decide whether to tell her of his faint disquiet about John's death. What he and Charles might have found plausible after a good dinner was too far-fetched to be presented as real speculation, although it didn't really seem to make much difference. Mary had still lost her only brother. Unless you were a policeman, the need to reveal and avenge murder was reduced almost to a philosophical enquiry after the losses of the last years.

CHAPTER TWENTY-ONE

While Laurence was mulling over Tucker's intentions and paying the bill, Mary's mood seemed to shift. She took his arm as they walked into the street.

'Have you ever gone to the films? I suppose you have, living in London?'

Laurence shook his head. 'Not recently,' he said. The only films he'd seen were flickering newsreels at HQ. 'Would you like to, next time, perhaps?'

'I'd love that,' said Mary. 'I saw Lillian Gish a while back, in *The Greatest Thing in Life*, and she was beautiful and funny. Or we could go to a play? *Heartbreak House* might be more your thing. More serious.'

Laurence relaxed into Mary's easy assumption that she knew what he'd like. He clamped his arm down a little so that her hand was caught between his upper arm and his ribs. He looked sideways at her, half hidden under the rim of her dark-red hat. She returned his gaze, apparently amused.

When they arrived at the station, there was an unexpectedly

large crowd by the platform. Laurence pushed himself to the front to speak to the stationmaster.

'No train,' he said when he'd fought his way back to her. 'There's been a landslip. Nothing until tomorrow. Do you want me to arrange for you to be put up at a hotel? Or can you go to your cousin?'

'My cousin's about to produce her fourth baby,' said Mary. 'I really don't think I could pitch up unannounced.'

To Laurence's relief she didn't look particularly bothered.

'Isn't your mother going to be worried?'

'No. She and Aunt Virginia are in Buxton. They're taking the waters in the hope it might help my mother's rheumatism.'

They had turned away from the platform. After a long silence, Mary said hurriedly, 'Look, would it be possible, say if it wouldn't, if I came back with you?' She looked slightly embarrassed.

'Yes. Of course. I just thought you wouldn't really want to. It's not terribly comfortable.' He was worrying that it might not be terribly clean, either.

'No, that's fine. More than fine. Anyway I'd love to see where you live. There's a limit to the appeal of teashops.'

He was about to tell her that she would have to sleep in his bed, and that he was quite happy to sleep in an armchair, but didn't want her to think his mind had raced ahead to the sleeping arrangements.

They stopped and bought roasted chestnuts on a street corner; the man who huddled over the glowing coals was wearing his campaign medals on his coat. Cradling the small, warm bags in their hands, they caught a bus that took them right up to Bloomsbury. Mary insisted she didn't want anything else to eat.

The house was in darkness but, as they climbed the first

flight of stairs, the door to his neighbour's flat opened. Laurence stopped dead, placing his hand on Mary's forearm.

'Good evening,' said his neighbour, his unkempt bulk filling the doorway. He looked Mary up and down.

'Ah . . . this is a friend of mine: Miss Emmett.'

'Yes. I see.'

'Was there anything?' Laurence began.

'No. I was just going out.' His neighbour stayed watching them as they climbed up to the next floor.

'Sorry,' Laurence said as soon as they were in his flat and he had lit the fire. 'Perfectly harmless. But something a bit odd about him.'

Mary looked amused. 'It's all right. He was just awkward in the way men are who live by themselves for years.'

She slapped her hand across her mouth.

'There I go again, piling on one insult after another. I hope you know I don't mean you.'

'One of your droopy widowers who, having the misfortune to be living a single life, has fallen into unsavoury habits?'

'You know I don't think that and I certainly don't mean you.' She lightly batted her fists on his chest.

He looked at her. Her eyes were only a little lower in level than his, grey-green and clear. Her smile faded a little and her lips parted almost imperceptibly. He held her gently by the upper arms, locking her gaze for what seemed like a minute but was probably no time at all, and then let her go. She looked away, apparently confused.

Laurence went through to his bedroom, leaving Mary to warm herself by the fire.

'May I play the piano?' she asked.

'You can try,' he called through, 'but it's probably unplayable. It hasn't been tuned since . . . for ages.'

He knelt down by his bedroom wardrobe to see whether he had any spare linen at the bottom. He heard her open the piano lid and pull the stool closer. Then the stool lid opened and there was silence. He rocked back on his heels to peer through the doorway. She was standing, leafing through some sheet music, staring at it intently with her head bobbing. Then he realised she was hearing the music in her mind. She looked up, saw him gazing at her and laughed.

'Sorry, just trying to work out what I won't disgrace myself with.' She paused and indicated the front sheet. '"Louise Scudamore". Scudamore? Was that your wife? Was she good? At the piano?'

'She practised a lot,' said Laurence, remembering her playing rather heavily, leaning forward with a look of fraught concentration on her face and her nose screwed up. 'Her biggest trouble was that she needed spectacles.'

He remembered how hard Louise had tried. Her mother had thought her exceptional.

'Actually,' he went on, with a sudden burst of honesty, 'she was probably a bit hopeless, but she enjoyed it and she loved the piano. That's why I've kept it, even though I can't play a note.'

'You should learn to play. It would relax you.'

'I don't know any teachers,' he countered. 'Anyway, I'm far too relaxed half the time. I need to be less relaxed.'

She looked at him knowingly. 'I don't think so, Laurie. I don't think you're ever truly relaxed. In fact, I seem to recall thinking you were a very coiled-up, contained man when I first met you.'

He was about to protest but she had already returned to the music.

'Right, Liszt. That's a good start,' she said, sitting down. 'I used to be quite good at this. Or perhaps not?' she said, as she began to play, faltering a little on the first notes.

He finally found a pair of sheets. They were old and had been neatly turned, sides to middle, but they were clean and without holes. While she was engrossed in the music he held them to his face to check they didn't smell damp. When he shook them out, they were plainly for a double bed. Swags of embroidered flowers and bows decorated the upper edges. He found one recently laundered pillowcase and for the lower pillow kept the case already on it, smoothing it with his hand.

She went on playing. Her touch was assured but the tone was pretty awful. When he'd finished making the bed — *her* bed, he realised with pleasure — adding an extra blanket under the eiderdown because she might not be used to a bedroom as cold as his could be, he stood in the doorway and watched her. She thudded on a dead key, and not for the first time.

'It's stuck,' she said. 'You really ought to get this tuned, Laurie. It's a good piano, a willing one. It deserves to be tuned.'

'Pianos have personalities?'

'Of course they do. There are good pianos and bad pianos, willing ones and disobliging ones, modest ones and blustering ones. And *this* one shouldn't be abandoned.'

She leaned over and touched a slightly warped panel on the front where a shell in faded mother-of-pearl inlay was contained in a cartouche.

'Nor should her finery be neglected. When we still lived in the country, I had a lovely piano: a small Blüthner. Well, it was my mother's, really. My paternal grandfather had given it to her as a wedding present. My mother could play beautifully, much better than I can. When I was very little we used to laugh when she played duets with my grandfather.'

'You haven't got it now?'

'No. No room and anyway it was too valuable. We had to sell it.'

'I didn't realise . . .' Laurence began.

'Actually father was dreadful with money,' she said. 'Hopeless. The house in Suffolk was in trust for John. My grandfather — my other one, my mother's father — must have seen the way things were going long before he died. My father was really kind — well, you know he was,' her eyes shone, 'but he believed everybody. Every chancer with a half-baked scheme to make money. Every tip on a horse that might reverse our fortunes. And he never learned. He always wanted to see the good in people. Like John, in a way.'

'I'm sorry. Your parents were awfully good to me.'

'They were good people. But my mother was always a bit disappointed. She would have liked more of London life, I think, and she got worn down by staving off one crisis after another. Although my father was a steadfast family man, he never seemed to notice the odd writ, or the grass three feet tall, or living on mutton and onion tart for a week, or the smell of boiling soap ends.'

She changed the music and played some Brahms he recognised. He opened a kitchen drawer, found some candles and inserted them in the piano candleholders; as he pushed them into place, he could feel the accretion of old wax on his fingers. Wax that had dripped there when Louise was still thudding through her Chopin. He put some more coal on the fire and lit the oil lamp that had been his mother's.

Mary played for a little longer; the soft light on her skin made her look as young as he remembered her from before the war. But after a while she stopped suddenly, and swung her legs back over the stool.

'No, the piano needs more love to do Brahms justice. I'll tell you what, you get her tuned and I'll give you a concert.'

'I don't have any wine, to reward your efforts, I'm afraid,' he said. 'But I've got gin. And biscuits,' he added as an afterthought. 'Sweet-meal. Mostly broken. Or would you like cocoa?'

'What a feast,' she said.

In the end he found some bottled plums and a loaf of bread, as well as the biscuit fragments. The combination had shades of a school midnight feast. While he put them on a tray, she was looking at his bookcase.

'A man's shelves reveal all his secrets,' she said as she pulled out a book.

After a second of anxiety, he felt pleasure at this strange intimacy. 'Mostly my father's secrets, in this case.'

'Fair enough for the Dickens and the Wordsworth, and I don't think you'd have chosen Meredith, but *The Return of the Native* is a bit racy for somebody's father, I'd have thought. And — goodness, Laurence — *Sons and Lovers.*' She looked back at him questioningly. 'Whatever next?' She squatted down to look at the lower shelf. 'Now we get to it.'

Again he felt a flicker of unease.

'*Three Men in a Boat* next to their natural companion-on-shelf, Foxe's *Martyrs.* The many faces of Laurence Bartram.'

'Foxe is for my book research.'

'But you don't like your book.'

'No, I do.'

'No, you don't. You never talk about it. We've passed scores of churches and you've never said a thing about any of them.'

He didn't like to say that he had assumed she wouldn't be interested. When he didn't answer, she got to her feet. 'I didn't mean to pry.'

'No. It's fine.' He forced a smile. 'I do like churches a lot but the book's an excuse not to have to do anything else. I haven't looked at it for weeks.'

'Am I an excuse?'

'No, of course not.'

'But helping me is?'

'You mean, is it a diversion? Well, yes, but not in the way you think.'

Fatigue and gin had relaxed them by the time she finally braved the iciness of his bathroom, took a glass of water and kissed him on the cheek. He waited until she'd closed the door of the bedroom before stripping down to his shirt, drawers and socks.

He could hear her moving about for a while and the creak as she got into bed. He snuffed out the candles and then stubbed his toe on the armchair he'd arranged. He pulled his dressing-gown collar up around his face, covered himself with a blanket and tried to settle for the next half an hour. Eventually he dragged the seat cushions on to the floor, lay down on them and rolled himself up in the old blanket. He had not slept on a floor for three years. He hadn't expected to do so again but he was quietly content and lay for a while, looking towards the grey shape of the window and listening intently to any noise from next door. Was she awake? What was she thinking? He fancied he could hear her breathe though he knew it was impossible.

CHAPTER TWENTY-TWO

*T*he deep contentment he felt in Mary's company lasted him all the next day, even when she'd gone. He thought how pretty she looked in the morning, dressed but with her hair loose and legs bare. She had insisted on assembling a rudimentary breakfast. Eventually he'd surrendered and watched her as she handled his china and put a kettle on the stove as if she had visited many times before. He ached for her, not just to possess her, although certainly that, but also to protect her and to know her with an absolute familiarity.

But she ate swiftly, returned to the bedroom and sat, tidying her hair in front of the looking-glass. He turned away. She emerged with her hat on and her bag in her hand. To his surprise, she now wanted to go to Charing Cross. She had decided not to go back to Cambridge yet, she said. She referred vaguely to cousins near Wadhurst. Instead of asking her about them quite naturally, he'd resisted, convinced it would sound like an interrogation.

When he eventually walked out of the station and turned up the Strand, it was a fine day with the sky bright above the piebald trunks of the plane trees. He was determined not to let his mind dwell on her unexplained times in Sussex.

He had decided to start looking for Inspector Mullins in the archives of the *Daily Chronicle*. The *Chronicle* had the sort of ordinary coverage he needed, but also he had once pencilled the words of one of its war correspondents into his day book. The man had written: 'As an outside observer, I do not see why the war in this area should not go on for a hundred years, without any decisive result. What is happening now is precisely what happened last year.' Laurence had found it comforting rather than depressing. It meant he wasn't going mad.

He had occasionally peered at the *Chronicle*'s offices tucked away in a tiny square to one side of Fleet Street. The building had a dark and elaborate brick façade with an impressive portico. He was taken immediately down to an airless basement room crammed with files. The woman running the library of back copies looked blank when he asked whether she remembered the incident.

'I don't *read* any of them,' she said, as if he'd accused her of idling. 'I just keep them tidy.'

His first problem was in remembering when exactly he'd seen the original article. It was recent, he thought, not long after he met Mary. He took out a month of copies and placed them on a long table, going through them a week at a time. He was pretty sure this would be front-page news. A violent attack on such a senior officer was almost unknown in England, though he vaguely remembered that the head of Scotland Yard had survived being shot by a madman not long before the war.

He found the first mention of Mullins' murder fairly quickly on an inside cover of a September newspaper, but it was obviously a follow-up story, considering whether Bolsheviks might have been behind the attack, so he kept going backwards. Finally he found the headline he sought. It was unequivocal: SCOTLAND YARD SLAYING. The accompanying photograph was a portrait shot of the officer in uniform. The date was Friday, 26 August 1921.

He ran through the columns beneath. Chief Inspector Mullins had left Scotland Yard as he usually did at five-thirty in the afternoon. He was walking down the steps accompanied by a constable who, although some way behind him, was to be the nearest witness. As Mullins reached the last step, a man came up and spoke to him. The constable thought he had addressed him by name and that, although the inspector had nodded, he did not appear to recognise the gunman. The assailant then pulled out his weapon from inside his coat and fired. Mullins fell to the ground almost immediately and the gunman fired one further shot, mutilating him. Mullins expired within seconds. With the element of surprise in his favour and because those nearest were attempting to provide aid to the dying officer, the gunman was able to escape apprehension. He was described as clean-shaven, of average build, possibly in middle age. He wore a hat, which concealed some of his features, and a British Warm, with the collar up. The piece ended: 'Chief Inspector Gerald Mullins joined the Metropolitan Police in 1900 and served with distinction within the Corps of Military Police from 1916 to 1919. He leaves a widow, a son who is a police cadet, and four daughters.'

Laurence was struck straight away by the similarity, albeit as much in its vagueness as anything more significant, in the descriptions of the murderer of Jim Byers and the assailant described here.

He went back to the desk at the entrance and rapped lightly. The curator appeared out of the doorway behind it.

'Do you know how I can find out who wrote this?' He laid down the paper and pointed.

She shook her head, much as he expected. But then she said, 'Please wait,' and went back through the door. He could hear her footsteps as she climbed the stone stairs. After ten minutes he began to wonder whether she'd gone for a tea break, but she appeared as suddenly as she'd gone and beckoned him to follow her.

The porter in the little cubbyhole by the front entrance looked up. He was holding the telephone receiver in his hand and after a couple of seconds said, 'Mr Peterkin? Gentleman here to see you, sir.'

CHAPTER TWENTY-THREE

*P*eterkin was waiting as Laurence extricated himself from the small cage of a lift on the first-floor landing. He was shabbily dressed, with a harassed expression.

'Yes?' he said. 'May I help you?' He sounded mildly resentful at any expectation that he should.

'I'm sorry. I just wondered if I could speak to someone about an article in your paper.'

'Today?'

'No. A while back. It's about the murder – of a police officer – last summer. I really have only a few questions.'

'You mean the Mullins case?' The man looked slightly more interested.

Laurence nodded.

'It's not me you want to see.'

The man turned and Laurence followed. They passed through a long, scruffy room, amid a low buzz of chatter from men and one woman working at typewriting machines behind half-height partitions. Screwed-up balls of paper littered the floor. A telephone rang as he passed. At the far end was a tiny office. Peterkin stood aside at the open doorway. The room smelled strongly of tobacco.

'Mr Tresham Brabourne,' he said wearily, and a younger man looked up as if strangers were bundled into his office every day. By the time he stood up from his desk and shook Laurence's hand, Peterkin was gone.

Even as he absorbed the extraordinary coincidence unfolding in front of him, Laurence remembered Byers commenting on Brabourne's youth. He still looked very young, though he had to be well into his twenties. He was dressed in baggy tweed trousers and a thick corduroy jacket, a Fair Isle jumper and a striped scarf. Brabourne shut the door and gestured to a bentwood chair while he sat astride a similar one, facing Laurence over its curved back. He was silent for a couple of minutes, patting various pockets and finally pulling out a rather crushed packet of cigarettes before selecting one and putting it in his mouth.

Laurence read a poster on the wall:

BLESS | cold
| magnanimous
| delicate
| gauche
| fanciful
| stupid

ENGLISHMEN.

'Wyndham Lewis,' Brabourne muttered, pulling strands of tobacco from his tongue as he followed Laurence's glance. He offered the cigarettes to Laurence, then lit his own. As he struck and discarded a succession of faulty matches, he gestured to Laurence to speak.

Laurence, still astonished that fate should have delivered Brabourne to him, tried to explain his presence methodically but, as he jumped from Mary to Holmwood to the execution in France, he realised how muddled he sounded.

Brabourne listened patiently and intently. 'So,' he said, finally. 'You came here wanting to find out about the death of a London policeman in the summer, but now you're here, you've discovered you'd rather talk about my part in a firing squad in France in 1917? You know, when they were rebuilding these offices, the first year of the war, they found an old stone lion – probably Roman – hidden beneath our site. You never know what you're going to find if you start digging.'

'It is all a bit odd,' Laurence acknowledged. 'I'm really only trying to find out what happened to a friend with whom I should never have lost touch.'

Brabourne raised his eyebrows.

'The thing is, his sister really needs to understand why he shot himself.'

Laurence was aware it all sounded a bit lame. Why a man being treated for mental distress might kill himself was not a very profound mystery.

'But then one thing has led to another; his story was tied up with other stories and everything became more complicated. Or perhaps I've simply complicated it. The policeman was one thread, a man shot for cowardice became another and finding you is just a stroke of unnerving luck.'

'And they're all connected.'

'I'm sorry?'

'They're all connected. John Emmett and Private Byers were part of the firing squad. Mullins was the APM there. Emmet was hit hard by it all . . . So we end up at this place Holmwood,' he went on. 'It's what journalists do: remember things.

Tie them together. However, I was hardly likely to forget those names. I never knew the names of the other soldiers involved but Byers had been in my platoon way back in 1915. And of course you probably already know that I met John Emmett, but not, perhaps, that I liked him. You may know that I defended Edmund Hart? In theory, at least.' He stopped abruptly. The ash fell from his cigarette onto the floor.

Laurence ran his hand through his hair. 'The execution. I've had one other account – from Byers, in fact, and he had tried very hard not to talk about it since.'

'Byers,' said Brabourne, nodding. 'Well, it was a bad business, in that all capital punishment is bad. The offence and the trial were both mishandled, frankly. And the execution was a complete travesty of justice and dignity. But to set the record straight, it was desertion he was charged with, not cowardice. For cowardice, you have to be within hailing distance of the enemy. Hart never got as far as the enemy. And there was the whole question of shell-shock.' He shook his head slightly. 'Hart had been treated for it the year before. In England. But there were those who said he'd faked it and that went against him. He certainly wasn't deranged enough when I met him to gather the medical evidence. Some doctors were sympathetic; some weren't and would simply hammer home the nail already in the coffin. That and the fact that he'd spent every moment since his arrival trying to leave the regiment and get into the navy. Not popular. Not a man you'd want to join your club.'

'And you? What did you think?'

'He was sane enough. A rather awkward, immature man. Not a leader. Hart repeatedly said he was nervous. But he managed to make everyone else nervous too. The colonel had been hesitant about sending him forward on the day in question but he had no other officer available. In my opinion, Hart was a liability in action. Not his fault. I didn't care if he was barking mad, neurasthenic or even a fake; he just wasn't officer material, as they used to say, or at least only, and redundantly, right at the end. But there was no question in my mind that he was, at the very least, confused and disoriented the night he disappeared. At the end of his tether; it's just his tether wasn't as long as some people's.'

He stubbed out his cigarette and threw it in the empty grate.

'We were at Beaucourt, late October. Three brigades, a ludicrously complicated plan of attack on enemy positions north of the river: a lot of pencil marks and stopwatches. The battalion moved forward. The men were overloaded with kit: it was a miserable evening; damp, foggy, no good for sleep.' He was lighting another cigarette as he spoke.

'We went forward as the third wave, with the German guns blasting away, and the wire in the fog like the tentacles of some hungry subterranean monster.' He added, almost with wonder, 'It was extraordinary: when the bullets struck the wire they sent diamond sparks into the mist: it was as if this monster we were approaching was electrified.'

Laurence didn't interrupt. He could see why Brabourne had done well as a journalist.

'It was chaos up there. Hart wasn't in my company — but after a bit I hardly saw anybody anyway. My colonel was killed; I saw two other dead officers recognisable only by their badges.' Brabourne drew in deeply on his cigarette, exhaled after a few seconds' contemplation and re-inhaled the smoke up his nose.

'At first there'd been something comic about my war. I joined in Monmouth. My father's family came from the South Welsh borders. Found myself with a bantam regiment. Byers too although he was transferred soon after. All these midget

Welshmen: five feet three inches or so. Until then I'd thought of myself as rather average build. Perhaps I was down under some mysterious military acronym: SFO, Short for Officer.'

Laurence guessed the man in front of him was about five feet eight inches.

'Suddenly I was a giant. We could go down an open trench and the men would be undercover, walking upright, and I'd have to bend down for safety. I needed to stoop to hear my sergeant if there was a bombardment. Then, in the first serious action, I put my pipe in my pocket and while we're heads down, crossing no-man's land, my jacket starts to smoulder. Gave me the nickname Fiery, of course. Even when I was moved, the name stuck. Trench humour. It must have run in the family: my brother Diggory started his war in Egypt, shifting mummies to Europe to turn them into paper – using the dead to make paper to replace the shortages caused by killing people. Though in my family, war was safer than peace. We're both alive. Our father died in 1906 in the Salisbury train crash; *his* father, a planter, bit of a black sheep, disappeared without trace in the eruption of Krakatoa.'

Brabourne looked quite cheerful as he contemplated his legacy of disaster.

Laurence smiled. He had liked Byers' description of Brabourne and he liked him even more in the flesh.

'I had this sense of being at this really momentous period in history and, what's more, right at its heart. I thought everyone at home would want to share it. I thought, in my innocence, that it was an opportunity.' He gestured with his cigarette. 'Spectacularly naive. But like everyone, I also thought it would soon be over and I was in a hell of a rush to get stuck in. I wanted to picture modern warfare with modern photography. Then, of course, it all became longer and tougher than any of us had dreamed, and I think taking photographs became a way for me to deal with things that were beyond anything I'd imagined. Or, at least, that's with the wisdom of reflection.' He grinned. 'I'm good on that. I'd had two warnings about taking photographs of sensitive subjects and I still couldn't resist it.'

'Yes. I heard. About the camera,' said Laurence. He pulled out of his inner pocket the photograph that Byers had identified as the firing squad. He slid it over the table and said nothing.

'God.' Brabourne picked it up. 'The very day. Hart. It's my picture. A bad one. It could be before or after. Not sure why I took it at all, really. The light wasn't good enough.' He looked chary.

'Byers,' Laurence pointed, 'said it was before.'

'Right,' said Brabourne, nodding. 'I think I was mostly concerned with getting my picture before I was lynched. Though it seems to be coming into its own, ghastly as the scene is.'

'You obviously knew Lieutenant Hart,' said Laurence, 'but did you know John Emmett? Before, I mean?'

'Well, yes and no. I'd never met him until then. But I had been in contact with him over something else.'

'Do you mind if I ask what? If it's not private?'

'It was another slightly frowned-upon activity. We both wrote poetry. Lots of us did — not just those chaps who've made their name now. Battalions of minor poets. I mean, you were hardly going to start producing a novel in those conditions. Emmett thought he'd pull some of the stuff together, circulate it. Same sort of diversion as mine with photography, I suppose. A bit like poor old Owen publishing *The Hydra* at Craiglockhart. Anyway, it got around. I can't remember when I heard of it — quite early on probably, because I think there were four anthologies and I got into number two. Emmett's mag was called *Distant Constellations* to start with, and then in later copies it just became *Constellations*. But we always called it *DC*. A slim first issue. The second was better produced because, I think, Emmett was on sick leave, then there were two more towards the end of the war. He was good. His details circulated by word of mouth and we could use noms de plume if we chose. The subterfuge wasn't because he was afraid, but because he didn't want to be stopped, especially as some of the poetry got more critical of what was going on. And maybe he was using army ink and paper. Probably made from the grave-wrappings of Nefertiti.'

Laurence pushed the photograph to one side and pulled out the small magazine Mary had given him.

'Good Lord. So you had one all the time.'

'Mary Emmett, John's sister, gave it to me. Is this one of the last issues?'

'Yes.' Brabourne looked again at the cover and blew his ash off it. 'It's *the* last one. He fell apart after that.'

He picked it up, turned the pages and showed a poem to Laurence; it was just two columns, headed 'Verdure' and 'Ordure'. Underneath were rhyming lists of loves and hates, wittily, if self-consciously grouped and cleverly rhymed.

'It's very — well, Wyndham Lewis again,' said Brabourne. 'Avant-garde. *Blast*. All that stuff. Better when it was original.' He turned over another page and grimaced. 'I can't say that revisiting my own youthful creation is always a great experience. Some of these poems stand up to the test of time. This one of mine was straining to do so even when I wrote it.'

Laurence followed his eyes. 'You were Hermes?' he said.

'Oh yes. I saw myself as the messenger, bringing news from the front to . . . well, I'm not sure who to. My mother, perhaps?

Hermes without a destination. More of a lost homing pigeon.' He turned back a few pages, pointed. 'That's John Emmett's work.'

He was Charon,' said Laurence.

'Charon the ferryman,' said Brabourne. 'How pleased my Classics master would be to know I remembered something. Rowing the dead to Hades.'

CHAPTER TWENTY-FOUR

'Why did you have to defend Hart anyway?'

Brabourne shrugged as he lit his cigarette. 'Well, somebody had to. He was in my regiment. My father died when I was young but he'd been a barrister. KC in criminal law. Mostly to please my mother I was supposed to be going the same route. I was a pupil in chambers: Paper Court, strings pulled, shoehorns applied. Outcome, disappointment all round. I hated it and suddenly the war came and there was a way out. So I'd had some experience of advocacy, though not much. Fat lot of good it did Hart. Frankly they were only giving lip service to the conventions anyway.'

'Was the court martial fair?' asked Laurence. He wasn't sure whether any of this was relevant to John but having heard Byers' disturbing version of Hart's execution, he wanted to get a sense of the whole episode.

'Fair? What a question. It was a full-field, general court martial, of course, as he was an officer. Would he have been convicted in a peacetime court? No. Would he have been shot if he were a private? Probably. Did guiltier men than he escape prosecution? Undoubtedly. Were there grounds for leniency? Certainly; the board made a unanimous recommendation for mercy. And I gather some, at least, were appalled to find the sentence had been confirmed. Were they out to make an example of somebody? Unquestionably.

'But was the sentence unjust in the circumstances?' He appeared to think it over. 'No, not really. But hard? Very. The evidence was hardly substantial. It was the handling of the whole affair that was cruel. They took six weeks to decide to act against him in the first place and that hiatus had persuaded him that there wouldn't be any court martial. In the event, he had less than two days to prepare a defence, though proper procedures were just about followed. A court martial isn't really an inquiry. It's not like a court case at the Old Bailey. There's no real cross-examining, just statements with an assumption the truth is being told – except by the defendant.'

He stopped and examined his cigarette, which was burning fast, and then drew on it almost experimentally. 'About a hundred years old,' he said, 'my brother got them in Turkey.' He paused for a moment. 'You know how it all came about?'

Laurence shook his head. 'I don't know anything about what he did.'

'Ah.' Brabourne said nothing for a while. The cigarette looked close to catching fire completely.

'Do you have the time for this now?' Laurence asked.

'I'll tell you what,' Brabourne said. 'I do need to meet someone actually. Old friend now at the Bar. Come with me. Have a quick drink at the Cock. He's invariably late.'

He stood up without waiting for a reply, took what looked like an old naval duffel coat from a hook on the back of the door and let Laurence follow him down several flights of stone stairs.

✳

228

They came out of the square and turned right into Fleet Street. Brabourne kept talking all the while.

'In a nutshell, Hart vanished when he should have been fighting. He started off in the rear. The CO instructed another junior officer to tell Hart to take some reserves forward to the green line. He didn't order Hart directly; every aspect of Hart's orders that day was equivocal. He should have got off the charge simply on that count. Anyway, they came under heavy fire and the group dispersed, some taking cover, some wandering about. Hart wasn't the only man to get lost. He told an NCO that he was going back to HQ for more orders. The trouble was that on his way back he met another junior officer who told him to go forward again with a dozen stragglers. There was bad blood going back months between Hart and this man. In court Hart argued — *we* argued — that technically Hart had seniority and the other officer had no right to give him orders, but it didn't look good. Hart not only refused to go forward again, but just turned round and walked away from battle by himself, in the opposite direction from his battalion and in full view of a handful of men.'

Brabourne was moving briskly, dodging pedestrians, and when he pulled ahead sometimes his words were lost. Eventually he stopped to cup his hands round a match. As he did so, three different sets of bells began to ring the hour. Laurence looked up with sudden pleasure at the congestion, even of churches, in the heart of the city. Although Brabourne appeared not to have noticed, he said, 'There was a time St Bride's and York Minster were the only churches to have a twelve-bell peal.'

Brabourne went on, 'Something else seems to have happened on that walk back: when Hart was found, he'd discarded part of his uniform despite the bitter cold. He said a shell had landed near him, opening a small mass grave, and that rotten fragments of bodies hit him. Who knows the truth? I didn't. There were graves everywhere, theirs and ours, rotting bodies everywhere, come to that. It might have happened that way. His story was semi-coherent. It was generally believed that he was trying to disguise the fact that he was an officer while keeping his head down until the worst of the attack was over.

'The trigger for Hart's absenting himself was undoubtedly the squabble over who had the right to give who orders. Puerile. This other chap – who was supposed to be in charge of ammo, not giving tactical orders – rushed back to report him. Pathetic and lethal. It was tit for tat really. Hart had reported him a while back for smuggling a woman into their shared quarters, said he couldn't sleep.'

Laurence recognised so much of what he was hearing: antagonisms, feuds, intolerance born of sheer fatigue, but rarely with such a fatal outcome. In his own regiment, Pollock – said to be the fattest, least fit soldier ever to be sent into action, and who was rumoured to have needed to have his uniform made specially – had been mocked relentlessly as he blundered and wheezed through his duties, always trying to deflect jokes made at his expense by being the funny man. To his shame Laurence had tried not to notice.

'But if Hart had gone straight back,' Brabourne continued, suddenly crossing the street at an angle between two motor buses, 'it would probably have passed over.' A car narrowly missed Laurence and the driver hooted his horn at him.

'When he drifted in the next day, his failure to account for his absence led the acting CO to put him under arrest. What happened to Hart between the moment he walked off and his eventual return to the battalion is anybody's guess. I don't think he planned to get out of a tough situation. I think he genuinely lost his mind. Just for a while. But that wasn't the majority view; they thought he was simply in a funk.'

Laurence nodded. In military offences that he'd witnessed, a lot depended on interpretation. However, the cases he'd dealt with did not involve officers, nor did they carry the death penalty.

They were outside a narrow building with a lead-paned bow window.

'Ye Olde Cock Tavern, no less,' said Brabourne, pushing open the heavy door. 'Dickens' favourite.'

The place wasn't busy and they took a table near the fire, facing each other on blackened oak settles. Brabourne insisted on buying the beer.

'There were two things that prejudiced the case,' Brabourne continued, tapping the end of a match on the table to emphasise his points. 'Firstly, Hart had never wanted to be there. He wanted to be in the navy. And he kept on and on asking for transfers, which, as I said before, didn't gain him any friends and of course the navy never took the casualties the army did. So rather than a genuine wish, I think, to be at sea, this looked like further evidence of cowardice. Secondly, the regiment was struggling. Very low morale. There were rumours that a handful of men had gone over to the Germans in the next sector. Junior officers were terrifyingly inexperienced as well as bickering among themselves.'

Laurence remembered how Byers had levelled the accusation of inexperience at Brabourne himself.

'But the real disaster for Hart was that one NCO, who spoke as a witness and had seen him arguing with the other subaltern, said he didn't even look as if he was in a funk; he simply looked as if he'd rather be off out of it. There was something a bit dodgy about that NCO and the other junior officer: they used exactly the same words and phrasing in their statements. In a civilian court we'd be on to that like a shot – obvious collusion – but such refinements didn't impinge on military proceedings.

'And of course his vanishing trick had left his men exposed and at risk. If his behaviour was genuine, then he was deranged. If he was faking it, then his acts were several miles beyond unbecoming of an officer and a gentleman. They thought he was faking it.

'Ultimately he *wasn't* quite a gentleman. It wasn't a particularly smart outfit, for God's sake, but he didn't have the background of the other officers and they let him know it. In fact, to start with, his unpopularity was what coloured my decision to defend him. I didn't think anyone else would even try. Not that I did him any good.'

Laurence watched the man's face. It was bleak. His cigarette burned away between his unmoving fingers. Laurence felt uneasy, as he had when talking to Leonard Byers, knowing that he was returning people to events they would prefer to put behind them.

'I thought Hart would get off, or at least get a lesser sentence, and Hart certainly thought so. I mean, in the entire war only two other officers ever went before a firing squad and one of those was for murder. Officers were found guilty of serious offences from time to time but the sentences were always commuted. *Nearly* always.'

Charles had said the same, Laurence recalled.

'But as the witnesses spoke, I realised he hadn't a hope. It wasn't the facts, meagre as they were. They just didn't like him. He didn't fit in. His commanding officer said he didn't trust him and everyone else took his lead. As for Hart, he wouldn't, or couldn't, even speak in his own defence. They sentenced him to death almost as a matter of course. Still, they made a fairly vigorous recommendation for mercy, on the grounds of his age and lack of experience. For all the good it did.'

He took another drink and wiped his mouth.

'God knows where my chum is.' He looked around as if his friend might be hiding in an alcove. Laurence drank slowly. He wanted Brabourne to complete his story and was glad the friend was late.

'Then, after he'd been found guilty but we were still waiting for the sentence to be confirmed, I was allowed to see him again. There was nothing to say, of course. Not easy to have a conversation with someone you've failed to protect from a death sentence.'

Brabourne took a deep breath.

'He said his nerves were bad and he wished he could have some books, especially poetry. I seized on poetry as something we had in common; we could hardly talk about the weather or the war. I expect you can see what came next: he turns out to have been one of John Emmett's group of poets. It was only then that I found out that he had written for *Constellations*. I'd read several of his poems. He may have been a pretty inadequate soldier but he was an extraordinary poet.'

Laurence felt his breathing slow, as he began to see things coming together, but he wanted Brabourne to tell it all in his own time. Hart must be Sisyphus. Only one poet in the magazine could be called extraordinary.

'So there we sit, a chilly evening in this room in a French farmhouse, which they've commandeered as a prison. Big old fireplace, black and cave-like: somehow it made the room feel colder, having it there unlit. They'd stuffed barbed wire up the chimney, presumably to deter anyone from attempting to climb out, and when gusts of wind were funnelled down, the wire made this whining sound. It made my hair stand on end. The room smelled of cold soot. A small casement window with wooden slats nailed over it and two guards outside the door, though God knows where he was supposed to run off to. Anyway, he still believed the sentence would be commuted. We both did. I think everybody expected it. I'm freezing, he's wrapped a blanket round his uniform in this damn awful situation, and we're discussing Masefield and Brooke and whether Bridges was a good Poet Laureate.'

He paused, tapped his cigarette packet.

'Bloody business. I'd had nothing more than a summary of evidence half an hour before I had to defend him and they told him the sentence had been confirmed only hours before they shot him. When they told him they had the formal confirmation of his sentence, they added, as if it would make a difference, that he was to be allowed to keep his badges and his rank. I mean, what kind of mind thinks up that nicety?'

After a while Laurence prompted him: 'And you saw him again?'

'The padre and the colonel arrived. I left. Hart was a waxwork. Next time I see him, he's tied to a post.'

'Which poet was he?' Laurence asked, certain that Brabourne would confirm what he already knew. 'Hart? His pseudonym?' He nodded at the magazine. Grey and dog-eared, its typing irregular, it looked like something a schoolboy might produce.

'Hart? He was Sisyphus. Perhaps he saw himself always struggling to no avail. We were all a bit dramatic and self-important at the beginning – we were very young. But by God he could write.'

'And the fellow subaltern who reported Hart – the one you said was his enemy?'

'Lilley, Ralph Lilley.'

Laurence felt a surge of disappointment. It was not the name he had expected.

Brabourne picked up the pamphlet of poems Laurence had put down on the table, turned over two pages and handed it back, open. 'Hart,' he said. It was the extraordinary poem Laurence had first seen in Cambridge. 'Streets ahead of the rest of us, wasn't he? He wrote in every edition bar the first.' Then he shrugged. 'But who's to know what dead men might or might not have become? Saints and prodigies in a very few cases, perhaps. Most would have shown an utter failure to fulfil early promise, that's my guess. Without a few howitzers, maybe even that creative response might have failed to ignite. Good thing in my case.'

'At least you tried,' said Laurence. 'My service was an intellectual desert. The only writing I did was letters to next of kin.' He grimaced. 'Art came down to nothing more than doodles of the colonel's extraordinary moustache. During my whole time in service I think I finished only two books: *King Solomon's Mines* and *The Good Soldier.* My wife had sent me her idea of suitable reading matter for a fighting man.' He paused. 'I don't think she'd read them herself, not the second, obviously. But the title sounded encouraging. I had a book on church architecture, but apart from that it was the *London Illustrated News*, always minus the best articles, which previous readers had taken a fancy to and cut out. No poetry magazines. I was no John Emmett.'

Brabourne laughed. Then he said, more seriously, 'I managed to get Hart his books; it was the least I could do.'

Laurence hardly took in what Brabourne was saying as the implications of the situation at the time of Hart's execution had suddenly hit home.

'So John knew who Hart was before that morning?' he said.

'No, not really. In fact, it should have been another officer who commanded the detail but he fell ill. The CO let him off and decided Emmett, who had just joined us, but was senior, could take it. A good thing too. The way they carry on, you'd think soldiers would jump at shooting an officer but of course the talk's all blather. I'm sure Emmett had previously never met him face to face.' Brabourne appeared to be thinking. 'No, I'm certain of it. Hence the shock . . .'

'Shock?'

'When he realised who he was. He knew the name, of course, but it's not that rare and he'd got his orders very late in the day.' Brabourne stopped, deep in thought. 'He was tired and it was all very tense. He might not have taken it on board. It was "unsatisfactory", that's the military term, but pretty bloody dreadful is more accurate. Hart found all the courage he'd hoped for when it came to it. The rest of us were novices except for the APM – Mullins – who couldn't be bothered to stay and see the sentence carried out. A couple of the men were in Hart's own company. I really thought the padre might faint. He'd been there only a month. I suppose I wasn't much better. The MO was grim-faced. He had to pin the traditional bit of flannel on Hart's chest – all that medical training to identify a route for a bullet to the heart.' Brabourne's lips twisted. 'The squad was subdued but hopeless, and apart from anything else they couldn't shoot straight. The sergeant was a nasty bit of work.'

'So did John know who Hart was afterwards?'

'He put two and two together. I'm not sure at what point. Do you know what happened? That day, I mean?' he asked cautiously.

'He wasn't killed outright.'

'I'll say he wasn't,' said Brabourne. 'But Emmett should have put him out of his misery instantly and the sergeant should have marched the detail off swiftish the minute they'd fired. Instead of which, everybody stood and watched. And Emmett . . . he would have done better by an injured dog. He dithered. No, that's not entirely fair: Hart was obviously trying to speak. Emmett was a decent chap. Probably his instinct was to let a dying man have his say.'

'Did John tell you this?'

'Well, afterwards he asked me whether I knew that the dead man had been a poet and I said yes. He seemed very cast down but then he was shaken to the core by what had happened. Literally shaking. I had to give him brandy. Emmett said Hart seemed to be saying that he loved his mother, and that his father would have been ashamed, or something along those lines. Not remarkable last words.'

Brabourne pointed to his tankard. Laurence shook his head. 'No, I really must go. But what about Tucker?'

Brabourne looked surprised at the use of the name. 'Tucker. Of course, he was the sergeant. You know him?' he said.

'No. But I know more than I like about him.'

'Well, he was cool as a cucumber. In control. Nasty, as I said. Walked up, took the gun off Emmett. Blasted young Edmund between the eyes. Hell of a mess. Deliberately, I don't doubt. One of the lads was retching. Extreme insubordination, I suppose. But somebody had to finish it. I'm not sure Emmett was going to fire at all.' The journalist was pale.

'That afternoon it was business as usual and having buried Hart we went off on a practice attack. Emmett spoke to me again a day or so later. I was on the point of going off for home leave. He asked if I knew anything else about Hart. I said I didn't know anything about his home life. Like Emmett, I knew much more about his poetry, but then I'd had years to read his poetry and only two days to familiarise myself with the case, much less the man. And I can't say Hart was very talkative. Not even in an attempt to save his own life. He no longer cared, I think.'

'I'm sorry to take you back to this.'

Brabourne shrugged. 'It's not something I was ever likely to forget. I gave evidence to an inquiry two years ago. Though I was mostly being questioned about being a Prisoner's Friend. It's said if you defended, you sentenced yourself along with the accused man.'

'So I heard. Was it true?'

Brabourne opened and shut his matchbox a couple of times. 'I'm still here. Though I think my CO was quite glad to have seen the back of me for a while. Whereas a month or so later his golden boy, the prosecuting officer, went out on a routine patrol and never came back. By the time I got back from leave the CO was happy to have any officer with experience.'

He glanced behind Laurence at a man coming in from the street. Although he was just a dark shape in the doorway, Brabourne waved. Laurence took this as his cue.

'I'll be off,' he said. 'Thank you for everything. It's been tremendously helpful. Perhaps we'll meet again.'

He felt sleepy from too much beer and longed to be outside. He nodded at Brabourne's friend who was buying himself a drink, still wearing his court wig and gown.

'Come back if there's anything else at all,' Brabourne said, standing up and shaking Laurence's hand.

As he was walking away Laurence turned.

'There is one other thing. Did you know that Byers' cousin had been murdered? Same surname, same home village?'

He knew instantly that this was news to Brabourne. The journalist became suddenly alert. At the door Laurence looked back and saw Brabourne still watching him. He stepped out into light that seemed astonishingly bright.

CHAPTER TWENTY-FIVE

*T*he next day he woke up with a headache and couldn't face his planned morning in the library. Eventually he decided to catch a bus to Marble Arch; he would go to his barber's and get some fresh air by walking in Hyde Park.

A couple of hours later he sat on a bench, relishing the crisp morning, watching the ducks on the ornamental lake and some elegant women on horses, trotting along the bridleways. Having now heard two versions of the events around the death of Hart, he thought he had a full picture.

He wondered how many executions by firing squad had taken place in the field. This made him think back to routine orders and how often he'd just passed over the notification of an execution. Hundreds, certainly, must have been shot. He hoped five hundred was too many. Say it was two or even three hundred soldiers. Only three officers in total, Brabourne had said. It seemed very few, yet he'd never heard of any until he had looked into John's troubled war.

Each execution would involve six officers or more for the court martial, officers for the prosecution and the defence, two or three senior officers to ratify the sentence, the assistant provost marshal, and six to ten soldiers on the firing detachment. An officer commanding the execution, medics, padres, guards, the burial party. Twenty or so men involved in despatching a single soldier of their own side. Even allowing for some duplication, four to five thousand or so men must have been involved between 1914 and 1918.

The only unusual element in Hart's case was that the condemned man held a commission. Did that make it harder for everyone involved, he wondered? He thought it probably did. Even so, the numbers of men caught up in trying and executing Hart made the notion that there was some sort of curse ludicrous. There was no reasonable way to check, but they couldn't all be dead. Nonetheless he wondered what had happened to the other subaltern who had reported Hart for walking away. Ralph Lilley. He, almost more than anyone else, would seem to be responsible for Hart's predicament. If Lieutenant Lilley was still alive, that would virtually confirm that the nexus of deaths, including John's, did not have Hart at its centre.

He was getting cold so he walked fairly briskly along the Bayswater Road. The Hyde Park Hotel loomed up behind the mottled plane trees and on impulse he turned in past the doorman. He asked to use the telephone and the concierge made the connection for him. Of course it was a ridiculous time to try to catch Charles at his club but he left a message with the porter, simply saying that he had a lot to tell him and that he planned to go to Birmingham the following morning. He felt slightly melodramatic as he ended, saying that he expected to return on the same day.

On the spur of the moment he decided to jump on a bus to Victoria. From there he crossed the river. Although Brabourne's account had hardly mentioned Byers, Laurence had been bothered by something in the way Byers told his own story. Now he had an excuse to speak to him again, even if a pretty feeble one.

It took him forty minutes to reach the lock works. The watchman came out.

'You looking for the major?'

'No, Mr Byers.'

'Not here, sir. Won't be until later.'

'How much later?' Not that he could hover in the yard to ambush him.

'Search me.'

Very briefly he considered leaving a note, asking Byers to contact him, but he was sure that he wouldn't do so. He might be able to prevail upon Calogreedy to speak to Byers again, but the reason for his visit was pretty tenuous. It had been a ridiculously impulsive detour and he knew it was largely because he had too much time on his hands.

He set off for home. The street outside the works was empty. He was approaching the bridge when, as he turned to cross the road, he almost collided with a man on a bicycle coming round the corner. He stumbled back over the kerb. The man half stopped and half fell off. As he picked up his cap from the road and straightened himself up, the cyclist apologised.

'Sorry, sir. Not usually anyone about. I should of looked. You all right?'

It was Byers. Slowly his expression changed. 'Mr Bartram.'

Laurence's reason for being there suddenly seemed even flimsier.

'I had some news.' He felt a fool as he said it. 'You might like to know the man you told me about – Tresham Brabourne, who defended Lieutenant Hart – he's alive and well.'

It sounded ridiculously thin. Why should Byers care? Byers stared at him, gripping the handlebars tightly.

'So not everyone's under a fatal curse,' Laurence said, trying to sound light-hearted.

Only a slight tension of his jaw showed that Byers had

heard but he didn't move on. He looked more uneasy than relieved at this information. One foot remained on the pedal, the other pressed down on the road surface as if he was about to push off and cycle away.

'Did he say anything?' Byers asked eventually, still wary.

'Well, more or less what you said. A bad business.'

'About me?'

Laurence thought back. 'Nothing in particular. I mean, apart from you, because you'd been with him before, he didn't even know the name of anyone in the firing squad.'

Byers looked as if he was engaged in one of his famous computations of figures. When he finally spoke, his voice was flat. 'Just before, when they were tying him up, Tucker leans towards me and hands me his pocket knife. He nods towards Hart and for a minute I think he's telling me to cut his throat but he just says, "Cut off his pips, son." I didn't get it at first and Tucker gives me a push. I look to the officer, that's your friend, the captain. But he doesn't seem to see what's going on. I stumble out towards the man. Half afraid someone's going to give the order to fire while I'm out there. Then I'm standing in front of him – the officer we're going to shoot – and I'm not looking at him and I think I says something like, "I'm sorry," very quiet so that Tucker can't hear, and I reach forward and sawed the pip off one shoulder and then he turns so I can get the other one. And I'm looking for the other badges when Emmett suddenly wakes up and shouts, "Byers, what the hell do you think you're doing, get back in position," so I do. I scarper back, clutching these pathetic bits of stuff in my hand. And when I get back, Tucker's there with his hand out and I just put them in his palm. I felt bad about it after because I thought it was a proper order, but later I heard that they didn't take the rank off a condemned man.'

He caught Laurence's eyes briefly.

'It was just another little game of Tucker's. Probably he sold them for a mint.' His shoulders slumped. 'I'm sorry. I am. I didn't know any better.'

Laurence wanted to reach out and touch Byers' nearest arm, stiff on the handlebar. But even before he could tell him that he had nothing to be sorry for, Byers was moving off, pedalling away without looking back.

Laurence got home feeling cold and dispirited. He had a glass of brandy to warm himself, then managed to settle to his own work. He wrote until evening before assembling his notes. As he tidied up, he gathered up his recent letters. He glanced down to Eleanor's, lying on top. Her handwriting was as determined as her character. Suddenly, he tipped out the odds and ends that Mary had given him. On top was the note about the birdwatching. His eyes went to the bottom and then to the letter. He was almost certain that the comments about somebody dislikeable in the guise of a bird were in Eleanor Bolitho's handwriting, as he had guessed. Eleanor had obviously been seeing John long after the war and had a close friendship with him. But she had chosen to lie about it to Laurence. Could the N be Nicholas Bolitho? Did William know that they'd both gone to Holmwood? He picked up the scrap and put it and Brabourne's photograph in his wallet.

When he'd left Brabourne the day before, he was reeling with all the new information but as he slotted each element into place he realised there were crucial questions he might have asked. Now he also wondered: why hadn't Brabourne mentioned Byers' actions?

CHAPTER TWENTY-SIX

Tresham Brabourne seemed keen to see Laurence again, although he made it clear that his time was limited. He suggested Laurence find his way up to the office he'd visited last time. Although the door was ajar, Laurence knocked. The floor was covered in open newspapers and Brabourne was kneeling in the middle.

'I'm checking your Byers bombshell, about his cousin,' he said. 'Turns out Mullins was looking into it. Curiouser and curiouser. There has to be a connection. A story.' He looked excited.

'There were two things I wanted to check myself,' Laurence said. 'Why on earth did John Emmett ask for a copy of your photograph?' He took it out of his pocket.

'He didn't. Nobody saw me use the camera. More than my life was worth.'

'But you gave it to him?'

'No. God, no. Hardly. Last thing I'd want him to know about.'

'Well, somebody gave it to him,' said Laurence. 'Are you sure this is yours?' He handed it to him. 'Could anyone else have been taking pictures that day?'

'Very unlikely,' said Brabourne, examining the picture. 'No, this is mine. Was mine. Look – my monogram on the back. I still have that stamp. P is my first name, Peregrine. Not very surprisingly, I opted to use one of my other names – Tresham. It was that or my third name, Everard, which wasn't a great improvement on Peregrine.' He looked down at the photograph in his hand. 'But God knows where the negative is.'

'When did you last see the picture? Do you have any sense of when it was lost?'

'No. I mean, no, it wasn't lost. It was hardly something I gazed at every day but it was with my things until I met Colonel Lambert Ward. I set up an interview with him a couple of years ago. Do you remember the Darling Committee? Suggesting reforms for courts martial?'

'Lambert Ward?' Laurence echoed.

'The MP. The parliamentary questions man. I was doing this big piece on him; I can probably find it. Certainly got the goat up plenty of our regulars. Letters came pouring in.' He looked happy. 'Especially from those who'd never fought, of course. Very keen on the ultimate sanction, our older readers. But the rest was pure coincidence. We were talking about the bee he's got in his bonnet about burying executed men alongside their more valiant comrades in arms. He's very old school in his ways but strangely vehement about keeping our dead together.'

He stopped, got up again, walked to a cabinet and pulled out a drawer. He seemed to find what he wanted almost immediately, ran his eyes over it and handed it to Laurence.

'Quotes. They were for my piece,' he said. 'I could hardly improve on their words. From Hansard or public speeches.'

Laurence looked down at the transcript. Two speeches had been marked in pencil.

'The first is Philip Morrell. The former MP. Liberal. I'd like to do a piece on him too. And this is the colonel,' said Brabourne. '"These men, many of them volunteered in the early days of the war to serve their country. They tried and they failed . . . I think that it is well that it should be known and the people of this country should understand . . . that from the point of view of Tommy up in the trenches, war is not a question of honours and decorations, but war is just hell."'

Laurence nodded. He sat back. Just hell. He was glad someone had spoken this truth in parliament.

'He told me that there was utter silence in the Commons after he'd spoken, and nobody would meet his eyes,' Brabourne added. 'But what I found interesting when I met him was his conviction that intolerable fear pushed some men into extraordinary acts of courage, and others into cowardice quite out of keeping with their characters. I think he was saying both extremes were a sort of madness. I liked him.

'I mentioned that I'd been personally involved in a court martial and a firing squad. He seemed quite interested – well, he would, of course. Much more so when he found the condemned man was an officer. He was the first person I'd spoken to about it since the war. Even my brother doesn't know. I didn't tell Lambert Ward about the photograph at first. Partly because it's not of the execution itself, thank God, but mostly it didn't seem fair to the other men involved, who didn't have any choice about being there.' He held the tiny stub of his cigarette between finger and thumb, inhaling before discarding it. 'And I felt that it looked a bit like a souvenir. That wasn't how it was, but I wasn't proud of it.'

Laurence asked, 'Are Lambert Ward and Morrell working together?'

'Loosely, yes. The colonel, Morrell, General Somers, and the man who's the member for North-West Lanarkshire, whose name I can't remember. Pringle? No, Thirtle; all good men of absolute probity, no axes being ground, I think. Somers and Lambert Ward were military heroes themselves in their time, which probably helped. The war and the public making subsequent attacks on them all were playing hell with Lambert Ward's health. But then there's Horatio Bottomley.'

Laurence watched, puzzled, as Brabourne slid his matchbox open and tipped his matches out on to the desk.

The name rang a bell with Laurence. 'Another MP?'

Brabourne gave him a wry look. 'Yes. "The Soldier's Friend". Among other things. Including being owner-editor of *John Bull*. It puts me in a difficult position. The *Bull* is a bit of a rag and Bottomley would stop at nothing to support his causes. And there's no end to the causes that support Bottomley. Our editor loathes him. He's had some murky dealings and he's rabid about Germany. I just thought the next thing would be that those men in my picture who had a right to remain anonymous would be plastered all over Bottomley's front page, *and* I'd also be in deep trouble here for not letting *The Chronicle* have the story. But I trusted the colonel. In the end when I sent him my meagre notes on Hart's defence, I also sent the photograph, which was with the file. He wrote back and said he'd like to talk to me properly about the execution. After all, on the previous occasion he was there for me to interview *him*, not vice versa.'

Brabourne was arranging matchsticks into an elaborate snowflake pattern. He nudged the final one into position and looked up.

'We agreed that we would meet again. In the event, he was

unwell; an ulcer apparently. Morrell was down in the country so it was Somers who contacted me and suggested we meet at a hotel, the Connaught. Lambert Ward had passed on the photograph. But I trusted him just as much as the colonel, who had given me his word that it would be seen only by him. Somers gave me an equally solemn assurance. Not that the picture was very informative in itself but I was confident that there was no possibility of it emerging in any public way. I didn't trust Bottomley an inch but I trusted Lambert Ward; he understands modern soldiering. Somers is utterly honourable, although from a different generation and a different war. And he'd lost two sons in ours so he had some idea of its realities. I knew one of his boys. At Wellington. You know how schools yoke you for life, willy-nilly? Why you're here for Emmett, really.'

Was that true, Laurence wondered?

'I told him who was involved, the names of the officers, at least. Again, Somers said he would never make them public. I couldn't remember those of the soldiers, apart from young Byers, if I ever knew them. To tell you the truth, I didn't particularly want to remember any of it. I didn't want the photograph. It's history now.'

Laurence watched with regret as Brabourne's elbow came down in the middle of his fragile matchstick creation. The sticks scattered.

'Somers listened, took a few notes.' Brabourne brushed a matchstick off his coat. 'Told me the Germans executed only a handful of men. Fifty or so. Makes you think, doesn't it?'

Laurence was astonished. Were British soldiers so much less disciplined than Germans? Everybody said they were the best army in the world.

He was about to speak when Brabourne said, 'I did in the end tell him about Emmett – that whole ghastly botch-up.'

Brabourne looked straight at Laurence when he didn't respond. 'You think I shouldn't have said anything?'

Laurence shook his head vigorously. 'You were the one who was there.'

'I thought about it after meeting Lambert Ward and decided it was the details that make a cause. Told him it was idiotic to mix up the rifles. Which was worse? Having to shoot him, or finding they'd mostly missed? Somers looked grim, although he said he'd seen men flogged and hanged in the war in Africa and he himself had even confirmed their sentences. But that was in the last century.'

He tapped out a further cigarette from the pack but held it without lighting it.

'He asked me a bit about Hart's background. He already had his name from the records but said he was interested because so few officers were executed on any side. He had details of one other case, a Lieutenant Poole. There wasn't much I could tell him except about the indecent haste of it all. And I tried to explain how the other officers took against Hart, and the tension between Tucker and Emmett, but it all sounded a bit thin if you hadn't seen it. I was biased in Emmett's favour probably. Perhaps one of the other commit- tee members had the photograph afterwards? Not Bottomley, I hope.' He grimaced. 'But I'll check I didn't have any more of them. It was all a muddle back in the war!'

'May I think about it for a while?' Laurence said. 'I'm going to try to trace Tucker — he seems to be the lynchpin for so much of this. He lives in Birmingham.'

Brabourne looked at him. 'You should be careful.'

'Because?'

'Because your friend John Emmett told me a couple of things about Tucker that were all too plausible, having seen him

in action myself. I don't think Emmett was trying to exonerate himself. He knew he'd messed things up — it was
undoubtedly a terrible burden — but he was trying to explain
Tucker. Ostensibly he hoped that because of my paltry experience at the Bar I might be able to advise him. Really, he just
needed to get it off his chest, I think. He was a man obsessed.
Also — and it sounded a bit melodramatic — he wanted to pass
on the information in case anything should happen to him.
Not at the hands of Jerry but of Tucker.'

'Anything I should know?'

'Tucker and Captain Emmett met long before. Perhaps you
knew that? Emmett joined the West Kents. Tucker was a sergeant. Tucker had a chum whose name I can't remember, a
corporal. The two had joined up at the same time. Tucker was
brighter than the average soldier and did well. But Emmett said
he was a bad influence over his weak pal.'

'Perkins?' Laurence said, remembering the name William
Bolitho had given.

'Possibly.' Brabourne shrugged. 'They were vaguely implicated in lots of minor trouble-making but none of it was
pinned down. But then, in spring the following year, not long
before things got really sticky, apparently they were running
out of wire. As they were everywhere. Two details went to get
wire from farms in the area. Tucker headed up one lot, John
said. They found precious little; the French were already hiding
stuff by then. Three days later a girl on one of the farms is
raped and murdered. She's very young: fourteen or fifteen.
Emmett said it was just possible the death itself had been an
accident — caused by an attempt to subdue her. But it was now
the third rape that had occurred near their positions.

'The French police discovered an army-issue canteen outside
the barn when her body was found. Tucker claimed he'd never

been near that farm, but the mother gave a description of a belt buckle and insignia she'd seen when the soldiers had come before. Her husband and son were serving with the French so she could identify the uniforms.'

Brabourne stopped and appeared to be thinking back.

'I think Tucker eventually conceded he might have been there — he took the line that one small farm was much the same as any other and all the French were devious, English-hating peasants. But of course he said he hadn't gone back. Emmett has a bad feeling about it all. Calls the friend in and it's obvious the soldier — Perkins, if that's his name — is uneasy. Keeps contradicting himself and both men are the only alibis for one another for part of the day in question.'

'I'm surprised that was enough to exonerate them; it sounds more a cause for suspicion, I'd have thought.'

'Indeed. To you, me and, especially, John Emmett. But not to a harassed CO, it appears. Emmett said he just knew, increasingly, that Tucker was involved and probably this Perkins too. And Tucker knew he knew and it amused him. The French gendarmes thought two men had raped her. Technically, one rape and one act of sodomy.' He looked up. 'Emmett must have spoken good French?'

He waited for Laurence to reply.

'Yes, he spoke nearly perfect French.'

'Emmett was the liaison officer. Perhaps he was more convinced by the police than his tired CO, who was trying to prepare his men for the next attack. And Emmett saw the body in situ; her own neckerchief stuffed in a mouth choked with vomit, though death occurred when her throat was crushed, possibly by a forearm during the act . . .'

Brabourne tailed off, stubbing out his cigarette in his overflowing tin ashtray.

'I'm sorry, this is probably more than you want to know about something that happened a long time ago,' he said. 'But when I met him, it had worn Emmett's nerves down. I think that the circumstances show that Emmett's failure in commanding the execution detail wasn't weakness and Tucker's promptness to step in wasn't courage. And Hart was going to be shot one way or the other.'

'It's helpful,' Laurence said. 'The whole picture, the way it fits together. John's state of mind. It's what I've been trying to get a grasp of.'

'The fact that he told me all these details is some indication that things weren't good. Though we did share a billet for a while and some wine — increasing quantities of wine, in his case. Emmett told me there were items missing off the girl's body: a comb, some ribbons and so on. It also seemed as if someone had cut off some of her . . . pubic hair.'

When Laurence looked surprised, Brabourne added matter-of-factly, 'I had actually come across this in my time at the Bar. These men . . . they do sometimes collect items from their victims.'

'But wasn't that incredibly risky?' asked Laurence. 'It was murder, after all, and the men all lived on top of each other, and were often on the move and had few personal possessions. Anyway, the colonel would have had a right to search Tucker's things at the time.'

'He might have done but it was hardly likely. Tucker was a sergeant; he wasn't some spotty private. And I do wonder if for Tucker it was the risk that made it attractive.

'So the gendarmes leave Emmett with a list of pathetic missing personal items. He took all the information to the colonel, but there was no other evidence. They were preparing for the big push and the colonel said Tucker was a good enough NCO not to be antagonised by excitable French women with vague accusations. "Against the general good" was the line, Emmett said.

'The colonel let it go. He refused to release the men for possible identification by the girl's mother, because that would merely confirm what Tucker had already given them: that he'd been at the farm in the preceding week. Emmett tried to take it further up the chain of command but the CO was getting increasingly fed up with the whole business and what he was beginning to consider as questioning his orders. Not long after, the Somme goes up and one dead French girl pales into insignificance beside fifty thousand British casualties on day one.'

Brabourne stopped again. He chewed on a matchstick.

'I have to say, it all sounded pretty circumstantial. I don't think there was ever a case, but Emmett was certain Tucker was the man, together with his faithful sidekick. And things changed between him and Tucker from then on, he said. Perkins stayed out of Emmett's way as far as possible but Tucker was always *in* the way, always hovering this side of insolence, but challenging him in subtle ways, always making things difficult. You know how it was? A good NCO and your problems were halved. With a bad one, life became hard: messages didn't get passed on, maps were out of date or dropped in the mud. Telegraph lines were damaged. Men were unavailable when Emmett needed them. Always small things, but they disrupted the running of the company and made Emmett's life thorny.

'Then, a month or so later, there was an outbreak of pilfering. Tobacco, sweets, small change – but causing trouble. There was bad feeling and some suggestion that a young soldier was being picked on as a possible culprit. Emmett and another subaltern decided to do a spot check of accommodation. Tucker was excluded from all this by virtue of rank; indeed, he was part of the checking. No sign of the stolen goods, but in his chum's knapsack there was a comb — a woman's hair comb. Ordinary, cheap thing, gilt, but Emmett said there was something distinctive about it.'

Brabourne closed his eyes for a second.

'I know. It was a unicorn. The pattern. Just like the one missing from the dead girl. Emmett thought it even had her initials on it. It was on the list the gendarmes had given him. He said Perkins was obviously shocked to the core. Swore blind he'd never seen it before. Tucker suggested to him that he might have bought it for a lady friend back home and the man eventually agreed. But Emmett said it was well worn. He knew the colonel thought he'd simply got a down on Tucker and it wasn't enough.'

'What about the corporal?'

'Tucker was naturally devious — Emmett thought he'd planted the comb to keep his friend in line — but he sensed Perkins was frightened and out of his depth. Over the next couple of weeks, Emmett kept Perkins in sight. By now the man looked haunted, and he and Tucker were no longer the mates they'd always been. In fact, Emmett thought he was trying to avoid Tucker. Then, right out of the blue, Perkins asked to speak to Emmett privately. Tucker was out of camp. The corporal wasn't specific but he hinted that it was to do with the murder. Perhaps he was going to confess; perhaps he thought he could turn King's evidence.'

'Didn't he say?'

'No. Emmett, who is off up to HQ, says he'll see him the following afternoon. But Tucker gets back earlier than expected — perhaps he didn't trust his old friend. The following morning, they're repairing trenches when, oh so conveniently for Tucker, you might think, there's a collapse and his chum dies unpleasantly but without a word. Emmett is sent off to the regimental first-aid post and then hospital, and the CO is killed within weeks.'

'I hadn't realised,' Laurence began. 'I knew about the individuals involved in the trench fall. A man called Bolitho told me. An officer. He was there.' He recalled Byers' sense that Tucker had let his friend die. 'But Tucker rescued John. Why would he do that if John had wanted to tie him to a murder?'

'God knows. Game playing? Power? Perhaps he was being watched too closely to finish him off when the fall didn't kill him. Emmett, of course, thought that the whole episode was about Tucker trying to murder him. And he was near as certain that Tucker had engineered Perkins' death. It wouldn't have been hard. Those old trenches were pretty unstable. But, of course, his accusations were in danger of sounding like paranoia. He kept the comb, the only evidence of the rape, in his pocket all the time. He said one day he would show it to the girl's mother for identification. But it would only have tied Perkins to the murder and he was dead. He showed it to me. I have to say, you needed to know what you were looking for to see any initials.'

'But John didn't mention a Bolitho?'

Brabourne shook his head.

'Being trapped was John's nightmare.'

'That fits,' said Brabourne. 'The good criminal mind is adept in sensing the weakness of others. Perhaps that was all Tucker intended – to torment rather than kill, and, by getting in there for the rescue, to have all the pleasure of watching Emmett suffer.'

'I think I know how the story went on from there,' said

Laurence, as Brabourne put his feet on the desk. 'John was injured. Sent to hospital. His battalion took heavy casualties. John went home until he was declared fit for active service again and then, finally, in 1917, his path and Tucker's crossed again.'

Brabourne shook his head and tapped his ash just short of the ashtray. 'With the subtle addition that Tucker had officially saved your friend's life.'

They both lapsed into silence. Laurence looked over Brabourne's shoulder to the window, trying to gauge the time by the light outside.

'Did you know that in John's account of the accident – if it was an accident – in the trenches, it was a Captain Bolitho who saved his life?' Laurence asked.

Brabourne shook his head. 'I can't swear to it but he didn't actually talk much about the incident at all, except to explain how Perkins ceased being a danger to Tucker. You have to understand that for Emmett it was all about the French girl's murder.'

'He left him some money. Quite a lot,' said Laurence after a short pause.

'Tucker?' Brabourne looked astonished.

'No. Bolitho.'

Laurence allowed this to sink in for a moment.

'And Byers,' Laurence said, more cautiously, 'seemed uneasy about the lead-up to the execution.'

It wasn't the whole truth but he wanted to let Brabourne tell him about Byers himself.

But Brabourne just looked blank. 'Byers?' he said. He seemed puzzled. But after a few seconds' thought, he seemed to realise what Laurence meant. 'Cutting off the badges? Poor man.'

Laurence wasn't sure whether he meant Byers or Hart.

'I imagine he thought he was supposed to for some reason,' Brabourne said. 'He wasn't a chancer of any sort. Emmett should have stopped him, of course.'

After a moment's further thought, Laurence asked, 'The article you did on the murder: the policeman? Did you think then that it could be connected to Hart or Tucker or John?'

'It honestly never entered my head. I didn't even put two and two together when the story first came in. I mean, I knew he'd served in France. I suppose it's odd that there are no leads and that it was so efficiently and coolly done. But if you want the truth, to start with I thought Mullins would have been on the take and had crossed some criminal bigwig. If there's anything that didn't fit, I suppose it's that, in military life, Major Mullins had a reputation of acting right by the book. A very tough man. I would have thought corruption would have been anathema to him.'

'Your piece said he was "mutilated"?'

'Newspaper dramatics. The second shot got him in the face. Very nasty. As much for onlookers as for Mullins, who could hardly have cared by then. Personally, I'd rather there wasn't a connection,' he went on thoughtfully, 'as the numbers of those present at the time of Hart's death seem to be diminishing rapidly.'

'Byers is well.' Having said that, Laurence was still nagged by the fact that Leonard Byers' cousin had been murdered.

'But his cousin was shot in the face. Like Mullins.' Brabourne indicated the papers on the floor.

Laurence nodded. He could see that Brabourne's newspaperman instincts sensed a connection. 'Perhaps you'll find the link,' he said. 'In the meantime, I'll let you know how I get on with Tucker.'

'Yes. Do. And be careful. I don't want to be running a piece on another mysterious but violent demise.'

Brabourne felt in his waistcoat pocket. More cigarettes, Laurence assumed, but instead he brought out a fine fob watch and opened the case.

'I'm going to have to . . .'

Laurence jumped up. 'I'm really sorry, I keep returning and seem to have tried to extract from you an entire history of the war. One thing seemed to lead to another.'

'That's the joy of my job,' said Brabourne. 'Connections. So many things do seem to link together so often.' He tapped the watch and turned it so that Laurence could see it. It was old and handsome.

'It was my grandfather's. He fought at Balaclava. Mind you, although I'm very attached to it it's not much good for actually telling the time.'

He smiled broadly, giving off the boyish energy that Byers had commented upon. He tapped it again, then started rummaging through one of the piles on his desk. Several leaflets and loose sheets slipped to the floor but he seemed unbothered.

'Take this.'

He handed Laurence a magazine. It had stark red and black print on the front and a title, *Post-Guard: The New Review*.

'Myself, I've given up writing poetry in favour of photography. If I get a lucky break I'd like to move into film. Movement: speed, machines, that's the future. But for now . . .' He gestured around him extravagantly. 'This might pay for my dreams. Really I'm better on murders, but I do bring out this periodical in my free time. It's subscription only and we haven't got it going regularly but one or two of the wordsmiths in the copy of *Constellations* that you've got are in my mag too. Writing very different stuff now, of course. None of that morbid sentimentality: summer, lilac, ancient warriors. None of that, thank God. Do you remember Frances Cornford on Brooke? "A young Apollo, golden-haired,/ Stands dreaming on the verge of strife,/ Magnificently unprepared/ For the long littleness of life." I mean, Brooke was hardly unprepared. He was at King's, Cambridge, for heaven's sake. And no innocent, one hears. And he worshipped the heroic littleness of life, clutching his Homer closer than his gas mask. I've nothing against the dead and nothing against Cornford: "the long littleness of life" – lovely line. Wish I'd written it. She was in love with him, of course, wasn't everybody? Perfect poetry. Means nothing and so everything. That's why people like it. Not everyone could cope with Sassoon.'

Laurence, who had known Sassoon at school and hadn't liked him much, didn't want to say so.

'There's still a taste for that sort of thing, of course. *Nostalgie de la guerre.* But not in this.' Brabourne tapped his magazine. 'This is *not* for everybody.' He looked proud. 'Not sure we've got the title right – it was supposed to be a pun on avant-garde.' He made a face. 'Picking up where Kandinsky and Co. left off.'

Laurence hoped he looked intelligently non-committal.

'I put two of Hart's in pride of place and there's one of Emmett's too. Of course we're not making a profit yet, but he deserved to be published. We're getting reviews.' Brabourne looked worried. 'I hope his sister won't mind. If a miracle occurs and the public suddenly develops a passion for proper poetry, then we'd pay his heirs, of course.'

They shook hands. Laurence walked down the stone stairs and out on to Fleet Street. Away from the heavy air of ink and machine oil and paper, London smelled light and cold. There was heavy traffic: trams and cars held up by a brewer's dray unloading near St Bride's. He looked up the street towards St Paul's and then up at the sky.

259

Sometimes he was not sure whether he was more disoriented by all that had altered or by how much had not. The view he had now – of the pale, graceful lines of St Bride's and then the uncompromising dome of the cathedral, rising grey above the City – was little changed since Wren built them. That, at least, was permanent. And yet this was also the street from which the great business of the nation's newspapers had told the modern world how it was changing.

As he walked back towards Aldwych, he turned on impulse towards the Temple church, almost hidden in its peaceful square. Finding no one else inside, he sat for a while, watching the faint sunlight warm the stone effigies of the Knights Templar.

CHAPTER TWENTY-SEVEN

*H*aving arrived at the station well before the train to Birmingham was due to leave, Laurence paused outside to look at the war memorial. Had it been here the last time he passed? Similar monuments were suddenly appearing everywhere, but the bare earth around this one suggested it had been unveiled only in the last few weeks. New roses, just a few dormant winter stalks and thorns, had been planted around it. For a second he tried to imagine his own name being chiselled out by a busy mason. But what place would have claimed him as its son and remembered him in death?

He went inside to the ticket office. The steam hanging over the platforms was mirrored in miniature above the large tea urn at the station café, where he sat at a corner table, clutching a cup of tea while he waited for his train. Strong and sweet, it was bitter with tannin. He held it more to keep warm than to wake himself up. He'd brought *The Times* to read and Brabourne's *Post-Guard*. He was just rereading one of Hart's poems when he felt a tap on his shoulder. He turned round to find Charles standing there, with an identical copy of *The Times* under his arm, the brim of his hat pulled down low, a dark paisley scarf round his neck and the rest of him swathed in a vast tweed coat that must have belonged to his grandfather.

'How the hell . . . ?' Laurence began, but swiftly realised that he was neither particularly surprised nor unhappy to see Charles. Had he hoped for this when he'd left his message? His smile acknowledged the possibility.

'It's good to see you.'

'Well, I wasn't having you setting out on a solitary encounter with Sergeant Tucker, old chap.'

'Oh God. You haven't brought a gun, have you?'

Theatrically, Charles opened the front of his voluminous coat, reached into a deep poacher's pocket and brought out a short, thick truncheon with a leather loop. He placed the loop around his wrist and slapped the truncheon down against the palm of his hand a couple of times. Laurence frowned.

'It's a priest,' said Charles. 'For despatching fish. I've gone off fishing but found this in a cupboard; better than nothing, I thought. And less provocative than a gun. I do have one or two other useful things here.'

He reached into another pocket, brought out a hip flask, which he waved vaguely and then put away, and finally dragged out a buff-coloured folded map.

'Birmingham,' he said, 'but I suppose you've got one already?'

Laurence smiled and shook his head.

'But you know where to find your man's drinking den?' Charles asked. 'It's a big place.'

'I know its name, according to his friend who told Leonard Byers. And I know it's a long shot,' he added, not that Charles had protested. 'It's not unreasonable to assume he'll be traceable from there.'

Charles raised an eyebrow. 'And you think his pals are going to tell you, just like that?'

'They might.'

Charles rummaged about in yet another pocket. This time he withdrew a thin, folded bundle of one-pound notes.

'Money?' Laurence looked puzzled.

'Quite right, old chap. Well done. See your detective skills are coming on.'

'You can't give him money. Well, it's very decent of you, of course, but I can't let you. I'd thought I might offer a very small amount, but if Tucker is half the rogue he's said to be, it might make the situation more dangerous, not less, if he thinks we've got full wallets.'

'My guess is that Tucker may have had his finest hours as a soldier,' said Charles. 'Once home without any real power, he's probably no threat at all. His sort need war. Still, I could be wrong. That's why I'm here.'

They walked down alongside two carriages of the train — handsome in its dark purple and cream. A gleaming peacetime train, Laurence thought, remembering the dinginess of trains in the war years. When they found an empty compartment, Charles struggled out of his coat and threw it up into the luggage rack. Laurence wondered briefly, and disloyally, how Charles's plus fours would blend into a working-men's pub in Birmingham.

The whistle blew and the train pulled out slowly, gathering momentum once it was clear of the first bend. They passed by the water tower, then under a viaduct and between high warehouse walls, all red brick and flaking painted advertisements. After a quarter of an hour they were carried over a bridge above an anonymous parade of shops. Then came row after row of terraces: narrow houses, their yards and washhouses a depressing patchwork of black and grey below the track. A solitary washing line bore dingy sheets that drooped heavily in the drizzle. The train had still not taken on much speed. A canal ran alongside the line for a while but, beyond the weeds in the crevices of decaying brickwork, there was no vegetation anywhere.

Only as they moved outwards from the heart of the city did larger houses appear, comfortably set amid gardens and parks. On a summer's day the prospect might be quite fine. Laurence suddenly recalled a childhood smell of suburban lilac and sticky lime trees. He had once lived and played in places like these. They roared on, passing a long strip of potato fields marking the transition from urban to rural landscape. Most of the holdings were tidy dark patches but others appeared long abandoned. The train speeded up across level earth fields as north London was left behind. Near the line the bushes were blackened with soot while further away the few bare trees were so misshapen, presumably by the prevailing winds across the open terrain, that they were unidentifiable. A small factory stood neatly to one side of the line at the edge of a small town. He wondered what county he might be in: Hertfordshire? Bedfordshire? Rain and smuts soon obscured even the monotony of the view.

They sat in companionable silence. Above Charles's head was a cheerful print of the Lake District. A man, a woman and a terrier strode forward under a perpetually blue sky with fluffy clouds. Charles was reading. Eventually Laurence must have fallen asleep because he was startled by the ticket inspector opening the door. Looking at his watch, he saw that they were halfway to Birmingham. The weather had improved slightly and they seemed to be passing through gentle hills. Laurence tilted his head to read the title of Charles's book: *The Mysterious*

Affair at Styles. On the cover, three or four figures, dressed in their nightclothes, their faces illuminated by hand-held candles, peered into the darkness. Laurence smiled. No wonder Charles had a taste for intrigue.

Soon they had outrun the rain and the sky showed patches of brightness. The train passed some ruins on one side and a large signal box on the other. They were making proper speed now and occasional sparks shot past the window. As they entered a long tunnel, the train started to slow. Charles put down his book.

'Good?' asked Laurence.

'Quite excellent. Mrs Agatha Christie. You think you know who did it and then you think, no, that's what she means you to think, and then, of course, it's going to be someone quite different. Which it is but not the one you've thought. Wonderful stuff. Haven't you read it?'

Laurence shook his head. It seemed ages since he'd read a novel and even then it was mostly Hardy or Trollope, all favourites of his father.

'A bit more thrilling than poor old John's death. Pure escapism. Strychnine, femmes fatales, lost wills, violent death. And it all hinges on chemistry. Stepson saved from the rope by a cunning Belgian.'

'But you haven't finished it,' said Laurence. 'How do you know?'

'Oh, I've read it twice before. First time, she had me believing it had to be the Belgian himself. Mind you, I've a lot of respect for the Belgians. Extraordinarily brave man, their king. You can't quite see our King George commanding a front-line action, can you?'

CHAPTER TWENTY-EIGHT

They arrived at Rugby on time and from Rugby, crossing pastureland, the train soon reached Birmingham.
The city seemed to appear quite suddenly. Laurence had never
seen England's second city before. His first impression was of
redness and solidity, dark bricks and heavy architecture. A new
city, not like London with its layers of existence, of squalor and
beauty: its fine squares, slums, parks and palaces spreading out
either side of the muddy grey Thames. Did Birmingham even
have a river? He didn't know. Almost all the buildings they
passed were small factories and workshops, although there were
some distant spires, grey-white and more graceful than the
buildings by the railway.

Charles pointed towards a clock tower in the same uncompromising style as the rest of the city. 'University,' he said. 'The
tower's supposed to be like the one in Siena. Can't see it myself,
but it looks better on a summer's day.'

Laurence laughed. 'How on earth do you know?'

'Family,' said Charles. 'We had a factory here. I thought I
told you.'

Laurence felt guilty. *Had* he known? Charles was probably his oldest surviving friend. Charles was straightforward, growing more bluff with the years, where Laurence had become increasingly intense, even melancholy. If he had to characterise the relationship, he would have said it was simultaneously sturdy but superficial. He could never imagine discussing anything about Louise, or even the war except as a sort of historic event. He'd never even had the sense of shared experience that he'd briefly felt with the injured William Bolitho or Tresham Brabourne. Yet the very fact that their friendship was one of the few that had accompanied him since childhood had its own power.

'You hardly need the map, then?'

'Actually I haven't been to Birmingham for years. The old man used to bring me, trying to get me interested. My birthright of housemaids' boots and gentlemen's cufflink boxes. Had the opposite effect: couldn't wait to distance myself. Every time we came up here and saw the factory — much the same colour as pickled beetroot — or the men: either cowed and overly respectful or surly and monosyllabic — my heart sank. He'd make me handle the slimy hides as they hauled them slopping out of the tanks. My father liked to feel he was in touch with it all, so we'd end each visit by going to a tripe and pig-heel shop. Absolutely foul, and all the while his man would be waiting in the car outside. But it was the smell at the works that was so truly appalling. Perhaps people who spent their lives there became hardened to it but it was the most disgusting stink. I could recognise a tannery a mile off. Probably shall, today.'

As if to make his point he stood up and loosened the window strap.

'When my father died, and I came into my kingdom, the first thing I could think of was: thank God I could rid myself of it. Mama was all for it, of course, she'd never quite got over marrying into trade. And in the war half the men in the works had gone to join the Warwickshires, while the underage ones and the women were off making ammunition at Kynoch's, and at the end few wanted to come back any more than I did. Though I got a good price for the place.'

Before he'd even finished speaking, the train was juddering to a halt, pulling in under the long glass station roof. Charles heaved himself into his coat; Laurence put on his hat and scarf. They went out into the corridor, stepped down and walked briskly along the platform and up the stairs, emerging on to a busy street.

Charles breathed in ostentatiously. 'Ah — best ladies' calfskin gloves,' he said. 'Now, as I recall, it's this way. We can walk,' he said. 'I don't think it's far at all.'

Although Laurence had no idea where Charles was heading, he was swept along by his confidence. As a tram clattered down the rise, a horse-drawn coal cart converged on it at an alarming angle, but one passed easily behind the other. It had turned into a crisp day and there were plenty of people about.

They walked for ten minutes between buildings that emanated an acrid smell of hot oil and coal fires against a continual din of metallic hammering and drilling. Through open doors they could see men working over benches and the glow of furnaces. They passed one courtyard that appeared to be full of prison grilles, until Laurence realised he was looking at bedsteads, piled up against every wall.

'You do know it's the Woodman we're looking for?' Laurence asked Charles.

Instead of replying, Charles rifled through an inner pocket, pulled out a leather-bound book — the sort they'd all had in the army — and undid a stained brown strap. He turned the pages to the end and tipped it towards Laurence to show him an address.

'Tucker's home when he enlisted,' he said.

For once he resisted looking pleased with himself. Charles's careful writing read 'Florence Place'. It rang a bell but Laurence couldn't think why.

'Doesn't mean he'll be there or ever was, but it's a start. And it's not far away,' Charles said.

They seemed to be zigzagging across main streets. In one small road two or three establishments sold nothing but hosiery, while another offered mostly household wares, with a cooper's sign over the door of the adjacent double-fronted store. Charles was moving steadily to the right. The shops displayed fewer wares in grubbier windows as the successive streets grew poorer, the houses in worse repair. Roofs bowed. Broken windows were papered over. Children playing in the street, some with bare legs in laceless boots, and women in dirty aprons over old coats, all stopped and stared at the two men. Charles occasionally said 'Good morning' briskly, but there was little response beyond a few nods of the head. There was a marked contrast between the poverty here and the busy industry only a few roads away.

Laurence was glad when they turned into a street at a right angle, away from the stares, but Charles stopped in surprise. The road ended in a bleak wasteland of rubble, laths and rubbish. Charles looked at his map.

'Well, I'll be . . .'

'What's happened?'

'He should be here. At least, Florence Place should be here but it's not.'

A few yards away an old woman leaned against the last standing building: a boarded-up tavern. She was wrapped in a shawl and had a clay pipe in her hand. She could have been a figure from fifty years before.

'Knocked 'em down ten years back. Pretty, in't it?' she said.

'Damn,' said Charles under his breath. 'We'll have to try the drinking den after all.'

Laurence felt something didn't quite fit. 'But if she's right, then this couldn't have been Tucker's address when he signed up, either.'

'No. Well, nobody checked, I suppose. But then nobody would have been able to notify the next of kin, either.'

'Which wasn't necessary in Tucker's case.'

'No, or he didn't care.'

'Or he didn't have any next of kin.'

However, Laurence remembered Byers saying bitterly that there was a Mrs Tucker somewhere.

'Or he didn't like people knowing where he lived. Even then!' said Charles.

A handful of children started to gather round. One small and grubby girl pulled hard on Laurence's sleeve, silently but holding out her other hand. He slipped her a penny, hoping the others wouldn't see.

Charles walked less confidently back up the road, then stopped. The children followed noiselessly.

'We can ask in there.' He pointed to the isolated public house. It was propped up by two wooden buttresses where neighbouring houses must have been torn down.

'It's closed,' said Laurence.

'I don't think so,' Charles replied.

There was no sign or brewery notice. Laurence crossed the road, walked up to the building and tried the door; it opened easily. Charles followed him in. Three men were drinking beer around an upended crate, while two others and a drably dressed woman sat at a window seat. The landlord stood behind a rudimentary bar. A dog snarled at them from beside a stove, but made no effort to get up.

Laurence didn't feel threatened; the drinkers looked guarded rather than intimidating. All talk had ceased as they came in. From what he could see of the landlord, he seemed to be dressed in part of a uniform: khaki trousers, topped with a collarless shirt and a waistcoat.

Laurence ordered two pints of beer. It came from a single unmarked keg. He handed over a shilling for the two. He doubted anyone else in there was paying the going rate. The landlord's unease might have been because the pub was open before drinking hours.

As if to read his mind, the man said defiantly, 'We keep to pre-war drinking in here, now it's not an official house.' Surprisingly, he had a London accent.

'I'm sorry to bother you,' Charles said firmly, 'but we're looking for an acquaintance.'

There was a snigger from the woman in the window.

'Tucker, Tucker's the name. Knew him in the war.' Laurence got out the photograph and put it on the bar. 'Used to live in Florence Place.'

The silence continued. Nobody looked at the photograph. Laurence looked round. No one met his eye.

Finally the landlord spoke.

'And you think your old army mate drinks in here?'

'So we've been told. Him or his friends,' Laurence said.

'Lots of Tuckers.'

'He was a sergeant.'

'*Sergeant* Tucker.' The landlord looked amused. 'Anybody know this *Sergeant* Tucker?' he said and without waiting for an answer asked, 'What makes you think he comes here?'

'Well, he said he used to live over there.' Laurence gestured to the derelict plot of land.

The woman in the window snorted again.

Laurence looked at her. She was small, probably not more than twenty. Her face, as she gazed at him frankly, was pinched and either bruised or dirty.

'You knew him?' he asked her.

'Nah. Jest he came from a stinking rotten place. Gone now. It's all going now. Even this home from home.' She grimaced at her own surroundings.

The landlord looked irritated. 'We're providing a service. Just for the last weeks,' he said. 'No point wasting the building before the wrecking ball calls time. After all, there's no sign yet of all their municipial improvements out there.' Although he mispronounced the word, he sounded angry as he gestured towards the door. 'They can take the houses away but where are people supposed to live? Even now they've had the exterminators in and taken out a few of our lads. Germans got the wrong people if you ask me.'

'You and the Bolshies,' a man muttered as he got up. As he wrenched the door open, a cold draught knifed in. The door banged shut behind him.

'Do you happen to know a pub called the Woodman?' Laurence asked in the silence that followed.

For some reason this seemed to amuse the group at the table.

'You could say so,' said the landlord. 'There's ten or so Woodmans around. God knows why. Munitions Man, Metal-Rolling Man, Lime-Kiln Man, or even No-Fucking-Chance-of-a-Job Man, you'd understand. Not much call for woodmen in good old Brummagem. Still, what's in a name?' He picked up the dirty mug on the bar, dipped it in a bowl of murky water, pulled it out and rubbed it with a rag. 'This used to be the Royal Oak.'

He looked up towards the men at the table. 'Fred, Ivor, you were soldiering men. Did you know this Tucker?'

One man was shaking his head before he even got to the end of the sentence, as if to deflect any involvement with strangers. The other appeared not to have heard at all.

'Sorry. Can't help you,' the landlord said. 'Me, I got a chest.' He thumped on his sternum. 'Missed the chance of a scrap. Was in stores. Never left the country. But good luck to you. Though I doubt you'll find him.'

They stepped out into the fresh air. A man stood against a boarded shopfront opposite, rolling a cigarette. Otherwise the street was empty. Charles was feeling in his pocket, obviously intending to return to his map. Laurence felt heavy after a pint of unfamiliar ale.

'What made you think that place was still in use?'

'Grey cells.'

'Grey cells?'

'That's what Mrs Christie's little Belgian has.'

Laurence thought Charles was fearless, reliable and like a child in some respects. He wasn't sure whether he was useful or a liability.

'And I saw a thread of smoke coming from the chimney. So somebody was in there. And there are two jugs hanging on a hook outside. That's a sign of a place to drink in these parts — and I imagine they'd have been long taken if they were simply there as ornament on a ruin.'

'I forgot you were the Sir James Frazer of local customs. They'd heard of Tucker all right, don't you think?'

As Laurence spoke, the man across the road detached himself from the wall. As he came towards them Charles looked momentarily puzzled but Laurence recognised him from the bar a few minutes before. He'd been the first one to leave.

As he reached them he said, 'This Sergeant-as-was Tucker you're after? What's he worth to you?'

Charles and Laurence briefly exchanged looks.

'My cigarettes?' Charles said, holding them out. The man looked doubtful. He rubbed his nose with his hand and pushed his cap back.

'Looks to me like you'se come a long way,' he said. 'Not from these parts, anyway. So you must be wanting this Tucker a mite more than a Frenchie fag or two. Price of beer's enough to turn you temperance around these parts.'

'You're right, of course,' said Charles. 'So what do you think would be fair payment, assuming you actually know where our man is, or have some pretty solid information as to where he lives now?'

'Oh, I know where he is right enough,' the man replied. 'I'll take you to him toot sweet. Mind you, can't guarantee he'll welcome you with open arms.'

'A shilling. How does that sound?' asked Charles.

Laurence thought of the fold of pound notes in Charles's inner pocket. The man looked doubtful but nervous, as if he didn't want to see Tucker but wanted more money. Finally he seemed to decide on tactics.

'Look, I'm out of work, three babbies at home. Wife's about to drop another. I did my bit in France and all and I reckon you did too, sir, so you know what I'm talking about. It in't easy. So how's about two bob? Something for the wife an' a bag of suck for the little'uns? For that I take you right to him. Nasty bit of work he is and all. Though not the scrapper he was, you'll find. Mind you, I'm not hanging around while you try and talk to him.' He barked – something between a laugh and a cough.

'Done,' said Charles. Laurence was surprised; he'd expected him to drive a harder bargain.

'This now' – he held out a florin – 'and sixpence when we get there.'

The man tucked the coin away and pulled his cap forward.

'It's not far. 'Course, they all knew Bert Tucker,' he nodded back towards the Public House, 'though it was his ma's address you had and she's been dead since for ever. But landlord barred Tucker a year back and he don't do that easy. Would serve Dr Crippen if he dropped by with small change. Same at the Woodman. Barred.'

He was walking slowly and obviously enjoying himself.

'But that lot don't like strangers even more than they don't like your man.'

They took a mean-looking street to the right and then, swiftly, a second, which passed under an archway into an alley so narrow that Laurence couldn't imagine it ever got sunlight. The cobbles beneath their feet were dark and damp. At small, irregular intervals, there were shallow doorways. Washing was strung across the street; despite the lack of light or warmth, people obviously lived here. A woman stood at a single water pump, talking to a young girl with a grizzling baby on her hip. They all fell silent as the men passed. Laurence hoped they weren't being led into some kind of dead end where the man or his friends would swiftly relieve Charles of the rest of his money, but eventually the alley came out in a wider, cleaner street with a neat row of small villas on one side.

They crossed over. To their left a cemetery spread out, covering a sizeable area of ground. Whilst there was no sign of a church, an apparently abandoned mortuary lodge stood at the entrance and beyond it sooty stones were arranged in tidy rows, with the occasional rusting iron cross or hefty stone angel. The man looked pleased with himself and pointed through the open gateway.

'There you are,' he said. 'There he is. And not likely to be leaving.'

'He's dead?' said Laurence, after a split second's confusion. 'You're telling us he's dead?'

He felt irritated but largely because it had never entered his head that Tucker might have died. All his reasoning needed Tucker alive. The man stepped away slightly as if nervous one of them would take a swing at him, yet still hoping for the sixpence.

Laurence was lost in thought. Somehow he felt the unknown Tucker would always have been protected by his own opportunism. He was trying to recalibrate every assumption he'd made. Even if Tucker wasn't directly implicated in John's shooting, he had associated him with the other violent deaths. Tucker's malevolence had been a fixed point in the story Laurence had built up.

Finally he asked, 'When?'

'Bert? Back last winter. December? January? February mebbe?'

'So where's his grave?' said Charles, looking towards the dismal rows of stones.

The man looked at them, almost amused. He waved towards the left of the grounds. 'Resting in the arms of Jesus. Bert's hardly one for a fancy stone. Not the type and not the money any more. He was peddling his own wife the last months.' He looked momentarily uneasy. 'Offered her to me once but you never knew with him what was a joke. But no way she was about to get him all the fancy trimmings when he copped it. No, there he is and there he'll stay, but I expect even she doesn't know exactly where he is. No change there.'

'How did he die?' Laurence beat Charles to it.

'Drowned.'

'Drowned?' said Laurence. 'What, *here?*' It seemed unlikely.

'In the canal. Down by the basin. Beyond the Tap and Spile. Near the Mission. He'd been drinking. Fell in or pushed in. Depends who you talk to.' He looked pleased at the effect of his information.

Laurence looked at Charles.

'Which?' Charles asked.

'Well, the police says fell. Drunk and drowned. They don't give a farthing. He was a bit of a villain and so, likely, was the man who done for him, so what should they care? Bert was a mean bastard, begging your pardon, but he knew the area and he looked after hisself. When he'd had too much – when he could afford to have too much – other people came out of it the worse. He didn't. More likely, somebody had enough of his schemes. His wife, mebbe?' He coughed. 'No, she's had all the nerve beaten out of her as well as her teeth. Would never have the guts to do him in. Besides she was wailing all night, they say, and what's she going to do now with her little 'uns?'

'So it's just you who thinks he was murdered?'

'Nah. Everybody knows it round here. For starters the killer was seen by a local. Police weren't having it because the man – bloke called Victor – was on the job with a part-timer, a girl called Betty Carew, and they'd been drinking half the evening. But not so drunk they don't remember a man hanging about. They were round the back of Mathieson's warehouse and they saw this stranger looking like he was up to no good, they tell it. A bit later they heard Bert singing as he went home. He was drinking in the Tap after he'd been banned from his usual. It was a pretty miserable night, they said – raining on and off. 'Course they didn't recognise him spot on – he had his cap and scarf on and head down, but it was him. He was a great man for a song, Bert. Few minutes later, Betty, not quite as occupied as old Victor, if you know what I mean, says she heard a cry and then a splash. Police said if she did, why didn't the two of them go see, but she was earning and it was a bad night and too cold not to get on with it.' He leered. 'Old Bert didn't look his best when they got him out.'

'These two found his body?'

'Some bargee the next day shifting pig iron. He was down by the lock. Face mashed up a bit. His own mum wouldn't hardly of known him if she ever did, but who knows whether he'd been thumped before he went into the water.'

'Was there any idea who did it?' Laurence interrupted.

The man shrugged. 'Like I said, there was plenty was glad to see him gone. That's not the same thing as knocking him off, though.'

'Had there been any trouble beforehand?'

'Always in trouble was Bert since the war. Never the biggest but he was the toughest before the drink started to get to 'im.' The man beamed – his pleasure in Tucker's malignity was obvious. 'Even 'is own officer hated him.'

Charles and Laurence looked at each other.

'He come up here, just like you, and gave him a drubbing. Williams – in the pub today but knows to keep his mouth shut – was in the same regiment, recognised the man. Bloke asked around like you have. One of the reasons no one's speaking: we aren't after more trouble. Specially after Bert's gone and got himself killed. Found him in the Woodman, the stranger did. He weren't barred then. Talked for a bit. Shouting the odds. Bert tells him to fuck off for a coward, 'scuse my French, dragged him outside. The landlord shouts he's barred. The gent calls Bert this and that and lays one on him. He's good.' The man's eyes sparkled in recollection. 'Time was, Bert would have put up a fight but he just goes down. Blood everywhere. The gent gets a bloody nose but Bert comes off worse. 'E's spitting teeth and tells him he'll get him. But as it turns out someone gets him first. I'm not saying it was him, though. This officer wasn't the only one had grudges against Bert, and him sorting out Bert was months before somebody sorted him out for good.'

'Did you actually see him get in the fight then?'

''Course I did. He didn't look much, the officer, but he laid Tucker out right and good. Some old grudge from army days, like I says. Friend of yours, was he?'

'He might have been. Can you describe him?'

'Middling height. Middling looks. Dark hair. Gent, like I said. Would've sorted out Bert right and proper if a copper hadn't been passing, nosing about, heard the racket. Bert was too pissed to fight proper. This bloke calls Bert a blinkin' murderer but he looked fit to do Bert in hisself. Made a mistake laying one on the copper, though, because then they took him in.'

Briefly Laurence wondered whether there was any way to check the truth of the story, although it felt real enough. The description of Tucker's first assailant fitted John but then it fitted him too, come to that. Yet Mary had spoken of an assault that had led to John's arrest.

Suddenly the whole scenario he'd constructed, with Tucker as a stealthy and methodical killer, seemed ridiculous. He was just a semi-criminal local down-and-out. He would never have had the means to travel to Devon and to Oxfordshire to kill former comrades, much less the ingenuity. Deflated, Laurence felt a fool for allowing himself to believe in the dangers of chasing Tucker.

He looked at Charles. 'I'm sorry,' he said. 'What a wild-goose chase.'

Charles still looked interested. He turned to their companion. 'Thank you,' he said. 'Very helpful.'

He handed him the promised sixpence and a further shilling. The man nodded, touched his cap, hovered for a few seconds and started to walk off before he turned and added, 'Tucker might quite have liked being called a murderer but then the man said Bert forced himself on some girl. No way Bert was going to take that one — used to fancy hisself with the ladies way back.'

'So,' said Charles, as they walked the slightly uphill route back towards the station, 'I assume we agree the man in the fight was John?'

'Almost certainly.'

'How did John find Tucker?'

'He got hold of his address, like us, I suppose. Florence Place — Florence *Street* was written down on a note in John's effects. He had Byers' original address too. It was in his pocket when they found him.'

'You're with our friend and think Tucker was killed deliberately? But was it the same man who did for the chap in Devon?'

'Jim Byers?'

'Yes, Byers Two. The cousin of Byers One. And Inspector Mullins? Or, just possibly, John Emmett?'

'*If* they were all murders,' Laurence answered. 'Yes, it's a huge coincidence. I can't think it's worth checking with the police here or trying to track down the couple who might have seen Tucker's assailant. The whole damn thing is vague.'

And, he thought, if the facial injuries in all the deaths, bar John's, were intended as a message, whom was the message for?

As they climbed on to the homeward train, Laurence said, 'You know, I'm completely losing sight of what I set out to do.'

'Find out what on earth the fair Mary Emmett's brother was thinking of when he pulled the trigger,' replied Charles as they were pulling out of the station in a carriage that smelled strongly of old tobacco. 'All pretty straightforward when you started. What a man will do for love.'

Laurence felt tired and irritated. 'I hardly knew her when I agreed to look into it,' he said. 'I just wanted to help her with a horrible event in her life. Tie up loose ends. I didn't know it wasn't going to be so simple. It isn't like your storybook sleuths. Everybody isn't either good or bad, with clues and a tidy solution to be unravelled. Everything here goes round in circles. There isn't going to be the clear answer she wants answered: why did John die? And if there was, it wouldn't be the sort of answer she'd understand. He died because he was born at the wrong time. Or he died because he crossed the wrong person. Bad luck. No more. For God's sake, we still don't even know there was a murder or a killer. Or if there was, only of a farmhand, and a policeman, both of whom might have nothing to do with anything. If we did, we'd have told the police.'

'Point taken,' said Charles. 'Though you underestimate Mrs Christie, by the by. It's not individuals but combinations of circumstances that lead to catastrophe in her books. A fatal collision of character and events.' He beamed. 'But I suppose Emmett's sister would be happiest with clarity. It was So and So's fault – George Chilvers, the late Sergeant Tucker, General Haig. If you could find a murderer, that would help everyone. Well, not the murderer; perhaps it wouldn't help him. But it would be simple. Emmett didn't kill himself. Someone else, the embodiment of evil, did. A homicidal maniac. Which means there was nothing anyone could have done and Miss Emmett doesn't have to feel guilty.'

'Why on earth should she feel guilty?' Laurence jumped in. 'She's the last person who should feel guilty. John was off in Germany before the war, then he was fighting in France, then he became ill. She'd hardly talked to him properly for years.'

'I rest my case!'

Laurence gazed out of the window. He didn't want to continue the conversation. But Charles, apparently oblivious that he was treading on eggshells, went on, 'The thing is that a murderer wouldn't really help. Murderers have their stories too. Their reasons. The people they crossed. The people who did them down. Mrs Christie can leave their world behind on the last page but a real murderer's story doesn't end on the gallows.'

'Extreme violence changes everything for ever,' Laurence said, and then, in a more conciliatory tone he added, 'There is one loose end, though. Tresham Brabourne gave me another name – the junior officer who sneaked on Hart to their superior officer and got him charged. If I could track him down and if he survived the war, that would be informative. Man was called Lilley, Ralph Lilley.' He looked at Charles expectantly.

Charles shook his head. 'Never heard of him. But I'll ask around.' He sounded tired. He fumbled for his pipe and then gazed out at the darkening day.

Laurence rested his aching neck against the back of the seat. He couldn't think straight. Was it possible the man who told them the news of Tucker's death had deliberately misled them to put them off the track? He thought not. He realised now that the landlord had been amused when they'd been making their not very subtle enquiries.

Charles had been right, of course, Tucker had provided the easy solution. But if Tucker was out of the picture, then the murder of Jim Byers and any possibility of John having been murdered became much harder to link.

On the blank margin of his paper he wrote down the name of everybody connected with the execution of Edmund Hart. It was an untidy list because in some instances he either didn't know the name or had only a rank or a partial name. He drew a line through those he knew were dead or disabled. The list became much shorter. He wrote down a second list of everyone he knew of who'd been there when John was trapped in the trench fall and repeated the process. Again, it was not a long list, though he had less information this time. Only Leonard Byers was on both lists. Then he added Eleanor Bolitho. She was not there but she'd nursed John at both periods in his life.

Finally he set down the names of anyone else he could think of who had been significant in John's life in recent years. After Eleanor this had just six names on it: Mary, Mrs Emmett, Doctor Chilvers, George Chilvers, Mrs Chilvers and an unknown army friend who had visited him in Holmwood. He added Minna's name at the top with two question marks. She was dead, but she was the only possible link with the word 'Coburg' on John's note.

Obviously John was the man who had attacked Tucker but it had happened well before Tucker's death. Could John have returned to Birmingham after the initial fight and killed him before killing himself? Everyone agreed Tucker had enemies but one of them was certainly John. Instead of looking for Tucker as a potential killer of John Emmett, what if he discovered it was the other way around? It was John who had been arrested for assault, John who had been put in a nursing home to avoid prosecution.

What if these enquiries turned up something worse for Mary? He knew that was one reason he'd avoided going to the police in Birmingham. When John went absent, could he have travelled all the way to Birmingham to deal with Tucker? Was that where he was in those missing days? If Tucker had died in January or February, it was too late, but if he'd died earlier, it was just possible John could have been involved and he certainly had a motive. It would help if he had the dates, which meant he would have to contact the police after all, although he would be surprised if they hadn't made their own inquiries as to whether the dates fitted, given the earlier attack.

He recalled the various descriptions of John as much improved in the last weeks before his death. He was talking more, he seemed to have had a burden lifted from him. Might it have been because he'd finally dispensed his own sort of justice? If John had killed Tucker, then his own suicide became more comprehensible.

By the time they pulled into London, Laurence was hungry and thirsty, and Charles was snoring. The air felt wintry. They shared a cab, which dropped Charles off first before going on up to Bloomsbury.

'Thank you,' Laurence said. 'It was much better having you there. If ever I can reciprocate . . .'

'You can,' said Charles, patting his pocket. 'Two tickets for the Varsity Match. First time at Twickenham. New beginnings. Come with me and cheer for the dark blues.'

Laurence smiled. 'Of course.' Then before Charles went in, he remembered one thing that had been on his mind since the morning. 'Is there a river in Birmingham?'

'The Rea, not one of the great waterways of the world or, indeed, England. Not, I'm afraid, one of which poets sing. Or can pronounce, really.'

CHAPTER TWENTY-NINE

*D*elicate ice crystals radiated across the inside of Laurence's bedroom window when he woke late the next day. As he waited for some water to heat for shaving – it must be the coldest day of the year so far, he thought – he picked up a monograph on the church of St Alfrege but soon found his thoughts drifting back to Birmingham.

The violence of Tucker's end added to a list of possible murders, yet removed the most likely perpetrator. It was just feasible that John could have killed Tucker, although the deaths of Byers' cousin and Mullins had taken place well after John's own. Laurence found himself more rather than less determined to get to the bottom of things.

When he reread the list he'd made on the train, his instinct was that Eleanor Bolitho was the key to it all. The more he thought about it, the more he saw a discrepancy between Eleanor's insistence that William must be protected from reminders of the war, and the feeling he got from the man himself who appeared to welcome company. Was Eleanor worried that Laurence might let slip something that she would rather her husband didn't know, or that William might tell him something she wanted to keep hidden? Eleanor had lied about how well she'd known John. What else had she lied about?

He decided that the only way to make sense of this was to try to see her again and tell her he knew she had been to Holmwood. If he could put pressure on Eleanor to help him, things might start to fall into place. Nevertheless, when he left his flat, he almost changed his mind. The sky was heavy; freezing rain was turning fast to snow and by the look of it there was much more to come. By the time he was on the bus, the snow was coming down heavily and they made slow progress.

He had come to assume that William, at least, would always be at home. But nearly an hour after he set out, he stood on the doorstep outside their flat, having rung the bell three times, feeling that certainty, among others, seep away from him. He had been fired up with a determination to confront Eleanor. She had, of course, a right to privacy, but he needed to be certain what her part was in John's death. What did she know? What had she guessed? He was convinced that she was withholding knowledge about John from him and, more importantly, from John's family. From Mary.

The weather continued to deteriorate. He stepped back to look up at the three-storey building; the Bolithos' windows were dark. He had been prepared for Eleanor to be angry or even to refuse to let him in, but not for her absence. He felt in his pockets for a piece of paper, but as the only pencil he had on him was broken, there was no way he could leave a message. Anyway, he had wanted to catch her without her being forewarned. The snow flurries were now obscuring the view to the end of the street: he couldn't just stand between the pillars of the stone porch and wait in the cold. The black-and-white lozenge-shaped tiles beneath his feet were already partly obscured by white and the street itself was completely covered.

He pulled the brass bell knob one more time. He thought he could hear it jangling somewhere in the building, but he moved away immediately, knowing it was no good. He slipped on the lower step and swore loudly.

Eventually he pulled up his collar and set off back towards Kensington High Street. An absolute peace descended as he walked by. He gazed into a bay-fronted room where a woman was already drawing the curtains. Smoke and snow billowed over a chimney. He turned the corner, into a street that bore slightly downhill, becoming aware that he had to be careful not to fall. He looked down at his feet. He could already feel the wet seeping in and cursed the fact he had not worn sturdier boots. As he trudged on, he wondered again why he was pursuing all this. There was nothing to pursue really. A man had died, one of millions in the last seven years or so. He had no moral imperative to find out exactly why or how; despite what everyone assumed, he had not been a close friend of John Emmett. There had already been a perfectly thorough judicial examination by the police and coroner. He felt cross with himself, with the situation and with the weather so early in the winter.

As he looked up, a cumbersome shape caught his eye between the swirls of snow. Whatever it was, it was moving slowly and unevenly towards him, though many yards away on the other side of the street. Thinking it was a woman caught out with a perambulator, he moved to help her, but even as he speeded up, the shape twisted, then seemed to sprawl sideways and stop. He tried to run towards what was evidently some kind of accident. As he got closer it dawned upon him that it was a wheelchair and before he could identify the faces he realised it must be Eleanor and William. Eleanor didn't see him, even when he was only a few yards away from where the chair had tipped over. William was still half in it and seemed to be trying to pull himself clear. Eleanor had her arms under William's and her elbows were tucked into her sides as she tried to move him. Her boots were slipping and she heard Laurence only when he spoke their names. He looked first at Eleanor. Her face was grim and determined, but was lightened by relief as she recognised him.

'Could you steady the chair?' he said as he leaned forward and checked that William was simply stuck, not injured.

He placed his arms round the man's waist, but when the weight of him started to shift, he staggered slightly before regaining his balance. The unfamiliar distribution of William's legless body caught him by surprise and he felt a twinge of pain in his back. Suddenly he was standing, bracing himself, legs apart, with William pressed against him and his arms round his waist almost as if they were dancing. He could feel the slight roughness of the man's cheek, the dampness of his scarf. Eleanor had got the chair upright; the edge of the tartan blanket seemed to have caught in the wheels and she tugged it angrily. Laurence lowered William onto the seat while she held the handles. He had always thought how well William looked but now he saw the invalid in him: his eyes were closed, his face grey and his lips blanched, only the tip of his nose a bluish red. Eleanor glanced at Laurence and for a moment there seemed to be unfeigned gratitude in her face. Though her eyes were fierce, there was something else there; she was biting her lip and looked close to tears.

William's eyes jerked open. 'Hello.' The bleakness of his appearance disappeared as he tried to smile. 'A knight in damp but shining armour,' William said. 'We hadn't quite foreseen the weather changing so swiftly. Stupid of us. Felt a bit like Captain and Mrs Oates. Noble but foolish.'

The snow was settling on him and the tracks behind them showing where they had come to grief were already vanishing. Laurence took the handles from Eleanor. She nodded.

'Hold on,' he said.

The chair jerked forward, slewing to the side, and William coughed, but then it came under control. Laurence kept going rather than risk it stopping. It must always be quite a heavy task, even without the snow, which had brought the couple close to disaster on this occasion, and Eleanor was far slighter than he. He manhandled the chair off the pavement and across the road, with Eleanor beside him. On the far side she took off her sodden gloves and stopped as he tipped the chair back a little, then helped guide the wheels to the pavement. Her knuckles were raw and red.

Finally they reached the bottom of the steps. There were only three but the snow had piled up against them. Laurence couldn't imagine how the Bolithos got in and out, even at the best of times. Should he try to lift William again? But Eleanor turned to the side, where there was a small tradesman's gate he'd hardly noticed before. He helped her pull it open against the snow and, once through, they were in a narrow but more sheltered passage. It led to a bolted door with two sturdy planks nailed to the step. For the first time Eleanor looked a little more cheerful.

'Ingenious, don't you think?'

It was a relief to get inside. No fires were lit but it was warm compared with the street. William removed his gloves and scarf with stiff arms.

'Go and sit down,' Eleanor said as she spun the chair

round towards the hall. 'I'm going to heat water and help William get into some dry clothes.' William made vague gestures of protest.

'Do you need any help?' Laurence said.

'Could you light the fire? Hang your coat there.' She gestured at a row of hooks.

He wandered into the dark drawing room and pressed his face to the window. The snow seemed to be stopping. He picked up some matches from a brass holder, turned on the gas tap and lit the mantles. They popped for a minute, then began to glow as he knelt to light the paper spills and ignite the coal already laid in the grate. He could hear Eleanor and William talking although their words were indistinct. The fire flickered and caught.

Even as the day outside finally disappeared, this room looked as bright and warm as when he had first come here. He looked at the drawings that had created such an impression on him on his first visit. There was a good head and shoulders one of Eleanor. Standing by it now, he saw that William had sketched her in red pencil. It was dated only the year before. On an oak side table his eye was caught by a snap of her that he hadn't noticed either; it was taken a while back — she was with a small group of nurses standing outside a building that from its shutters looked French or Belgian. He had to look hard to pick her out with her linen veil low on her forehead. On the other side of the table was a formal photograph of her and her son. He bent over to see Nicholas looking rather solemn as he sat on his mother's knee. Eleanor, too, looked a little sombre as she gazed down at her child, her arms encircling him. Laurence focused on her image: she was quite different in stillness. In the flesh, the impression she gave was dominated by animation and intelligence and, of course, her striking colouring. In repose and in monochrome, she looked quite ordinary: just a mother with her son.

He didn't hear her when she came in the door behind him. There were spots of colour high in her cheeks and he waited to gauge her mood. She fiddled with a small silver brooch that held her blouse collar together at the neck.

Eventually she said, 'Thank you. I've helped William to bed to rest with a hot-water bottle.' A smile flickered. 'Do sit down, Laurence. I'm not about to show you the door this time. We wouldn't have got back without you.'

She sat down heavily in a deep chair with her legs straight out in front of her and her head back against the cushions. Her shoulders slumped. She gave him a rueful look.

'Obviously I would never have left the house with him if I'd thought it was going to snow, but these shorter days drive William mad – just sitting at the window watching the moving world. He needs to get out. He can go short distances on his own but only in fine weather. Winters are long for us.'

'It must be hard,' Laurence said, meaning for her, but she took it as referring to her husband.

'It is. Very. William is only thirty-two. He's intelligent, curious. What's he supposed to *do* with the rest of his life?' She jumped up, as if putting an end to reflection. 'Now, I'll fetch you some tea. I expect you're as cold as the rest of us.'

She was gone for another ten minutes or so. He pulled his chair nearer the fire and held out his hands to the flames, though there was no real heat in them yet. He stood up when she came back and took the tray from her. She poured from an old ironstone teapot and they sat opposite each other.

'He's asleep, thank heavens,' she said. She still looked very pale. Her eyes were red-rimmed. 'Now – presumably you were trying to find us at home this afternoon?' she said. 'Unless, of course, you've got other friends in the area?'

He nodded. 'Yes, I'm sorry. I know you don't want to speak to me. I don't usually pester people but I just sense you know more about John Emmett than I do. Probably, more than anybody and I don't even know what kind of thing it might be and now's not the time.'

This evidently amused her. 'Well, I'm hardly going to attack you now, am I? And obviously you are never, ever going to give up. You're deceptively determined, Laurence. You must have made a formidable soldier.'

Laurence explained briefly about finding Calogreedy and then Byers. He didn't protect Eleanor from the details and he could tell that she had not known the whole story. Her face twisted in shock and disgust but then she surprised him.

'"We were together since the War began,/ He was my servant and the better man."'

He must have looked perplexed because she said, 'It's Kipling. Your Calogreedy and Byers. They reminded me of it.'

It lightened the atmosphere. He liked the lines.

'Look,' she went on, 'I'll try to help you although there are things you simply have to swear not to share unless I say. But I don't know where to start. Why don't you ask me questions?'

He thought for a minute.

'Did you know about the execution?'

'Only the fact of it. No details. Not that it was an officer. He told me once and never spoke of it again. He didn't speak much by then.'

'Do you think John killed himself?' he asked, after another pause.

'No, the war killed him,' she answered quickly, 'whoever pulled the trigger. In himself, I think he was getting better. Next?'

'Did something happen at Holmwood?' he said and then added, because it seemed unfair to mislead her, 'I know you visited him.'

'Yes, I did,' she said, without hesitation. 'He asked me to, so I did. Twice. As for Holmwood itself, I hated him being there but honestly it was no worse than many places and better than some. The old chap —'

'Chilvers.'

'Yes, Chilvers. At heart he genuinely cared, I think. I mean, he liked having his own little kingdom but, unlike his son, he wasn't interested in the things money could buy — and, believe me, money there was, aplenty; they charged a fortune, based on a few good results. I think Chilvers believed in what he was doing. He was interested in them all, which is a good start.'

'I thought you'd complained.'

'It was young Chilvers and poor staff that let him down. I suspect they didn't pay well enough to find the right men after the war. Chilvers *fils* was too greedy and Chilvers *père* too oblivious to the realities. George Chilvers caused problems that his father was too blind or too weak to see and which the staff were too intimidated to bring to his notice. He was an unpleasant man. He loved the luxuries but, unlike his father, he didn't give a moment's thought to the inmates. In fact . . .' she stopped and seemed to consider her next words. 'I think he actually enjoyed their predicament. I mean, I didn't see him with them very much but what I did see, I didn't like. You get a feeling for such things in my line of work. You'd think everyone working with the sick would be kind, or at least decent, but there's something about vulnerability that attracts the rotten sort too. He was rotten through and through.'

The vehemence of her words left Laurence expecting more but she lapsed into silence.

'Did he hurt John in some way?' he asked.

'Not physically. Even at his worst John had a sort of strength. He had a dignity that never left him. George Chilvers' sort go for the weak.'

Laurence found himself hoping George Chilvers had never known about John's failures during the execution of Hart.

'Of course Chilvers hated the fact that they'd all seen active service,' Eleanor said, pulling on a spiral of hair, 'while at the same time gloating over his own cleverness at avoiding it and somehow believing he would never have crumpled as they did. I know for a fact that where procedures were unpleasant or painful, Chilvers would always be overseeing them or pushing the limits: straitjackets, electrotherapy, cold hoses, enemas, that kind of thing. He'd use therapeutic treatments devised by his father as weapons against the most fragile. Of course, then they'd come to dread them. In fact, one poor young man threw himself off the roof when he'd thought he was going to be discharged but his family insisted he stay a little longer for more treatment.' She sat forward, her cup cradled in both hands. 'I loathed George Chilvers. Did you know that Chilvers has a wife — Vera?'

Laurence nodded. 'She was a patient once, wasn't she?'

'Had been. Before the war, when they took women as well. She was only young, delicate, and had the misfortune to be an heiress with no living parents. Her uncle had her committed after a suicide attempt and George Chilvers moved in on her. Poor little thing basked in this worldly young man's interest, no doubt. Eventually, around the time she turns twenty-one, Chilvers *père* is prevailed upon to pronounce her of sound mind and discharge her, just in time for Vera to use that sound mind to pledge herself to his son. She was away from home when John was first there. In Switzerland in an institution, he thought — all very circumspect. When she returned, John met her a few times. She was sweet, he said, and liked to pick the roses and so on in the gardens.

'He was kind to her; John was always so nice to anyone in trouble; that was his downfall. I don't think Chilvers was treating her very well. That's what John thought. He said she was like a child in many ways and terribly lonely. But his help misfired as poor Vera fell madly in love with him and trailed around after him, posting billets-doux under his door. Of course it soon became obvious. George Chilvers was furious. He might not have been interested in his wife beyond her fortune but he wasn't about to be humiliated by her flagrant obsession with John. John, of course, couldn't go off anywhere else so he was a sitting duck, first for Vera and then for that vile man.

'George had restrictions put on John's movements. That's why he was pushed up to the poky rooms on the top floor under constant supervision. The ones where the lights were left on all night. Where doors were locked from six to six. It wasn't because he was at risk. It was to punish him and to stop Vera getting to him.'

She leaned forward and her voice became more indignant.

'John wasn't that ill when he was sent up there. But he deteriorated. He was in a room where the previous patient had been driven to kill himself. They removed everything with which he could hurt himself, from shoelaces to china plates to tin spoons — even his pen. The sheets up there were made of canvas, which couldn't be shredded. It was definitely not a situation that John in particular should have found himself in; George knew it, too. It wasn't about an illicit trip to London.'

Brabourne had said much the same thing about Tucker, Laurence thought. The deadly intuition of a sadist.

'But it was more than that,' she went on. 'Chilvers actually threatened him. His weapons were formidable: restraint, drugs. Some of the other staff were kind but Chilvers held the power.'

'But you went out with John?' Laurence was sure Eleanor had accompanied John on his birdwatching walk down the river.

'On my first visit we could walk about – even outside. I took Nicholas with me, but on my last visit there was nothing like that. No freedom.'

'Did George Chilvers speak to you?' Laurence said.

She waited a long time before answering. He had the impression she was trying to decide whether to tell him the truth.

'Yes. He had seen us walking in the gardens the first time I went and something in our demeanour made him suspect that I wasn't John's sister. He had an eye for these things.'

'What did you say?'

'I protested and played the outraged relative. Well, it was either that or tell the truth and I wasn't about to gratify him with that. But I was nervous that his real sister – your Mary – would turn up and he'd mention me to her. I could imagine him forbidding me from visiting.'

He had the impression she was about to say more but when she didn't Laurence finally brought himself to say what he'd come for.

'It was you John left the money to really, wasn't it? I mean, it was nominally left to William, because he could justify that, but it was because of you, I think. You and William were a married couple. It didn't matter who got it, you'd both have the benefit of it without William being humiliated.'

'What on earth gave you that idea?'

'Because the incident in the trench collapse was nothing in

the scale of things. I kept thinking it felt wrong. Men were dying or being injured, horribly, every day. Trenches collapsed pretty often. Probably the death of a man called Perkins, Sergeant Tucker's partner in crime, was the most significant aspect of that accident. And William's part in pulling John out was prompt and efficient, but he didn't do most of the digging. In fact, it was Tucker, John's enemy, who extracted him and saved his life. I kept thinking, why did William get left money when Tucker didn't. And then I thought – forgive me, Eleanor, but it's true – it was simply because William was married to you. John wanted you to benefit, either because you nursed him when he was injured or, perhaps quite simply, because he loved you.'

She didn't answer at first. Then she looked up and, to his surprise, she said, 'No. He didn't leave it for me. I promise that wasn't why.'

He was embarrassed. He'd been certain John was in love with her and she with him.

'I'm awfully sorry,' he said.

'No, don't be. There's some truth in what you think, but the bequest wasn't because of me, or only obliquely.'

'Did he write you a letter? At the end?' It was a sudden guess. Could he have posted one to her before he died?

She sighed. 'Yes. Yes, he did, although I never read it fully. I saw it only when George Chilvers brandished it at me some weeks after John's death. He'd stolen it somehow. I think he half hoped I would try to seize it and then he could have all the fun of seeing how far I'd go to read it. Perhaps he was hoping I'd end up wrestling him for it. Odious, odious man.' Her apparent sarcasm was belied by the slight wobble in her voice.

'I think other letters may have gone missing. Correspondence to him as well as from him.'

'Of course they have,' she said. 'When John absconded, I imagine Chilvers was terrified he'd tell people outside what had been happening. About Chilvers' personal vendetta. John still had contacts. Visitors. I'd posted letters for him once. Probably his sister did too. Ones he didn't want to leave in the hall at Holmwood for posting.'

She paused and poured them both out some more tea.

'John was melancholy, damaged, but extremely rational. He believed in justice. So I bet Chilvers made a clean sweep of John's belongings. Then when John was found dead, well, Chilvers probably destroyed them to save Holmwood's reputation. They'd already had a couple of suicides apart from the one I've told you about. And what if John revealed Chilvers' treatment of his wife or Vera's love letters to John turned up? George Chilvers might even have seemed like a suspect. Not for murder, necessarily, but it would seem like provocation. John kept a diary from time to time too when I knew him. Do you think his sister has that?'

Laurence was almost certain she didn't. 'How do you know all this?' he said.

'Because the letter Chilvers was taunting me with was one John had left for me, and not yet posted. Chilvers was almost proud of his daring. He never even let me see it properly, just one paragraph while he kept hold of it, so I don't know if it talked of suicide. On the whole, I think it was just a letter. I'd had others. Because if it was a suicide note, the coroner would have had a right to it and its contents would have become public and there were things that John had written in that paragraph that he wouldn't have wanted revealed publicly. But Chilvers stole it and blackmailed me with the contents. That's the kind of man he is.'

'Blackmail?' Laurence was startled.

'Yes. Plain and simple.'

'But you were supposed to be John's sister – or was he black-mailing you because he'd discovered you weren't?'

She gave him a slightly pitying look. 'Well, hardly, I don't think it's a crime to claim to be someone's sister.'

'But you hadn't got any money, then,' he said.

'He didn't want money. He wanted me. To take me to his bed. He wasn't put off by my hatred. He was aroused by the idea of my loathing him and still having to give myself to him. That's how he was. I only agreed to meet him because he led me to understand that he had held back some letters of John's to protect the family. He thought he could coerce me because there was information in the letter that was potentially very damag-ing to someone I love.' She blushed, but not at the revelation that Chilvers desired her, Laurence thought, but with anger.

Laurence frowned. 'William?' he said, slowly, wondering what on earth John might have known about William that might be damaging.

'You're dogged but you're not a natural detective, Laurence,' she said. 'If it wasn't for the simultaneous pursuit of true love – I assume you *are* in love with Mary Emmett? – I'd sug-gest you gave it up. No. Not William. Or William only in part. Nicholas. My son, Nicholas.'

Suddenly he understood. How stupid he had been. But he waited for her to tell him.

'Nicholas isn't William's son. He's John's. John was acting as a father in providing for a son. He saw him only a couple of times but he did love him. In that paragraph Chilvers was bran-dishing, John said that loving me and becoming Nicholas's father, even though it had not been intentional, had been the one good thing in his life. Chilvers was jubilant to have that knowledge.'

'Does William . . . ?'

'Does William know? Well, yes, of course he does or I wouldn't be telling you.' She looked amused. 'Nicholas looks pretty much like his father.'

Laurence thought back to his brief glimpse of the child and the photograph on the table. Nicholas was darker haired than William or Eleanor, certainly, but perhaps you saw what you expected to see. However, his overwhelming feeling was one of happy surprise. She obviously noticed because she looked more relaxed than he'd ever seen her. The fiery intensity faded from her eyes.

'I think there's a picture of him with John's things,' he said. 'I'd assumed it was John himself, but it is probably Nicholas.'

She nodded. 'I gave him that the last time I saw him. I'm glad he had it.' Then she added, 'The discretion is for William's sake, you see, not mine. That was the mistake George Chilvers made. He thought I'd deceived William. But William and I could never have had children. His injury was widespread to his back as well as his legs. We can never have a marriage in that sense. But in other ways, we are very happy. He has been immensely kind to me. I was pregnant. He was an invalid. We take care of each other and he loves Nicholas as his own. He understood my feelings for John. He is an exceptional man and I am very lucky.' Her face was calm.

'I called George Chilvers' bluff,' she said. 'Refused point blank. Told him there was no secret there. Threatened to report him to the police, and like all of his sort his threats melted away. I wouldn't have reported him, of course. William knows, but everyone else believes Nicky to be his own son. I don't imagine William ever told you I knew John Emmett? He wouldn't have wanted to you to make any connection.'

Laurence thought how open and frank William had seemed. But now it appeared even he had things to hide.

'You never wrote to the Emmetts after John died, did you?'

'No.' She looked embarrassed. 'William asked me to but I couldn't risk contact.'

'But if George Chilvers panicked and drove around for hours searching, before calling the police, it does suggest that even though he might have worried that blame for John's death might be laid at his feet, he certainly wasn't directly responsible for his death,' Laurence said.

Then, realising that he had never told her of his suspicions, he explained, as simply as he could, the strange coincidences that he had uncovered while trying to understand John's state of mind. She did not look scornful as he would have feared before today; instead she was obviously concentrating.

'In fact you were the first person to suggest he might not have killed himself deliberately,' he said. 'An accident, you thought.'

She smiled. 'An accident I hoped, I think. Even murder would, oddly, be a lot better than having to accept that someone at the centre of your world, your son's father, would rather be dead.'

'So you don't see Chilvers as a murderer?'

'Much as I'd like to lay it all at his door, I don't. He's greedy and a bully, not a killer, though his actions might well have contributed to John's state of mind.'

'When did you hear from John for the last time?'

She thought for a minute. 'I had a letter from him about this time last year. He sounded better. I think because he was in London, meeting someone who he thought would help him. He'd been moved or disturbed – I'm not sure which really – by all the hoo-ha in the papers about the Unknown Warrior. He was more open, more reflective. I was surprised he'd got away though.'

'Was that allowed, generally?'

'Rarely, I think. It must have meant he'd eased himself from George Chilvers' clutches. Dr Chilvers used to encourage patients to walk locally with family or friends who visited, as long as they were well. We had gone out to walk along the river together on that first visit eighteen months ago. Nicholas was very little. It was lovely. George was away.'

Again, Laurence found this picture of normality comforting.

'But of course they were very careful at Holmwood and I can't think they would have countenanced a trip away unless it was crucial — a family funeral, perhaps — and, I imagine, accompanied by a trusted family member. I suppose he simply picked his moment and left.'

'Do you know what he was doing in London at all?'

'No. I have a sense that the other person wasn't a close friend but I don't think that's because of anything specific. He thought it would be a turning point. But who knows what of?' She screwed up her eyes, thinking, then jumped to her feet. 'Wait. I've got some letters in the other room.'

She disappeared out of the door but was gone only a short time. She came back carrying a small box, set it down on the table and began rifling through it. She took out a tied packet of letters, pulled out one, then another, read a couple of lines and smiled. Laurence longed to be able to read some but knew he couldn't ask. They were part of an intimacy she had struggled to maintain. She held one up and he saw the large, slightly childish script.

'He had pretty dreadful writing,' she said. Very quickly she picked one out. 'He went to a hotel, I remember now, though I've no idea if he actually got there. The Connaught. That's it. Hotel writing paper.' She looked down. 'He just says he's looking forward to a good tea. He's almost jolly. But then I never heard from him again and he killed himself a few weeks later.'

Laurence could hear in her voice her attempt to be matter-of-fact.

'He could have been seeing lawyers or something, I suppose?' he said, although Mary had said he'd remade his will after the war and there was no indication he had revised it. He tried to picture the hotel. 'Where is it?' he said. The name rang a bell.

'Carlos Place, it says, Mayfair.'

He shook his head, trying to remember where Brabourne had been interviewed about Hart's execution.

'It's called the Connaught now, after some useless princeling,' she said. 'But before the war it was the Coburg. Do you remember? They had to change it because it was German. Pretending all the time that the veins and arteries of our own dear royal family weren't running with German blood. I still think of it as the Coburg, though.'

'The Coburg?' he said.

Eleanor was still looking at the letters.

'The Coburg. Of course.' He almost laughed. 'John wrote down the name on a note in his room at Holmwood — Mary had it — and there I was dreaming up an international conspiracy.'

'You idiot,' she said, visibly amused.

'Well, it was always possible he might have drifted into something through Minna. Or through other people he met through her in Germany.'

'Possible, Laurence, but not really very likely,' said Eleanor. 'Did he seem like a spy to you? Minna died young and, anyway, he didn't meet her in Germany; he was at university with her brother.'

'At Oxford?'

'Yes. Her brother was a philosopher, I think. The two men met through a love of rowing, as far as I can remember. There were plenty of Germans there before the war and the Baumeisters were a very pro-English family, John said. Minna was visiting her brother, she met John and they fell in love.'

'I hadn't realised.'

Laurence was thinking that, if they had met in England, the fact that none of the Emmetts had ever met John's fiancée spoke of a wider estrangement than he'd understood from Mary.

'Minna died not long after they broke off their engagement. He felt very bad about it. And her brother was killed in the war. John felt bad about that too. But then he'd reached the point of carrying the whole world's troubles on his shoulders. And there were plenty to carry.'

'There was something else, in German,' he said, trying not to sound defensive. '"*Gottes Mühle mahle . . .*" is all I can remember now.'

'"*Gottes Mühle mahle langsam . . .*" I expect?' Laurence smiled at her. 'It's a film,' she said. 'But also a German proverb that means something like God comes at last when we think him furthest off.'

He sensed she was about to speak again but they heard William coughing from down the corridor, so she left the room. Although he had been caught out by the relevance of the name Coburg having a more innocent explanation than he'd dreamed, the location connected it unequivocally with the execution of Edmund Hart. Was John giving evidence as Brabourne had? It was the same hotel.

He heard Eleanor open a door down the corridor, but although he listened carefully, he couldn't hear her speaking.

After a while a door closed and a few minutes later she came back holding a steaming jug.

'Hot water,' she said. 'I could do with more tea.'

When they'd sat back in their chairs she spoke again. 'I expect you're wondering why I didn't marry John.'

'I suppose I was.'

'I was terribly in love with him. I always was from when I first nursed him. I think he was remarkable, quite different from anyone else I'd met. He was intelligent and kind and aware. He was a man of the world in the real sense and he was a man quite outside his time. Solitary, self-sufficient, but not, or not yet, shut away. I nursed him again when he had pneumonia and he had his breakdown. I expect you know that one of his men raped and murdered a young girl and nobody would bring the man to book? Then that execution. He would never discuss it but I think it finished him really. The two things just preyed on his mind all the time. That the guilty lived and the innocent died and all because of the war.

'He could never have married. He felt he was too damaged and there was something, an absolutely impenetrable barrier, that no one could break through. He said he was cursed. That people who came too close to him suffered and he couldn't make things right. He said everyone he'd ever loved had died. I think he was fond of Minna, and he had been close to his father, though not to his mother or, I suppose, his sister.' She glanced at Laurence. 'I'm sorry; it's not what you want to hear. In many ways he was so rational but in others he had a dark, almost medieval sense of guilt and self-denial. He was quite ascetic. I think he could have lived contentedly in a hermitage or a cave by the sea or even a monastery.

'Our relationship was never going to exist in the world beyond the two of us and the present. I was posted to the

305

Second London General Hospital. When he came home he didn't want to see me. He never answered my letters. Meanwhile, I had started visiting William in a convalescent home. I liked him a lot. He made me laugh; he too was intelligent, although less complicated than John. After a bit it was obvious he had feelings for me but he was never going to say because of his condition and also it was such a cliché to fall in love with your nurse. But William brought me serenity and, despite everything, a sense of optimism.'

'But you did see John again?'

'Well, obviously,' she said. 'Eventually he got back in touch with me. I think perhaps he felt he had to. I'd nursed him and we'd been lovers.' She delivered this nugget in an absolutely matter-of-fact way. 'Perhaps he felt he owed it to me. He was nervous, diffident. Not like himself at all. A stranger to be seduced. I saw myself as a sort of Orpheus to his Eurydice, fetching him back from the underworld.' Suddenly she laughed – the first time he'd heard her do so. 'No, that *does* sound preposterous. But I hoped that some kind of intimacy, warmth, might break through to him. It didn't, of course. He wasn't even really there.

'I must have been mad myself, or at least terribly naive to prescribe myself like some quack medicine, but then I loved him. Quite quickly, I realised I was pregnant. *Not* part of my cure. In some ways finding I was pregnant made me less desperate to be with John. I couldn't care for a child as well as him and by then I knew he would break my heart. I would never be able to *have* him, you see.

'I spent ages trying to decide whether to tell him, to tell William, or to run away and tell neither. In the event I told William first and he immediately offered to marry me. Then, a little later, I thought John should know; I'd been worried he was in too precarious a state to hear the news — he'd been arrested for assault by then — but in his way he was pleased, I think. And very relieved when I said I intended to marry William — not because he was off the hook,' she added hurriedly, 'but because the baby and I were safe.

'I saw him three times after I had Nicholas. He was like an uncle, I suppose, rather than a father to him. William was and is Nicholas's father. But then John left us the money. He'd never mentioned it. It's sad. All of it.' Her head dropped.

By the time he left, stepping out under a sky full of stars, Laurence felt he had finally grasped the mood of John's last months, and the man he had become between leaving Oxford and dying. He crunched off down the street as briskly as he could, hoping to find a cab on the main road.

He was determined to find out why John had gone up to London. The reason was apparently so compelling that he would risk a return to the draconian regime that young Chilvers had imposed on him before and which he so loathed. Whatever it was, the fact was that, once in London, away from Holmwood, John could have done or met anybody, and so soon before his death. It had to be significant. Obviously he could hardly write to Holmwood himself to ask what Dr Chilvers knew about John's visit to London. But Mary could.

CHAPTER THIRTY

*I*t took only a day or so for Laurence to decide to return to Fairford. He had already written to Mary, suggesting that she ask Dr Chilvers for more information about John's visit to London. He tried to convince himself that it was simply the possibility that George Chilvers had useful information that necessitated the journey to see him face to face but underneath he was driven by his fury at Chilvers' treatment of Eleanor and John. He knew that he'd transferred his anger, anger which he had rarely allowed himself to feel, from the dead Tucker to George Chilvers. He didn't want to tell him he was coming as he suspected he'd simply decline to see him. He decided to catch a train down to Fairford and risk George Chilvers being away.

On his way out to Paddington he picked up his post. Until recently correspondents had been few and far between. Now there were invariably letters for him.

The first was a complete surprise. It was from Westminster School. They were seeking a temporary replacement history master for the Lent term, with the possibility of a permanent position thereafter. His name had been suggested to them by an old boy, William Bolitho. Although completely out of the blue, an offer that he would have rejected out of hand a few months ago suddenly seemed like a godsend; he knew he could not and should not pursue a dead man indefinitely. It was time he left the confines of his flat and a book he doubted he would ever finish. He would go and see the school. He was also strangely touched by William's recommendation. He remembered telling him briefly about his pre-war enjoyment of teaching but was surprised Bolitho had taken it in.

There was also a letter forwarded from Mary. Dr Chilvers had written by return in answer to her enquiry. He was brief, she said, but there was no sense of him withholding anything. He confirmed that John had wanted to go to London in late autumn the previous year. The reason John had given was that he had been asked to appear before members of Colonel Lambert Ward's commission. However, Dr Chilvers felt that revisiting the circumstances in which he had first become unwell would be less than helpful for John at this stage of his recovery. Nevertheless, Dr Chilvers had said (and Mary had scrawled beside his comment, 'Oh, one's disappointment at the ingratitude of one's patients!'), Mr Emmett had taken advantage of a delivery of provisions to hide in the back of a lorry and had managed to catch a train to London. In the event he had returned in his own good time and in equable spirits, but it was felt he should be more closely watched after that. However, Dr Chilvers had taken the liberty of writing to Colonel Lambert Ward, who assured him no meeting had been requested, nor had one taken place. Dr Chilvers had not confronted John with this by the time of his death. And although he could not have answered if it had breached confidentiality, in answer to her second question he could tell her that he had never had a patient called either Lovell or Hart. Chilvers ended his reply, pleasantly enough, by hoping that Mary was in good health.

Laurence grinned at Mary's initiative. Her enquiry resolved one loose end. Neither Lovell nor Hart had ever been treated at Holmwood. But neither had John seen Lambert Ward. Had he met Somers like Brabourne had, or possibly seen Morrell or Bottomley? Or had that simply been a plausible excuse?

On impulse he decided to telephone Brabourne. He went into a hotel on Russell Square on the way to the station. The lobby was silent and the desk was unattended but after a few minutes' wait a porter arrived and made the connection for him. Brabourne soon answered.

'I've put together some cuttings,' he said. The line was crackling. 'You can pick them up any time you're passing. But there's not a lot to add. The Darling Committee presented its findings two years ago now – I was one of the last contributors, although Lambert Ward is certainly still heavily involved in all kinds of issues connected with military justice. Bottomley's still out there, shouting the odds through the mouthpiece of his paper. Quite brave; they all come under assault, even from fellow MPs. For Bottomley it's part of his trade, but some quite nasty stuff comes Lambert Ward's way, and Morrell's and Somers' too.'

'Do you think it's possible John Emmett was giving evidence in much the same way that you were?'

'Possible. As I said, the Darling people wrapped up their report at the end of 1919. The Southborough Committee is still taking evidence. Perhaps I should be in touch with them myself. Might be a new story brewing.'

Laurence thanked him, then added, 'John never mentioned a man called Meurice? French?'

'No, I'm pretty sure not. Very faint bell but not in that context. By the way, a snippet for you. I got hold of Jim Byers' photograph. Pre-war but he's as like cousin Leonard as peas in a pod. Could just be someone mistook one for the other, don't you think?'

'Thank you,' Laurence said. 'Interesting.' He paused briefly while he considered whether he was leaning too heavily on a new acquaintance, then continued, 'I've got something for you too but there's a snag, I'm afraid. Could you check one other thing for me? I think you'd know how to get the information I need without having to give too much in return. Tucker was killed last winter. In Birmingham.'

'Was he, by God?'

'I need to know the date but I don't want a fuss.'

He expected Brabourne to question him, to try to see a story in the enquiry, but he simply said, 'All right. Not difficult.'

Laurence wrote a short message to Charles before leaving the desk, and paid a boy to take it straight to his club. Yet again he had a feeling that he was getting further away from a simple answer to Mary's question, which was probably just: 'What was my brother like?' or 'Why did he die?' Instead, he was following wild-goose chases: intruding into lives that were already bruised, seeing anomalies where there was only the discontinuity of lives disrupted by the chaos of the war.

Laurence walked out into Russell Square. Even though it was milder again and the sun was shining, the brief outburst of prematurely wintry weather had left the trees bare. He liked this time of year when the bones of London appeared, no longer hidden by foliage. Now the shape of the square was plain. Tall, red-brick houses stood solidly around the huge area of gardens with every detail of arch, balcony and portico seen as the architect intended. A haze of branches still stopped him being able to see right across the square as he set off across it. At the far corner, cabmen were drinking tea by a dark-green hut. They nodded in response to his greeting.

The journey to Fairford seemed much shorter when travelling by train than it had done driving in Charles's car and he made the connecting train at Oxford with quarter of an hour to spare. There was even a carrier at Fairford Station who agreed to take him to George Chilvers' house for a small sum.

'It's not far,' he said. 'Just out of the village.'

The cabman offered Laurence a blanket smelling strongly of horse, which he refused; it wasn't cold. The horse plodded on as if it had done the journey a thousand times. There were two possibilities looming and Laurence considered them both: either Chilvers wouldn't be there and his journey was wasted or, if he was, there would be a row. As they bumped along, he steadied himself with his hand on the edge of the seat, realising he was looking forward to the confrontation. Would George Chilvers recognise him, he wondered? If he was able to extract the letters or garner the smallest piece of information it would be a bonus but he was quite content just to rile him.

The house had pretensions to grandeur but lacked charm. Laurence guessed it had been built within the last century. The front was dressed in Bath stone, from which a heavy wooden porch protruded outwards, its supports painted a dull green. It looked out of place on its site: neither within a village nor clearly at home in a fold of countryside. To either side were rather desolate flower beds, tidy but understocked. Laurence remembered Eleanor telling him how Chilvers' wife, Vera, had loved roses. He presumed her money had bought the house.

A maid in uniform opened the door. She was very thin and very young, probably no more than fifteen, and sounded as if she had a cold. Mr Chilvers was at the hospital, she told him, but if he liked he could wait in the drawing room; Mr Chilvers usually came back for tea. Laurence looked at his watch. He had plenty of time; the train connecting to the Oxford line didn't leave until five-thirty.

'Would you like tea?'

'No, thank you.'

The maid took him into a room with parquet flooring and half-height, varnished-oak panelling. There were some brocade chairs with crimson cushions arranged carefully on their tasselled corners. He chose the chair nearest the unlit fire with its bright brass scuttle of wet coal. The chair scraped on the floor as he sat down and his foot clanged against the fender. This was a room in which nobody could ever move about silently. The girl went out, sniffing. He gazed out at the desolation of the lawn and wished he had brought a paper.

He was miles away in thought when a woman's voice said, rather breathily, 'Are you all right? Have you come to see George? I don't know where he is, he's usually back by now.'

Laurence jumped up. The figure in the doorway was slight; a girl, he thought. She looked more surprised to see him than he was to see her.

'I'm Mrs Chilvers,' she said.

She was older than he had supposed. Her figure, voice and bearing were of a young woman but her face, though pretty, was not. Fine lines crossed her forehead and her lips were chapped. She had mousy, straight hair and was dressed in a rather smart, long-sleeved blue dress with a wrapper. He wondered whether she had just come in. Then, as she stepped forward, the fabric dropped a little and, under a string of plump pearls, he could see what looked like an old bruise, yellow and violet, between her neck and her shoulder blade.

She sensed him looking and shrugged the wrapper up again, clutching it to her as if she were naked underneath. Tiny blotches of pink blossomed on her cheeks.

'I'm sorry. I was asleep,' she said. 'George will be back soon.'

She was still framed in the doorway, apparently uncertain as to whether to come in.

He put his hand out. 'Laurence Bartram,' he said, in what he hoped was a reassuring tone.

She stepped forward and put out her hand awkwardly to shake his. 'Vera,' she said. 'I'm Vera.'

She was staring at him while keeping hold of his hand. His glance flickered downwards to register long pale scars between the buttoned cuff and her hand as she pulled it away.

Almost immediately, and while he was just beginning to wonder whether he could ask Vera about her friendship with John, he heard a car outside. Vera seemed startled and looked behind her to the doorway although there was nothing she could possibly have seen yet. A few minutes later a door slammed and George Chilvers strode into the room. He made no attempt to disguise his irritation at finding her there.

'Shouldn't you be resting?' he asked his wife. 'Haven't you taken your medicine? Where's Rose?'

'I have. I *have* rested. Rose gave me the new cordial at lunch. Sorry, sorry. I just heard Rose let someone in and I came down because I thought it might be you—'

'Well, as you can see now it *is* me. So there's no need for you to hang about.' George raised his eyebrows at Laurence, inviting him to share his amused exasperation. Vera had hardly left them when he said, 'Women, eh? But I'm afraid my poor wife suffers from her nerves. Scared of her own shadow but what can one do?'

He smiled, man to man. Laurence did not smile back.

'I didn't catch your name,' George said, extending his hand, evidently more relaxed now his wife had gone. 'But don't I know you already?' He looked puzzled.

'Yes and no. My name is Laurence Bartram. We met when I came to look round your father's nursing home. But the person you met was, to a certain extent, a fiction.' He had decided to come clean about his original visit. 'I was ostensibly looking for residential care for my brother then. That brother doesn't exist. The person I am now is a friend of the late John Emmett.'

For a few seconds Chilvers looked genuinely surprised, but he recovered fast. 'Of course. I thought there was something fishy about you then. I'd guessed you might be a newspaper journalist but perhaps you're simply a habitual fantasist, Mr Bartram?"

'I represent the family of John Emmett and, to a secondary degree, Mrs Eleanor Bolitho.' Laurence ignored George Chilvers' raised eyebrow. 'It is possible I made a mistake in approaching your father in the way I did but my motives were to clear up some questions that remain over the circumstances of Captain Emmett's death. I'm sorry that I felt it was necessary to deceive him. It was not lack of respect but necessity. As it happens, I thought him a good man doing an important and difficult task. I don't want to have to tell him of my fears that a patient's belongings were misappropriated.'

Chilvers still looked comfortable. 'Good he may be, indeed, a saint he may be, but a businessman he is not,' he replied smoothly. 'But actually it's irrelevant. The thing is, my father's dying. He's not likely to see the summer. A large tumour. Quite untreatable in the long term. Well, in the short term, to tell the truth. Once he dies I might just sell the whole place as a going concern, and go abroad. Or I might let it continue to bring me in a tidy income. Though some things will have to change. I haven't decided, but either way you running to my father is hardly going to hurt me. It might hurt him, of course. Perhaps that would be satisfaction enough for you, having already led this "good man" down the garden path?'

When Laurence didn't reply, George Chilvers went on, 'The thing about my father is that, despite his strange passion for invisible illnesses, he's a traditionalist at heart. Takes everybody's story at face value. Gives hours of his time, even now that he is a very sick man. Indulges the deluded, the weak, the malingering, the storytellers: he never discriminates. Has been known to reduce fees for long-term favourites. All very noble but, in the end, this isn't an order of nursing nuns. And too much coddling makes it far too easy for a man to stay ill.

'So, take the matter of suicide, which I am sure you intend to do sooner or later. Almost all the suicides connected with Holmwood have been patients who had been forced out into the considerably less tolerant world outside. It wasn't Holmwood they had a problem with, it was returning to their so-called nearest and dearest. Or they loved melodrama, as many of these types do, and simply miscalculated.'

Laurence remembered the description of the young man throwing himself head first over the banisters on to the flagged hallway. It seemed all too carefully calculated to him.

'But mostly they could see eviction from our little Eden looming and couldn't face it,' Chilvers went on. 'After all, they were men who had already proved themselves unable to face adversity in other spheres. I'd include your friend Captain Emmett in this. My father seemed to think he was turning a corner. He was certainly getting restive and becoming a damned nuisance, frankly.'

'He went to London,' Laurence interrupted.

'He went to London and caused us all a hell of a bother. We were responsible for him. Pulling these stunts was the sort of selfish act Emmett specialised in. His suicide was all of a piece with this. My father was ill in hospital in London. I had to deal with Emmett and keep Holmwood running.'

'What was Captain Emmett doing in London, do you think?'

'I have no idea and, frankly, I don't care. Picking up a tart and taking her to a hotel? Fornicating with another man's wife? His sort preyed on women. He even brought Mrs Bolitho to Holmwood, trying to pass her off as his sister while she slavered over him. He must have thought we were fools. Well, my father may react like a fool through his own innocence, but I am no man's patsy. Then she had the impertinence to complain about our treatment.'

Laurence was determined to keep his temper. What he needed was information. He recognised nothing of John in Chilvers' view of him but he remembered Eleanor describing Vera Chilvers' crush on him.

'Treatment?'

'We kept him in the custody of his room. If he couldn't be trusted to respect our boundaries, then he needed to be restrained. It wasn't the first time. He was always challenging our decisions.'

'Restrained?'

'Not a straitjacket, I'm afraid, if that's what you were hoping for. Locked in. Constantly supervised. He cut up about it, of course. For a period of time — a very short period of time — I had to sedate him with veronal. He could get quite violent when crossed.'

'You had the training to make such decisions?'

'I hardly feel I need to justify our regime to a self-confessed liar,' Chilvers retorted, and to Laurence's satisfaction he now appeared to be only just keeping his temper under control. 'Each patient has a broad range of medication and treatments written up by my father at admission, which covers all conceivable possible future requirements. The day-to-day treatment plans are a matter of discussion and we tend to pick and choose from what was prescribed in the patient's file. There can't be a doctor here every minute of the day.

'In this case, when my father returned to Holmwood he reversed the treatment decision. He likened Emmett's troublesomeness to pins and needles in a dead leg when circulation returns. My father's trade lends itself to metaphor. Unfortunately, and foolishly in my opinion, my father always had a soft spot for the man, but you only have to see what Emmett was capable of when he attacked our attendant outside the church. He may well have been your friend, but he was violent, dangerous even. Assault is what saw him admitted in the first place. You would have thought he would have had a better war.'

'You knew him in the war?' Laurence said, attempting to sound surprised. 'I hadn't realised. Were you in France?'

Chilvers flushed. He recovered almost immediately but Laurence knew he'd scored a hit. 'I knew of his war. It precipitated his illness,' said Chilvers. 'Much to my regret I was unable to fight myself; I have a degree of scoliosis.' His hand curved towards his spine. 'One has to accept the limitations it imposes and move on.'

'It must be hard.'

'I fear I'm revealing a side of your friend that you didn't know?'

'I didn't actually know him at all well,' said Laurence. 'I know his sister.'

Something approaching amusement crept into Chilvers'

voice but it made him if anything less attractive. 'Ah, yes. Emmett's sister. Or should I say "sisters"? I'm reminded of that little ditty: "The bible says to love my brother but I so good have grown,/ That I love other people's brothers better than my own." So are we discussing his real sister or the one who prefers other people's brothers?'

'If you mean Mrs Bolitho then, yes, I know both women. I count them as friends.' Laurence was still trying to keep his voice under control. 'But at present it is Captain Emmett's possessions I am interested in.'

'All returned to his family, such as they were.'

'Not all, I think. I believe you retained some letters.'

'And your belief rests on what facts?'

'Because Mrs Bolitho tells me you have some correspondence from Captain Emmett to her and possibly from her to him.'

'Well, I hardly think Mrs Bolitho can set up her camp on the high ground. Both of you playing your charades, but I imagine you're aware she's an adulteress, as well as an impostor. A woman full of tales and accusations. I hope she hasn't wrapped you around her little finger, Mr Bartram. Are you a married man?'

'The letters?' said Laurence, crisply. 'They are legally the property of the family.'

He wanted to protest that Eleanor had had no further physical relationship with John once she decided to marry William but sensed that Chilvers would be more gratified than rebuked by any discussion of Eleanor's private life.

'No letters, I can assure you,' Chilvers said. 'Why should I lie? Violet ink and lascivious thoughts are hardly my reading of choice. If there ever were any letters, I can assure you they must have been long destroyed.'

319

'If there were letters, they should have been put before the coroner after John's death.'

'Indeed? I do have some grasp of the law, including that of defamation. Perhaps you have forgotten, or didn't know, despite the richness of your information, that I am a solicitor?'

'Does the Law Society know of the wills you've drawn up for patients and the bequests profiting you or your father?'

Chilvers shook his head. 'Clutching at straws, I think, Mr Bartram. The few wills I made are all quite in order, I think you'll find. The legal position of lunatics is entirely clear. No wills were made when any testator was of unsound mind. But some legal assistance with all kinds of matters is part of our service to our unfortunate guests.'

'And your wife?'

'My wife? Mr Bartram, are you now going to insult my wife? Or are you simply going to continue to insult me?'

'You drafted her will?'

'I certainly did. And it was witnessed. You are obviously aware she was, for a while, a patient of my father's: a delicate woman, Vera, but, as you can see, she is still very much alive. Because she is my wife, and as we have no children, if she died intestate her property would come to me in any case. However, any will I drafted initially for her was made void by our marriage. I fear I may be missing some point here?'

'You were blackmailing Mrs Bolitho,' Laurence said, nettled that the conversation was not going as he intended.

'That is quite an offensive accusation to make against a professional man. I'll let it pass but I think it is time you went, Mr Bartram. Quite why I would want to blackmail a woman like that escapes me.'

As Chilvers turned away, Laurence said, 'You wanted to blackmail her firstly because you were anxious that your cruelties at Holmwood should not be given any publicity, particularly by an experienced nurse. Even the most indulgent father might think twice about leaving an enterprise that he had built up with care and kindness in the hands of a cruel, dishonest owner. Secondly, your wife's attachment to John Emmett, though unreciprocated except in terms of friendship, might have provided him with evidence of your shabby treatment of a woman you had a duty to protect. Thirdly, and crucially, I believe you had a strong physical attraction to Mrs Bolitho, which you wished to consummate in any way you could. You were yourself a married man at the time. Mrs Bolitho might have needed coercion, even had she not found you repellent.'

He looked steadily at Chilvers, who stepped forward, clenching and unclenching his left hand as it hung by his side. Laurence was willing him to lash out. It was twelve years since he had won his house cup at boxing, but he was leaner and perhaps fitter than the man opposite him. Chilvers may well have made the same judgment, as he stepped back slightly.

'I am not going to stand for one more minute of this. You may have been bewitched by Mrs Bolitho and her bastard child, but I most certainly have not. You have no proof of the existence of any letters. All this is conjecture. Fantasy. I might remind you that the first time I met you, it was you, not I, who were acting under false pretences. Kindly leave my house. If you return I shall call the police.' He rang the small bell on the table.

'I'm not sure you would actually want the police here and I may well visit them myself as Miss Emmett's representative, but I'm leaving anyway,' Laurence said, more calmly than he felt. 'Should you want to reconsider your statements, here is my card.' He laid one down on the table. 'Should you remember that, after all, you do have any of Captain Emmett's possessions, perhaps you would contact me?'

321

Chilvers picked up the card, looked at it briefly and threw it on to the coals.

Laurence had an overwhelming urge to punch Chilvers, regardless. His fingers curled into a fist as he measured up the precise spot on Chilvers' jaw where he would land it. Chilvers licked his lips and the corner of his eye twitched.

'I warn you to stay well away from Mrs Bolitho,' Laurence said, taking a small step forward. 'You may be right in thinking I could not make my accusations stick. You may well have destroyed the letters, once they were no use to you as an implement to batter Mrs Bolitho into surrendering. You may not be a thief and a predator, but, I think, collectively these accusations might do you harm if brought to the attention of the right people. A fusillade. It's a military term. You won't know much about its effects. Wise men under such fire keep their heads down.'

Chilvers started to speak but Laurence wouldn't let him interrupt.

'John Emmett was unwell and unable to defend himself. Mrs Bolitho is all too able to defend herself, but vulnerable because of her circumstances. I, however, am neither unwell nor vulnerable. I have absolutely nothing to lose, whereas you, I think, do. I can assure you I shall do the very best I can to bring you down without a moment's hesitation if you cause Miss Emmett or Mrs Bolitho any further distress. I shall speak to your father, the police, the Law Society and my friends in the national newspapers.'

Laurence wondered briefly whether he could indeed presume upon his very new acquaintance with Tresham Brabourne.

'And you may find that the reputation of Holmwood and, indeed, its history come under intense scrutiny. Maybe even enough to make your dying father reconsider his disposition of his property and save his patients from your attentions.'

Laurence reached the front door before the maid who was hovering uncertainly with his things. His last words had been pure bluff, a performance fired by adrenalin, and his heart was beating heavily and fast. As he took his hat and scarf from the girl, he was unable to resist looking back to see whether Chilvers was still in view. The man had followed him into the hall but now stood with his back to him, looking upwards. His spine, Laurence noticed with a small satisfaction, seemed straight. At the top of the stairs he caught a flash of blue on the upper landing. It was Mrs Chilvers, he thought, moving out of sight before her husband could see her.

CHAPTER THIRTY-ONE

*A*s he strode down the drive he wasn't sure whether he had achieved anything, yet he felt invigorated. He was quite happy to walk the distance to the station in the fresh air. Having taken such an instant dislike to Chilvers the first time he'd met him, there was a sort of gratification in finding his first impressions borne out by everything Chilvers had said during this encounter. Laurence had accomplished nothing of substance, yet he felt pleased with the day. He suspected Chilvers was a man few people stood up to. His only worry was whether the man was capable of taking out his ill temper on his wife. Laurence recalled Vera Chilvers' bruises. The thought of her husband with his hands round her neck was too imaginable, but how could she escape from him and would she want to?

He had clarified to his own satisfaction that there had been a letter or letters belonging to John; that Chilvers had indeed appropriated them; that he had discovered the nature of John and Eleanor's relationship as well as Nicholas's parentage; and that, once the letters had failed to bring about the desired outcome with Eleanor Bolitho, he had probably destroyed them. Whether they gave any insight on John's state of mind would never now be known. Yet George Chilvers' very hostility made his depiction of John convincing. If John was restless, challenging the staff, wanting to go to London, and had risked being imprisoned in his room, then he was no longer the withdrawn, silent man Mary had spoken of. Things had changed. Laurence was glad that old Dr Chilvers, at least, had seen something special in John, that he had moderated his harsh treatment and had perceived an improvement. All this would be happily received by Mary.

Yet his triumph began to fade as he realised that any doubts as to John's death being suicide were borne out by this new account of his last weeks. George Chilvers had made no effort to hide his dislike of John. Was that dislike sufficient for him to have wished him dead? Mary had said that Chilvers had driven around in his car looking for John after he got away. Was it possible that, far from intending to take him back to Holmwood, he had set out to remove him permanently? Could Chilvers have taken a gun from a previous patient?

By the time the train came, the adrenalin had subsided. He dozed, off and on, much of the way back to London. Feeling more or less revived when the train drew in, he decided on the spur of the moment to take a diversion past the *Daily Chronicle*'s offices. He knew it was a gamble. It was far too late to find Brabourne there but the paper itself was presumably open at night and it would be worth the cab fare to pick up the cuttings the journalist had promised. Brabourne had been as good as his word and the doorman handed him a plump brown envelope. Opening the flap, Laurence saw it contained several folded pages of newsprint. He tucked it into the inside pocket of his coat.

His flat was cold when he got in and the larder was distinctly bare, but he prepared a plate of cold mutton, some pickles and bread. He picked up a solitary pear, trying not to notice how shrivelled it looked. Just as he was settling back in his chair to eat it, he heard a knocking downstairs. He listened again. He so rarely had a visitor that he had never bothered to mend the broken bell pull. The knocking grew more insistent. He opened his door and went down the stairs to the street door. It was even less likely that any visitor would be for his downstairs neighbour. On the doorstep stood Charles. Wordlessly, he followed Laurence back up to his flat.

'Sorry, old chap. You did say you wanted to see me. Were you in the middle of dinner?' He looked over Laurence's shoulder at his plate. Laurence pushed the half-eaten pear deep into his pocket.

'Come in. It's not very warm, I'm afraid.'

'Hell's bells, man. Are you in training for an Antarctic expedition? No, I'll keep my coat on, thank you.'

Laurence poured out two tumblers of whisky as Charles riddled the grate and shovelled the coal over balls of screwed-up newspaper in the fireplace. He bent over with his lighter.

'Shan't stay long,' Charles said as he got to his feet again. 'But I wanted to tell you what I've been up to. Had to hurry round. Great news. Significant news, that is. You asked me to find out about Lilley. Lieutenant Ralph Lilley, principal author of Edmund Hart's misfortunes. It wasn't hard to find out that he made it through the war. He left the army, hale and hearty, in 1918, and went back to his parents. Only child. His mother was a Berridge — one of the Shropshire Berridges, so plenty of money coming young Lilley's way. Father has a small estate and officially Lilley returned to manage it. A keen sportsman, our boy, who became youngest ever master of foxhounds of the local hunt. In fact, along with shooting and fishing, that's how he mostly passed his time.'

Laurence spotted the past tense and felt a flicker of anticipation.

'Until?'

'Laurence, you bad man. You're already wishing harm to come to young Lilley. Well, you won't have to wait long. I found he was in the Ox and Bucks. So I started asking around and hit gold with my second cousin, Bim.'

Laurence marvelled, not for the first time, at the names of individuals in Charles's circle, names that rarely indicated their sex.

'Bim's wife, Didi, is quite a horsewoman. Marvellous seat, side-saddle. Formidable in top hat and veil. And she hunts with the Old Berks. As does – or did – their late lamented master, Ralph Lilley. Didi was terrifically happy to find someone who didn't already know the story.'

Laurence knew the hunt from his school days.

'The Old Berks have their stables at Faringdon. The Lilley estate is near by; it stretches along the Vale of the White Horse. In fact, do you remember when we used to take picnics out from school and go to Dragon Hill?'

Laurence nodded, memories suddenly flooding in. Legend had it that the hill and gully were where St George had finally slain the dragon and no grass had grown there since the dragon's blood soaked into the earth. When he was thirteen he had believed this to be fact. Even when he knew it wasn't, the place was still atmospheric.

'But what's the connection?' he said.

'No connection with Dragon Hill, per se, except that the Lilleys lived close by. But also near by, as I'm sure you've realised, is the spot where John Emmett died.' Charles drank his whisky very slowly. Laurence knew he was savouring the moment to come.

'Faringdon Folly.' Laurence said.

'And, indeed, near the small station at Challow where, early last spring, Ralph Lilley fell to his gruesome death under the London-bound train.'

'Good Lord.'

'Of course you're wondering: did he fall, jump or was he pushed?'

'I suppose so. Which, then?'

'Rather as with Tucker, the official verdict was that it was an accident. They said he fell when somewhat under the influence. He went up most Wednesdays, quite late, to dine with friends in London. It was getting dark. He'd been hunting and had had a stirrup cup or two. There was certainly no hint of suicide. Far too much self-regard, young Lilley, and life was going well for him. He'd just got engaged to the younger daughter of Lord Fitzhardinge, though Didi implied he had rather an eye for women. Plural.'

'But?'

'But there were only four witnesses of any kind. Six, if you count the driver and fireman, though the engine was past the spot by the time Lilley went under its wheels. Train almost empty and nobody on that side of that carriage. On the station: a pregnant woman and her mother. Neither woman actually saw him fall and the one who was with child passed out. The porter was inside and the elderly stationmaster was at the near end of the platform, looking at the engine, not at the people waiting to board, when Lilley tumbled on to the line.'

'That's three,' said Laurence.

'Yes. But there's the rub. Lilley was talking to another chap just before the accident. That same man jumped down to help the mortally injured Lilley after he fell. He wasn't yet dead but was not a pretty sight. The driver and fireman stepped down too and the stationmaster ran off to call for a doctor, though there wasn't much a medic could do with a man who'd gone under a train. By the time they returned, Lilley was dead. The doctor had his work cut out, dealing with the pregnant woman and the distressed driver. The stationmaster was trying to keep the few passengers on the train and eventually the local bobby arrived. By then the other man was nowhere to be seen.

'I actually drove over on my way back from Bim's to London and had a word with the stationmaster. Both he and the two women had been able to give only the vaguest of descriptions of this other man, and although the stationmaster had a faint feeling he'd seen him travel from there before, he was utterly unable to add to the basic description they all put forward. You'd probably be able to provide it yourself by now: a man in a British Warm and hat. A gentleman, the stationmaster thought. A soldier, the women had thought. The fireman saw that someone was crouched over, dealing with Lilley, but he couldn't describe him at all. He thought it might be the young porter. Nobody got a clear look at his face. The stationmaster thought he was middle-aged, the women that he was quite old.'

'So not an octogenarian grandmother, at least, then?'

'Quite honestly, Laurence, it could well have been a giraffe for all the powers of observation of those on the platform. The stationmaster said the mystery man hadn't bought a ticket. Not that day, anyway, but he could have had one already.'

'Then Lilley wasn't shot in the face?'

'No, but his legs were cut off by the train.'

'So,' Laurence summed up, finding himself indifferent to

Lilley's horrible end, 'if we assume that Lilley was no accident, and that the same man was involved in Lilley's death as with the others, which is a bit of a leap but not a huge one, then it seems he manages to avoid attention because he has no particular distinguishing features and he dresses in clothes worn by half the men in England.'

'It has the feel of your man. Your unknown man. Although the police would have liked to speak to him, of course, they believed it was just the typical modesty of a decent Englishman, slipping away to avoid thanks, having done all he could. But this is a small station. Not many people use it. Lilley did, regularly, but did the unknown man know this? And if he did, how did he know it? It could be that he lives near by.'

'And it could, just possibly, be why John ended up where he did.' Laurence heard the excitement in his own voice. 'But this man, he couldn't have used the station regularly or the stationmaster would have recognised him.'

'He did recognise him, of course,' said Charles, 'if only slightly. Perhaps he's got a motorcar.'

Laurence thought for a minute. 'The murder of Jim Byers seems likely to have been committed by a man with a car. No other way, really. That bit of Devon's pretty isolated. He wouldn't have needed one for Mullins or Tucker. I think we do have to include those two on our list.'

Laurence began to calculate the distance from Fairford to Challow: fifteen miles or so, he guessed. George Chilvers had a car. Could the fact that the presumed murderer had always been seen in a military greatcoat be a clever ruse? Unlike most men of his age, Chilvers had never been in the forces. However, in all other ways Chilvers seemed an unlikely killer. He was too fastidious and although a bully and a thief, he didn't seem like a man with the ruthlessness to carry out so many murders and, with some regret, Laurence had to accept that he had no conceivable link with any of the other dead men.

'I'm too tired to think all this through,' he said finally. 'But I don't think there's much doubt that we're looking at murder now. Probably four murders, maybe more. I'm going to go back and talk to Mrs Lovell. She must know more than she's letting on. To start with, I wondered whether Hart could be her son, but it doesn't fit. All the same, I do think her son's story may be mixed up with the execution and its aftermath. I might get a picture out of her on some pretext, though I can't think of any now, and she won't be letting any photographs far out of her sight, I imagine.'

Charles nodded, holding his glass with both hands. 'You could say you thought you might have known him, I suppose?'

It was obvious, yet Laurence had more of a problem with the idea of lying to Gwen Lovell than to the others he had deliberately misled. He didn't answer.

'You're thinking, what if the old girl is excited at being able to exchange recollections of her boy?' said Charles.

'Yes, I suppose I am. But also we aren't even absolutely certain he was ever in the army. The records don't show it.'

'Difficult one. Perhaps Lovell lied to his mama? Ran away to avoid being called up? Perhaps she lied to you? Not impossible. If you want me to come along to see Mrs Lovell, I will.' He looked at Laurence expectantly.

Although tempted for a moment, Laurence sensed he would get more out of Mrs Lovell if he were alone. Force of numbers might cause her to be suspicious and he thought Charles's jocular confidence might grate on her. Nevertheless, if her son had not been a soldier and she knew it, then she had lied persuasively about receiving the telegram.

Just as Charles put his glass down and stood up, Laurence

said, 'Why do you think Somers, if it was him, took Emmett to the Connaught instead of his club? It's a bit furtive.'

'The Connaught is hardly a Limehouse opium den. And skulking about is not really in his character, I'd say,' Charles replied.

'You know Limehouse well, then?' Laurence asked, keeping his face expressionless.

'Of course.' Charles was struggling into one arm of his coat. 'Opium dens – just the sort of place the really depraved murderer plots his crimes. Ask Sherlock Holmes and Dr Watson. Or there's Fu Manchu – you don't have to have smoked an opium pipe to know where to find trouble. To get inside the mind of a drug fiend in his lair, you just need to read a few books. After all, you haven't been to the Connaught either but you know how it'll be in there. Palms. Tea. Cocktails. A grand piano. And plenty of people who don't know one another. That's the key to anonymity.' He finally heaved his coat over his shoulders. 'Actually a chap I knew from Birmingham days – Arthur Ward – his father was our works foreman – he wrote the Fu Manchu stories.'

'I could have sworn the author was——'

'Rohmer. Sax Rohmer. German name, but not his real one. "Arthur Ward" carried too much of the smell of the tannery for tales of the Orient. Taking a German pseudonym was an odd sort of choice, but there we are. Damn good yarns.'

CHAPTER THIRTY-TWO

*F*or a while Laurence had considered it just possible that the tensions between John and Sergeant Tucker had become lethal. Now that he knew that so many of those involved were dead, the situation seemed unreal, something out of Charles's detective novels. Leonard Byers' rueful comment about a curse was close to the truth but there was nothing supernatural about these deaths. Neither John nor Tucker could have killed all three men: Lilley, Jim Byers and Mullins, because both were by then dead themselves. So who else knew them all and could have done?

He realised now that what they ought to be looking for was not a message but a motive. A motive should lead him to the man to whom this violence made sense. A sense driven by hatred or greed or jealousy, perhaps, or even a sort of biblical retribution, but a sense that Laurence currently couldn't begin to grasp. If the motive was to remove everyone connected with the firing squad, then he needed, urgently, to find out more about young Hart himself.

Yet not everyone connected with the execution was dead.

With a suddenness that made his hair stand on end, he realised how stupid he had been. John had died at the end of December. Tucker had died the same winter, Lilley in April, Byers in early summer. Mullins had been murdered in August. Whoever was carrying out these killings had not necessarily stopped. The arrangements just took time. The killer needed to track down his quarry, to undertake his mission and then return to normal life without arousing suspicion. It was not necessarily over.

Who else might be on the list? Was the lost legatee of John's will, the Frenchman, Meurice, already one of the victims or could he have been the assailant all along? More than ever, he was aware that his enquiries had always been patchy.

What about Leonard Byers? Was he in any danger now? Laurence also had an increasing sense of unease about the safety of Tresham Brabourne, even faintly considering whether he might be at risk himself. Had he even met the murderer already as he lumbered around with his questions?

Thinking about Brabourne, it occurred to him that Charles's unexpected visit had diverted him from looking at the bundle of cuttings he'd picked up at the *Chronicle*. He laid them out on his table. There were articles on parliamentary debates, a few letters, mostly from *The Times* rather than the *Chronicle*. There was a profile of Colonel Lambert Ward and blurry photographs accompanied an older article on General Somers when he was fighting in Africa. There was a vast front-page headline from Horatio Bottomley's *John Bull*: TRAGEDY OF A BOY OFFICER. The only bit of the page not covered by the headline was an advertisement for Excelda handkerchiefs.

He turned over and skimmed through the article. It concerned the death of one of the other two officers executed. The journalist was in full flow but the case against the hapless lieutenant of the Naval Reserve seemed as weak as the one against Hart. What surprised him was that the piece had been published in March 1918, before the war had even ended. He imagined the fury it must have caused in the War Office.

He read through the letters. Despite a few enraged denunciations, there was nothing here that hinted at future violence. Laurence noticed that several of the letters were from the fathers of sons who had been killed while obeying orders and they didn't want their boys buried next to a coward. While he could understand their point of view, he didn't think their sons would agree, were they to rise from their ranks of stone in France. What had John wanted to add to all this?

Brabourne, who had known John Emmett as a fellow officer, was the one person who seemed to accept all along that John might well have killed himself. He was an intelligent observer and had seen John at his worst. Laurence had liked Brabourne – he was a man facing forward, he thought, and for that reason he had an energy that Laurence could only recently detect in any measure in himself. He thought of Brabourne dressed for the outdoors in his bitterly cold office with its ill-fitting window, or striding down Fleet Street at one with his world, but otherwise apparently immune to his surroundings.

Something had rung a bell when he'd seen him and it burst upon him suddenly what it was. The scarf Brabourne was wearing was, he was almost certain, a school sporting colours scarf, but he was equally certain it was the same colours as the one John had with him at his death. The one that had been returned to the Emmetts, not his own school scarf, but another man's.

Another man's school. It meant nothing: hundreds of boys had joined up from schools like Eton and Harrow, Rugby and

Wellington — Brabourne's school — and, indeed, like John, Charles and Laurence himself, from Marlborough. Brabourne too had commented on this. No doubt this was how it had always been: he had read the memorials to the battle dead of the Crimean and Boer Wars during interminable sermons in the college chapel. As a schoolboy he would try to make anagrams of their names to pass the time. But each of these previous conflicts accounted for only a handful of old boys. The memorial boards erected now would list tens of names for every house in the school. And there was Brabourne — not, as Byers had predicted, dead in the mud, a casualty of his own sense of invincibility, nor reduced to gold letters on a plaque to create wonder in generations of boys to come, but moving on, away from the war. One day he would be an old man, with no doubt a fine career behind him, while those three or four years in uniform would be no more than one brief, if distressing, episode in a life rich in adventures, challenges, sorrows and joys. It wouldn't be the first and the last thing he thought of every day. Laurence doubted it was, even now. It would be history. Brabourne would tell his grandsons about it.

He realised that it was quite possible that Brabourne had lent John a spare scarf, though it was unusual to have two, and in peacetime no public schoolboy would wear the colours of another school. War, however, was a colder, more pragmatic way of life. It was even easier to imagine that Brabourne would have given his own scarf to Edmund Hart. Laurence remembered Brabourne commenting on the cold in the room where they had imprisoned the condemned man as they waited to hear his fate.

He reflected just how many young officers had known one another. He was always amused by Charles's social networks but they formed the web that both trapped and supported people like him; people like himself, too, Laurence supposed. It was that society that men like Edmund Hart were excluded from. Even as the war progressed and more officers had been promoted from the ranks, there was a gulf between the traditional officer class and those on whom war had bestowed a grudging commission. If Edmund had been to Eton or Marlborough or Harrow, he might well not have died for his offence. It was a chilling thought.

When he picked up the envelope to replace all the cuttings, he could feel something still inside. He had missed a rough note from Tresham Brabourne, folded round a photograph. It was of a very young, light-haired man, with a blanket round his shoulders; he was sitting at a table with what appeared to be a plate of bread and cheese. The background was very indistinct but, although the photograph was quite dark, the man's fatigue was obvious. He looked solemnly at the camera. Along the top of the scrap of paper Brabourne had scrawled in pencil, 'Vis Tucker's death. Police records state it was in late February.' Laurence registered that it let John off the hook for Tucker's murder and that he owed Brabourne a drink. Then all other thoughts drained away as he read the note that had enclosed the photograph. Brabourne had written:

I checked again if I had another photograph of the firing squad. The one you have is definitely the only one and was previously in my possession (not that I want it back). I had absolutely forgotten I also had this picture. It's Edmund Hart on the night I told you about: bitter cold, poetry, a mistaken, though shared, belief that his sentence would be commuted, and all the rest. I took this at his request; he wanted to reassure his ma. A day later he was shot. The film hadn't even been developed. I could hardly give it to the padre to send home with his effects — and yet it seemed wrong to destroy it. You might find that it makes the whole affair more real to have a likeness of a man much more sinned against than sinning.

Laurence could not take his eyes off the picture in his hand. Hart looked about seventeen. His hair was tousled, his eyes wide. Laurence immediately grasped that his task had become easier. Here was a picture he could show to people. Somebody out there who might not have known his name might yet recognise his face. He would show the Bolithos, Mrs Lovell, even Charles. Either of the Bolithos might have come across him in France. Mrs Lovell had said her son had brought home a friend or two and it was possible this man was one of them. Although Charles was a remote chance, he seemed to know so many more people in the army than one war would normally make possible. Laurence would take it to Holmwood and try Dr Chilvers; after all, Brabourne had said Hart had been treated for shell-shock in England. He might just have been at Holmwood despite Chilvers' assurance that he'd never treated a Hart. Could it have been under an assumed name? Some family shame protected?

He hadn't expected to hear from Mary with any speed. Yet on the Friday he received a letter by the afternoon post, post-marked Sussex, saying that she would be in London on the Tuesday and why didn't they catch up. He felt a familiar pang of jealousy at her continued journeys to see an unknown friend and was irked by her casual offer to fit him in with her existing engagements in London, followed by an equally famil-iar irritation with himself.

But a second letter soon took all his attention. The envelope was larger with round, neat writing. Inside were two sheets of writing paper. It was, to his astonishment, from Vera Chilvers.

Dear Mr Bartram,

I couldn't help but overhear you talking with my husband yesterday and afterwards when George had gone out I found your card in the grate. Please don't tell him I have written to you or he would be very angry with me and the post-boy for taking my letter.

You were right, he did take some of Captain Emmett's things. There was a watch on a chain and the letters I think you were looking for. I hadn't realised why he took the letters. I thought it might be that John was complaining about how my husband treated him and it might have got him (George, I mean) into trouble. George can be quite unkind.

He hated John because John was kind to me. John Emmett was my only friend, when he came it was the best time in my life. I miss him all the time. He just talked to me and he gave me a poem he'd written in the war but George tore it up. He gave the pieces back to John. I think George has burned all the letters a while back and now the watch is gone from its usual place so you must have scared him. He was in a furious mood after you had gone.

Before the letters disappeared, they were in his desk. It was the day John went missing and there was such a brouhaha and George was in and out, but he had left these on the top when he was suddenly called away. I only had time to read the one which seemed to have been by John because he had that odd writing. Mostly they were to him from a woman called Elly. I didn't dare take any. They had gone by the evening. I never saw any of them again.

John didn't complain about his treatment in that letter. In fact he said after he'd been up to London he'd got a lot of things off his chest. He'd been in touch with a man he needed to speak to and also a woman he'd done a great wrong to, he said. He talked about hoping his son would never see the things John had seen. John never told me that he had a little boy or even that he'd been married and I was sad that he hadn't. I didn't know he loved someone called Elly. I would have kept his secrets whatever George did. I hope you will tell his little boy that his father was a very special person.

I had nothing else left of John since George tore up my poem so I hope you will not think wrong of me that I read them. I just wanted to have him for a bit. But <u>don't let George know</u>.

Yours sincerely,
Vera Elizabeth Chilvers

As he read her rather childlike letter, Laurence felt overwhelmingly sorry for Vera whose life, he thought, must be hell. He wished he could report the theft of the watch, which Mary had said right at the start was missing, though it would probably simply make Vera's life worse. He had been unable to question her as he'd wished, yet she had still come up with crucial new information.

Vera implied that John had met a woman while he was in London. Had this been Eleanor? Was John's inability to marry her when she was pregnant this 'great wrong'? He didn't think Eleanor saw it that way. It could have been Gwen Lovell. But then he stopped himself; John's world was infinitely larger than the fragment he had been exploring. There could have been many women wronged, though he smiled to think of John as a voracious seducer.

Nevertheless, the train of thought this opened up, no matter how fantastic, raised one other question. Was there any possibility, however unlikely, that the killer, if there was one, could have been a woman? All the accounts of the deaths came down to a faceless figure in a heavy coat. Eleanor, as fearless as any man, seemed quite capable of subterfuge and, given her experience in the war, was almost certainly familiar with guns. Gwen Lovell, who had once been on the stage, was tall and well built with a low voice. He tried to imagine either woman in a greatcoat and hat with their hair up, and visualise whether they could possibly have masqueraded behind the anonymously familiar outfit. It was not impossible. What might drive them to it? The answer was the same for both of them: to protect their sons. But the image that returned to his mind's eye was of Hart, friendless and alone as he went to his death.

CHAPTER THIRTY-THREE

The first person he showed the photograph to was Mary, whom he had arranged to meet in the Lyons teashop in Piccadilly in the early afternoon. He thought it would be very hard for her to see a picture of the man her brother had been ordered to shoot. He had found it hard himself, gazing on that boyish face while it still held a little hope. When it came to it, he held back despite Charles's admonition not to treat her as a child.

From the teashop they took a cab as rain was falling heavily. The driver insisted on dropping them at the end of Lamb's Conduit Street. They half walked, half ran down the street, trying to avoid the deepest puddles, and when they reached his flat they were cold to the bone. Mary had a bag with her and he hoped that meant she intended to stay.

He lit the fire and brought her a towel. Her hair fell in dark curls about her face and the tip of her nose was as pink as her cheeks but her eyes were bright and she looked amused. He hung her coat over a chair near the fire. When he came out of the kitchen she was sitting on a hard chair with her back half to him, rolling down a woollen stocking. She looked up.

'I hope you don't mind,' she said, easing it over her foot and wriggling her toes before hanging the sodden stocking over the arms of the chair seat next to her coat. Her calf was slim and white.

He sat down on the floor. She rubbed her leg with the towel, then reached up under her skirt and undid the other stocking. Her hair tumbled forward. Laurence was transfixed by the curve of her nape and the taut wool of her cardigan across her back. Her hands smoothed the stocking down over her knee. She sat up abruptly and he thought she had caught the intensity of his gaze before he looked away.

'I like being up here in your eyrie,' she said, rubbing her hair briskly. 'It's simple and it's cosy by night and the light pours in during the day. If you were reduced to a couple of trunks — like poor John — you'd be all nicely bound books and sheet music from Chopin to 'Roses of Picardy' — yes, you have, Laurie,' she said, as he shook his head, 'I saw it — and some impressively obscure pamphlets on churches plus those heavenly watercolours of Arabia' — she pointed to the far wall — 'a good Persian carpet, worn but serviceable, French linen and the basic ingredients for a gin sling. What a cultured man he must have been, they'd say. How eclectic. Whereas I'd be all party frocks from before the war and too many hats and unsuitable novels and solidified paint brushes I forgot to clean and ticket stubs for *Oh! Oh! Delphine* and so on. Hmm, they'd think. What a flibbertigibbet.'

He felt his heart lurch as she tugged at the knots in her hair. She had regained some of the spirit he remembered from years ago, and with her hair loose, she looked young and vulnerable.

'You've never showed me any of your paintings,' he said.

'Ah, the man of culture speaks. You don't want to see my hats, I notice. But I can do better than paintings. I'll draw you.

You've got a handsome face – good bones. I'd enjoy it. I like doing people I know well, whose layers can be explored.'

'It sounds a bit forensic.'

'Oh it is. You'll be squirming under my all-seeing eye.'

She pulled her bag towards her and put away her comb, then took out a woolly scarf. For a second he was puzzled, until she said, 'It's the one John had. I thought you might be able to find who owned it? From the number,' she added eagerly.

He took it. 'I can try.' Of course he could. Brabourne might be able to tell, he thought. But where did it get them?

He had hesitated to show her the photograph, not wanting to break into her happy mood, but as she drank her tea he finally passed over the picture.

'I've never seen him,' she said, quietly, without him having to explain who it was. 'He doesn't look old enough to be called up, let alone shot.' She shook her head slowly. 'Poor him. Poor John. It's not the way we were told things were.' She rubbed her nose with the back of her hand, like a small child. 'They're past caring now, I suppose, but for every one of them there's a family who are destroyed too. And how could you bear it if your son hadn't been killed by a German but in cold blood by his own side? You'd have a lifetime of nightmares, I would have thought.'

Laurence nodded and took back the photograph. 'I suspect nightmares were what broke John,' he said.

'Do you know anything about his parents?' Mary looked back at the photograph in his hand. 'Lieutenant Hart's? Perhaps he had brothers? Or a sister?'

'It's a good question. We know the area he came from but it's quite hard to find out. Even families often weren't told for ages.'

It sounded feeble, even to him. He urgently needed to find Edmund Hart's family. Once he'd shown the picture around, he would focus on that single task. Nevertheless he felt uneasy.

What right had he to intrude on grief or shame or anger? Even if the parents were alive, what if they were trying to hide the truth from neighbours or friends and he blundered in? He recognised that it was this that had previously deterred him from trying harder.

'There are lots of things no one can ever know,' she said. 'I'm only getting to accept that now. John was always so self-contained, the more so when he went away to school. He was probably fond enough of us all but, except for my father, he never let us in. John dying was almost a part of that: not leaving a note, not letting us even try to understand.' There was a trace of bitterness in her voice. 'You probably know more about John now than any of us ever did.'

'I'm sure that's not . . .'

'Oh, not from want of trying, just because John didn't want to be known. Not in life. Not in death. Probably my father understood him, though even he didn't always. Take his engagement. He wrote back to my father a few times when he was travelling and then the next thing we hear is that he has got engaged to a German girl. We didn't even know about her and there was already a lot of bad feeling against Germans. So my parents either kept it quiet, as if they were ashamed of it, or found themselves defending someone they'd never met. Then somebody told my mother that John's fiancée was in England, had visited him, yet he had never brought her home. It felt like a rejection. And by the time we knew, he'd left Oxford without a degree and they were both back in Germany, staying with her parents.

'And while he was away things had got really difficult at home. It was all to do with money. My grandfather – my mother's father – died when John was abroad with Minna's family and left John quite a large bequest. I think neither my

345

mother nor my father had realised none of it would come to them. John hadn't expected it either, of course. He hardly knew him. My grandfather was born a working man but had become rich in later life from buying and selling metals. But neither side approved of my parents' marriage, my father's family being higher class than my mother's. Ironically my father was much poorer than my grandfather became. We seldom saw either grandfather; there'd been some falling-out when we were young. But still, my grandfather must have liked the idea of a grandson. What with my parents and Minna, and my grand-father and John, we seem to be a family where the most powerful relationships exist only at a distance.'

'Given I didn't have a proper home myself, I would never have noticed,' he said. 'I thought it was just a bit . . .' He paused to think of a word that wouldn't hurt her.

'Bohemian. You thought we were charmingly bohemian, from the uncut grass to our apparent imperviousness to cold, the leaking roof, the lack of staff for a biggish house, our old-fashioned dress sense and the strange potato, windfall and scrag-end aspect of our diet? No, we simply had no money.'

Laurence didn't reply. What she said was more or less true. The intermittent metallic echo of rainwater, dripping into three or four zinc bowls in the conservatory, and the women being swathed in Indian shawls on chilly summer evenings had had no significance to him then. He had liked the silent long-case clock, minus its hands. He had thought it all rather romantic. A small part of him was disappointed when Louise didn't seem to want that sort of life.

'. . . and of course John was a long way away,' Mary was saying, 'but he did have money after grandfather's death. I think he was just caught up in Germany and Minna and so forth. But my father, though kind in every way, was so hopeless, and in the end had to ask John for help when creditors threatened to overwhelm us. And John didn't reply. Of course, he may never even have got the letter. But, urged on by my mother who was really upset, my father wrote him a second, very hard letter. Although John paid off their debts then, for a while there was a kind of a rift. My father was humiliated and who knows what John felt? He'd always looked up to my father, was almost oblivious to his weaknesses, and suddenly there he was, begging, and my mother resentful that they should have to. My father was walking the dog one evening soon afterwards and he didn't come back. He'd had a heart attack. They found him dead in a field the next day. The dog had stayed with the body. John had never seen him again to make up. After that the war began.'

'I'm sorry. I didn't know.' He paused. 'I would never have guessed John would be someone who'd be queuing to volunteer. He never seemed the sort.'

'Not a fighter, you mean.' She smiled. 'Or not a patriot?'

'Not taken in by politicians. Certainly not the sort who might have thought war was an adventure. Particularly as he had German friends, had been going to marry a German girl.'

'I suppose,' Mary said, obviously still thinking aloud, 'that he might have reached a point in his life when he wasn't sure *which* way to go. His pieces of writing from Germany weren't selling any more. His relationship with Minna ended when hostilities became inevitable. War had come and, having been in Germany, he'd probably got a better view of what it was likely to mean for us. Because he'd travelled, his German was pretty well flawless — he was an internationalist in lots of ways — so maybe that made him try to pre-empt the inevitable? He hadn't just hidden in Minna's pro-British circle; he'd written in the papers about the clamour of the Prussian warmongers. I don't think he ever thought it was just going to be a short thing. But he never explained directly.' She looked puzzled and he guessed it was the first time she'd ever considered John's early volunteering. 'I hope it wasn't because he didn't care what happened to him.'

'People admired the first men to go,' he said.

'Yes,' she said eagerly. 'We were proud you know, in an unthinking way. But now, looking back . . . You know, even though my father loved it, John would never go shooting. He didn't like killing things. Not even wasps.'

Her eyes flicked back to the photograph. For a moment she looked distressed, then went on, 'If my father had lived he would have been fearfully proud. He always said he'd wanted to join the army himself when he was young, but his heart wasn't good from a fever he'd had as a boy. The only books he read were always about battles and heroes. Ancient Greece, Agincourt, Waterloo and the most dreadful memoirs by stuffy old generals.'

The silences that fell between them now were companionable, Laurence thought, not the awkward breakdowns in conversation or head-on collisions when both had talked at once when they were trying to get to know each other. Now silence seemed more of a measure of closeness than speech.

Eventually he said, 'So that's where the bequests came from? John was wealthy?'

'Fairly. He supported my mother after my father died. And when John died himself he left my mother provided for and left me enough to ensure I could be reasonably independent. If I didn't have commitments here, I'd go to Italy and study in Florence. Art. Italian. I'd always hoped to do that before the war but it wasn't possible.' She seemed to rush past this reflection as if it pained her. 'And now I'm not free to go.'

He was surprised by the degree of her loyalty to her mother.

'I don't know why John left money to Mrs Lovell, but I'm glad he remembered William Bolitho,' she said.

'I imagine he liked him, and Eleanor Bolitho befriended him when she was his nurse. Also, he probably wanted to help someone who had ended up in poor shape.'

He still didn't tell Mary that Eleanor had seen John at Holmwood and had passed herself off as his sister. She might even have been the last visitor he saw before he died. Nor did he mention Nicholas. He felt uncomfortable lying by default but he had made a promise.

'That must have made a difference to them,' said Mary. 'I mean, it must have given them hope. Especially for William Bolitho, given he was unlikely to work again. They at least had something to live for. That little boy.'

Laurence looked down and Mary took it for distress.

'Oh my God, Laurence, I'm so sorry. I forgot. I mean, it's awful that I forgot.'

'It's all right. I forget myself sometimes. It seems a long time ago. But I just can't imagine it. It's not real. I can hardly remember what Louise's face looked like and I never even saw the baby.'

'Your son.'

'I wish I had,' he heard himself saying without acknowledging her. 'I wish I knew what he looked like. Though he would have looked like all babies, of course. Small. Round. Cross.' He attempted a laugh.

'Did he have a name?

'Christopher Joseph Laurence. Christopher after my father and Joseph after hers. We were going to call him Kit. For short.'

He stopped, the brevity of everything concerned with his unknown son suddenly overwhelming him.

He took a couple of deep breaths. 'He did all right at first.

Louise was virtually unconscious by the time he was delivered. She had a massive haemorrhage, though she did see him, or so her mother likes to believe. He just succumbed. No will to live. A big baby,' he added. 'No real reason for him to die. Not enough oxygen, perhaps, they thought.'

'Oh Laurie,' said Mary, moving to sit on the floor next to him and rubbing his hand. 'You must have been so sad. To lose them both. You must have loved your wife very much.'

'That's the really awful bit of it. I'm not sure I ever did. Not enough. I married her because I was lonely. That wasn't what I thought at the time but looking back I think that's why. I didn't have a family so I thought I could share hers. She was utterly without malice but she was just a girl, unformed. I couldn't talk to her.' He stopped. 'And she didn't like me, not as a husband. Not in a physical way. She liked me as a friend, as someone to be beside her, to sit in a nice house, to tease her and admire her. But me as a man she found very difficult. She was young. She knew nothing at all really about the realities of love or marriage. I think part of her couldn't believe I could want to do something so horrible to her. I didn't have time to get to know her before she was pregnant. Then she lost the baby and was devastated. All she wanted was another baby. When she knew she was pregnant again, that made her happy. Totally, utterly happy.'

He wondered whether he was entering territory that was far too personal to discuss with a woman he had not known long, however intensely he had felt a connection, but he kept on talking. Mary looked interested but not shocked at his openness.

'Once she was pregnant she didn't want me to share a room with her. Of course she was terrified about losing this baby too but it was more than that. I think it all revolted her. All the same, I hated myself for being dissatisfied with her, and yet wanting the comfort of her so much. And meanwhile the war had come.

'When I came back on leave the gulf between us was even greater. All she talked about was the baby or if she discussed the war it was simply how we were winning every battle. She wouldn't hear anything that contradicted that. She wouldn't see what was right in front of her eyes. A couple of times I read reports to her from *The Times*: all highly watered-down versions of what I'd been part of, but she actually put her hands over her ears.'

'Perhaps she was frightened to bring a baby into a world where victory wasn't a certainty?'

Mary stood up as she spoke and he thought she was going into the kitchen. For a second he thought his frankness had disappointed her or even repelled her. However, she leaned over to touch the side of his face. When he didn't pull back she put out her other hand and raised his face to look at her. Then, astonishingly, she bent down and kissed him gently on the lips. 'I'm so sorry,' she whispered.

He looked back at her and her gaze didn't waver. She walked on into the tiny scullery and ran herself a glass of water. He loved watching her take his rooms for granted.

'It was the war,' she said as she came back through the door, 'and it was like nothing else. It complicated things. Not just for soldiers.'

He sensed she was pondering whether to continue.

'I wasn't honest with you,' she said finally. 'Sins of omission and all that.'

His heart sank. He wasn't sure whether, after all this time, he wanted to know any secrets she'd been holding back.

'There was somebody.'

Laurence felt a terrible sadness, then simultaneously — and, he knew, demeaningly — a hope that the past tense meant just that.

'He was married,' she said, sitting down next to him on the floor, her back against a chair. 'It was a very unhappy marriage. Among other things, his wife found she couldn't have children. Very sad for them both. Although she found someone else, they were Catholic; hers was a very old recusant family so the world turned a blind eye. Richard found himself sort of in limbo. He loved the estate — just two farms and a beautiful Tudor house, though a very dilapidated, very cold house.'

She smiled, apparently in recollection, and Laurence's heart sank again.

'My father was dead. My mother, well, you've seen her. She seldom thinks of anyone or anything outside the effort of just living her life. So there was nobody to inveigh against my unsuitable relationship.'

She looked straight at Laurence but he found it hard not to avoid her eyes, hoping she didn't mistake jealousy for disapproval.

'Nobody to tell me that my reputation would be besmirched or that I'd never find a decent husband. Of course we didn't know there'd be a war, but if we had, we'd probably just have seized the day.'

Although the grin she gave him was partly bravado, he thought, it made her look like a schoolgirl.

'Anyway, Richard was as much a husband as I can imagine any man being. Not at first, not for a long time — I was quite young, of course, and he was dreadfully anxious about protecting me from scandal, whereas I didn't really give a fig myself — but, in the end.'

Laurence desperately wanted to swallow but she was looking

at him too closely. She seemed to be testing his response despite her apparent certainties.

'Anyway he stayed in the country in Sussex, in the old, cold house overlooking the Downs. He'd been born in that house. His wife, Blanche, lived in their flat in London. He was lonely but he loved the countryside. The cloud shadows over the hills, the foam of hawthorn in spring: he used to say the whole landscape echoed the sea. His house was a bit like an old ship, stranded inland. It was all faded reds and silver wood, over-hanging upper storeys, barley-sugar chimneys.

'We met at the house of mutual friends one weekend. I think we each sensed loneliness in the other. We took to meet-ing just to walk and talk. Over the next months and years we must have explored the whole county in every season and every kind of weather. He liked the crumbling cliffs, the sea mists and the rattle of the sea on the shingle; he tried to go into the navy when he saw the way things were going, but it was quicker' — she grimaced — 'and easier to get a commission in the army. My own favourite place was the Long Man of Wilming-ton — a huge chalk figure with a stave in each hand — and a little medieval priory or something near by. A place of ancient peace. I often go back there now.'

Laurence felt the tiny satisfaction of incorporating another bit of her life into his understanding of her. This was the scan-dal Charles had spoken of and also why he had bumped into her in Sussex. He wanted to ask the identity of the man she had met but not introduced him to at the Wigmore Hall, but it still wasn't the right moment.

'I expect people talked,' she said. 'But it was a long, long time until he asked me if I would consider being his. He was such an extraordinarily decent man. He told me he could never offer me marriage. Never bring me to his house as its chatelaine.

Not in his wife's lifetime. That people might despise us and we would have to be terribly careful not to have a child. But he loved me. He loved me and I loved him, so it was an easy decision. And I was never happier.' She stopped. 'Do you think the less of me?' she said almost triumphantly.

'Of course not,' he said. His chest hurt with it.

'Well, it's different now. Since the war. These times we live in. But it was a bigger thing then. My mother wouldn't speak to me when the penny dropped. Not for about three weeks. Which is ages in her book.' Her lips twitched and a small dimple showed that she was trying not to smile.

'What happened to him?' asked Laurence. 'Was he lost in the war?'

'Yes.' Her animated face seemed to freeze.

Then, seeming to think this inadequate information, she added, 'At Vimy Ridge. Just a tiny piece of shrapnel. A lethal sliver of hot metal burning its way through his brain. He wasn't touched otherwise.' She seemed momentarily lost. 'He was very . . . beautiful,' she said.

Her head was resting on his shoulder. He stroked her hair with his right hand and absent-mindedly tucked a strand behind her ear. She turned her face towards him just as his arm gave way and they both fell to the floor. He was more or less on his back, rubbing his arm to restore circulation. She pushed herself up to a half-sitting position, leaning over him. For a second she just looked at him. The fire popped. Then she reached out and dragged a cushion off the chair, putting it behind his head. The top of her own was framed by the window and the light of the sinking sun illuminated individual hairs like fine copper wires. He pulled her towards him and kissed her. It was clumsy, the adjustment of unfamiliar bodies. Her mouth was little and controlled at first and then became softer as he kissed her. His hand curved round the back of her neck and he moved it downwards, feeling the depressions of her collarbone, sliding under the neckline of her dress with his fingertips.

She pulled away slightly but still lay with the top of her body over his. Her eyes were grey and solemn, her eyelashes surprisingly dark. He noticed she had tiny freckles on her nose, so faint he had never seen them before. He watched himself touch her. She had looked so boyish, yet felt all curves and pliancy in his arms. This time she kissed him.

'This isn't about Richard,' she said after a long time. 'It isn't even about John. It's certainly not about Louise or the war or either of us feeling sorry for the other one. It's just about you and me.'

She traced his lips with her fingers. She was smiling.

Many hours later he woke in bed feeling cold. It was just light and at some point in the night they'd moved from the floor to his bed. Mary was nestled, fast asleep, between him and the wall, with his arm under her neck and her back curved into him, but the blanket had barely covered them both and his naked shoulders were cold. He propped himself up awkwardly on one elbow and looked down at her. His fingers hovered over her ear; although he longed to touch her, he didn't want to wake her up. Her curls lay flat against her cheek. He felt a charge of happiness. It was as if the intensity of his gaze reached her because suddenly she gave a sigh, turning over and nearly knocking him out of bed. He held on to her and her eyes opened. She blinked a couple of times.

'Ooh, you're cold. You'd better kiss me.'

'Such self-sacrifice,' he said, pulling her towards him.

She smelled warm and musky. His hand followed the

355

contours of her neck and shoulder. Moving to her breast he was filled with joy as well as desire when he felt her nipple harden again beneath his fingers.

It was nearly lunchtime when they finally got up. As she sat on the edge of the bed she picked up his copy of *The Jungle Book*. He was about to justify it being there when she said, 'I love these stories. I've still got mine. Rikki-Tikki-Tavi was my favourite. That's why I kept a ferret; it was the nearest I could get to a mongoose in Suffolk.'

Once out of bed he felt slightly awkward, although Mary seemed completely at home, both with him and with the acceleration of their relationship. He'd intended to make breakfast but by the time he had washed and shaved she had already pulled the bed together, gathered up their discarded clothes off the floor, cooked scrambled eggs on toast and made a pot of tea. She was walking around in his dressing gown. He picked up a piece of hot bacon between his fingers. They had eaten nothing the evening before and he was famished.

'This is a good thing that's come out of all this unhappiness,' she said, her knife and fork clattering on the plate. 'One really good thing. Us finding each other.'

He looked at her but didn't speak. He was happier than he could remember being in ten years but despite it all he felt an underlying disquiet.

When he returned from seeing her off at the station, the flat seemed quiet without her, yet it still held echoes of her presence. He felt calm and hopeful. He was able to settle to work for most of the day. For the first time he could see that he might write his book and return to teaching. All the while he deliberately left the washing-up, the two plates, two teacups, two knives and teaspoons, on the side.

CHAPTER THIRTY-FOUR

*C*harles's disappointment at finding that Laurence had dealt with Chilvers by himself was palpable. As a result, he insisted on accompanying him around during his next day's errands. Despite Laurence's half-hearted protestations that it would be too cold and too boring for Charles to drive him to the Bolithos', he was glad to have him as a chauffeur. Charles could even take him on to see Mrs Lovell, leave him there and still have time to see his tailor as he'd apparently planned, while Laurence could go on to Fleet Street by bus. He had woken up determined to catch Brabourne at the paper at the end of the day.

First, however, he wanted to show the photograph to the Bolithos and Mrs Lovell. Even if they didn't recognise Edmund Hart, that would at least clearly exclude him from certain places and events. Tomorrow he intended to show it to Major Calogreedy, although he hoped to avoid Leonard Byers. Dr Chilvers could wait a week or so.

Before Charles started the car, Laurence handed the photograph to his friend without speaking.

'And this is?'

'You don't know?'

'Presumably it's Hart?' He shot a look at Laurence. 'Poor bugger. But no, I didn't know him, I'm glad to say.'

They reached the Bolithos' house at three. As he hadn't warned them he was coming, Laurence went in alone, leaving Charles in the car. For once Eleanor seemed as pleased to see him as William was. She took him into the sitting room, and there, playing with a toy car, was Nicholas, who looked up curiously as Laurence came in. He stood up, knocking over a line of painted toy soldiers as he did so. One rolled under a chair; another was clasped in his small hand. The boy's sturdy legs emerged from corduroy shorts, his socks had fallen down and he wore a blue cardigan that emphasised the colour of his eyes. Laurence bent and picked up the car.

'Aha, an Alvis. Now, if you look out of the window you'll see a big one.'

Nicholas ran to the window. Eleanor lifted him on to a chair where he could gaze out at Charles's car parked in the street. Laurence watched him for a few seconds. He had the shape of John's brow and chin, yet his eyes were unquestionably Eleanor's. But above all, Nicholas Bolitho was simply himself, pointing and chattering away excitedly.

While Eleanor held Nicholas up to see the Alvis, Laurence spoke to William.

'I'm sorry to rush in and out,' he said, 'but I simply wanted to see if you recognised a photograph. A man called Edmund Hart.'

He saw that Eleanor had her eyes on them, even as she was responding to her son. William nodded, took the picture, looked at it in silence and finally shook his head.

'I don't think so. I'm pretty certain not, but of course there were so many faces. And because of the blanket you can't see what regiment he is in here.'

'He wasn't there when the trench collapsed?'

'No. Not that I saw.'

Eleanor came over, leaving Nicholas with his face pressed to the windowpane. Laurence scanned her face closely as she took the picture from her husband, but she gave no indication that she recognised the man in the photograph, though she took longer than William to shake her head.

'I was wondering if I'd nursed him,' she said. 'For a minute I thought it was a boy I'd cared for in France. But there were so many who looked like this. Schoolboys.' She tipped it to the light. 'Sorry. No. Anyway, I would have remembered the name — when I was at Cambridge just before the war I toiled for hours over *King Lear*. I'd remember an Edmund.' She looked up at Laurence. 'Is he the one?'

'I'm afraid so.'

Eleanor's first reaction was to look over at her son, still kneeling on a chair, staring into the street, one small hand still clutching a solitary red guardsman. When she turned back she had tears in her eyes.

He felt embarrassed at marching in and then leaving so abruptly, and he would have liked a chance to see more of Nicholas, but he didn't want to arrive at Gwen Lovell's house too late or miss Brabourne at his office. He wished he'd taken Brabourne's home address.

When he left, Eleanor brought Nicholas down to see Charles's car. Charles shook her hand in greeting and then swung the little boy into the passenger seat. Although Nicholas's lower lip wobbled for a moment, he was smiling within seconds as Charles flicked switches on and off. Eleanor looked chilly; she wrapped her arms around herself and took her eyes off her son only briefly.

'Laurie,' she said, in a low voice, leaning towards him. 'It was one thing to tell you a secret of my own after I'd judged you could keep it but there's something else I ought to tell you if you want to understand John. Because it's someone else's secret, I hope you can give me your word, even though it involves someone you know, that it will go no further?'

Laurence could only nod agreement to her solemn entreaty. Her glance flickered to her son and Charles, tactfully engrossed in the dashboard.

'John loved his father very much – you may have gathered. But when he was still a boy – thirteen or fourteen – he discovered a letter from his grandfather to his mother in his father's gunroom, of all places. It was hidden; he was young and curious. I don't know the exact contents but it made it clear that Mrs Emmett had had an affair in which she conceived her daughter. The father of Mrs Emmett's child was John's grandfather, Mr Emmett Senior.'

Laurence was stunned for a minute. 'But I gathered the older Emmetts were against the marriage?' he said.

'Well, unsurprisingly, if Emmett Senior was in love with his prospective daughter-in-law he didn't want his son marrying her. But there was no living grandmother. John's mother had been a housekeeper to his widowed grandfather and probably rather more.'

'Good God.'

'She married, impulsively, her family thought, then had a child who died in infancy. Born prematurely, John said, but it makes you wonder who its father was. Then she had John, unequivocally his father's son, the letter confirmed . . .'

Laurence was glad of that, remembering the bond between the two.

'And then at some point soon after that the marriage evidently cooled and the relationship with John's grandfather resumed. She bore him a daughter – Mary. John's father was not Mary's father.'

'How dreadful for John finding out, though. Did he tell his father he knew?'

'No. Impossible. But it was a terrible burden for a young boy to bear. It ruined his relationship with his mother.'

And his sister, Laurence thought. The living evidence of what had gone wrong with their family. He was certain Mary did not know. Did the maternal grandparents know or suspect? Was that why all their money had been left to John?

'Look, I have to go in,' Eleanor said. 'I'll keep in touch but it's too cold for Nicholas to be out.' She leaned forward and kissed Laurence on the cheek. 'I'd like to meet your Miss Emmett,' she said. 'Perhaps it's time she was introduced to Nicholas. If you want to tell her I knew John, well, you can, of course. If it would help.'

Then she bent over the car and exchanged a couple of words with Charles as she retrieved her son to wails of protest.

Charles was obviously delighted to have met Eleanor whilst simultaneously disappointed that she had not exploded into anarchy on her own doorstep. He had kept shaking her hand until she had had to withdraw it. As they drove away Laurence knew what Charles was going say next, but it was not until they had turned the corner that he finally spoke.

'You know what they say about redheads?' he muttered, his teeth clenched on his pipe.

When they drew up at the Lovells' small house, Charles let him out on the opposite side of the road, a little way down the street. Charles suggested waiting in the car but it was far too cold and Laurence had no idea how long he might be. If Mrs Lovell was in, he hoped the photograph might serve as an excuse to ask her some more questions. What regiment her son had been in, for a start.

Laurence braced himself. He crossed the road and walked up to the front door. The house was almost in darkness although a very dim light shone from a small window that he thought must light the stairs. He knocked, waited. Knocked again. Listened.

The paint was peeling on the front door. The passage to the side was shut. He had a sudden vision of her standing on the doorstep with pistols stuck in her sash and a dagger between her teeth like a pirate queen. At the same time he knew that if he really believed she was a murderer, he would hardly be here alone on a late winter's afternoon. He took two steps back to look up at the upper windows. He looked back over the road. Charles had gone. As he was about to knock again, he heard footsteps inside. Somebody was coming slowly down the stairs. The chain was removed and finally the door opened.

CHAPTER THIRTY-FIVE

*G*wen Lovell stood framed in the doorway, her face in shadow. For a split second he took her for her daughter, but it was an impression caused by Mrs Lovell's hair falling loose over her shoulders. As soon as he saw her, reality hit him. She was just one of tens of thousands of mourning women.

'I'm sorry. It seems as if I've come at a bad time.'

'No,' she said vaguely, but made no attempt to ask him in. She rubbed her face. He wondered whether she had been asleep. When he had first met her, her melancholy had had a sort of vigour. That was all gone now. His visit began to seem thoughtlessly impulsive.

'I'm really sorry to bother you, but I have a photograph and it's possible it might be someone your son knew — you said you'd met a few of his friends — and I wanted to check with you. I could come back at some other time.'

'No. Come in, Mr Bartram.'

Her voice was quiet. She motioned to him to follow her into the front room and lit the lamps, leaving the curtains open. He put his coat down over a chair. Finally, a smile flickered briefly, although it was as if she was having to make an effort.

'Are you well?' She said it with a tone of genuine concern.

'Quite well, yes, thank you. And you?'

She shrugged. 'Well, you know . . . it is not easy. Not at all. Do you have any news of your friend?'

'I think I know some of what happened to him,' he said. It was too complicated and too private to start to explain it to her. She seemed to understand this and inclined her head slightly, but her eyes were alert.

'But you have something to show me?'

He pulled out the photograph. She sat down and picked up some half-moon spectacles from a small table. He watched her face as he had Eleanor's but was absolutely unprepared for what followed. She put her hand up to her mouth. Her eyes opened wide. Her silence was unnerving.

Finally she spoke. 'Oh my God. What is this? Where did you get it?'

'I was given it.' He knew the answer was inadequate – she was so pale he was afraid she was about to faint.

'Harry,' she said.

Laurence's head spun. Was the condemned man not Edmund Hart but Harry Lovell after all? Had Brabourne lied and, if so, why? Why hadn't he checked first with Leonard Byers that this was indeed Edmund Hart?

'Harry?'

Gwen Lovell gazed at the picture.

'Where have you got this?'

'Is it really your son?' It was a ridiculous question. She was so obviously shocked. 'Can I get you a drink of water? I'm terribly sorry, I hadn't realised for a minute . . .' He felt cold with horror and angry with himself. Did she even know the man in the picture had been executed? But then, had he?

'Harry,' she said, then was silent. He became aware she had started to cry only when some of her tears fell on the picture. He heard a faint noise upstairs. Catherine was obviously at home; he hoped she wouldn't come down.

'You can keep it,' he said hurriedly, regretting it immediately when she threw him a look of disbelief.

She pulled out a handkerchief and blew her nose. 'Who did you think it was?'

'Actually I thought it was a man called Edmund Hart.'

She looked at him, pityingly, he thought. Her shoulders lifted as she took a breath.

'It is. This is my son — Hans Edmund Hart. He was never Lovell. Only Catherine is Mr Lovell's child.' She brought out the words slowly. 'My name was Hart before my marriage. I named him after my father. My father was German. I am German, although my mother was Welsh. We came to call him Harry. A diminutive. But also because — Hans — well, living in England, you can imagine; it would not have been easy.'

'And when he took a commission, he used his second name for every formality?'

She nodded. 'He had been brought up in England. He felt English. He was prepared to fight as an Englishman. But not as Hans.'

'You have no other photographs of him.' It was a statement but she took it as a question.

'I have pictures of Harry. I see him before I go to sleep and when I first wake up. When you have a child, they are your calendar, your measure of time passing. I see him in his christening robes, I see him as a little boy with his hoop. I see him building castles on the sand. I see him play the piano.

I see him at school. And now,' she glanced at the photograph again, 'I see him at the end . . . No, don't explain. I know what I am seeing. I am seeing what I already know.'

Laurence stood just inches away but with a continent of distance between them. He noticed that her accent was stronger in her distress. He wondered how he could have thought it insignificant before. He could think of nothing to say.

Yet as he stood there and watched her stroke the image of her son's face with her finger, it dawned upon him that if she had known all along how Edmund Hart had died, then she also had a much stronger motive for killing John than he had thought. Had he made a sentimental misjudgment?

After a long time he spoke. 'Did you know how he'd died?'

She shrugged. 'Not at first. Not for a long time. Not when your friend Mr Emmett wrote to me or when he left me the money. Not when I first met you. But now, yes. I know it all.'

'And Edmund's – Harry's – real father is dead?'

She looked up, alarmed, not by his question, but by something she had seen beyond him.

'Captain Emmett.'

The words came from behind Laurence's back. A man stood in the doorway to the room. Laurence hadn't heard him. He stepped forward and stood beside Gwen Lovell. In the better light, Laurence guessed he was in his late fifties. He was of medium height, strongly built and had an authoritative presence. He was familiar yet Laurence couldn't identify him. Where had he seen him before and why, given that he had obviously been in the house all the time, did Gwen look worried to see him?

'May I have it?'

Gwen Lovell handed her guest the picture. He looked at it, his expression impossible to read. Finally he looked up. All the while, Laurence watched Gwen Lovell who was shaking her head almost imperceptibly. The man handed the picture back to her. Although Laurence knew he was on the point of placing the stranger, he was sure he had come across him in a completely different context.

'Harry,' the man said.

Suddenly Laurence realised with astonishment that he had seen the man before him at Charles's club. He was the man pictured in the articles Brabourne had given him. It was General Gerald Somers.

Laurence was briefly puzzled but then understood. Somers was already investigating executions during the Great War. If Gwen Lovell's son *had* been shot, then there was a logical reason why Somers was here. Laurence's anxiety receded. Mrs Lovell was no killer.

'If I'd known Mrs Lovell's son . . .' Laurence started. Somers began to speak almost as if he hadn't heard him.

'Sit down, Mr Bartram. You see, I know who you are and why you are here and now you know why I am here. Or, if you do not, I shall tell you.' He indicated a chair at right angles to Gwen Lovell and then sat down himself.

Somers started to speak a few times and then stopped, not as if he was nervous but as if he didn't know where to embark on his story. When he did so, it was neither with the official inquiry nor with Edmund Hart, but with his own eldest son.

'When Hugh died – in the family tradition he was a career officer – it was quite early on, February 1915,' said Somers. 'Extraordinary to think of it, but we didn't then know a great many families who had lost sons.

'I never saw my wife weep. She acted on instinct. It helped her, perhaps. She wrote her black-bordered letters. Ordered her mourning from Peter Robinson. She remained, head to toe, in deepest black, just as her mother or grandmother might have done. She was a figure in a landscape that had become history and she was left stranded, nowhere. Then, I think, she realised everything had changed. It seemed almost greedy to claim so much visible grief just for oneself. So with exquisite mistiming she found herself setting aside her Victorian veils and her crape just as every collier's wife was clutching at a worn black shawl. After 1916, mourning became a way of life.'

Somers paused and looked towards the window. 'She never spoke of Hugh again. All pictures of him disappeared. She refused to engage in any discussion about him. It was hopeless. Impossible. I never knew what became of his possessions. When Miles, my younger son, came home on leave, he was furious about this and would try to force Marjorie – my wife – to acknowledge Hugh's life and death, but she would simply leave the room. Miles and I would talk of him late at night – in low voices as if he'd done something unspeakable.

'And yet she had been – we all had been – so proud of Hugh: a handsome young man, our brave boy. How naive we were. Now he was buried in another country and even more deeply in our memory. Neither place was to be revisited. The care with which we negotiated our daily conversation in order to expunge Hugh eventually caused any real communication between us to cease altogether.

'Then when Miles was lost, there wasn't even a body. Suddenly the circumstances of Hugh's death seemed almost luxurious. Somebody had seen him and handled him, laid him down and read prayers over him. He had a grave.'

Somers got up, walked to the window and gazed out.

'"Missing, presumed killed in action". My wife didn't hold out hope, as some mothers did, that our son would be found. I think she felt a degree of contempt for me as I tried to extract from the War Office information they didn't have, trying to raise the dead. For her it was over. She had no sons left. No children. More picture frames vanished. With Miles gone, I lost my last link with Hugh. Yet, unlike her and unbeknown to her, *I* had one son left, whom I had betrayed many years earlier and whom I could hardly claim now. Harry Hart was my son, Mr Bartram. Harry Hart should have been Harry Somers.'

Somers had returned to stand behind Gwen Lovell, his fingertips on her shoulders.

'You didn't realise?' Somers was saying to Laurence. 'About Harry? I've known Gwen for twenty-five years. Gwen should have been my wife — if I had not been a coward and a scoundrel. I met her when she was nineteen. Innocent, sweet, with all her life before her. I was already a cavalry major. Family tradition. I was keen on tradition then. Went to Berlin with some chaps in the regiment and one took me to hear Gwen sing. She captured my heart.'

His face softened.

'I went to her dressing room with my friend. We had some champagne and lingered a bit that evening. She was amusing, gentle, kind — and her voice was lovely.' He looked happy, remembering it. 'I wanted to see her again. On my own.'

Gwen tipped her head back to look at him.

'I didn't want to seem like some stage-door Johnny so I just took her for tea and for walks in Babelsberg Park. The next year I went back. One hot May day I bought her a yellow parasol and we took a boat on the Havel. I could see she was fond of me. Although the relationship was still just a friendship, I had to tell her that I was engaged to be married. The terrible thing was that she had never entertained any thought of us having a future together; not because of a betrothal she hadn't even known about but because she assumed a man like me would never have serious intentions about a girl like her. I was ashamed when she told me.'

Gwen shook her head again.

'But we carried on, by letter, through visits, for weeks, months, a year. Mine was a lonely sort of marriage even before we lost our boys. Gwen had a Welsh mother; I had had an Austrian nursemaid. We corresponded in both languages. Time passed. Eventually things changed. Her father died. She came to London. We became much closer.'

He looked down at his lover but she was gazing at her hands. Laurence stayed silent, not wanting to interrupt the flow of speech.

'I set her up in a tiny flat. It was a compromise. I hoped she knew I loved her as she did me. But just when I thought we were most happy, Gwen decided to end our relationship. She wouldn't explain why. I was upset and angry — though I had no right to be. She went abroad. Within the next year or so trouble flared up in Africa. I finally left England with my regiment in 1899. I was worried about how she would manage. I'd been helping her financially. I wrote to her, care of her father. She never answered. When I returned in 1902, I heard that Gwen had managed fine: she'd returned to the concert hall and was engaged to be married to a widower.'

He drew breath and looked down at Gwen for a few seconds.

'I went back to the formalities of my marriage and the compensation of my sons. I thought of Gwen every day: what she'd think or say. Things that would amuse her. It wasn't until a year or so later that I was walking up Piccadilly and bumped into a friend of hers, a fellow musician. Of course, I asked how Gwen was. Her friend said she was back in London and the marriage was a success, but the husband was not in the best of health. Although he had not adopted her child, he took good care of both him and Gwen. I was reeling. The friend was talking as if I knew all about the situation. I don't know what I said then but I managed to extricate Gwen's address with a plausible story and wrote to her the following day.'

He smiled again.

'And so I discovered that the dear girl had ended the relationship because she was expecting Harry and didn't want me to feel obliged to her in any way. That was how much she loved me. When Mr Lovell offered to marry her, she accepted. Harry's name remained her maiden name – Hart. She told her husband that the man who had fathered her boy was from Germany and was dead.

'Which I might as well have been. I made contact with Gwen and from then on she kept me in touch with his progress as a child, and then as a schoolboy. I stayed away as she asked – she had a daughter by then – though over the years I saw the boy from time to time from a distance. He was musical, like Gwen, and I would attend his concerts, but I never made myself known. Gwen was not prepared to tell him his real father had risen from the dead and was a married man. Understandably.'

Laurence glanced at Mrs Lovell, whose intense gaze was now fixed, unmoving, on the general.

'And then came the war,' said Somers. 'Harry failed to get a commission in his first attempt. Gwen was sensitive to questions about his background, so I wrote on his behalf, saying I was the boy's godfather. I succeeded: he was commissioned three months after his eighteenth birthday, despite his German roots. Despite his lack of a father on his birth certificate. Not in the best of regiments, not like Hugh and Miles, but, as it turned out, fighting on the same blasted river plain. The same gas, the same wire, the same guns. The same rudimentary justice. The same muddy graves.'

'He joined the moment he could,' Mrs Lovell said, softly but firmly. 'He hated the idea of war but he wanted to do his bit.'

The light was starting to go, yet it was impossible to leave. Somers took his hands off Gwen's shoulders; he had evidently not finished unburdening himself.

'Might I speak to Captain Bartram alone, do you think?'

'Of course,' she said, although her eyes stayed on his face while she rose from the chair. Laurence heard her footsteps as she went slowly down the hall, followed by the muffled bang of a door shutting. Then silence. Somers hardly seemed to have noticed her going.

'Suddenly, Gwen asked to meet me. She had never asked me to leave my wife's side, even for an hour. She had borne Harry alone and she was alone in bearing the knowledge of his death. She had been so patient, so undemanding, for years. She was as she had always been: a good woman.'

Laurence had a sudden vision of Louise, curled up in bed with her back to him, more like a child than a wife despite being five months pregnant. She was soft and relaxed, trying to get him to discuss choices of names for their unborn child before he left for France. Her hair had been in a loose plait and stray strands had tickled his nose. He thought what single word he would use to sum her up. She was not what Somers might call a good woman. Nor was she undemanding. She was, he realised with an unexpected lurch of loss, sweet. Just a sweet girl.

'Yet when I went to see her,' Somers said, 'and she told me that Harry, my only remaining son, was dead, it felt like a kind of justice. For a moment it seemed reasonable that *I* should suffer. What incredible selfishness, eh, Bartram? Three boys gone, the two women who had borne me sons both dismantled by loss, and I could think only that some celestial justice had been meted out to *me*.'

Somers got up again and walked about; he had the very slightest limp. The room seemed hardly large enough to contain the two of them and all the ghosts of the dead.

'Over the next few months there were things Gwen could not understand. The telegram notifying her of Harry's death had no details beyond the location where he'd died and it had initially gone to the address where they lived when Harry enlisted. His effects were eventually returned to her and a slightly strange letter followed from him, written shortly before his death, saying he was in a "spot of trouble" but she was not to worry. There was no subsequent letter from his CO or the adjutant. She wrote to the War Office after a while, yet received the reply only that they would forward her further details of his death once they had them.

'More months passed and no pension was forthcoming. It struck her as odd but she was always rather diffident with authority, perhaps because she was part German, and Mr Lovell had left her a little and I was happy to support her. But she asked me to see if I could use my contacts to find out anything about our boy's death. She didn't even know where he was buried.

'It took me a little longer than I had expected to find out the truth, though I already had a bad feeling about the whole business. Harry should never have been a soldier. Hugh, Miles — were different sort of men — sportsmen, confident, forceful.' Somers continued, his voice low, 'But Harry was too sensitive, too imaginative. Always had been. More like his mother than me. He could sing. Was a chorister at St Paul's. I went to hear him a couple of times, although I never told Gwen.'

His eyes flickered downwards.

'She was so generous about describing his life without ever expecting me to share it. He was like her in so many ways. He could write; he produced a libretto while he was still at school. Poetry, too. It was fine stuff.'

Laurence, observing him closely, saw a muscle in his cheek twitch.

'Not just a father's pride . . .' Somers faltered.

At last Laurence spoke. 'I know,' he said. 'I read some of his work once.'

It seemed years rather than months since he had stood next to Mary in the Emmetts' attic room and first read the young poet's work.

Somers blinked. He looked surprised, then resumed speaking almost immediately.

'The war took my boys and then the influenza took Marjorie. Which was a mercy, I think. She had no wish to live, as far as I could tell, and the illness was shockingly quick. But the effect of seeing my whole family vanish in four years slowed me down and I took too much time in pressing for the truth about what had happened to Harry. Perhaps I was putting off the day when I would acquire unendurable knowledge.

'The truth was told to me in a room in Whitehall on a fine summer's day. I doubt the civil servant who eventually communicated Harry's ignoble end believed a word of the story I had concocted.

'After I left Whitehall, I walked down Horse Guards to St James's Park. I sat on a bench and watched a mother with her little boy, throwing bread for the pigeons, and he was laughing and running up and down, and suddenly I was aware of the most tremendous rage. Not sorrow — I was past all that, except in anticipating Gwen's reaction to my news — but fury. Rage at my country, which I had served with pride and to the best of my ability; which had demanded my sons' service and seen all three of them act, I truly believe, to the best of their ability. Two had been taken from me in circumstances beyond anybody's control but Harry had been taken, from Gwen and from me and from his own future, by his country. *My* country. Quite deliberately. He was shot by men who had served under him. They'd buried him perfunctorily — the battalion was moving on — and, in the resulting mêlée, even the exact location of his grave was lost.

'On leaving, I had said to this young mandarin, comfortable in his pleasant office with its views of the park, that in the conditions that prevailed at the time, and given both Harry's length of service and his youth, I felt it was quite possible still to say to his mother that he had served his country. He answered, sombrely, but evidently thinking I was deluded, "You may say whatever you feel will comfort the lady, but I fear the truth is that this officer died failing to do his duty and, indeed, putting the lives of his men at great risk."'

Laurence was silent; there was nothing he could say.

'But it took a chance meeting to make me see the way ahead. You might describe it as an act of God.'

CHAPTER THIRTY-SIX

'*I* hadn't been idle since the war. I'd needed to do something. I'd met Philip Morrell many years before. My wife was a distant relation of Lady Ottoline, Morrell's wife. He had odd views, frankly, but was well meaning and well connected. He talked to me round about the time of the Darling Committee. Asked if I'd be involved. They needed reliable factgatherers. People who could talk to people.'

He looked up as if checking whether Laurence knew what he was talking about.

'I was an experienced military man, I'd lost sons in the war, but I was broadly in sympathy with his views. Horatio Bottomley, the newspaperman, was with us. Obnoxious, but a force to be reckoned with. His interest was not simply altruism, of course; for him every cause had material value. Cruelty and injustice sold papers. He was raising questions before the war even ended. Damn lucky he wasn't prosecuted. But he correctly gauged a slight shift in mood and he's a useful man – he ensured we stayed in the public eye. Colonel Lambert Ward kept us respectable and we had

Ernest Thirtle, the MP, as a parliamentary link to the ordinary man.'

Somers could have been speaking to an anonymous interviewer, now that he had gained momentum.

'Morrell was asking questions in the House about the military handling of capital sentences before the war ended. Just a year later the Darling Committee accepted that there were grave problems in the system. Rather too late, of course, for those affected by it.'

'Yes, of course.' Laurence tried to feel soothed by this account of public service.

'And when the Southborough Inquiry reports next year, it will certainly confirm the validity of shell-shock. Not before time. The government are currently refusing to pay pensions to men who have broken down mentally without also having been physically injured.'

Somers was animated by indignation.

'They invited me to be a member of the board. And that's how I first encountered the journalist.'

Laurence was startled. For a moment he thought he'd lost the thread.

'Journalist?' he asked, with a shiver of apprehension.

'He'd contacted Lambert Ward while researching an article for his newspaper but when he let slip that he'd witnessed a firing squad, Lambert Ward persuaded him to talk at the Darling Committee sessions about the experience of being a Prisoner's Friend. He gave Lambert Ward a photograph of an incident he'd been involved in. For him, I gather, images speak louder than words. Eighteen months or so ago, we thought he might have further information for us, so Lambert Ward asked to see him again. Lambert Ward fell ill. I didn't trust Bottomley. Morrell was abroad. Thirtle was in his constituency so I said I'd see him. The colonel gave me the photograph and his file.'

Laurence was becoming increasingly puzzled. Where was the story going now?

'God sent his messenger in the form of Mr Tresham Brabourne. A man who bore witness, who watched my son go to his death. A man who'd been to school with Miles and Hugh. You've met him, I know.'

Somers looked straight at Laurence, who felt a degree of foreboding.

'Keen young chap,' said Somers. 'Reminded me a bit of Miles, to be honest. But now, slowly, agonisingly, I really learned about Harry's death. I began to get some idea of the paucity of what passed for evidence, of the flimsiness of the case against Harry. Of the carelessness with which they took his life. Speaking to Mr Brabourne took me to the firing line, as it were. But Brabourne was – and remains – quite oblivious of my connection with the man he knows as Edmund Hart. I very much doubt he would have supplied so much detailed information if he'd realised he was speaking to Edmund's father.' He gave a wry smile.

'Young Brabourne had excellent recall of the trial but he couldn't give me all the names, only those he'd served with. However, he did identify Emmett in the photograph.

'Until I spoke to Brabourne, I had no idea who the officer who commanded the firing squad was, or even if he'd survived the war. But just as I was moving towards Captain Emmett, he was moving towards me.

'The final reckoning began in November last year,' Somers said, pre-empting with his slightly raised hand Laurence's attempt to interrupt. 'The homecoming of the Unknown Warrior. A warrior still fighting, it seems. Rising from his grave, journeying home, welcomed by the greatest in the land, sleeping among kings? Moving stuff, fine spectacle: caught the mood of the nation.'

Laurence nodded. It had all happened at a time when he was scarcely reading the papers, yet the event had slowly seeped into that selfish, armoured part of his life. Although he hadn't been inside Westminster Abbey since then, he did sometimes think, as he walked past, of the anonymous, broken corpse in the vault.

'I went and stood by the track at some small Kentish station,' Somers said, 'and I watched the train pass from Dover to London. Five seconds of light in the darkness. He was in his box of oak, known only to God and certainly never to be known to anyone on earth. Maybe he was one of the criminal, idle sort: stealing food, cheating at cards, clipped with his head down, trying to keep out of it. Maybe he was a hero who laid down his life for his friend. All the same, I thought my wife might have liked me to be there. Three-quarters of a million or more British dead, ten of thousands of bodies never found, and just one man on the train. They weren't good odds but there he was, for a fragment of time, hurtling past in the dark. The possibility of Miles. The shadow of Hugh and Harry. It was foolish, of course, but I was in good company. I stood there and a made a vow to myself: Harry's death would not go unanswered.

'I wasn't the only one who had fancies after that dead man's journey,' Somers said, still matter-of-fact. 'There was Gwen getting more concerned that she knew so little about Harry's death. But then there was Emmett himself. Things were unravelling. The turning point came when she received this letter—'

'From John Emmett,' Laurence broke in.

'Captain Emmett, on his own inexorable crusade for truth and justice,' Somers said bitterly. 'Emmett had pored over the hullabaloo in the papers. He too had been thinking about the unknown dead. In fact, it turned out he seldom thought of anything else, although at the point of contact with Gwen he was vague and said only that he had information about Harry's death.

'Gwen wrote to me. She assumed, rightly, that it was a fairly standard communication from a surviving comrade in arms, but she was puzzled by the intensity of the tone. I realised the letter's significance immediately and told her I would contact him. I didn't know what to do. I hadn't even told her the truth yet, but it was obvious Emmett fully intended to do so. I knew then that I couldn't bear the thought of her finding out about her dear boy's sordid end yet.'

In the few minutes' silence that followed, Laurence strained to hear movement. Wherever Gwen had gone, she was silent. He was cold and his back was stiff; his leg was going dead. He had a feeling that a dark shadow was falling on them all.

'I had waited two decades to do the right thing by Gwen and Harry. It was too late now, of course, so all I could do was intercept Emmett. So I wrote to him, expressing an official interest in his actions. I threw the names in – Darling, Southborough. Mentioned Lambert Ward,' Somers explained. 'Said that I had his name on record as commanding a firing squad. I hoped I might draw his focus away from Gwen for a while. I claimed his testimony would be invaluable.

Laurence could only imagine the effect this interrogation would have had on John, whose memories had never left him. His heart sank.

'I wrote to his Cambridge address – it was on the letter to Gwen – and he replied. I asked him to meet me in London.

When he arrived and revealed that he was currently incarcerated, I was surprised. His letters were untidy but rational, and the man himself anxious but entirely sane.

'I had arranged the meeting at the Coburg – somewhere I had taken Gwen, long ago. Nicely anonymous place. I did promise him discretion. A promise I suppose you could say I broke?'

Just for a second his eyes met Laurence's.

'He told me everything. I promised him a meeting with Mrs Lovell – I said I'd met her in the course of building up a file for the committee – meeting her was the thing he most wanted. What *I* wanted was information. He provided it. After he was dead, I was left to deal with the guilty men. But I still couldn't tell Gwen the truth about Harry's death. I dreaded an official letter coming. I hoped my interview at the War Office had pre-empted the possibility. But then came Emmett's letter and then, afterwards, you came too.'

He stopped, then said, abruptly, 'Do you know about how Harry died, Bartram?'

'Yes, I think so. Tresham Brabourne told me.'

'My boy was ill. In mind and body. He'd been treated for shell-shock and for dysentery. He'd not long been back from sick leave. Do you know what condition he was in when they arrested him, Captain Bartram?'

Laurence thought he detected a slight tremor in Somers' voice.

'He was very distressed, I think.'

'The official report says he had discarded part of his uniform,' said Somers. 'He had taken off his Sam Browne and his tunic. They argued that he was trying to hide the fact he was an officer. His CO said Harry had been jittery beforehand. They'd been close to a shell burst. The men dispersed into foxholes. Harry had blood and bone fragments on his uniform, on his face. Another man's blood and bone. A witness had seen him rubbing at his jacket, spitting on a handkerchief, like a mother wiping her child's mouth. Another junior officer, a bumptious young subaltern, Lilley' – he spat out the name – 'told him to pull the rump of his group together and continue the march forward. Harry told him that he didn't have to take orders from him. It was a schoolboy spat – not the stuff of heroes, but neither was it desertion.

'Harry turned on to open land and walked away towards HQ. There was no protection and constant German shelling. It was hardly the act of a man running for safety. If anything, it was suicide. The other subaltern reported his disappearance the next morning but by that time Harry had come in, half dressed. There'd been sleet all night. He'd got lost, disoriented. He'd spent the night half naked in the mud. He had to be treated for exposure.'

Somers came to a halt. He looked tired, Laurence thought, although he still held himself erect. They sat, almost companionably, their knees only inches apart.

'My whole career was about making correct military decisions.' Somers shook his head disbelievingly. 'I was a soldier myself, damn it. Some of the men were animals: looting, pillaging, making brutal assaults on each other – worse, on the local population. Rape. Murder. They'd have hanged in England and we despatched them just as soundly overseas. Hard men. A hard life. Swift justice, often as not. But we gave even them a hearing.'

His legs were set wide apart, his fingertips splayed deep into the arms of the chair.

Laurence was about to speak, but Somers stopped him again. It was as if he was anxious that he might lose track if he was interrupted.

'I imagine Brabourne told you about the sergeant – Tucker?'
Somers didn't wait for a reply.

'He was a bully and, Emmett believed, a rapist, probably a murderer, who found entertainment in an execution. If anyone should have been before a firing squad, it was Tucker. The minute it was done, Tucker should have got the men out of sight and marched them away. This is the army. Executing soldiers is nothing new. There's a procedure for all these things. But Tucker wanted to relish it. Harry's suffering, the soldiers' suffering and Emmett's destruction.'

'Tucker was killed.'

Somers nodded. 'Vermin,' he said. 'Emmett had already tracked him down. Gave me the details of his whereabouts. But the Tuckers of this world enjoy violence and degradation. Why should Tucker repent? I didn't have to shoot him. He was so drunk that he put up no kind of fight. I did little more than destroy his face as he destroyed my son's, then I rolled him into the canal. He deserved worse.'

Somers' confirmation that he had killed a man was delivered so matter-of-factly that it took some seconds for it to sink in. It had long been obvious what Somers was leading up to but it was so hard for Laurence to absorb that a deadly curiosity now overwhelmed the enormity of what he had been told.

'The police officer in London?'

'Mullins? Yes, of course.'

'And Byers?' he asked, slowly. 'In Devon?'

'Yes.'

'It was your revenge for your son?' said Laurence. 'That was why?'

Outside the window, on the other side of the tidy hedge, lay a small London street where darkness had fallen. Across it, under the streetlight, two women walked by and their animated chat was quite audible through the window. Laurence thought the room seemed too ordinary to contain the man in front of him.

'Yes,' said Somers, finally. Then he repeated himself, 'Yes. Wasn't that enough?'

Wasn't that enough? Leonard Byers had said that the last time Laurence had seen him. It was an epitaph for the whole grim mess. He waited for the other man to collect himself.

'Tucker died too easily,' Somers went on. 'Corporal Byers, too: a man more used to making beds and heating an officer's canteen than putting his life on the line. Your friend Captain Emmett said Byers was fussing about his wet feet while they were waiting to shoot my son and then he walked up to my boy, a condemned man within seconds of death, and tore off his badges. It was simply an act to humiliate him. Gratuitous.'

He was white-faced.

'As for Inspector — late Assistant Provost Marshal — Mullins, he was a cold, hard man who believed the worst of everybody. From my committee work I know that more men, whether guilty or simply unfortunate, were ensured of capture, arrest or execution under Mullins' aegis than any other. Although I took enormous risks in shooting him in broad daylight, so close to Scotland Yard, it was worth it. I was never worried for myself but simply that I would be prevented from finishing off my work.'

Laurence could hear his own breath. It sounded uneven and he hoped it wasn't audible to Somers. The last time he remembered feeling like this was in France. He shifted slightly to ease the pressure on his spine. Somers' revelations were exactly what he had feared, yet could never possibly have expected from a man of his standing.

'You wanted to remove everyone involved in your son's death?'

'Of course not.' Somers looked surprised. 'I accept military necessity. I only ever wanted the guilty to be punished. There were six officers of the court martial. Despite sentencing my son to death, they recommended mercy on account of his age. For this, I spared the four who had survived the war: Ryecraft, Vane-Percy, Goose and O'Shea.'

Somers recited their names effortlessly, ticking them off on his fingers. How many times had he gone through the case papers, Laurence wondered? He doubted whether even Brabourne would have known the name of every member of the board.

'Harry's CO — a chap called Gooden, whose evidence damned Harry — died in an accident on the grouse moor on the opening day of the season in 1919.'

Somers smiled, without showing his teeth.

'Shot by a keeper. Presumably in error. My only targets were Emmett, Tucker, Byers, Mullins, Lilley and General Hubert Gough. All, bar Gough, are now dead. The Honourable Ralph Lilley — the subaltern who had been so eager to condemn Harry, simply from spite and dislike — lived conveniently close to my home. We knew the family slightly, though of course he had no idea of my link to Harry. I followed him for a while, observing his habits. Watched my quarry settle back into the comfortable life he'd led before the war. Lilley took a regular train from our local station. It was the most natural thing in the world to join him, talk to him on the platform and then push him under the incoming train. These things are never quite straightforward: he fell too far out and the train merely cut off his legs rather than killing him outright. But I jumped down on to the tracks and was able to tell him why he was dying, before help came and he bled to death. I was the unknown hero of the hour.'

Laurence found it hard to process what he was hearing. How long had he been here, listening to a man who should have been the sanest of individuals, and whose demeanour and tone were indeed utterly reasonable, talking of madness?

'I can see your skills deserted you there,' said Somers. 'Perhaps you didn't get as far as Lilley. You didn't use your imagination.'

'Do you know, I've had enough of people telling me what I should have done,' said Laurence, fatigue and discomfort crushing the instinct to placate the man in front of him. 'I now know why John Emmett died, even if I don't know exactly how. I set out to unravel that and that alone. John's path crossed, disastrously, with your son's and with you, but all I ever wanted was an answer for his sister. I have that answer. And for her it may now be much simpler to come to terms with her brother's death. Knowing his life was taken by you, not thrown away by him,' he said, recalling both Byers' and Eleanor's comments about the relative pain of the suicide or the murder of a loved one.

Somers' face contorted slightly. He looked puzzled. 'You think someone killing someone you love is easier to bear than knowing they took their own life?' For the first time, he fell silent.

'Yes. However you might have chosen to punish the men you condemned, for John Emmett's sister, at least, I think the truth will be terrible but less hard than it was.' And then, still angry, he added, 'I did know about Lilley and *you* got the wrong man in Byers. He wasn't the man on the execution detail.'

'There you are wrong. Emmett identified Byers on the photograph. Described him. Told me precisely how he'd fussed about his wet feet — had degraded my son in his last minutes. I tracked him down to the very farm he'd enlisted from.'

Although Somers spoke firmly, a faint doubt showed in his face.

'That was his cousin,' said Laurence. 'There's a family resemblance, I'm told, but he was a cousin. You killed Jim Byers. Jim Byers just did his bit in France for three years. Leonard Byers is alive and well.'

He was angry because Somers was wrong. In this war every man's life had been on the line. Batmen and bandsmen had fixed their bayonets alongside their comrades. There was no escape.

Somers looked disconcerted only for a second and then, unexpectedly, he laughed, a laugh that filled the room with something like normality.

'Of course he's well,' he said, with just a trace of bitterness. 'Mr Leonard Byers, successful civilian. Of course he is. I told you he was a man with an eye for the main chance. Warm feet now, no doubt. Still, I'm sorry about the cousin if it's true. Dismal, run-down place the farm was, too. Not much sign of Mr Lloyd George's land fit for heroes down there. Scarcely fit for cows. But I am sorry. Not that any of it matters now.'

'And you were seen,' Laurence said, realising that for all his reasonable manner, part of Somers was irreparably and unpredictably damaged. 'Byers' old uncle, semi-bedridden, was at a window when you arrived with your gun. He was a weak witness, shocked and bemused, but he was still a witness.' His words came out more strongly than he'd intended.

'I was *seen*, as you put it, before I pushed Lilley under the train. I was *seen* by plenty of people when I shot Mullins. There's seeing and not seeing. Age, expectation and authority: they're all surprisingly effective disguises, Mr Bartram, especially to certain witnesses.'

Laurence looked at the window. It was now completely dark outside. Where was Gwen Lovell?

'I wasn't merciless, you know. I checked them all. The other men connected with my son's death are more or less blameless or dead. One — Private Watkins — endures a living death in the North Wales County Lunatic Asylum.

'Since the death of Mullins, things have become harder but my hand was forced before I was ready when I realised Mullins might be piecing things together. It was Gough I wanted, above all. Gough served with me in Africa. I *knew* him. He deserved to die. An ambitious man. An incompetent commander. Callous, arrogant; I doubt he even bothered to read through Harry's defence.

'In those crucial days when the top brass were weighing Harry's fate in their hands, even General Shute, who had no respect for Harry's division and whom the men hated, pointed out that Harry was very young. So I let Shute live. The request for confirmation of sentence rose upwards until it reached Gough. Gough rejected a unanimous call for clemency by the officers of the court martial. Gough said with zeal that he "recommended" that sentence be carried out. Only rank distinguished him and Tucker: brutal men who revelled in war's cruelty and humiliations. He's been in Switzerland. But now he's back. And I have waited for him.'

There was absolute silence. Laurence had heard a single car pass by and a door slam across the road; the sounds provided a comfortable, though brief, assurance that there were people out there. Was Gwen Lovell listening to all this? Had she known all along what Somers was planning or what he'd done? While he was certain she hadn't known when he had first come to her house, he sensed that she did now. She had aged twenty years since then.

'Mullins came to see me after Emmett vanished. Very polite, of course. A favourite nephew had been a patient at Holmwood, as bad luck would have it. The late Inspector Mullins was obviously a very well-connected man. The boy had no father so Mullins was up and down to see him. He made a miraculous recovery. So Dr Chilvers, not putting vast store by the local constabulary, had asked Mullins to cast an eye over Emmett's disappearance as a personal favour. Bad for the place's carefully built reputation to lose a patient. It was Chilvers who told Mullins that Emmett had been in touch with members of the Darling Committee and was obsessed with the Hart execution. All the same, it should have been a formality for a busy senior police officer from another force. Eventually I had to concede to Mullins I'd visited Emmett at Holmwood. Chilvers was bound to tell him. I said Emmett had been a friend of Hugh.'

The army friend that the staff at Holmwood had described, Laurence thought. He had simply assumed it was a wartime contemporary of John's. How careless he'd been.

'Mullins was sharp. He seemed to be satisfied but he obviously kept turning it over. He remembered Hart's execution, of course. Then Emmett was found dead and Mullins thought a little harder.'

'And Mullins was briefly involved in investigating Jim Byers' death,' Laurence said.

'I didn't know that,' Somers said, obviously digesting this new information. 'Perhaps he was already looking out for connections? A clever man. But Dr Chilvers knew of Emmett's assault on Tucker — it was why he had been admitted: to escape prosecution for assaulting a policeman in that fracas — and that, too, Chilvers passed on to Mullins. Tucker was also dead, as Mullins discovered from the Birmingham force. Too many coincidences. At some point he commandeered Harry's file and tracked down the letter I'd written, pushing for him to be given a commission. He came to talk to me. I don't know if he ever knew about Lilley. His death was carried in *The Times*, so it was likely. Lilley lived and died just two miles from my house. Sooner or later Mullins would have approached Gwen because of Emmett's wretched bequest. Then, a week before his death, he asked me to come and see him again when I was next in London. Nothing urgent, so he said.

'I couldn't risk it any more but, anyway, he'd always been on my list. The perfect public servant. Duty and inflexibility. I went up to London, and the rest you know. The police were always going to go flat out once nemesis had caught up with Mullins. He'll have kept a record. Today it's you on the doorstep, tomorrow it will be them.'

Somers got up and came towards him. Laurence tensed himself, but Somers simply walked unevenly past him to the window. Charles had said he had been wounded in South Africa. Somers stood looking out at the darkness, with his back to Laurence. Laurence wondered whether he should make a run for it. With his back so stiff, he doubted he'd get far. Who would win if it came to a tussle, and what part might Gwen Lovell play?

'Brabourne was so clear about what happened at the trial but I smelled a rat when he became vague about the execution itself,' said Somers, still gazing out. 'I didn't want to alert him with too many questions, and I had to keep my emotions tightly under control. Eventually he revealed that Harry hadn't died immediately. It had a taken a *coup de grâce*. Which meant Emmett should have put the last bullet in his brain. Except that Brabourne's essential decency covered up Emmett's disgrace. It took Emmett himself to tell me what had really happened.'

Laurence was finding it increasingly hard to concentrate. He knew how the story Somers was now telling would end. He wished he hadn't sent Charles away.

'Emmett and I talked for an hour or so at the Coburg in the first instance,' Somers continued, 'just establishing the outline of it all. I couldn't push him too hard as I didn't want him to be uneasy, and he needed to get back to Holmwood before the police were called to find him. I put him on a train. Made arrangements to meet again. I wanted to get him to my own house, away from onlookers, with time to go through it all. I wanted to make sure I got every fact, every name. To know exactly what happened and who was involved.'

He glanced at Laurence more directly.

'But Emmett knew it would be very difficult to escape from Holmwood a second time.'

He paused.

'And I knew that once I'd persuaded him to come to see me, he would have to disappear, you see. He was a link to me and I had my mission to complete. I didn't care about surviving myself but I did care about justice.'

Somers was almost persuasive, his tone of voice reasonable.

'I told Gwen to write to him. To ask to meet him. To suggest myself, as he had already met me, as an intermediary. To say that I lived not far from Holmwood, that I could arrange it. She wrote in good faith, believing it would happen — and Emmett had absolutely no idea that I knew Gwen other than professionally. But, as I said, he was desperate to see her. She was the lure. However, I had absolutely no idea that he had left Gwen a bequest, which meant that his death would lead straight back to her.

'I set up the final meeting at my house in Oxfordshire. When he arrived, Gwen was not there, needless to say, but

Emmett didn't really seem surprised. He just wanted to talk. He told me every damn thing about Harry. His poetry. His trial. His death. Harry's persecutors and those few who tried to help him. Above all, Emmett gave me the names and each individual's portion of guilt became clear. I promised to tell Harry's mother everything.'

He stopped again, and then he said in a slower voice, 'I have thought about it since, of course. Did I feel pity for Emmett? Obviously he had suffered. Nerves, mostly. His right arm was useless, you know? When I had seen him for the first time, I assumed he'd been wounded but it wasn't that. Nothing really wrong with the arm at all, but plenty wrong in the mind.

'But, do you know, during the long hours he was with me, I thought there had been some sort of lightening of his spirit, as if by telling me everything he had rid himself of his guilt. In the end I told him the truth. He had been so honest. He had emptied himself out. So I told him Harry was my son. I wanted to tell somebody at last.'

'What did he say?'

'He asked me to forgive him.'

Laurence felt numb. It was so simple.

'I told him there was nothing to forgive,' said Somers. 'It was war.'

'But you didn't forgive the others?'

'The others didn't ask.' He paused.

'Emmett told me that at the last minute he realised that he knew my son. He'd actually met him once. They shared a deep love of poetry. Harry's last words were supposed to have been, "For God's sake shoot quickly and get it over with," but when he fell to the ground he was only injured. Refused a blindfold.'

Pain was unmistakable on Somers' face. His speech slowed. 'He had blue eyes, like his mother.'

He wiped his forehead, hesitated.

'Emmett just stood there. Frozen, he said. Harry tried to speak. Emmett had his gun in his hand; everybody waiting for him to do his duty. He said Harry was unintelligible. Then Sergeant Tucker, who hadn't marched the men away but left them gawping, quit the line, came forward, cool as you like, took the gun from Emmett, who put up no kind of resistance, and he shot Harry straight in the face.

CHAPTER THIRTY-SEVEN

*T*he two men looked at each other. Both started to speak at once, then stopped. It was as if all the chaos of murder, adultery, suicide and illegitimacy had been reduced to mere social awkwardness.

Finally Laurence said, 'And now? What do you intend to do?'

'I imagine if you leave here you'll go straight to fetch the police?' Somers looked up. At last Laurence could hear Gwen Lovell move at the back of the house.

'I just didn't really think . . .' Laurence began. Did Somers intend to let him go and if not, what would he do?

'Oh, you think,' said Somers. 'You're a brave man. Brave and dogged. An excellent officer. Acting major. Twice mentioned in despatches and holder of the Military Cross. How does the citation go? "For conspicuous courage under fire. Leading an attack against considerable odds, in which the battalion sustained heavy losses, he returned to retrieve the injured at considerable risk to himself." You *think*, Captain Bartram. You think very carefully and you act decisively. If you didn't count on my finding you, you certainly knew it was a possibility you would find me.'

He was trying to heave the dead weight of Pollock, pitiable, fat Pollock, back across the churned-up terrain. Bent half double, he strained to drag him by the legs. Pollock's weight made a trough in the mud and as Laurence leaned forward he could smell the urine soaking through the soldier's trousers. He hoped the man was unconscious — the body kept lurching to the side and every time he managed to move him more than a few inches, Pollock made a wet, wheezing sound and red froth came out of his mouth. The front of his tunic was black and tarry. Laurence hadn't dared open it in case it was all that was keeping Pollock's guts inside his body. Suddenly the ground fell away and they were both tumbling into a crater of mud and water. The tremendous weight of the injured man landed on top of him. For a minute he lay winded and nauseated, then panicked and struggled furiously to get a purchase on Pollock's jacket. At last he tore himself free but his legs had lost all feeling. He sat in the slime holding the man's head in his lap. There was faint sunlight now, piercing the smoke, as the water around the soldier turned reddish brown and strings of pink saliva congealed between his bloody teeth. He sat and stroked Pollock's cold face until someone came and found them.

Somers was still talking.

'Did you really believe you were the only one capable of a bit of detective work? It's not hard to find a man's records, you know. To talk to a few people.'

He was getting up as he spoke. He returned to the bureau and opened a different drawer. Laurence wondered what he was about to show him. Somers rifled through some papers and turned round. He was holding a gun.

'Believe it or not, I regret the need for this,' Somers said. 'But, you see, Brabourne contacted me a day or so ago asking what had happened to the photograph he'd given me. Emmett stole it from my house, of course, after I showed it to him. I never even noticed its absence. I gather it came home with his effects? I had to improvise, say there'd been a burglary. But it wouldn't do. I knew you'd come back to Gwen sooner or later and now the journalist was suspicious too. He asked me if I had known Mullins. If I knew that Emmett was dead.'

He sat down, still holding the gun. It was hardly different from the Webley that Laurence had used in the war.

'Did John take anything else?' Laurence thought Somers hesitated but realised the man was simply tiring. Somers shook his head and carried on talking.

'Gough. He was the ultimate arbiter. He had my son's life in his hands. I simply want him now. After that, I don't care. What difference does it make to me? I'll hang, Gwen will be disgraced either way. If I shoot you now, I might get Gough and we might just get away. I have tickets for Gwen, Catherine and myself to sail to Canada in January. I chose the anniversary of Harry's death. By then it all needs to be finished.'

He looked at Laurence almost questioningly as if asking for his approval.

'I can't let you stop me before I've dealt with Gough.'

'I think there would be a difference to you in killing me,' Laurence said steadily.

The Webley looked well maintained. Was it loaded? Somers was not yet pointing it at him, but held it by his side. Laurence was surprised to find just how much he wanted to live. He wondered what Mary would feel if he died.

'As you say, it all depends on motive,' he continued, amazed that his voice was steady. 'In war there's little choice. We both know that. Killing is abhorrent to start with, but it becomes routine. Possibly you felt you had no choice with the men involved in Harry's death, which makes it a noble cause in your eyes. But shooting me would be for nothing more than your own convenience. You might justify it on the grounds of protecting Mrs Lovell, but I don't think that's what she'd want, certainly not here in her own house and probably not anywhere, for that matter. I don't think you want to shoot me. I suspect you're weary of the whole thing.'

He hoped it was true.

'You could be right,' Somers said slowly. 'I lied even to her. Denied I'd ever seen Emmett. It can't be done here.'

He stopped speaking and seemed to be finding it hard to concentrate, though the gun was now pointing directly at Laurence, who was now sure it was loaded.

'It's a bad business about Byers. But it doesn't take away the justice of my mission. If you'd had a son, you'd understand.'

'Actually, I did have a son,' said Laurence. 'He died too.'

In the end it was such a simple thing to say.

Somers seemed distracted by his response. The gun dropped again.

'I'm sorry. This is a bad business.'

He rubbed his eyes. Any energy in him was suddenly gone. He deflated almost visibly.

'Do you know, I feel terribly old all of a sudden? I thought I'd fought my wars long ago. I'll be glad when all this is finished . . .'

Then he seemed to recollect himself and looked straight at Laurence.

'Because you were so close, I finally had to tell her,' he said bitterly. 'Telling Gwen the truth, was the worst thing I've ever had to do. Not Brabourne's truth, and certainly not Emmett's truth in all its searing detail, but a truth of betrayal. A truth she would have found out anyway. The scene that followed was every bit as distressing as you could imagine. But she was no

397

Marjorie, stoic and withdrawn. Gwen just wept in my arms. She got out all the photographs from when Harry was a little boy. There were not a great many but she had kept them carefully, and there were his letters home.'

He gestured to the bureau in the corner.

'Catherine was away. We sat until it became dark. Eventually she lit the lamps, set the fire. I talked about Hugh and Miles for the first time really since their death. Her tears were for them as well as for their unacknowledged half-brother, Harry. Our sons. Some time after midnight we went up to bed.'

Instinctively Laurence looked down at the weapon, which Somers was holding without wavering, then made himself return to the other man's deeply furrowed but still handsome face. The clock on the mantelpiece whirred but did not chime.

'Perhaps it would be for the best . . . ?' Somers began slowly.

Laurence jumped as the door, which had been ajar, opened. For a moment he thought the gun had gone off. Gwen stood there, her face blotched, her hair unkempt.

Somers looked up and attempted a smile. 'Come in, my dear. We're nearly done.'

She walked slowly into the room. Directly behind her was Charles. Gwen stared at both men in front of her with horror and then glanced behind her at Charles, who, Laurence now noticed, was holding his own gun – the Luger – his usual affable expression replaced by one of alert hardness. Laurence's eyes went from Charles to Somers, then to Gwen, who had moved swiftly towards the general. The situation was both farcical and potentially deadly. For a moment her body blocked Somers' weapon, but he drew her to his side.

'Put down your gun,' Charles said firmly.

Somers stared at him, his gun as steady as ever, the barrel still pointing at Laurence.

'I'm afraid it's not possible,' Somers said.

'Please, Gerald,' Gwen said. She reached out and placed her hand on top of Somers'. 'It's over. Enough people have died.'

Somers resisted for only a second. Then his right hand swung up and, holding her to him with his other arm, he pressed the barrel to Gwen's head.

'I'm sorry, my darling,' he said. 'How I wish you had never met me.'

Laurence sensed Charles's finger tighten on the trigger, bracing himself for a shot. Gwen's face drained of colour, her eyes wide.

All of a sudden, Somers' gun arm fell to his side. Slowly Gwen Lovell reached over and took the weapon from him. She gazed down at it in her hand, weeping, and then, gingerly, laid it on the table. Laurence picked it up. It was loaded. He emptied out the bullets and put the gun in his pocket.

When he looked back, Gwen had her arms around her lover and his head was bowed on her shoulder. She was trembling but stroking his head as if he were a child. Her eyes met those of Laurence. He could not read her face. Finally, Somers lifted his head. Charles glanced at Laurence, still firmly holding his own gun.

'Would you accept my word that I will turn myself in? It has a little more dignity about it.' Somers appealed directly to Laurence, sensing that the decision ultimately lay with him. 'Let me have twenty-four hours here, so that I can see Gwen straight. Her family in Germany can't forget she took the other side in the war — her nephews were killed. She has no one else but Catherine. Tomorrow, on my honour, on that of my three sons, I'll let justice take its course.'

Laurence thought quickly. If Somers didn't turn himself in within twenty-four hours, they could tell the police, who could protect General Gough until Somers was found. However, he couldn't think how they would explain the delay and what if Somers went through with the murder of Gough before then?

Charles raised an eyebrow; he too wanted it to be Laurence's choice.

Eventually Laurence spoke. 'All right.' He was so weary. He doubted that Somers had the energy to continue his campaign; he doubted that Gwen would let him out of her sight. Despite having other reservations, he didn't want to be the one to turn a decent, honourable man over to the hangman. Gwen Lovell had already lost so much. It all sickened him.

Somers seemed to sag and Gwen helped him into a chair.

'But just as you wanted your truth, I want to be able to tell John Emmett's sister what happened to him,' Laurence said firmly.

Somers stiffened slightly and looked uneasy. His glance flickered to Gwen, then back to Laurence.

'How did you get him to your house?'

'By car. I visited Holmwood a week or so before Christmas. Drove around the lanes not far from the village. Parked the car half a mile away behind some abandoned farm buildings, with a blanket over the engine. Couldn't risk it not starting when it was needed, though in the event the weather was mild. Walked to Holmwood. Went through the motions of having a meeting with Chilvers. Met my poor old friend Emmett: all sanctioned by Chilvers, with tea and cucumber sandwiches. The good doctor was keen to accommodate the valiant but shell-shocked son of a titled friend that I'd mentioned to him. Emmett thought I was there to represent Mrs Lovell. He was longing to see her; never was a man so obliging in the arrangements for his own removal.'

Gwen shuddered. Laurence thought she might faint, but she clung to Somers' arm.

'I wanted more information. I wanted *him*. Told them all at Holmwood that I'd arrived by train. Gave Emmett the directions to the car. Young Chilvers, an egregious braggart, even took me to catch a train home.

'Nobody to notice at home whether I had or hadn't got the car: one of the few advantages of having lost your entire family. Told my gardener it was being repaired. Agreement was that Emmett would get away when he could, pick up the motor car and drive over to my place at Fawler. He was still confined to his room, more or less, or under constant supervision, but this suited me, as he was hardly likely to tell anyone of our plan. He thought Christmas Day would be his only chance to get away as he knew they'd all be taken to church. As far as I was concerned, Christmas was ideal as anybody who had a family would be with them. He thought I'd drive him back eventually, of course. I left a map in the car but he said he'd been at school not so far away and knew the area.'

'Yes,' said Laurence. 'We were at Marlborough together.' Then he suddenly remembered. 'May I get something?' Gwen nodded. Laurence went over to his coat, felt in the deep pocket and pulled out a grubby striped scarf. 'This was yours, wasn't it?'

Somers looked down and touched it. 'Miles's scarf, from Wellington. His team colours.' He turned back the corner, looked at the school number, then took the scarf in both hands. 'Thank you,' he said. 'I'm glad to have it.' Laurence could see him making connections. 'Was it with John Emmett when he died?'

Laurence nodded. 'I came here on my way to see Tresham Brabourne — taking it to see whether he could confirm the school and identify the initials.'

Somers didn't respond for a while. Finally he said, 'I gave it to Emmett as we left the house because he looked so cold. Miles didn't need it. I wasn't going to need it again.'

Gwen made no move to touch Somers. Laurence felt indecent, watching her world collapse.

'I don't believe John had to die. I don't understand why,' Laurence said.

'It isn't hard,' Somers replied. 'He died because he killed my son.'

Laurence was struggling to see this rational, decent man as an unstable, flawed avenger. He thought to himself that, if anything, John had died because he had *not* killed Hart.

'There was no connection in all this with a Frenchman called Meurice?' he asked on the spur of the moment. Somers' expression was uncomprehending and his head shook almost imperceptibly.

As they reached the front door, Laurence turned to Gwen Lovell. She hadn't put on the light in the hall and in the open doorway her face was dark.

'Your son was a wonderful poet,' he said. 'He had a magical gift and he spoke for all of us. He should have lived.'

She was silent.

He followed Charles down her chequerboard path and didn't look back. Even as he shut the gate behind him, he still wasn't sure he had made the right decision. Would Somers have shot him but for Gwen Lovell and Charles's adventitious arrival? How close had Somers been to shooting Mrs Lovell?

He stood for a second, feeling the weight of Somers' gun in his pocket, and looked in through the open curtains. Somers and Mrs Lovell were sitting opposite each other in the front room. They could have been any middle-aged couple about to make cocoa and go to bed.

As he and Charles trudged up the street towards the car he spoke. 'So, what made you come and find me?'

'Saved by an old soldier. You were hardly through Mrs Lovell's door,' Charles said, 'when I noticed Nicholas Bolitho had left his wooden guardsman in the footwell of the car. I thought I could just whizz back and give it to Mrs Bolitho and still get to Savile Row. But Mrs Bolitho – Eleanor – wanted to give me a message for you. It was something she'd remembered. She thought she might have come across the man in the photograph. She was thrown when you showed it to her because he was so much thinner in the picture than when she'd nursed him, and she'd known him as Harry not Edmund. But it was the name that niggled at her, because Hart was a German name as well as a British one, and that made her think, because she'd once had a British patient with a German name. And she thought it was him. She remembered that, because they'd had prisoners of war as temporary orderlies and she had heard Hart joking with them. Harry spoke perfect German, she said. When she warned him to be careful who overheard him – feelings were running high after some bad losses – he told her his mother was half German and had been a classical singer in Berlin and that he'd been born in Germany. Well, after we'd left – what a mind that woman has – Eleanor starting putting two and two together. Almost as good as Mrs Christie. Apparently you'd told her Mrs Lovell had once been a singer in Germany?'

'I've no idea. I may have done.'

'So I said, "But our Hart was born in England. We checked. In Winson in the Cotswolds. Can't get much more British than that." She gave me a very long, teacher-like look and said, "Winsen is a city in Lower Saxony." But the next bit's interesting. She said that illness and long, sleepless nights often had the effect of causing men to unburden themselves of secrets. At one point, the lad had also told her that his father was a famous British military man, but that he had never met him and that his mother didn't even know that he'd found out. Eleanor thought it was a fantasy – a product of fever and unhappiness.'

'He knew Somers was his father all along?'

'Well, possibly not all along. But he knew. It can't have been that hard for a enquiring boy.'

Laurence thought of that other enquiring boy, John Emmett, who had discovered that his sister was not his father's child. He also remembered puzzling over Brabourne's account of Hart's dying words. So the boy died believing that his father, the courageous officer, would be ashamed of him. Laurence was glad Somers need never know.

'Once she'd remembered the name,' Charles said, 'she recalled that, like Emmett, he was something of a poet. She didn't know whether they'd met but thought John might have seen some of Hart's work.'

'Dear God. But what made you break in?'

'Well, Eleanor was suddenly uneasy. Mostly because she was sure you were going to blunder in, oblivious, waving your waiting-for-dawn photograph at the mother of a dead man, which of course was precisely what you did.' Charles looked smug. 'But partly she, and I, just had a bad feeling about it. About Mrs Lovell, to be honest. Had a hard time stopping Eleanor coming along. Thought I might as well come to the house, gun in pocket; knew you wouldn't approve if you saw it. If all was well, or you'd just got yourself in an emotional pickle with Mrs L, I could have done my "can't sit freezing my bollocks off in the car any longer" speech. If all was not well, then I could weigh in. QED. Looked in through the window, saw Somers. A famous military man, no less, in Mrs L's parlour. And then I saw the gun in his hand. Pointing at you.'

'Thank you. You may just have saved my life.'

'I don't think so for a minute,' said Charles. 'I don't think he ever intended to hurt you and I'm certain he wouldn't have done anything more to hurt Mrs Lovell. I think you just caught them unexpectedly. He improvised while he decided what to do. The gun simply gave him time, although I thought better of announcing myself by the front door once I'd seen it. Went round the back. Found Mrs Lovell sitting at the pantry table, all these papers and photographs spread out around her, and her head on her arms, weeping. I just tapped, smiled. She jumps up, very embarrassed to be caught red-eyed and wild-haired, and lets me in, easy as you please. Neither of them exactly has a criminal bent. My guess is she wanted it stopped.'

'Your rescue mission could have gone hideously wrong.'

'Hard to see Somers as a killer.'

'I think he saw himself as a warrior. Soldiers at war aren't murderers. They're heroes. Somers was fighting a battle.'

'I don't expect Mrs Lovell knew?'

'Not at first. Later she may have suspected something was amiss but it's not as if Somers was living with her or as if the news of each death was a headline murder until Mullins. She didn't even know the names of the men involved in her son's execution. She didn't even know he'd been shot at dawn. I think Somers only told her when Brabourne contacted him about where the photograph was.'

'But she knows now,' Charles said grimly. 'She heard much of your conversation.'

'I think she already knew. She may have found out only recently. But she knew.'

He remembered the sad but calm, candid woman he had met a matter of weeks ago. Since he first saw her, her spirit had been crushed.

'But what *I* want to know,' Charles went on, more slowly, 'is how did the general persuade Emmett to break bounds and meet him, then go off to some godforsaken wood in the middle of winter?'

'The meeting was easy. He simply asked him to come. Said Gwen Lovell would be there. John could tell her everything, as he longed to do. Why John then went with him to such a remote spot, I don't think we'll ever know. He knew the Folly from school, of course.'

'When did Somers shoot him?'

Laurence shook his head, still unable to understand why it had ended there. Somers obviously wanted to kill him away from the house and presumably John just trusted him.

'Probably a couple of days after they met. He didn't want to interrogate John at Holmwood, apart from anything else. He certainly didn't want him reaching Gwen and giving her every miserable detail. He'd promised she'd be at his house. How long could he stall, even when he'd told John the truth about his son? Yet John was torn apart with remorse, did what he could to make some kind of restitution. Was honest with Somers himself. I should think Mrs Lovell was horrified to know Somers killed him. I don't think she knew *that* until tonight. After all, Emmett had only wanted to help her.'

Nevertheless, he reflected that Somers, who had gone out of his way to mutilate the men he'd killed, had been careful to leave John's face untouched.

'What are you going to tell Mary?'

'The truth, I suppose. Before anyone else does.'

'And the police?'

'I'll give him his twenty-four hours.'

Charles shrugged. They sat in the car and still he made no move to go. Three girls passed them, arm in arm, singing a Christmas carol.

'You don't really believe that there'll ever be a trial?' Charles said.

'No.'

'Will he do the decent thing?'

'Possibly.'

'So you think that him putting an end to himself would be a better outcome than the gallows?'

'Yes, I do, actually. A trial would only injure more people.'

'And you don't think there's a risk to Mrs Lovell and the girl?'

'No,' said Laurence, trying to suppress a flicker of uncertainty. 'He had his chance and he couldn't face it.'

Nevertheless, whatever happened to Somers, he thought, the future looked bleak for the Lovells, both mother and daughter.

Charles started the car and they drove on slowly out on to the main road, following a tram into the heart of the city, and in all that time they never exchanged another word.

CHAPTER THIRTY-EIGHT

*L*aurence lay awake for hours, going over and over the previous evening, trying to understand what had happened. He had a profound sense of having made a serious mistake. Was it a failure to imagine the impact of his questioning on those he spoke to? He had been too ready to treat them as one-way conduits of information, never considering that the flow of information might run both ways. Why *hadn't* he called the police? Although he had felt reasonably certain that Somers was of no further danger, it was a huge and possibly dangerous assumption. He had been numb and exhausted at the time but now anxiety crept in.

Laurence would never be sure whether he had acted correctly. And what would Somers do now? For all his chivalric instincts to unravel John's death for Mary, it was she who had asked the one question he should have looked into early on: where were Edmund Hart's family? There was in itself nothing sinister about anglicising German names in war. It was common sense. The Coburg Hotel, the Bechstein Hall; even the royal family had dispensed with Saxe-Coburg-Gotha in favour of Windsor. Anyone with British loyalties or interests shed a name that tied them to an enemy.

However, even if he'd laid his hands on every bit of information; even if he had persuaded the police in the beginning that there was a link between the deaths – and perhaps he should have done this – they would only ever have succeeded in tracking down Somers slightly earlier than they had. Almost all the killing had already been done. Charles and Laurence had, perhaps, saved the life of General Hubert Gough, a man for whom Laurence had little respect. He wondered whether, had Somers' intended ultimate victim been anybody other than Gough, he would have been so willing to walk away the evening before.

His thinking was cut short by a hammering on the street door.

'Telegram,' the lad said, handing over the familiar envelope. 'Your bell needs to be fixed.'

Laurence's heart raced for a moment. Telegrams were always bad news. He walked back into the bedroom and sat on the edge of his bed, just holding it. He dreaded finding that it was from India.

Finally he tore it open and forced himself to look. It was from Mary. PLEASE MEET TOMORROW EASTBOURNE STATION MIDDAY REPLY ONLY IF NOT AVAILABLE M.

Sitting there, all alone, he beamed.

Travelling to the south coast was easy. The day was clear, the train was on time, the carriages half empty. As he stepped from the train, seagulls were wheeling and screeching overhead. Even on this December day he could smell salt in the fresh air.

Mary was waiting outside in a small car.

'See, I drive *and* punt,' she said, as he slipped into the

passenger seat and finally succeeded in shutting the door after banging it three times. 'I was taught during the war.' The car smelled of leather and mould and her. It creaked every time he moved. 'And I've borrowed my doctor friend's car so that we can get about. We've got it for only two hours, though, while he's on duty at the cottage hospital.'

She leaned over and gave him a kiss. He nuzzled into her hair and tried to clasp her neck beneath the folds of scarf. She twisted round awkwardly, burying her face in his coat with her arms around his neck. The embrace was bulky and marvellous and safe. Then she pushed him away from her slightly.

'You've got things to tell me,' she said. 'Important things. I can see it in your face. I'd asked you here because I had something to show you but now you must tell me what's happened.'

And so, not at all as he had planned, he sat in the Austin on the station forecourt and told her everything that had unfolded and much, though not all, of what he knew. She didn't stop him; indeed, her expression scarcely changed. Mostly she gazed full at him, a little anxiously but concentrating. After a while she looked down at her gloved hands on the wheel and moved them to her lap.

'I'm not sure whether my intervention helped, really,' said Laurence. 'I'm afraid the truth is as dismal in its way as how things originally looked.'

'Not for me,' she said.

Laurence didn't respond.

'Which doesn't mean it isn't just as horrible and sad. In fact, because it involves more people and more destroyed lives, it's sadder really. But, in a selfish way, for me, it's a kind of easing of the heart. An enemy killed John as surely as they might have done at any time in the war. The motive was desperately unfair.' Her voice was slightly hoarse. 'But this way I can think about

John without struggling with the fact that after all he'd been through he chose to leave us.'

He was immensely relieved that she felt the same as Eleanor, although something had bothered Somers about John's death and that something was bothering Laurence now.

'How do you think the general thought it would end?' Mary asked.

'I'm not sure. Somers certainly intended to kill General Gough. Who knows whether that would finally have been enough?'

'Why did he leave Gough until last?'

'My guess is that it was tactics. If he went for the high-profile people first – Gough and, to a degree, Mullins – there would have been many more questions asked and the risk of him not finishing his self-imposed task would have been increased. After all, if you hadn't wanted to understand John's death, not even dreaming that he'd been murdered, Somers would presumably have got away with it all.'

'And then what?'

'He said he dreamed of taking Gwen and Catherine Lovell abroad to start a new life. But I don't think he believed it really.'

'And all for revenge,' she said.

Laurence was silent. As well as vengeance, John's death and the pattern of his own life were simply about fathers and sons, and the struggle to make things right.

He looked at Mary. Quite late on, he'd grasped that her real question all along, even if she had never known it herself, had been why her brother had rejected her. He had an unequivocal answer to that now: her father was not who she believed him to be and, to the young and imaginative John, she was the living proof of his mother's infidelity. It was an answer he could never give her.

Instead he said, 'I hope you'll meet Eleanor Bolitho. I think you'd like her and she could tell you much more than I can about John. She looked after him during the war and even when he was really unhappy, quite cut off from the world, she cared for him.'

He was sure Mary would realise the truth about Nicholas Bolitho as soon as she set eyes on the child, but thought Eleanor would eventually tell her everything. The likeness between the little boy and John was remarkable.

Laurence thought of his own father. He couldn't remember his voice or his face, just his singing in the bath and his strong, square hands. Strangely, he could recall Mr Emmett more clearly. The affable smile, the absent-minded pats as he passed by; the sudden appearances and disappearances always with a dog or two beside him; the nightly toast to the survivors of Omdurman, at which they had all giggled.

He must have smiled at the memory because Mary asked, 'What are you thinking about?'

'Nothing. Vague memories. Your father, funnily enough.'

Something was bothering her, he could tell. Finally she said, 'John's willingness – his need – to give General Somers every last detail of the execution: the names of those involved, the circumstances, grim as they were. It probably sealed the fate of all of them, I suppose?' There was something in the tone of Mary's voice that made him think she hoped for contradiction.

'I think John's way out of despair was scrupulous honesty,' he said. 'He needed to make his peace. He could hardly guess that Somers was using his list to conduct his own war. He wasn't just speaking to a very eminent and much more senior military man, but one who had an official role, assisting a parliamentary committee. He also thought he was bringing some sort of help to Hart's mother.'

Suddenly he thought back to Somers' last conversation with him. 'You know, I think John held back on telling him of Hart's last words. Somers had told John he was Hart's father but that the boy never knew him. To discover his son knew who he was all the time and believed he'd be ashamed of him, would have been too terrible to bear. John told Somers that Hart was incoherent after the first volley. It must have been one of the few times John evaded the truth.'

Mary's face cleared a little. 'I'm glad,' she said.

Within minutes they had turned off into a village. Thatched cottages bordered the main street, with a small brook on one side. After they passed a couple of larger red-brick houses, the village petered out by a flint-and-stone church and a field gate. Laurence guessed the small church to be very old, possibly twelfth century. His eye was taken by the vast, white-chalk figure that rose up in front of them, dominating the grassy hillside above the church.

'The Long Man,' Mary said with almost proprietorial pride.

The outline, clutching a stave in each hand, was obviously pagan in design and spirit. Laurence's spirits lifted. God knows how old the figure was, or what it meant to its creators, but undoubtedly it had stood on its hillside for millennia and would stand there long after they and their strange world were reduced to dust. He found the prospect of his own irrelevance comforting.

They left the car and walked across the churchyard in which grew a yew, also of great age, its wide branches propped on wooden supports. He could see why Mary liked this place. Ahead of them lay a medieval building with a long barn at an angle. As a dark figure carrying a box across the courtyard drew closer, he saw to his astonishment that it appeared to be a nun.

'Wilmington Priory. It's a nursing order,' Mary said. They crunched across the gravel and he prepared himself for the explanation that he sensed would follow.

'The thing is,' she said very slowly, 'that when I told you Richard was lost, I meant lost. It wasn't a euphemism. He isn't dead, you see. Not really.'

Instantly Laurence felt his hair prick on the back of his neck. Mary pulled on a metal boss next to a studded wooden door, silver-grey with age, and waited. The door was opened by another nun. She left them in a dark hall, whose only ornamentation was a black oak table, two upright chairs and four religious paintings.

'Everything I told you – how he was injured – was all true.' As she spoke, Mary wouldn't look at him.

'In a sense he died the minute the shrapnel hit him, but although his injuries were terrible, he survived.'

Finally her eyes moved, almost pleading, to Laurence's.

'He was brought back to England. It became obvious that he would live, but also obvious that he would never be able to do anything for himself. The damage to his brain was never going to heal. He was a child. An infant. He knew no one and nothing, he could not move. He –' She paused. 'He even has to wear baby napkins. So he *was* lost, you see – the man he was, the man I'd loved. He came here and here he will stay for the rest of his life. He will never walk, will never see his lovely Downs or winter seas again. A few friends come from time to time, but less and less often. His doctor is an immensely kind, wise man. It's his car, actually. I bumped into him at the concert we went to. I thought you'd seen us talking together; I wanted to explain but to start to tell you the whole story was too much then. I didn't know you well enough and I wanted you to like me, and the alternative was to lie, which I didn't want.'

He stroked her arm. 'It's all right.'

'As for his wife, despite her scruples before, she eventually divorced him and married her lover. I would have married Richard then, even as he is, *especially* as he is, but legally he can't make the vows. She can divorce him, but I can't marry him unilaterally. Besides, he has no idea who I am.'

She looked at Laurence and shrugged.

'So that's that.'

He removed his hand as an older nun, wearing a white apron, came into view and beckoned them to follow her. They went up a shallow flight of black oak stairs and turned into a long dormitory. The first thing Laurence noticed were the large Gothic windows, which filled the long room with light. The views over the hill and past the Long Man in all his vigour were superb. The second thing he noticed was the row of beds and the peace. Younger nuns in slightly different habits attended the patients. One man groaned as two nuns turned him from his back on to his side. The occupant of the bed nearest the door lay on his back, one eye half open, his hands moving jerkily under the sheets. A shining line of saliva ran down his chin. Laurence looked away, feeling embarrassed.

He had thought their guide might have taken a vow of silence, but now she was talking quietly to Mary as they moved down the beds. Finally she left them at the last one, under a window in the corner. Mary leaned over and kissed the supine form, his head supported on either side by pillows. She looked back at Laurence, who was hovering uncertainly, and motioned him over.

'Richard, this is Laurie Bartram,' she said in a low but even voice.

Sitting down on a plain wooden chair by the bed, she brought the man's hand out from under the covers and held it.

'He's been wonderful in finding out what happened to John.' She leaned forward to do up a pyjama button that had come adrift. Then she sat in silence for a while, stroking his fingers.

Laurence studied Mary's lover's face. He was freshly shaven and his hair was slightly damp. Mary was right: he was a handsome man. He looked well, were it not for the puckered crater of healed tissue visible on the nearside of his head and the absolute lack of any facial response. His eyes were open, his irises very blue, yet Laurence could detect not a single indication that he had any awareness of their presence. When Mary let go of his hand, it fell loosely to the cover. She tucked it away, under the blanket.

'I can't stay today. But I went to see the house this morning and it's looking at its best. They've repaired the window frames and since the boys came home from the war, the gardens are getting back into shape. Mr Strangeways tells me they've had a wonderful year for roses – most of them still blooming until the last few weeks.'

She stood up, bent over and stroked Richard's brow, then looked down at his face intently, as if she couldn't believe what she saw. 'Bye bye,' she said, finally. 'I'll be back to see you soon, darling.'

She nodded to a nun by the door. 'Thank you,' she said simply.

They walked down the stairs and out into the open towards the church.

'The house is gone, of course,' she said. 'I haven't seen it since before the war. Strangeways, the head gardener, has gone to work at Compton Place. The court-appointed guardians decided that, as Richard had no heir, they needed to raise

416

funds for his care throughout his remaining life and the house was too dilapidated to leave empty.'

She walked down the path between gravestones made smooth by time and through the Saxon doorway into the church. He followed.

'Then there was a fire. Some mischief by local lads.' She wrapped her arms about herself. 'Not that he will ever know.'

They sat in the empty church. It was cold. The tiny vestry held one of the most beautiful stained-glass windows Laurence had ever seen, simple and full of colour. St Francis stood among butterflies and birds, all depicted as identifiable specimens. Beneath its rich light, the parish registers lay on a table.

'So you don't consider yourself free to make a life with anyone else?' asked Laurence.

'No, I don't. I'm not. Who knows, one day . . .'

'It's fine. You don't have to say anything. I should have liked . . . Well, you must know . . . But I'm sad. Not mostly for me,' he hoped this was true, 'but for you and for him.'

'It was one of the reasons I wanted to know more about John,' she said. 'I was so angry when he killed himself. Perhaps not with him but with God or fate. There was Richard, a body without a working brain, and there was John, only slightly injured, with a proper life if only he'd grasp it, and it seemed that he'd just thrown it away. I know that's unfair. I knew his mind was probably as damaged in its way as Richard's, but I needed to know that for certain. I needed to grieve, not rage. That's why I got in touch with you, I suppose.'

'Yet I turned out to know John a lot less well than you thought,' said Laurence. 'Less than you, certainly. And Eleanor Bolitho knew him best.'

She looked at him questioningly. 'But you were the only

friend John ever brought home. It had to count for something. I'd very occasionally seen him with others, heard him mention names, but you'd been to our house. Anyway,' she smiled rather sadly, 'you and I — we saw something in each other ages ago, didn't we? Back then? Something that might have been but wasn't?'

'I wish I'd been braver.'

She headed him off. 'And of course, you took finding John so much further than I'd ever intended and I became much more involved with you than I'd ever dreamed. And because you found out the real story, I have General Somers and the odious Tucker to feel angry about, instead of my own brother, and that's easier.'

'I'm not sure you'd feel angry at General Somers if you met him,' he said. 'Angrier at circumstances. Sad, even.'

Then he added, 'I've been thinking about our first meeting, that summer — when I was at school. I suspect John's invitation came from the same instinct that he showed in his bequest to William Bolitho, and to Edmund's mother, and probably to the unknown Monsieur Meurice. He may have been a solitary man, but he was a kind one, you know: a man who wasn't very good at intimate friendship but was very aware of others' unhappiness. Not an easy combination. And I was a very lonely boy after my parents died.'

'Have you exorcised your ghosts?' sad Mary, so quietly he almost didn't take it in.

'Ghosts?'

'You said earlier that John and, to a degree, Tresham Brabourne, were exorcising ghosts by speaking up. Somers was too, I suppose, in a ghastly way. Even Byers, in talking to you, from what you say. Are you the only man who walked through these horrors unscathed?'

'I was lucky,' he said, though he knew it sounded implausible. 'I was ill with pleurisy once and in hospital, and I hurt my back helping an injured soldier, but apart from that I was lucky.'

'But you lost Louise?'

He was quiet for a very long time. Finally he said, 'I was never sure whether I loved her, you see, so I couldn't really grieve for her.'

'And your son?'

The silence seemed to go on and on. She didn't come to his rescue. He looked up at the glass butterflies. He tried to remember Louise as he had last seen her. She was standing on the station in a summer dress and a straw hat. She wore white stockings and button shoes, and her pregnancy showed. It must have done because he suddenly remembered that she'd placed his hand on her hard belly.

'It's moving,' she'd said, her face bright with excitement. He had pulled his hand away too soon.

'There was an attack in France, you see.' He stopped, then started again. 'Well, there were lots of attacks, of course. It was only if you weren't there that you could think in terms of battles. The Battle of the Somme, the Third Battle of Ypres and so on. It wasn't really like that; there were all-out attacks and unexpected skirmishes, and they all led one into another. Just one attack stands out. It wasn't the worst, though it was bad. But it's the one that stands for all the rest. Rosières. It was the end.'

He felt a sharp and terrible ache. Love and failure and betrayal. Fathers and sons. His chest felt tight and his eyes were sore. The memory that he had tried so hard to suppress welled up. The darkness of the hours before morning. The discomfort, the cold and the insomnia.

✳

If only he could sleep he knew he would cope better.

Twenty minutes to go.

As the creeping barrage had died away, he found himself with hypersensitive hearing. All around him the shuffling and muttering of weary and scared men. Someone having a piss. A cough, the rasp of metal against a flint, the flat noise of rain falling on waterproof capes, and the occasional innocent snore from the rare soldier who could sleep despite everything. He had indigestion and was trying to find the bismuth that the MO had given him. The MO thought he had a peptic ulcer but could offer no better treatment until Laurence returned to England. A few weeks ago one of the regimental majors had collapsed and died of a heart attack. He'd been complaining of pains in the chest for months. Laurence slipped his fingers between his tunic buttons and rubbed the centre of his chest tentatively through his shirt and vest.

He felt awful: sick and sweaty. His neck ached and he rotated his head a couple of times to ease it. He was conscious of every breath forced in and out. If he couldn't control his breathing, how could he hope to control his behaviour and that of a whole platoon of men? He could hear Sergeant Collins moving up the trench, murmuring; he couldn't distinguish the words but the tone was of reassurance and encouragement. They had two new lads; both said they were eighteen but Laurence doubted they were.

Fifteen minutes.

The barrage had found its new range. He hoped it was accurate. His fingers were tingling and the tips had no feeling at all. He had been turning over the signal whistle in his hands when his fingers lost the ability to hold it and it fell to the length of its lanyard. What would happen if he couldn't keep hold of his rifle when the time came and had to cross no-man's land unarmed?

Ten minutes.

The barrage stopped. He looked along to his right to check that his nearest NCO was ready. He could hardly see him but eventually he did and nodded. He took a furtive swig from the tiny bismuth bottle. He polished his watch face with his handkerchief. His eyes scanned the men closest to him. Who would make it? Jones, the temperance ranter? Gaseley, the loner? The unfit, overweight Pollock who had successfully lumbered his way in and out of two years of action? Sergeant Collins, once a stationmaster from Bromley? The East End scrap dealer, Levy, only twenty-two and yet already the father of four children? Who else was out there? What else was out there? He had studied the maps, read the reconnaissance reports, but things changed; whole landscapes altered in battle. They had seen aeroplanes, of both sides, crossing the sky during the late afternoon on the day before while it was still light. He could hear that high, distant noise of them even now, their apparently unhurried movements seeming to have nothing to do with what was going on below. Even when one of them was shot down — though they'd seen and heard no firing — and fell to earth in silent flames, he had no sense that a man like himself was being roasted alive.

Five minutes.

He cleared his throat. Licked his lips. He had no saliva. The bismuth clogged his mouth. What if he couldn't blow the whistle? He felt for it again. The pain in his chest was excruciating. He looked up, exchanged grim smiles with Collins who had taken a position down to his left. Watched him pat one very young soldier — was the boy's name Russell? — on the shoulder. Looked at his watch. For a moment the numerals blurred.

Two minutes. He could hear Pollock's adenoidal breathing.

His arm rested on the ladder; momentarily he laid his forehead against it. He could sense every pore, every nerve ending and every alert hair on his body. How could all this suddenly cease in oblivion? It was unimaginable. Please God, he wasn't about to be sick. To his right one man crossed himself and he could see his lips moving in prayer. Now his heart was thudding so hard he could hear nothing else. The field guns stopped. Would they have cut the wire? Would they?

One minute.

Pollock belched. Someone sniggered. He kept his eyes on his watch, steadied a foot on the lowest rung of the ladder, raised the whistle to his mouth and started a prayer of his own. Please God, he said, keep me safe. Please don't let me die.

Ten seconds.

Take someone else this time. Not me. Take someone else. Anybody. I just want to live. Please. Don't let it be me. He looked at the slight, fair-haired boy to his left. At Pollock, gasping, mouth open. Made his glance pass by Levy. Felt Russell watching him. Gaseley's eyes were shut, his face white and inscrutable. Not me. Not now. Please. The whistle was in his mouth; he could feel its vibrations but heard nothing. They started to climb.

Anybody.

'I remember a sergeant shouting at the men not to bunch up – it was human nature to cling together, a lethal instinct – and then I remember seeing Jones, a Welshman who'd been praying just before we went over, moving ahead of me even while the men to each side of him fell. I passed a soldier called Levy lying on his back, the top of his head blown away. And then as we came towards the enemy lines, suddenly this German was right in front of me and he saw me and was so close I could see the muzzle of his rifle as it found me. I dropped down and got him as he fired, and a man called Pollock, who was right behind me, was hit. He went down clutching his belly and he just said "ouf" like a monstrous cushion deflating. I felt guilty and yet simultaneously elated. I thought God had answered my prayer; he'd taken Pollock, not me. That was bad enough. But it was worse than that.'

Laurence leaned his head back against a pillar.

'We broke through. We overran their position. It was bayonets for hand-to-hand fighting. But the casualties were terrible. There were two lads, friends who had joined together . . . I knew they were underage but we were short of men; it was easier not to ask. One of them was shot only feet from our position. His war had lasted less than five minutes. We never saw the other again. Eventually we crawled back. Tried to pull in our wounded. A few days later – a lifetime later – we were back in billets. We'd lost over half of our officers, nearly a third of our men. My men. I was drinking myself to sleep each night.

'A few days later, the colonel sent for me. I was hung-over and I thought he was going to promote me simply through lack of alternatives. But no, he had a telegram. Rather than look at me, he read it through without raising his eyes until he ran out of words, though it was so short he must already have known it by heart. It said that Louise had died giving birth and the baby had died with her. And they had died on the morning I was going into battle. Louise died – I made it my business to find out later – almost at the very hour I went over. When I was begging God to take another life instead of mine. The colonel's giving me a tot of his special scotch and apologising that he can't send me home quite yet and I'm realising that I sacrificed my wife and my son and the whole long life he might have had, just so that I could go on living my pointless existence.'

'Laurence,' Mary said gently but protestingly.

'I know. I know. It's a terrible, cruel, Old Testament God who would accept such an exchange. I *know* that. But *I* offered them up.'

'Laurence,' said Mary, putting her hand under his chin and forcing him to look at her. Her eyes were shining brightly. She blinked several times. 'Thousands – *millions* – of prayers must have been said by desperate men in desperate situations. You think you were the only one who, faced with horrors I can't even imagine, asked to be spared at any cost? And what about all the mothers and wives and sisters back home? Do you think that perfectly nice mothers didn't hope and, yes, pray it would be someone else's boy? Their friend's son? Their sister's fiancé? I prayed and prayed for Richard. I went to church, and I went through the motions of joining in prayers for victory and prayers for peace, but, selfishly, the only thing I wanted was Richard. I didn't care whether we won or lost. When he was horribly injured I prayed for him to survive, when, seeing him now, I should have wished for him to have been spared the living death he has. But I wanted him back. I didn't want to live in a world without him.'

When Laurence didn't answer she said, 'You weren't thinking of Louise then. You weren't suggesting a sacrifice, one for another; you wanted to live. It's a powerful instinct. Then you got the news of Louise's death when you were away from home, under enormous stress, and it's hardly surprising you made a link.'

'It was cowardice. Plain and simple. Not the sort that gets you publicly condemned and shot like Edmund Hart. Mine was the tidy, private sort. His broke out, mine ate into me. My punishment was living. I found it wasn't that important. When Louise died she took a bit of my past – she was, *is*, part of my memories and of other people's. But when the baby died . . . He wasn't part of history, he couldn't be a memory; what he took with him was our dreams. His future . . . my future . . .'

He could barely make it to the end of the sentence; his voice was hoarse and he could feel his eyes filling with tears. He wanted to tell her that the earthquake of grief that was suddenly threatening to sweep him away was not about his son. Or that it was not only about him but about everything that was gone, even about Somers and the hollowed-out man who now lay in the corner bed only fifty yards away from them.

'I was so frightened,' he said.

She put her arms round him, knocking some hymnbooks on to the floor as she did so.

'Laurie, whatever you believe or part of you believes, the best thing you could do in your son's memory now is to live.

Work. Explore. Marry again one day. Have more children. Forgive yourself. Laugh from time to time.'

She kissed him on the forehead and held his head to her. He could smell her, wonderfully warm and familiar.

'But not to you or with you?'

'No. Not with me. Not now. But you're still quite young. Don't punish yourself for being frightened in intolerable circumstances. I don't mean to sound like a prig but when so many are dead like John or, like Richard, as good as dead, you have a chance to be part of this new world, unnerving though it is. I wish you would. And I hope you'll always be my friend. I need a special friend.'

'I'd like that,' he said. She handed him a ridiculously small, embroidered handkerchief that had been carefully ironed. He pressed it first to one eye then the other without unfolding it. He no longer cared whether he looked stupid.

'The rest – it's not quite as easy as you think. I can't see it another way; I can only learn to live with it. And I'll try. I'm thinking of going back into teaching. Apparently they're terribly short of schoolmasters and they're using men in their sixties and seventies to make up numbers. They need some new blood. I might even be quite good at it. I've been asked if I'd be interested in a History post at Westminster. They want to see me next week. They need someone to start next Lent term.'

'That's marvellous,' she said with real enthusiasm. 'I think you'd be brilliant at it. And we could meet and talk, and go to see Charlie Chaplin, even – and eat respectable crumpets and walk in Green Park. One day soon I'll move to London. It's hopeless living with Mother and she has Aunt Virginia who is the mainstay of her life. From London I could see Richard more often. I could work for a living. I want to do that. Anyway, if I stay in Cambridge, I'm going to wake up one day and find I've turned into a stuffed owl or a weasel inside a glass dome.'

'A weasel?' He ran his fingers through her hair. 'I don't think you're very weaselly, Miss Emmett. More of a mongoose: intelligent, mischievous and loyal.'

'Destructive and noisy, but good for keeping down vermin?'

'All useful skills in their place.' He laughed. 'I love you, weasel or not,' he said.

'Thank you,' she said and kissed him one more time, gently but with certainty. 'If it wasn't for Richard,' she began.

He put his finger up to her lips. 'Don't,' he said. Then pulling her to him, he buried his face in her hair. 'I love you,' he said again.

There was no longer any game to play so honesty could not damage him. She whispered something back into his shoulder but he didn't catch it and it didn't seem to matter.

CHAPTER THIRTY-NINE

*H*aving gone to his interview straight after lunch, at which the Board of Governors at Westminster School made clear his appointment would be a foregone conclusion, Laurence came out as the bells of the abbey were chiming three. As he passed through the Sanctuary, pupils stood aside to let him by. One or two smiled tentatively. This would be his life from next year onwards, he thought with pleasure. It was the second week of December, the last day of term and excited boys of all sizes teemed around him in black jackets and stiff white collars.

He went home to change out of his smartest suit, then left his flat in a panic, afraid that his sister would be standing bemused and alone on Victoria Station, not knowing how to reach her hotel. The second post had arrived. He went through it quickly, discarding an obvious bill. A letter from Charles lay on the hall table with a parcel. He tore it open, though it was clearly meant as a Christmas present. G.K. Chesterton's *The Wisdom of Father Brown*. He laughed, left the book on the side table and took the handwritten envelope, only opening it when he was sitting on the bus.

Two buses arrived together, both of which were crowded, so

he was lucky to get a seat. Outside it was already dark. Seen through the condensation running down the windows, London was merely a blur of red and yellow lights. He rubbed the glass with his coat cuff. Through the smeared, wet circle he saw they were at the back of Buckingham Palace, where the traffic had almost ground to a halt. He couldn't see whether the royal standard was flying. Perhaps the King and Queen were already at Sandringham; he thought that was what they always did at Christmas. He looked at his other letter. It turned out to be a dinner invitation from a Mrs Tresham Brabourne. He was caught by surprise; so the boyish Brabourne was married. At the bottom of the card, Brabourne had added his own postscript: 'If you would like to bring Miss Emmett, please do so.' Laurence smiled to himself.

As he walked into Victoria Station in a mist of drizzle, he was met by the sight of a scrawled headline on a paper stall, SUBMARINE LOST IN THE NORTH SEA. He was curious; he had never even seen a submarine. He bought a paper without stopping to read it and moved on towards the platforms. It was ten to five by the clock. Her train was due in at five. He tucked the ends of his scarf into his coat, buttoned his gloves. His eyes flickered down to the headlines. Beneath the submarine tragedy was a short report on an inquest. The coroner had opened the inquiry into what the paper called 'the tragic accidental death of the hero of Mafeking, General Somers'. He looked up at the board, feeling dizzy as he tipped his head back.

After he'd heard the news originally he had gone up to the Lovell house, taking with him the copy of Brabourne's magazine, *Post-Guard*. He had wanted Mrs Lovell to know that her son's poetry had been published, but the house had been all closed up. He squeezed his eyes tightly shut and the giddiness passed. Opening them, he saw with a start that the train had come in early. Putting the paper in a bin, he elbowed his way urgently in the direction of the platform.

Although his greater height gave him an advantage over the people ahead of him, he felt nervous as he tried to pick out his sister from the mass of travellers crossing the concourse. Around a bushy Christmas tree the station band was playing 'O Come All Ye Faithful'. They had drawn quite an audience, some of whom were singing along. Two policemen passed behind them, their eyes scanning the crowd. People were moving sluggishly because so many passengers were loaded with parcels or stopping for emotional reunions with arriving passengers. Above them all, the vault of the station was clouded with breath and steam.

He tried to imagine what his sister looked like now. It was eighteen years since she had disappeared to India. War had blocked her intentions to return once her children were less dependent. He could hardly remember her features; it was easier to recall her bossy presence: a big sister both loving and admonitory. He took off his gloves. Two or three women passed him with sons of approximately the right age in tow. He was looking across the platform when he felt a tug on his sleeve.

'Laurie?' asked the woman beside him, smiling tentatively.

He realised in an instant that he would have changed much more than her and felt a surge of warmth at her courage.

'Oh Millie,' he said, holding the sister he recognised instantly – smaller, rounder, but just as he now remembered her – first at arm's length and then pressed to him, so swiftly that her hat was knocked sideways and she had to extricate a hand to hold it on to her head. Her thick hair – pinned up in rather an old-fashioned way and much as his mother had styled hers – escaped in curls. She still had such a pretty smile.

He was suddenly aware of the boy standing next to her. Taller than his mother, indeed nearly as tall as Laurence, dark-eyed in a way that instantly reminded Laurence of his father. He smiled nervously and shot out his hand. Laurence took it and held it with his other one.

'Hello – Uncle Laurie,' said the boy. He had nearly said sir.

'Hello, Will.' He was suddenly and simply a man with a family, getting ready for Christmas.

'It really is so very good to see you, Millie.'

Their eyes finally met. Impulsively, he flung his arms round her again, then pulled back slightly and looked down at her. Her eyes were brimming with tears; she fumbled in her bag. He felt in his pocket and gave her his handkerchief, grateful that he had ironed it.

'I'm sorry,' she said. 'About everything,' she added, in a muffled voice, as she wiped her nose.

Laurence imagined the scene through her eyes. At twenty-six she had left England, her home, friends, parents and brother, for the furthest shores of the empire. He suspected that by then she had begun to think she would become an old maid and was glad to be married even to a man nearly twenty years her senior. However, she could never have guessed how completely her world would crumble behind her. During her long sojourn in India, she had lost not just both parents but a way of life they had all shared. The family home was long gone; friends had gone; the brother she had left as a schoolboy was a widower, not far off middle age.

'And how old are you now?' said Laurence and before his nephew could tell him fourteen, which he knew perfectly well, he laughed. 'I'm afraid I'm being a complete ass at this – you must be thinking I'm the most pompous uncle you could imagine.'

'No,' said the boy, a smile hovering, 'definitely not.'

'You must remember Henry's brother Norton? Will's other uncle?' Millie said. 'It's hardly a fair competition.'

Now she had linked her arm through his, yet still grasping his hand. Hers, gloveless now, was warm and dry. A porter hovered with a trunk and two cases, leading the way as they began to push a path through the crowds.

They were level with the station band when Laurence saw a face he recognised. Standing, listening to the carols, was Leonard Byers. Byers hadn't seen Laurence, who paused, just for a second, taking in the hatless young woman with bobbed hair, clinging to Byers' arm. As the porter parted the crowds, Laurence saw her in profile. She was very pregnant. She said something in Byers' ear, he grinned down at her and she laid her head against his arm.

One minute Laurence, Millie and Wilfred were having to muscle their way through the mass of people and the next, having come through the great arches, they were free, standing on the edge of the shining black street, where streams of cabs and dark cars moved swiftly in both directions. His sister looked from her brother to her bags and back to him again, as if she couldn't bear to raise her eyes and encompass the vastness of the new life around her. The boy looked in every direction: at the entrance to the underground station, the advertisement hoardings, the chestnut-seller, the clerks and shop girls getting off the bus, the passers-by slightly bowed under black umbrellas. His face was alert and excited.

In a way Laurence was glad that proper conversation was still impossible; the carols had died away behind them but now there was a constant hiss from the wheels of the traffic and a paper boy still shouting out the late headlines. They found their cab, loaded the bags, he tipped the porter and they were away, sucked into the city and the winter's night, with the bright shop windows and the slanting rain moving faster and faster behind them.

Epilogue

WEDNESDAY, 28 DECEMBER 1920

*T*hey were about twelve miles from Fairford now, approaching Faringdon. He could tell by the sinking sun that the road was heading almost due west. On the left, stunted willows marked what must be the distant course of the Thames or one of its small tributaries. This was countryside he had once known well. To the south there was a gentle sweep of open land and a wide view through leafless trees rising to hills on the horizon. The temperature had dropped fifteen degrees in the last twenty-four hours and there was a dusting of snow on ploughed fields tinged faintly pink by the sun. To his right, John could see a small mound, almost artificially neat, with a cluster of dark trees on its summit. Somers looked straight ahead as the road curved in front of them. From the trees rose an extraordinary tower. It seemed to stand alone, its castellated battlements clear against the sky.

'What's that?' John asked. 'Is it a castle?'

He remembered from his Oxford days that there had been skirmishes fought around here in the Civil War, although this looked more like a building from a fairy tale.

The general turned his head briefly. 'It's a folly. Faringdon Folly. Just a tower. Decorative but useless. Four empty rooms stacked one upon another,

Gothic windows and a marvellous view from the top. When I was young you could see into three counties from up there, though it scared us all to pass by it at night. The boys too in their turn. It's all locked up now, I believe.'

John recalled there having been a folly here long ago when he was a school-boy. Was this it? It was summer then and everything had looked different.

'Could we go closer?'

'I'll drive as near to it as I can.'

He was grateful that the general asked for no explanation but simply added, 'I think the last stretch is just a bridle path.'

They bumped their way up a rutted lane. It was only a few minutes before the car stopped.

'I'd like to get out here,' John said. 'I'll walk the rest of the way.'

The general looked mildly surprised. 'I'll come with you.'

'No. All the way back to Holmwood, I mean. I'd like a chance to think.'

'Good God, man, it's ten miles or more to Fairford. It'll be dark in two hours and bitterly cold by the look of it.'

'Don't worry,' John said, evenly. He opened the car door. 'I've walked all my life in all kinds of weathers. Like this' — he indicated his greatcoat and borrowed boots — 'I'll be fine. It's a good road. If I reach Lechlade and it's too cold, I'll put up at the New Inn. Might even get Chilvers on the telephone and make his son fetch me.' He almost smiled. 'I'd like to walk, to be honest. After this, I'll have precious little freedom.' He ran a hand through his hair. 'No solitary excursions for me for a while, I imagine. I'll see the Folly while it's light and then follow the road back. I feel better than I have for an age. Free.'

The general looked at him. John was very pale, but calm: a man who had finally relieved them both of an intolerable burden.

'Take this,' he said, handing him a hip flask, from under his seat. 'I keep it in case of the car stranding me somewhere inhospitable. Oh, and this' — he unwrapped the striped woollen scarf from around his neck. 'It was Miles's scarf. House colours. Still serviceable, you'll find. You'll need it.'

'Thank you.'

433

John thrust the flask in the less bulky of his pockets. He opened the door, then paused.

'You will tell her everything?' he said.

'You have my word.'

It was certainly cold and he was glad of the scarf. He had once owned one like it, a long, long time ago. He wrapped it round his neck and ears, stuffed his hands in his pockets and started to walk uphill, unsteady on the frozen, roughly ploughed ground. General Somers waited for some minutes, the engine idling unevenly. Then, when John had climbed over a stile and looked back to wave with his right hand, clutching the cross-bar with his left, he turned the car and drove slowly away, bumping down the frozen track.

As he drew closer to the copse, John could see that although it contained a few bare sycamores and elms, it was mostly fir trees, which made it dense even in winter. For so long he had avoided thick undergrowth, afraid of what violent surprise might be concealed there. But there was nothing to hurt him here. The war was over. It was all over.

A slight wind stirred the upper branches. It had been achingly cold in the open and the grass crunched under foot; once he was in the trees, he had some protection. The ground was softer here and covered in pine needles. By the time he reached the tower, he was slightly breathless; the bitter air, coming on top of the months of virtual confinement, had left him slightly out of breath. All the same it was good to be out of doors.

The tower loomed above him: dark brickwork with greenish streaks running upwards from the base. Had he been here before? He walked right round it and found a single door, heavily padlocked and offering neither protection nor imprisonment. He looked up; the empty, mullioned windows reflected the red sun, giving the impression of a fire burning at the heart of the building, while orange-streaked clouds moved slowly overhead. With his head tipped back he had a momentary illusion of the tower falling. He looked down and steadied himself with his fingertips on the damp brickwork. He inhaled deeply and the effort made him cough.

He sat down with his back against the tower. The hefty material of his coat would protect him for a while from the iron cold behind and beneath him. So much cold in his life. He turned his collar up. He wondered where he had left his gloves. The sky, which had been so blue, was turning a soft violet; the fields were losing their colour. Rooks were wheeling about the tallest elms. After some time — he had no idea how long he had been there — he saw a single star come out. Venus. The next time he looked there were hundreds; thousands, in a clear night sky. He could still identify the constellations his father had shown him as a child on night walks in Suffolk. It was August — the dog days, his father had said, stroking the panting Sirius on the head. High above him was Pegasus, the winged horse, with Orion the hunter and Canes Venatici, the hounds of the hunt. He felt the close hug the old man had given him as a consolation for his sudden terror of infinity; safety smelled of tobacco and elderly terrier.

How proud his father had been to see him an officer. He thought again. That was wrong; his father had never known of his choice but he had made it, hoping to please him. To make up for leaving him, just like everybody else, and going so far away. War was something his father would, at first, have understood, had he lived to see it. But what followed would have been incomprehensible.

A half-moon shone over the monochrome landscape. Miles away, a few lights marked an unknown hamlet. Had he fallen asleep? His breathing was shallow and his chest hurt slightly. He couldn't really feel his feet. He felt in his pocket for paper and a pencil. Hadn't he had a pencil when he set out? It was gone. Instead he found the hip flask and, opening it with stiff fingers, he took a drink; it was brandy, which made him shudder but warmed him. He set the flask beside him, felt in his other, heavier, pocket and drew out a package wrapped in cloth, which he set on his lap. The rooks had quietened now. A pale barn owl skimmed across the fields, suddenly swooping to reach its prey. From time to time small creatures scrabbled in the darkness around him. Not rats, he hoped. Then a larger animal passed behind the tower: a badger or a fox, maybe, busy in this other world. He was glad to be here. He knew it was where he should be.

He thought of Eleanor. Her hair, her smell, her comfort. He remembered walking with her in France. He had been sitting on a bench outside the hospital. She came out, put up a hand to the side of his face.

'Oh you're so cold,' she said. She rubbed her hands briskly up and down his arms.

'May we walk?' she said. 'Are you comfortable enough?'

'Of course.'

Her head was swathed in a hood and she had a thick man's coat over her uniform, coming down to her boots. She pulled gloves out of a pocket. Looking at her made him feel warm.

'Come on, race you to — wherever it is we're going.'

She ran ahead clumsily, laughing, and then she was gone. He called her name.

He opened and closed his fingers a few times to get his circulation going. Both hands. Both perfect hands. He poured some brandy on them and rubbed his palms together. She wasn't here. He looked at his fingers, spread widely and white as bone and opened his coat; he was not so cold. Then he unwrapped Miles Somers' scarf, folded it and set it down carefully a little way from his legs. He felt bad enough about stealing the photograph and package from the Somers house, but he didn't want to keep the scarf from its rightful owner too.

Then he took the small comb out of his pocket. He could hardly see the initials but he traced the unicorn with his finger. AM: Agathe Meurice. He set it down softly on the scarf.

He pressed his head back against the stonework and closed his eyes. He thought of other unreal worlds, other decisions, other possibilities: the shadows of faraway lives that had, briefly, crossed with his; of Eleanor, of a mortally wounded soldier trying to speak, and of a small boy startled by the cry of a red kite; but finally of his own hand in the dry comfort of his father's as they gazed up at the summer sky one Suffolk night.

When the shot came, the rooks rose outward from their roost with coarse cries of alarm, but in a few minutes they returned, settling back into the bare branches until the first light of dawn.

AFTERWORD

'Craven fear is the most extravagant prodigal of nervous energy known. Under its stimulus a man squanders nervous energy recklessly in order to suppress his hideous and pent up emotions and mask and camouflage that which if revealed will call down ignominy upon him and disgrace him in the eyes of his fellows. He must preserve his self-respect and self-esteem at all costs.'

Billy Tyrell, a military doctor and victim of shellshock, in evidence to the Southborough Committee. Report of the War Office Commission of Enquiry into 'Shell-Shock' (London, 1922), quoted by Ben Shephard in *A War of Nerves: Soldiers and Psychiatrists in the Twentieth Century*.

Only three British officers were executed in the First World War. On the other hand, over 300 British and Commonwealth private soldiers met this fate, although of the 3,080 death sentences handed down, most were commuted.

My novel is loosely inspired by the executions of Temporary Sub-Lieutenant Edwin Dyett, Royal Naval Volunteer Reserve, and of Lieutenant Poole of the West Yorkshire Regiment, both shot for desertion. The novelist A.P. Herbert, who had encountered Dyett while himself a junior officer in the same division, wrote a novel based on the case: *The Secret Battle* (1919). Leonard Sellers has produced an account of the Dyett case in *Death for Desertion*, first published in 1995 as *For God's Sake Shoot Straight*. Further reading in this area includes *Blindfold and Alone: British Military Executions in the Great War* by John Hughes-Wilson and Cathryn Corns, and *Shot at Dawn: Executions in World War One by Authority of the British Army Act* by Julian Putkowski and Julian Sykes. Ernest Thirtle MP published a pamphlet in 1929, *Shootings at Dawn: The Army Death Penalty at Work*. The terrible effect on families of losing husbands and sons in this way is revealed by surviving letters.

There are, of course, a great number of excellent books on the Great War. I am particularly indebted to the following: John Keegan, *The First World War*; Richard Holmes, *Tommy: The British Soldier on the Western Front*; Max Arthur, *Last Post: The Final Word from our First World War Soldiers*; and Neil Hansen, *The Unknown Soldier: The Story of the Missing of the Great War*. Gordon Corrigan has assembled a critical look at some of the myths of the war in *Mud, Blood and Poppycock*. Dominic Hibberd's biography of Wilfred Owen, Jean Moorcroft Williams' work on Isaac Rosenberg and Nicholas Moseley's book on Julian Grenfell are among many that I have read, as well as Vera Brittain's *Testament of Youth*, a vivid account of her experience as a volunteer nurse on the Western Front. *A Deep Cry: First World War Soldier-Poets Killed in France and Flanders*, edited by Anne Powell, is superb on the lives and deaths of less famous poets. Diaries, novels, plays and poetry of the period, as well as some comprehensive websites, have helped my understanding of the varied experiences of those who lived in the first quarter of the twentieth century. Above all, for a wonderful survey of the Great War in the popular imagination, there is Paul Fussell's classic: *The Great War and Modern Memory*.

For the care and understanding of men with shell-shock, I have used several sources of which the most valuable were the papers of W.H.R. Rivers who treated many of these psychiatric casualties, and the publication in 1917 of *Shell-Shock and its Lessons* by two doctors, Grafton Elliot Smith and Tom Hatherley Pear. Daniel Hipp's *The Poetry of Shell Shock: Wartime Trauma and Healing in Wilfred Owen, Ivor Gurney and Siegfried Sassoon* was invaluable in providing the connection between poetry and mental fragility. There was a hospital for shell-shocked officers in Fairford, Gloucestershire (now Coln House School), but Dr Chilvers and his son are entirely fictional. Ben Shephard's *War of Nerves: Soldiers and Psychiatrists in the Twentieth Century* and Jonathan Shay's *Achilles in Vietnam* were moving accounts of war and mental illness.

Sir Hubert Gough lived until 1963.

I have taken a liberty in placing the Faringdon Folly within the late nineteenth-century landscape. It was, in fact, built by Lord Berners in 1935, although the atmospheric hill upon which it stands is the site of settlements dating back to antiquity. Other locations all exist, although, as far as I know, Wilmington Priory was never used by a nursing order, and the beautiful 'butterfly' window at the church of St Mary and St Peter was lost in a fire a few years ago.

The Darling Committee (1919) and the Southborough Committee (1920–1922) both existed and examined questions of military courts martial and shell-shock, though I have added to their members and to their proceedings. Philip Morrell MP raised questions on these topics in the House of Commons as early as 1918 before standing down for the

December election. In 1919 an army officer, Colonel Lambert Ward MP (who had, like Sub-Lieutenant Dyett, served in the RNR), requested that there be no differentiation between the graves of those executed and those killed on active service. Many individuals volunteered to give evidence to the Southborough Committee.

ACKNOWLEDGMENTS

I am extremely grateful for the perseverance of my agent George Capel and her assistants Abi Fellows and Rosie Apponyi in getting the first draft of this book to a state where it could be considered a novel. My thanks too to Lennie Goodings at Virago; her confidence and continued investment in it were hugely encouraging. I also owe a debt of gratitude to her assistant, Victoria Pepe, who read the manuscript first and whose belief in it pushed it forward, and to the sheer stamina of my assiduous copyeditor Celia Levett. George Miller and Katharine Reeve provided technical advice throughout the writing of the book.

The assistance of Richard Holmes was invaluable; he headed off my worst military blunders with patience and good humour. Alwin Hutchinson also advanced my military education. Any remaining mistakes were entirely dreamed up by me.

Lucy Cavendish College, Cambridge, has, as always, been an inestimable resource for information and ideas, as well as providing the enduring friendships that have sustained my writing career.

Finally, my thanks go to the trustees of the Hosking Houses Trust who provided the 2008 Residency that allowed me to get the bulk of this book written in the peace of the Trust's Church Cottage on the banks of the River Avon near Stratford.